TARK'S TICKS VALOR'S GHOST

A WWII NOVEL

CHRIS GLATTE

SEVERN RIVER

PUBLISHING

Severn River Publishing
www.SevernRiverBooks.com

ISBN: 978-1-64875-564-4 (Paperback)

ALSO BY CHRIS GLATTE

Tark's Ticks Series

Tark's Ticks

Valor's Ghost

Gauntlet

Valor Bound

Dark Valley

War Point

A Time to Serve Series

A Time to Serve

The Gathering Storm

The Scars of Battle

164th Regiment Series

The Long Patrol

Bloody Bougainville

Bleeding the Sun

Operation Cakewalk (Novella)

Standalone Novel

Across the Channel

To find out more about Chris Glatte and his books, visit

severnriverbooks.com/authors/chris-glatte

For my Family,
Thanks for your unwavering support

1

APRIL 1942, MARIVELES LUZON, PHILIPPINES

Captain Gima of the Imperial Japanese Army sat in his high-backed wood and leather chair and stared down his nose at the pathetically emaciated US Army Captain. "Captain Glister, is it?" His English was nearly flawless after four years in California, attending and graduating from, Stanford University.

Captain Glister, the commander of Hotel Company, looked up quickly, noting the Japanese officer's perfect diction. He'd heard rumors about this captain's US education but didn't believe them until now. "Yes. Captain Eugene Glister, Serial number..."

"Stop," interrupted Gima, holding up his hand. "I know all that." He stood and slapped his hands hard on the wooden desktop, leaning forward. "I'm not interested in your serial number. Even in defeat you think you can make the rules and hide behind some asinine document. You've no idea the peril you're in. I'm the most lenient of my comrades. I'm outnumbered by officers who will kill you for a sideways glance." He stepped around the desk and stood in front of the tall officer. He puffed out his chest, slowly walked away and leaned on the front of his desk. "You have a unit in your company, a unit you command, First Platoon, Second Squad?"

Glister looked straight ahead and considered. This was an odd question; everyone commanding a company had a first platoon with a second squad. He nodded, yes.

"And this platoon and squad was special, I think?"

Glister scowled thinking of the men. Lieutenant Smoker's face appeared in his mind and his jawline flexed. He'd heard the lieutenant's body had been identified. His final mission, stalling the Japanese on the main road, had obviously been his last. It had been successful in the short term, allowing most of the division to retreat to Mariveles. In the end though, it had all been for naught as the surrender came soon after, but he had no doubt the mission had saved lives. Glister continued staring ahead Silently. Gima continued, "Was Second Squad of First Platoon special, Captain?"

"They were good men. If that's what you mean, yes."

Gima shook his head. "I mean, they are special enough to have their own name." Glister looked at him and scowled, obviously confused. Gima continued, "*Tark's Ticks.* They call themselves *Tark's Ticks.*" He flicked a playing card at Glister. It bounced off Glister's nose. He made no move to block it but fire raged in his eyes for a moment. Gima pointed, "Pick it up. See for yourself."

Glister picked it up and looked at both sides. Scrawled on the front was a death's head and the words, 'Tark's Ticks'. He kept the smile off his face, but barely. *Has to be Staff Sergeant Tarkington,* he thought.

Gima took it from him and paced. "I took this off one of my men. He'd been shot several times. He and nearly his entire squad were ambushed and killed. I keep it in my front pocket to remind me." He stuffed the well-worn card back into his pocket. "After my four years at Stanford, I left America with nothing but admiration. At first, I was against all this aggression, but I'm Japanese. It is my country, my duty, so I took up arms. When we swept through you and your puppet Filipino Army with such ease, it made me realize that you were not supermen. You were simply astoundingly arrogant. When the defense stiffened, I regained some respect, but when I came across that slaughtered unit and saw *this,*" he patted his shirt pocket, "I knew your core was rotten. I've promised that dead soldier and all the others, that I'd find all the members of *Tark's Ticks* and destroy them."

Glister's jaw rippled but he kept his composure and stared straight ahead. He had no idea if Staff Sergeant Tarkington and the rest of Second Squad were alive or dead. He only knew the commander of their platoon was dead. "What do you want from me, Captain?"

Gima struck like a cobra, slapping Glister's face with an open palm. "You will address me as, sir!"

Glister's head snapped to the side, but he didn't cry out or touch his face, just slowly brought his face back to center and stared ahead, his eyes, slits. "What do you want from me, *sir*?" he corrected, venom dripping from every word.

"I want to find them. I want to punish them. I want to know where they are, and I don't want any of your bullshit."

Glister braced and considered repeating his name, rank and serial number, but instead said. "Lieutenant Smoker, their commanding officer was killed trying to give us time to retreat here. I assume his men died with him."

Gima nodded, "I'm aware of the officer's fate. The other soldiers were buried in a mass grave after their dog-tags were collected. I've questioned many other soldiers from your company and know the leader of your second squad is a Staff Sergeant Tarkington. Thus, the ridiculous moniker, *Tark's Ticks,* no doubt." He squared on Glister and thrust his face forward, coming to his chin. He seethed, "Tarkington's dog-tags weren't there."

Glister shook his head slightly. "And you think I would know his whereabouts? How could I?"

Gima slapped the other side of Glister's face and Glister's jaw clenched as he restrained himself from strangling the smaller man. He doubted he could best the man in his emaciated condition, but he'd like to give it a try. Instead, he calmed himself as best he could. Gima spit, "I will ask the questions, *Captain.*"

Gima took a step back, shook his head and composed himself. "I don't like all this unpleasantness. I'd like to get you back to your men, but I cannot let this insult go." He touched his front pocket. "This must be avenged. I made a promise to my men. You can understand that. Tarkington, and whoever else is still out there, needs to be brought in." He raised a finger as if scolding a child. "You and your sixty-thousand cowardly comrades will be escorted north, to the railway station in San Fernando, where you'll be transported to Cabantuan and will spend the remainder of the war as guests of the rising sun. If I don't have Staff Sergeant Tarkington by then, I'll hold you accountable for his sins and will take necessary action."

Glister's cheeks still burned, and he was sure they were red as beets. "I am accountable." He said it as a statement, not wanting to be slapped again.

Gima looked at him as though teaching a simpleton. "This walk north won't be pleasant for your men. Command underestimated your cowardice and doesn't have the means to transport so many men. But they congest this area, and we need it cleared out. Many of your men are weak, sick and wounded. Many won't make it to the trains." He shook his head, "I've already told you; most officers are ready to kill with very little prompting. I've no doubt this migration will be unruly. I know you have the means to relay messages. You can get word to Tarkington to surrender himself. He'll take a direct order, even one passed along the grapevine." He went behind his desk and sat. "If he doesn't, you and your men will suffer the consequences. Dismissed, Captain."

Glister snapped off a perfect salute, spun on his heel and marched out the door, fantasizing about all the ways he'd like to kill Captain Gima.

Captain Glister left Gima's office wondering what he should do about Staff Sergeant Tarkington. He concealed his glee at hearing Tarkington wasn't among the dead. He'd had virtually no information about any of his units since the surrender and had assumed First Platoon had either been captured or killed in their mission to delay the Japanese. To hear otherwise was the best news he'd had in weeks.

He'd lied to Captain Gima about the moniker Tark's Ticks. He'd heard about it. Under normal circumstances he would've squashed that sort of thing before it got off the ground, but in the final chaotic days before the surrender, he'd let it continue. It seemed to increase the men's morale during a time when they needed it most. He understood Gima's reaction; it was like being taunted, which he had to admit, would piss him off too.

Now he needed to figure out what to do about it. Gima wanted Tarkington's head and he didn't doubt the Stanford educated officer would follow through with his threat. He wasn't necessarily worried for his own sake, but he doubted he would be the only one targeted.

He saw Lieutenant Govang sitting on the ground, his back against a low wall, surrounded by other officers. Like everyone else, his uniform was in tatters and he'd lost at least twenty pounds since December. He had his head resting on his arms, which were draped across his knobby knees. "Lieutenant." Govang's head snapped up and before he could get to his feet, Glister slid in next to him. Govang looked at him sideways. Glister kept his voice low. "Can we get word to someone still out there?" Govang's brow furrowed. "I mean there must still be soldiers out there who evaded capture. Is there a way to get word to them?"

Govang looked straight ahead. There was a guard holding a long Arisaka rifle pacing twenty-yards away. The order of the day was no talking and the bow-legged bastard had already reinforced the order by thumping one of the GIs in the face with his rifle butt. The GIs nose broke and his eyes turned deep shades of black, blue and purple. Govang leaned in, keeping his eyes on the guard then spoke low, "Not sure, Captain. Probably pass something to one of the Filipinos and they could pass it to a civilian."

Glister nodded. "Just met a Jap Captain. He's pissed at Staff Sergeant Tarkington. Guess he was on the receiving end of an ambush and found those playing cards they were leaving on bodies."

Govang smiled, despite the blistering sun they were forced to sit beneath. "*Tark's Ticks?*"

Glister nodded but waited until the Jap turned away. "Told me Tarkington wasn't among the dead. Wanted me to send an order for him to surrender."

Govang flicked a centipede off his arm. "Be his death sentence."

Glister nodded, "That's why I'm not sending that order." Govang looked at him and nodded. Govang knew his company commander to be a good officer and a better man. "I'm sending an order, but not what that son-of-a-bitch intended."

The bowlegged guard lunged forward suddenly and struck a GI who'd got to his feet. The butt of the rifle dug into the GI's gut, and he doubled over and fell to the side, trying to catch his breath. The Japanese yelled at him and it reminded Glister of a crazed squirrel chittering from a tree as he walked through the woods back home.

With the Japanese guard distracted he said, "Get word to Tarkington if at all possible: Keep fighting."

"Yes, sir. I'll see what I can do."

The guard continued his tirade, threatening other men with his long bayonet. Glister took the opportunity to pass along more information. "The captain told me we'll be moved north on foot to some train station, then onto a prison camp somewhere. Expect we'll leave soon. Warn the men when you get a chance."

Govang nodded. "Be better than cooking in the sun here, I expect."

Glister shook his head. "Captain warned me this won't be a walk in the park. Says most officers would rather kill us and be done with it. You know the stories out of China as well as I do."

2

Staff Sergeant Tarkington along with the six GIs leftover from First Platoon, and the Filipino, Eduardo, had fallen into the daily flow of life in the isolated village in southern Luzon. The sounds of battle had faded away like the setting sun, replaced by chittering monkeys and the incessant chirp of insects.

Nearly a month had passed since the battle on the road had taken most of First Platoon. PFC Vick's wound was healing well. He'd avoided infection and even expedited his recovery by insisting on walking around the perimeter at least twice a day. He walked slowly, making sure of every step, but every day he improved.

The GIs hadn't regained their pre-Japanese attack weights, but the plentiful food provided by the local hunters brought them to better health. Even their runny shits had solidified somewhat.

Eduardo appeared from the jungle, along with three other villagers. He held his Springfield rifle; the others held bows and arrows. They'd been on a hunting expedition and didn't like using guns for fear of drawing the attention of the Japanese, not to mention spooking their prey. Each villager had pouches brimming with dead animals.

Tarkington waved and Eduardo spoke in Tagalog to his fellow hunters, before they peeled off in separate directions. Eduardo's normally grinning face was a mask of concern as he approached. "Something wrong, Eduardo?" Tarkington asked.

Eduardo said, "We had a good hunt, but heard disturbing news from other hunters."

"What news?" growled Tarkington.

"The Japs are moving captured GIs and Filipinos by foot. They say they are being treated bad."

Tarkington scowled. Other GIs noticed Eduardo's return and joined them. "What kind of bad?" asked Tarkington.

Eduardo's lips pressed together and he shook his head then continued in his broken English. "They saw many dead. Filipino and American. Saw prisoners bayoneted when they fall. Made to walk in middle of day. Too hot and no water."

A wave of guilt swept over Tarkington and he could see it in the others too. They'd been living like kings while their fellow soldiers were being butchered. Sergeant Winkleman, his second in command, spat and uttered, "Barbarians. All of 'em, fucking barbarians."

"Where is this happening?" Tarkington asked.

Eduardo pointed south, "They started in Mariveles. They march north to a train station, San Fernando. Long walk. Over seventy-kilometers. Groups of one-hundred."

Tarkington shook his head. "Those men are malnourished, barely able to stand, let alone walk. How do they expect them to make it?"

Eduardo looked him in the eye. "Forced to march. If they fall, they die."

Winkleman gasped, "Jesus, it's probably their way of killing them without wasting ammo."

PFC Skinner rubbed his short-cropped hair. "We've gotta do something. Can't sit by while they murder our men."

The others murmured their agreement. Tarkington nodded, "Guess it's time to get back in the war."

That evening, Tarkington and the others met with the village leader inside the thatched main hall. It was a long building, able to accommodate all the villagers and was used as a communal dining area as well as a place to conduct meetings and even criminal trials if needed.

The village elder, Vindigo, sat at the head of the long table, his wife beside him. She was the only woman in the meeting. They were an old couple, but the epitome of health. Their skin was dark with deep creases crisscrossing their faces, but their eyes sparkled with life and good living. Tarkington had gone hunting and patrolling with Vindigo and had nothing but respect for the man's ability to move soundlessly through the jungle. His advanced years hadn't slowed him at all, as far as Tarkington could tell.

Eduardo sat in the first chair to Vindigo's left acting as a translator. After the usual greetings were out of the way, Tarkington stood and addressed Vindigo and his wife, Mona "Your hospitality over the last month is very much appreciated." He paused to let Eduardo translate. The Tagalog language wasn't as mysterious as it had been upon first hearing it, but Tarkington still had little idea what was being said. Vindigo understood English but translating assured accuracy.

Vindigo nodded and Tarkington continued. "Vick is recovering well thanks to you and your healers. He's not quite ready to leave, but we," he indicated the six other soldiers, "need to get back in the fight."

Eduardo translated and Vindigo nodded and spoke. Eduardo translated, "Vick can stay as long as needed. Vindigo will help. He offers to send guides."

Tarkington smiled. "That would be appreciated."

Vindigo spoke and there were more translations. "He warns of capture. The village will be destroyed if its location is known."

Tarkington nodded. "I understand." He looked around the room at the grim-faced GIs. "We're a small force. We only want to see what's going on with our fellow soldiers. None of us have any doubt that if captured we'll be tortured and killed." He paused looking around the room. "I, for one, won't be taken alive."

After the translation, Vindigo looked to the other men. Each stood and announced, "Nor will I." Over the past month, the GIs had plenty of time on their hands to discuss such things and, though it was easier said than done, Tarkington didn't doubt their resolve.

Vindigo nodded, stood and spoke in broken English, "You have honor. We will help you kill Japanese."

Tarkington nodded and smiled, "This will be a sneak-and-peek mission. We simply need to know what we're facing out there. If there's an opportunity to kill Japs — well, we'll take it — but only if we think we can get away with it. If we do though, there's no turning back. They'll hunt us." He paused to let Eduardo translate but Vindigo waved him off, understanding enough on his own.

Tarkington continued. "I've no doubt the reports of Jap cruelty are real, but remember, there's no backup, no Navy, no Army, no air support, nothing. As far as the Japs are concerned, all allied forces on Luzon surrendered. As I said, once we attack, *if* we attack, the cat's out of the bag. We'll be considered criminals and hunted mercilessly." He paused letting the point settle in. "If we do nothing else but witness atrocities — someday they'll be accountable, and we'll be there to verify their barbarism. But in order to do that, we have to survive."

It was decided; they'd leave as soon as they had eaten and gathered their things. The meeting broke up and the men filtered from the room, muttering among themselves.

───────────

Tarkington went straight from the meeting to PFC Vick's hootch. Stollman had been at the meeting, leaving his best friend alone with the lie he was going hunting. Vick was sitting on the edge of the thatch bed struggling to get his boots on, when Tarkington walked in. "What are you doing? Going for a walk?"

Vick stopped trying to pull the boot on and shook his head. "Nope getting ready to move out with you."

Tarkington grinned and looked at the wooden slats of the floor. "Can't fool you I guess."

"Nope. I'm fine, Tark. I can make it."

"Look Vick you need to sit this one out. We're not going into combat...at least I hope not. This is reconnaissance. The need for stealth is paramount and you're simply not ready for that yet. You were shot a month ago, for chrissakes. You need to heal."

"Bullshit. I'm good to go."

"Yeah? Let's see you put your boot on then."

Vick's face blanched a little, but he grabbed the boot and nodded, "Okay." He leaned over to steady himself; the movement put pressure on his wound and he couldn't keep from gasping in pain. Beads of sweat appeared on his forehead and he grimaced and grunted, desperately trying to push his foot into the boot without success.

Tarkington put his hand on his shoulder and Vick sat up straight, relieving the pressure from the gunshot wound. His face was pale and his eyes bloodshot from the effort. "It's not your fault, Vick. Your body just isn't healed yet. No one can heal that fast."

Vick spat, "Eduardo did. You didn't leave him behind."

"Eduardo should still be in the hospital. He's a freak of nature. Besides, he didn't have a choice. If he'd stayed, he'd be a prisoner by now or worse. You stay here, get better and when we come back, we'll see where you are."

Vick took a deep breath and let it out slow. "Stolly and I are a team. He'll be lost without me."

PFC Stollman burst through the thatch door. "Jesus, Vick. Tark's gonna think I've gone soft or something."

Vick shook his head. "Can't anyone have a private conversation anymore?"

Stollman shook his head and gave a sideways grin. "The walls are made of leaves. I was passing by, heard my name used in vain."

Vick mumbled, "Bullshit. This is bullshit. I should be going with you guys. I'm part of Tark's Ticks."

Tarkington still wasn't comfortable with that moniker but didn't say anything. Stollman chimed in. "A founding member. Lifetime membership." He leaned in close, "Which wouldn't be long if you gave us away out there cause you weren't able to move well."

"Fuck you, Stolly. I can move fine."

The glint in Stollman's eye vanished, he was no longer joking around. "It's true. I'll tell it like it is; you're a liability out there. You're not coming, Vick. I'll be fine without my nursemaid."

Vick finally nodded his head, acquiescing. "How long'll you be gone?"

Tarkington answered. "Figure at least a week. We'll move at night, lay up during the day. It'll be slow going."

Vick nodded and stuck his hand out. Tarkington took it and they shook. "Well, don't get your fool heads shot off. I'll be expecting you back here in a week."

Tarkington straightened, "Yes, mother." He stepped around Stollman who nodded. Tarkington looked at his watch, "We'll leave in two hours. Rest easy, Vick."

"Will do, Tark." he said, then addressed Stollman. "Watch your back out there. I won't be there to protect your useless ass."

Stollman shook his head. "I will. You know I'm the one that's gotten you through all this so far, right? Way you act, you're the only reason I'm alive."

Vick shook his head. "Just watch your back, okay?"

Stollman nodded. "I won't be lugging the BAR around on this one at least. There's no ammunition for it anyway."

"Yeah, that's one good thing, I guess. Good luck, Stolly."

"No problem, Vick. See you in a week."

Two-hours later, the six GIs and five Filipinos, including Eduardo, were standing in the center of the village. The GIs' packs were stuffed — mostly with food and ammunition. They carried two canteens each and would refill them at creeks or any wells they happened upon.

Tarkington addressed them one last time before they entered the wilds of the jungle. "Remember, reconnaissance. We get spotted by the Japs; we're done for." There were nods all around. "Let's move out."

PFC Vick stood in the door of his hootch, a village woman nearby, making sure of his balance. Stollman waved and shook his head, then murmured to the rest of them, "While we're going out to meet the enemy, old Vick's gonna be bumping uglies with all the women."

Skinner shook his head and pushed Stollman forward, his hand on his back. "He's the only one that has a chance with 'em anyway. You're way too ugly."

Stollman, following Sergeant Winkleman, pulled his straw hat off his head, and tossed his wild, curly red hair. "You kidding me? Those gals love my long locks." He brushed his hand over Skinner's stubbled scalp. "You should let yours grow out. Help you get laid, maybe take the edge off your shitty attitude."

Sergeant Winkleman was unable to keep from grinning. "Knock it off you two. No talking from here on out."

Stollman's face went serious and he nodded but lunged his boot back in a mock kick. Skinner smacked it away with the stock of his Springfield.

They left the safety of the village and entered the jungle. Over the past month, they'd all ventured out helping the hunting parties. The hunters didn't need their help — indeed they thought of the loud Americans as liabilities — but they went along anyway, to keep their patrolling skills sharp. Venturing out this time, however, felt different somehow: more permanent and ominous, and they'd be leaving the valley for the first time.

Tarkington was ten-paces behind his lead scout, PFC Henry. The four Filipinos from the village were out of sight, well in front. In the darkness and tight confines of the jungle, Tarkington could only see Henry's dim outline occasionally. He moved through the jungle with skill and silence and was the only soldier the village hunters didn't mind coming along on hunts. He also had the uncanny knack of sensing trouble. More than once they'd averted certain annihilation due to his sixth sense, which was why he was the squad's lead scout.

They moved through the hidden valley relatively quickly, maneuvering over ground each of them was familiar with. Once they topped out over the highest hill and descended toward the main highway, their progress slowed. The night was hot and humid, but the GIs were used to it by now and were relatively comfortable. They barely noticed the jungle's night sounds anymore, but when there was a slight change, each soldier felt it in their subconscious and before Henry held up a fist to halt, they were already slowing and paying more attention to their surroundings.

Tarkington listened intently, trying to decide what he'd noticed. He couldn't put his finger on it, but something was different and everyone felt it. After five minutes, he inched forward until he was beside Henry's crouched form.

Henry held his rifle at port arms and was as still as death. Tarkington waited. Henry knew he was there and would speak when he thought it appropriate. They'd been together since the beginning and knew each other's idiosyncrasies.

Tarkington held his captured Arisaka rifle over his knee and felt the pressure of his Japanese Samurai sword digging into his hip. He adjusted it slowly as he took in his surroundings. He couldn't see the Filipinos he knew to be in front and wondered if Henry could. Finally, Henry pointed into the gloom and Tarkington saw one of them emerge like a ghost. He came to them in a crouch, making no noise at all; his sandaled feet may as well have been floating over the ground.

Tarkington nearly jumped out of his skin, when Eduardo was suddenly beside him. The Filipinos spoke, their sing-song voices blending with the surrounding jungle sounds as though they were jungle animals themselves.

Eduardo nodded and the villager disappeared back the way he'd come like an apparition. Eduardo relayed the message. "Village ahead. Full of Japanese. We go around."

Tarkington nodded and retreated back to the nearest soldier, Sergeant Winkleman, and passed on the information. Soon the rest were bunched near Henry. He pointed right and moved off. They stayed in single-file, ten paces apart.

They passed closer than he would've liked. The dark shapes of thatch huts only yards to the left. He thought he could hear snoring and felt his ears warm as his heart rate increased. He realized it was probably the same village they'd fled through after losing most of the platoon on the road beyond. It had been abandoned then.

The image of Lieutenant Smoker's dead eyes flashed in his mind and he ground his teeth. Was his body still out there? His blood still pooled and congealed where he'd fallen? Had the Japanese bothered to bury him, along with so many others, or had they simply left them to rot and be picked apart by animals and insects? The thought made him yearn to enter the nearest hut and kill the snoring Japanese, but he reigned it in and slipped past without a sound.

Once safely past they moved parallel to the road, keeping to the jungle. The smell of rot was unmistakable. The jungle always had a hint of rot, but this was more pronounced — the smell of rotting flesh. He thought about the retreat along the road. It had been marked with constant Japanese air strikes and accurate artillery fire. He knew there had to be countless bodies scattered throughout the area, quickly becoming one with the lush jungle soil.

Tarkington glanced at his watch. Dawn was coming. They would need to find shelter before too long, somewhere well hidden. He increased his pace and soon caught up with Henry. He relayed his thoughts, Henry nodded and moved off, Eduardo right behind him. Tarkington shook his head, realizing he hadn't even seen the stealthy Filipino.

3

They spent the day in dense cover along the bank of a tiny creek. The air was slightly cooler and the impenetrable canopy overhead kept the sun from frying them too badly. They slept in shifts, although Tarkington wasn't sure if their Filipino guides actually slept at all. Whenever he saw them, they were vigilantly watching their surroundings. He wondered if perhaps they were like ducks and could sleep with one eye open.

They were close enough to the road to hear the distant sounds and feel the vibrations of vehicles passing by, but not close enough to see them. At one point they heard the unmistakable clanking of tank treads. All traffic was moving south toward Mariveles. Occasionally they'd hear the chatter of Japanese voices. The victors obviously weren't worried how far their voices carried.

As dusk was descending, they ate smoked meat and drank and refilled their canteens from the relatively cold creek. They didn't have purification tablets, but they'd been drinking from various creeks and rivers for months now and most had already experienced multiple bouts of sickness. The last thing Tarkington wanted was to be inflicted with what most of them had lived with the past few months, unrelenting diarrhea. If this little creek held a nasty bug, there was nothing he could do about it, so he drained his canteen and refilled it, hoping for the best.

As the GIs stuffed their food back into their packs, one of the Filipino guides appeared from the jungle. He sought Eduardo out and soon they were talking and gesturing in an animated conversation, which caught everyone's attention.

Eduardo nodded his understanding. Soon, another Filipino appeared and crouched, leaning on his Springfield rifle. Eduardo spoke to Tarkington and the rest of the GIs huddled closer to hear better. "Samir says there is a group of Filipino soldiers ahead a few kilometers. It appears they are waiting to ambush a Japanese convoy."

"Soldiers?" asked Tarkington.

Eduardo nodded but clarified, "He says they wear uniforms he's never seen and are very young."

"Did he talk with them?" Eduardo shook his head. "Do they look like they know what they're doing?"

Eduardo exchanged Tagalog with Samir and shook his head. "He says the ambush will likely fail. It is not a good spot."

Tarkington looked at Henry who was chewing on a long blade of grass. "Let's put a stop to it. If they attack, they'll tip our hand too." Henry nodded his agreement. Tarkington was the highest-ranking man, but over the past month, each soldier had realized they were playing a different game now. The massive military machine they were used to, didn't exist any longer, so they'd become a closer-knit group. Everyone's voice mattered in decision-making. Tarkington simply had the final say.

He clutched Eduardo's arm and spoke. "Go with the guides and keep the soldiers from attacking. Tell them to come back here so we can talk things over." He looked at Henry and PFC Raker, the other scout. "Go with them, so they see American faces." He tapped Eduardo's shoulder, "Hurry." Eduardo nodded and spoke quickly to Samir, who nodded and moved off back the way they'd come, disappearing in the darkening jungle.

The group didn't return as quickly as Tarkington thought they should and was wondering if something had gone wrong. He was pondering sending more men, when there was a rustling of jungle and he saw Raker and

Henry move into the small clearing, followed by unfamiliar Filipino faces. It was nearly dark, but Tarkington could see their uniforms were indeed different than the standard Filipino Army uniforms.

Tarkington counted fifteen young men, all holding Springfield rifles. They were thin from lack of food and glanced nervously left and right as though afraid of being attacked.

Tarkington stepped forward and stood in front of the lead man. The boy snapped off a salute and Tarkington nodded back. "You speak English?" The young man nodded and Tarkington continued. "I'm Staff Sergeant Tarkington and this is what's left of First Platoon of Hotel Company." He gestured to the GIs' grim faces. They looked ancient in comparison to the Filipinos. "What unit you with? I don't recognize your uniforms."

The soldier looked around the surly-looking group and finally nodded, as though deciding they weren't trying to trick him. "I'm honorary Lieutenant Fernandez and these are my men. We are from the Army Academy. These," he touched his tunic, "are school uniforms."

"Honorary?"

"Yes, we have ranks like the Army, but my rank means nothing outside the academy."

Tarkington nodded. "What are you doing out here? My scouts said you were in an ambush position."

His lips thinned and he nodded, a flash of anger in his brown eyes. "Yes. We were waiting to engage the next Japanese that came down the road when your men interfered."

"Don't want to tip our hands." Fernandez gave him a curious look and Tarkington explained. "Don't want the Japs to know we're out here."

"The Japs would be dead," he said as he puffed out his chest.

Tarkington shook his head and lowered his voice so only the lieutenant would hear. "From what my men saw, the ambush wasn't in a good place. You might've killed a few, but you probably wouldn't have survived."

Fernandez scowled and shook his head. "It was a good position. It would have been successful."

Tarkington held up his hands. "Okay, okay if you say so. Point is, we don't want the Japs to know we're here just yet. Not until we have a better idea what we're dealing with."

Fernandez's eyes clouded and he gnashed his teeth. "We are dealing with sons-of-bitches." The flash of anger mixed with his uncertainty in cursing in English made his words sound funny, but he was dead serious. "We must kill them all."

Tarkington kept the smile from his face. He put his hand on the young man's shoulder. "I understand. I really do, but we need to do it smart. We can't go off half-cocked." He saw the flash of confusion but ignored it. "We need a plan so we can cause damage *and* fight another day."

Fernandez stared at Tarkington in the fading light while chewing his lower lip. Finally, he nodded. "Okay. What plan?"

Tarkington nodded and gestured for the young Filipinos to make themselves comfortable. They sat in a semi-circle facing him. His eyes drilled into Fernandez's, "You and your men have any combat experience?"

Fernandez's gaze dropped slightly but he recovered and looked Tarkington in the eye. He shook his head slightly. "Our commander would not allow it. By the time the Japanese swept past, it was too late. We blended with the other refugees and walked south. When it was obvious the battle would be lost, we left our commander and have been in the jungle ever since."

"Are you hungry?" Lieutenant Fernandez couldn't hide the feral look from his face. Tarkington nodded and the men dug into their packs and handed out cured meat, left-over cans of food and whatever extra they could spare.

While they devoured the food like hungry beasts, Tarkington leaned toward Sergeant Winkleman. "What d'you think?"

Winkleman shrugged, "They're green as grass but they wanna fight. Their military school background will make them teachable, I guess. Damn, they look young though."

"Yeah, feel like it would be best to keep them out of this. They're kids."

Winkleman nodded. "Good luck. They're determined. The leader has that hungry vengeful look."

"I'm sending them back to the village."

Winkleman rubbed the back of his neck, flicking a long centipede into the brush. "Seems best."

Tarkington let them finish devouring the food then addressed Fernandez. "Your men need rest and food. I'm sending you back to the village with one of my scouts." He pointed at Francis. Eduardo went to his side and translated. Francis nodded. Tarkington continued, "There's plenty of food and water and most importantly, it's isolated and safe. You can get your strength back."

Fernandez's eyes flashed anger and he looked around wildly, like a caged animal. "No! We fight."

Tarkington was done. He lunged to his feet and lifted the boy off the ground, holding him up by his tunic. Fernandez struggled, thrashing his legs and gripping Tarkington's arms, trying to break free. "Keep your voice down, boy," he seethed, inches from his nose. He waited until the thrashing stopped then set him back down but kept his grip on the tunic. "You'll follow orders. You'll get your chance, I guarantee that, but as a leader you have to put your men's safety first and right now, they're tired and hungry. We're rested and in fighting shape and don't need your men giving us away because they're too weak to move quietly." He released Fernandez's tunic and stepped back. "Go with Francis. Get your men rested and fed and be ready to fight in a couple of days."

Fernandez's shoulders slumped forward as he accepted Tarkington's words. He nodded and passed an order along to the nearest man, whispered in Tagalog. Eduardo listened in, making sure the feisty student was passing the correct order. He gave Tarkington a quick nod.

It was fully dark when the ragtag group of students followed Francis back toward the village. Henry shook his head and spoke in a low murmur to Tarkington. "Some of those rifles weren't even loaded. Those boys would've been slaughtered if we hadn't happened along."

Once the academy students were out of their hair, they moved to the edge of the road and watched for Japanese traffic. They waited ten minutes and saw and heard nothing but the jungle's night sounds. The Japanese had nothing to fear from the allies any longer and would most likely do their traveling during the day.

They crossed the road in pairs while the rest covered them. Once across, they paralleled the road, moving along the less dense east side. The Filipino scouts moved quickly and quietly and the GIs were hard pressed to keep up while still maintaining noise discipline.

They came across the occasional dark building and bypassed them all without further investigation. When they came to a village alongside the road, they lingered on the outskirts looking for signs of life.

The front door of a hut opened and they watched an old man come out and move around the side to take a leak. He gazed up at the star-filled sky and swayed as his piss barely cleared his bare feet. He had no idea there were so sets of eyeballs watching him.

Tarkington nodded to Eduardo, who touched Samir's shoulder. Samir stood slowly and moved out of concealment, quick as a viper and was suddenly behind the villager with his hand over his mouth. He whispered into his ear and soon the man's rigid body went limp and docile. Samir released his grip and the old man followed Samir into the jungle and was soon standing in front of Tarkington and Eduardo. The rest of the squad was crouched out of sight, keeping a secure perimeter. The old man's smile was unmistakable, despite the lack of teeth. "Ask him if he knows where the Japanese are."

It was done and Eduardo relayed, "He says there are many Japanese on road every day. They go to Mariveles to invade Corregidor."

Tarkington nodded. "Ask if he knows where the American and Filipino prisoners are."

The man spoke long, using sweeping hand gestures. "He says they are marching them north. He doesn't know where they are going."

"How many?"

The old man shrugged then spoke one word. Eduardo nodded, "hundreds."

"Marching? Are you sure he doesn't mean transported by trucks?"

Eduardo clarified then answered, "Marching. He's sure of that. His son told him they are forcing them to march all day."

Tarkington nodded and thanked him, giving him a piece of dried meat. The man held the meat to his nose, sniffed it and closed his eyes as though it was heaven-sent. Tarkington smiled and motioned Eduardo back into the jungle. The old man watched them go.

The night's piss had been an eventful one and the old Filipino woke his wife from a deep slumber. She jolted awake, her deep snores stopping abruptly. She fixed him with a venomous stare. In the dim light of the lantern, she could see her husband of forty years sucking on a piece of dried meat. He moved it around his mouth, his lack of teeth keeping him from biting down. She muttered, "Where did you get that?"

He pointed outside and smiled. "The jungle gave it to me." She glared at him, knowing from long experience he'd tell her the rest of the story if she waited long enough. When she didn't take the bait and ask again he shrugged and said, "An American soldier and a Filipino."

Her interest piqued, she sat up in bed, exposing her low-hanging, wrinkled breasts. "You are lying." But she could see he wasn't and he did have the meat. "Will you tell the Japanese?"

He lay down on his thatch bed, still sucking on the meat and nodded. "In the morning. They'll give us rice." She reached for the meat but he turned his head, keeping it for himself. "Good night, wife."

She grumbled and uttered, "Don't wake me again, you old fool." He ignored her and made sure she could hear his loud sucking.

4

After encountering the old man, they continued south, avoiding villages and structures. They didn't see Japanese but heard the occasional aircraft buzzing overhead. The rumble of battle, which had been a constant part of their lives for so many months, was now a dim memory.

When the sky to the East lightened, threatening dawn, they found cover near another small creek and hunkered down. The long night of silent patrolling had drained the GIs. They gladly found cover, dipped their heads into the stream and drank their fill before digging into their packs for food. By the time it was fully light, they were well-concealed. They took two-hour blocks for guard-duty. Those not on guard cleaned their weapons and slept. The day warmed and the trips to the creek became more frequent.

They could hear the distant rumblings of truck engines and tank treads on the main road, despite being far away. It was nearly constant and they wondered if it meant the allies were still putting up a stiff resistance on Corregidor, or if perhaps the Japanese were using Mariveles harbor to move war material off Luzon to places with more need.

Tarkington didn't care one way or the other. The most pressing question for him was what was happening to his fellow soldiers. It was midday and he and Winkleman were chatting with Samir and Eduardo.

Tarkington cleared off a layer of rotting leaves and branches until he found dirt. He pressed his finger into the far upper corner. "We're here. Ask where Mariveles is in relation."

Eduardo asked and Samir leaned forward and punched a hole in the dirt a foot away then traced the road, connecting it to his depression. He spoke Tagalog and Eduardo translated. "He says we are ten-kilometers from Mariveles. The road is full of switchbacks. Much of it can be avoided by going overland." He pointed south. "There are low mountains overlooking the harbor. It will give us a good vantage point to see what is happening in the harbor."

"We can't do shit about the Japs in Mariveles. I want to know what's happening with the prisoners. Where would we most likely find them?" asked Tarkington.

Eduardo conferred with Samir. Both were familiar with the area and they talked for a minute between themselves before Eduardo answered. He drew another line in the dirt further east and moving north. He pointed to the line. "There's a road here. It leads to San Fernando. It must be where prisoners are being marched. There's nothing else. Only animal trails."

Tarkington studied the handmade map and pointed to an area on this side of the road. "What's here? Is there a good vantage point? A spot to see from?"

Eduardo didn't need to ask, "Yes. The road is surrounded by low hills. There's been tree cutting. We have good view here," he pointed to a spot in the dirt. Samir put his finger beside Eduardo's and nodded and spoke in Tagalog. Eduardo nodded, "He says he knows the area. He can get us there before dark."

Tarkington straightened and looked around at his soldiers. Some slept, but most were up and fidgeting with their weapons or tearing off chunks of dried meat. Henry was sharpening his knife. Raker was off with the other Filipinos checking the perimeter. Tarkington nodded and glanced at the scratched face of his wristwatch. "Okay, we leave in ten minutes. Let the men know, Wink." Winkelman nodded and moved off.

Dakil woke from sleep just as the sun was cresting the eastern horizon. His wife was already up and outside collecting kindling from the side of the hut. She wobbled inside, knelt in front of the old stove and shoved small pieces of wood inside. The teapot was already starting to whistle. "Get up lazy bones. We are nearly out of food. You need to find some."

Dakil smiled, remembering his good fortune the night before. "I will stand in the road and flag down the first Japanese officer I see."

"What if they don't find this American? They'll believe you are lying and come back and punish you."

Dakil's toothless smile spread across his face and his eyes creased into deep slits. "They'll come after you too, my dear. The Japanese will torture you in front of me to make me talk, even though I've already told them everything. It is their way."

She shook her head, marveling at how she had stayed with this man so long. She'd been with him since they were children, he was all she had ever known, but his detached cruelty never ceased to amaze her. "Then don't tell them. What they don't know can't hurt them or us."

He shook his head. "I'll make them believe. Perhaps they'll pick up their trail from here. You said we need food. The livestock's been butchered and all the young hunters are gone. I'm too old. You're too old. If we hope to survive we need help. The only way I see is the Japanese."

She was going to protest again but he waved her to silence and held out his empty cup. She dropped in tea leaves — nearly the last of their supply — then poured the steaming water. He blew over the top and walked to the door. There weren't convoys this early, but he knew there soon would be. Gripping his cup, he walked through the mostly-abandoned village until he stood at the edge of the busy road. He settled onto his haunches and sipped his tea, while watching the sun's rays filtering through the trees.

A half-hour passed before the first convoy rounded the corner. Dakil set his empty cup in the dirt and stood to his full height, searching for an officer to flag down. An armored car was leading the convoy and Dakil smiled and waved his withered arms. He stepped further onto the road and waved with more vigor as they approached.

The Japanese officer looked none too happy but directed his driver to pull to the side and see what the old man was getting on about. He ground his teeth, knowing this delay would mean he would be eating road dust until his driver was able to maneuver his way back to the front of the line.

The black car with the blazing red sun on the hood slid to a halt, throwing up a wall of dust enveloping the old man, who kept smiling and waving. Captain Husukima lurched from the passenger seat and strode to the old man, his sergeant by his side, holding his rifle at the ready. The driver stayed put, watching the big trucks trundle past.

Captain Husukima addressed him in broken Tagalog. "What do you want?" Dakil bowed over and over, not sure of the etiquette but knowing that Japanese culture was full of bows. "Speak!" Husukima barked.

"Sir, last night I met an American soldier and a Filipino fighter in the jungle, sir."

Husukima's eyes widened. "An American? Where?"

Dakil pointed toward his hut. His wife was on the porch sweeping. She watched them with a wary eye. "Near my hut. I was outside relieving myself. They jumped me and," he hesitated. "Forced themselves upon my wife."

Husukima looked past him to his wife. She looked even more stooped and elderly than he did. "They *raped* your wife?"

Dakil tried to keep the glee from his eyes. He nodded, then shook his head and added, "She is whore. She enjoyed it very much."

Husukima's face reddened and a vein on his forehead popped out and pulsed. "Are you playing games? Do you know the consequences of such actions?" He gripped the handle of his pistol while his sergeant clutched his Type-38 rifle.

Dakil held up his hands and shook his head. "I tell the truth. I saw a GI and Filipino fighter." He amended his story. "They *tried* to rape her, but I fought them off." The officer was about to pull his pistol and shoot the dithering old fool in the forehead, but Dakil turned and waved them to follow. "Come. I show you their tracks."

Captain Husukima glanced back at his sergeant who was ready to kill the old man and his pathetic wife if he so commanded. He held up his hand, "If there are no tracks, old man, you *and* your wife will die this morning."

Dakil looked back and shrugged. "We will die unless we eat, so it makes no difference. A bullet would be quicker than hunger."

Husukima and the burly sergeant followed the diminutive villager to the edge of his hut. Husukima glared at the woman as he passed, and shook his head speaking to his sergeant. "I'd sooner screw a knot in a tree than that old crone."

"Say the word and I'll end their miserable existences," muttered the sergeant.

"Not yet. We'll see what he has to show us."

Dakil stopped at the edge of the jungle behind his hut and pulled back the brush. The ground was slightly damp and in the morning light there was a clear boot print. "Here, see?" He pointed.

Husukima knelt and ran his hand over the print. He was no tracker — he'd grown up on the city streets of Tokyo — but even he could tell the track was fresh and, judging by the fact it was a boot tread, and fairly large, it could very well be an American's.

He stood and looked around for more. Nodding, he barked an order, "Get trackers out here. I want whoever left this track hunted down." Sergeant Junu stiffened and trotted off toward the car.

Husukima gestured to the patio where Dakil's wife still labored. "Come, sit. I want to know everything you saw last night."

Dakil nodded and went up the two steps and sat on the rickety chair, leaving the more robust one for the officer. Husukima sat and smiled at Dakil. His wife was inside tinkering with the teapot.

She came out holding a steaming cup of loose-leaf tea. Husukima took it, not bothering to hide his disgust. He sniffed it and put it on the floorboards next to his chair. "Did you see the American too?" he asked her. She shook her head, knowing the Japanese had strong views about women speaking. He redirected his gaze back to Dakil. "Tell me what happened."

Dakil told him everything that transpired and Husukima nodded when he was done. "So, no attempted rape," he said.

Dakil's toothless grin split his face. "I didn't think you wanted to hear that part, sir."

The old woman guffawed and slapped her husband's arm viciously, yelling rapid-fire Tagalog that Captain Husukima couldn't keep up with. Dakil clutched his arm and cowered.

Husukima stood abruptly and shouted, "Stop! Enough." He had his hand on his pistol. The old man was a character, no doubt, but he didn't have time for such nonsense. He pointed toward the tracks. "Stay away from there until my men show up with trackers. I don't want you spoiling the trail." Dakil nodded, Husukima stood, ignoring the tea and straightened his khaki pants. "Stay here until my men arrive, they may have more questions for you."

Dakil nodded and ventured. "We were told we'd be rewarded with rice if we told Japanese of enemy soldiers."

Husukima stopped at the bottom of the stairs and nodded. "I'll have the men bring you two sacks of rice. You will be properly rewarded."

Dakil's eyes lit up but his wife saw something else in the officer's gaze which worried her. As Husukima walked to his car, Sergeant Junu joined him halfway, having relayed his orders. Husukima leaned close and said, "Stay here and lead the squad of trackers once they arrive." He tilted his head toward the old couple, "and once they've showed them the tracks, put bullets in their fool heads. They wasted too much of my time."

"Yes, sir," smiled Sergeant Junu. "My pleasure."

The Filipino guides led Tarkington's squad through the jungle, avoiding roads and villages as much as possible. They were forced to cross some well-worn paths, but didn't see anyone, despite it being the middle of the day. Normally, there would be villagers around but many had fled before the advancing Japanese. Tarkington wondered how long before the villagers would filter back. He wondered what the Japanese would do with so many potential threats. Would they allow them to return, or keep them locked up? It would be a logistical nightmare to house and feed so many.

They were able to move relatively quickly and were soon at the top of a hill. The trees had been thinned — as though from a recent logging operation — giving them an unobstructed view of a small dirt road weaving through the lush valley. They found cover on the frontside of the hill, easily concealing themselves in the thick brush and leftover detritus.

Eduardo was between Tarkington and Winkleman. He pointed and whispered, "Mariveles is that way about twenty kilometers."

Tarkington nodded. The lush grass and jungle looked endless as it sloped toward the sea. "What if they've already passed?" he asked.

Winkleman shrugged. "They say it's groups of a hundred or so. I think the road would show more use if they'd all passed. I mean, it looks used, but not thousands of soldiers used."

Tarkington nodded. The dirt road still had a strip of grass growing in the center which he doubted would be there if thousands of shuffling feet had passed by recently. "Good point," he conceded. He glanced at his watch, "We've got another coupla hours of daylight. If they're coming today, we should see them soon."

They spent the next hour making sure they were well concealed. Raker, Henry and the remaining guides moved south, following the road toward Mariveles and were soon out of sight.

As the day was tilting toward evening, Skinner, on the right flank, signaled that the scouts were returning. Soon Raker and Henry were reporting to Tarkington and Winkleman. They were out of breath and had a sense of urgency about them. Raker was the first to speak. "They're coming." He pointed, and Tarkington realized he could see a hint of dust over the valley. "Lots of 'em."

Tarkington nodded. "Are the Japs sweeping their front?"

Henry shook his head, his breathing under control. "Nah, there's a jeep but they're acting like they don't have a care in the world. From what we saw, it's a group of American GIs. I'd estimate about a hundred. They look haggard."

Tarkington nodded. "Makes sense, I guess, splitting 'em up like that. Easier to deal with a hundred rather than thousands all at once."

Winkleman asked, "Any chance of breaking them out?"

The question was directed at the scouts, but Tarkington answered. "What the hell'd we do with a hundred POWs? We don't have anything to give 'em. Not enough anyway. At least with the Japs they'll get food and water and maybe medical care."

Henry shook his head slightly. "Doesn't look that way to me. We're what...twenty kilometers from Mariveles? Figure this is their second day of marching? They look like shit. Like dead men walking."

"Fucking Japs," seethed Winkleman.

A half-hour later, a Japanese vehicle came into view. It was a captured US Army Jeep. Where the white star of the United States had been, there was now a blazing red dot. There were four passengers, the soldier in the front passenger seat, obviously an officer.

Tarkington crouched and peered through a slot in the cover and watched the Jeep come to a stop. It was downslope fifty-yards or so. He had his Arisaka rifle up but had no intention of firing and giving away their position. He'd relayed that message to the others. This was a reconnaissance mission only.

The officer got out of the Jeep and stretched his back, twisting from side-to-side. He motioned and the other three soldiers joined him and spread out. They soon returned and had a brief conference, then the driver saluted, got back into the Jeep and pulled it off the side of the road and parked

Soon, around the corner came the lead element of the column. Two Japanese soldiers with slung rifles, bayonets attached, came into view. Tarkington pointed and whispered to Winkleman. "Bayonets...like they're expecting trouble or something."

The prisoners shuffled behind in a line three abreast. They wore what was left of their shredded uniforms — the beige long faded to almost pure white in the harsh Luzon sun. Tarkington pointed at the leading three. "That's an officer on the left." He wished he had a pair of binoculars.

"How can you tell?" asked Winkleman.

"Just by the way he's carrying himself. I don't know, but I'd bet a year's wage on it." As the rest of the group came into view Tarkington hissed, "They look ready to drop." The men in the middle were being held up by the men on either side. Everyone seemed to be limping. Their rags hung off their skeletal frames and they were obviously suffering in the blazing sun.

The lead guards stopped when they were near the Jeep and the officer stood in the middle of the road with his fists on his hips, facing the ragtag group. He yelled and the long, ragged line of POWs stuttered to a halt. Even from here, Tarkington could hear their agonized moans. There were guards along the outside of the lines and they had their bayoneted rifles off their shoulders.

An American GI from the center of the mass, suddenly broke away from the group and staggered to the side of the road, falling to his knees. He gagged, convulsed and finally toppled onto his side.

The Japanese officer unsheathed his sword and pointed at the man, yelling something. Two of the nearest guards hustled to the GI and leaned over and yelled, but the GI stayed down. The guards kicked him hard from both sides and the man curled into a ball to protect himself. They continued to yell and kick.

Another GI broke from the line and went toward the injured GI. A third guard stepped forward and slammed the butt of his rifle into the side of the would-be rescuer's head and he dropped too, clutching his face. The first GI rolled onto his back and held up his shaking hands. Both guards raised their weapons and thrust their bayonets into him, screaming. The GI's body curled around the blades and he clutched at the cold steel. His mouth was open, his swollen, grayish tongue out like he was screaming, but he made no sound. The guards pulled their bayonets back and the GI rolled to the side and went still.

The GI who'd been hit in the face got to his knees and reached again for his dying comrade. He was rewarded with a kick to the gut. Another GI ran to *his* aid and before the guard could kick again, helped the GI to his feet and they shuffled back into line.

Tarkington was stunned. He and his men had just witnessed a cold-blooded murder of one of their comrades. A defenseless, sick, American soldier; bayoneted. He clutched his rifle, wanting to kill every last one of them, but Winkleman squeezed his shoulder and whispered, "Not now, Tark. Not yet."

Tarkington snapped out of his rage and nodded. He could hardly speak, "Make — make sure the others don't attack." Winkleman nodded and signaled.

The Japanese officer sheathed his sword, got back into the Jeep and it lurched forward, kicking up dust. The procession continued shuffling past and Tarkington and the others watched in morbid fascination. They tracked the guards with their rifle sights, wanting to pull the triggers, but knowing it would end in their own deaths and probably many of the POW's.

When the procession rounded the bend and all that was left was their dust and the dead GI, Tarkington seethed. "They left the body to rot. Sons-of-bitches."

They waited twenty minutes before breaking cover and moving down-slope to the road. No words were spoken, each man trying to come to terms with what they'd just seen. The Filipinos went up the road, making sure the Japanese didn't return, while Tarkington and the rest went to the body.

He was still curled in a ball, the ground in front awash with his lifeblood. His gray skin and his staring eyes left no doubt he was dead. They stood around him staring grimly, memorizing his tortured features. He had a filthy rag covering a gash on his arm, and signs of spreading infection. He was rail-thin and badly bruised. He'd been on his last legs and the Japanese hadn't done a thing to help him.

After a few minutes, Tarkington pointed up the road. "These are the animals we're fighting." He shook his head. "I'll never surrender to those *savages*." There were nods all around. "See if he's got anything on him we can save for his parents. We'll bury him off this godforsaken road."

He watched them lift the body as though it was made of fine china. They entered the jungle, the sound of entrenching tools unmistakable. "What now, Tark? Do we hit them?" asked Winkleman.

Tarkington shook his head slightly. "Not yet. Much as I'd like to, we're not ready. Once we do, we'll be hunted, and I'd like to have an exit plan of some kind." He paused as he watched the men lower the GI into the scraped-out hole in the jungle. "Now that we've seen what we're dealing with, we'll move back to the village and come up with a plan of attack. We can't sit idly by while this goes on, but we can't run headlong into it either. We need to be smart."

He stepped into the jungle where his men were looking down at the corpse. Someone had closed the soldier's eyes and crossed his thin arms over his chest. He looked almost comfortable, before they shoveled dirt over him and laid a makeshift cross over the top. Nearby rocks were stacked over him to dissuade the jungle animals from digging him up. No words were said, but they all said silent prayers to themselves. After a minute or two, Tarkington waved them on, "Move out. We need to get back to the village and figure how to best hurt these sons-of-bitches."

5

After the old man told them of his encounter with the enemy, Sergeant Junu waited for the soldiers from the reconnaissance squad to show up. When they did an hour later, he led them to the old man who showed them the boot tracks in the jungle.

Before setting off in pursuit, Junu put his arm around the old man's shoulder and asked in his limited English, "Where wife?"

Dakil answered in his own limited English. "I not know." He looked around wondering where she'd disappeared to. He wanted her to see the two bags of rice being delivered. He wanted to gloat that he was taking care of her, making her rich.

She'd spouted nonsense about not trusting the Japanese officer, that she had a bad feeling about him. She begged him to leave before they returned. Did she leave? She'd be back and it would make it even sweeter when he not only had enough rice for a year but proved her wrong. The day couldn't get much better.

Sergeant Junu squeezed his shoulder and asked, "You want reward now?" He smiled at him kindly, like he was a child eager for a new toy.

Dakil's toothless smile lit up his eyes and he nodded. "Rice," he uttered and looked around as though perhaps the two bags were sitting nearby. When he didn't see them, he asked, "Where?"

Junu's smile turned dark and he said, "Better than rice." He pulled his knife from the sheath on his belt and held it up for Dakil to see. There was an instant of confusion, then fear. The knife plunged into his gut and sliced sideways, severing his abdominal aorta, the largest artery in Dakil's frail, old body. His eyes rolled to the back of his head as the blood washed over Sergeant Junu's hand.

Junu withdrew the dripping blade and let the old man's body topple to the ground. At that instant, there was a crash from the jungle and a bullet creased Sergeant Junu's cheek. He spun with the impact and fell to the ground clutching his face. He rolled on the ground, the pain washing over him in waves of agony. Out of the corner of his eye, he saw the old man's wife stepping from the jungle holding an impossibly long rifle. She was struggling to work the bolt, to chamber the bullet which would end his life.

He clutched at the rifle strapped to his back, but it was pinned beneath his body, digging into him. Normally, it would've caused him pain, but it was muted by the fire coming from his face.

He rolled to his stomach and got to a knee. The woman had succeeded in reloading and was bringing the rifle up again. There was a shot, and Junu thought he'd feel the lancing pain of a bullet, but instead she dropped the rifle and stepped toward him, her white top blossoming crimson from the bullet which had entered her back and exited her chest. She flopped forward and landed nearly on top of her dead husband.

Behind her, one of the reconnaissance squad soldiers held his smoking rifle. "Are you okay, Sergeant?"

Junu nodded and clutched his face, feeling the stickiness of his own blood mixing with Dakil's. "I need a medic. Hurry!"

Sergeant Junu didn't let his face wound delay the reconnaissance unit too much. He insisted they wait while the medic cleaned and stitched the wound. He used the old man's front porch, despite the medic urging him to go to the infirmary.

The gash required twenty stitches and each time the needle nudged and pulled the frayed edges of his skin, he winced but forced himself to remain quiet and take the pain. He'd take his wrath out on the renegade American.

Twenty minutes after the medic had started sewing, he was done. Junu's face felt hot, as though it were flaming. The medic bandaged his face as best he could and told him to keep it clean and replace the bandage with a fresh one as soon as he got a chance.

Junu dismissed him and gingerly touched the bandage. He could feel his face swelling, stretching the stitches. It throbbed, but he tried to ignore it and grabbing the barrel of his rifle, joined the reconnaissance team. Sergeant Hirosuku reported, "I sent two of my best trackers forward. There are more than just two sets of prints."

Junu looked surprised and asked, "How many are we tracking?"

"Difficult to tell for certain, but at least six, maybe more. There are boot tracks mixed with tire-tread tracks." Junu looked confused and Hirosuku explained, "The villagers use old tires for the soles of their sandals sometimes."

Junu nodded his understanding. "So not Filipino soldiers."

Hirosuku shook his head, "Likely villagers."

"Resistance. We'll make examples of them," Junu sneered. He looked Sergeant Hirosuku over. His reputation preceded him. He'd seen a lot of combat, even more than Junu himself. He noticed he carried one of the new Type-100 submachine guns, a rarity. He pointed at it, "How'd you come by that?"

Hirosuku brought the weapon off his shoulder and let Junu hold it. "A few were passed out to reconnaissance squads for testing. I was fortunate enough to be chosen."

Junu hefted it, grunted and gave it back. He tapped his Type-38 rifle. "I prefer my rifle. More accurate. You look like a yankee gangster with that."

Hirosuku shrugged. "Not as accurate but for close combat, I like it," He answered, ignoring the yankee gangster jab.

Minutes later they caught up with the two trackers. Their progress was slow, testing Sergeant Junu's patience. His face throbbed. At one point, he felt dizzy and pulled his canteen out with shaking hands, kneeling to hide his discomfort.

Sergeant Hirosuku saw the senior sergeant's obvious pain but knew if he mentioned it the surly soldier would reprimand him harshly. He'd watched Junu kill the old man and he knew a sociopath when he saw one. The Imperial Japanese Army was full of such men, unfortunately. He'd seen their atrocities countless times in China.

He saw no honor in killing defenseless villagers, particularly ones who were helping. Most Filipinos he'd encountered hated them with unfettered passion. Indeed, the Filipino Army had put up a stalwart defense alongside the Americans and from what he had seen, the consensus that they were an inferior, untrained force, was wholly wrong.

To find a helpful Filipino was an anomaly. For the senior sergeant to kill him was, in his estimation, counterproductive, but he'd learned to keep his opinions to himself.

The rest of the day was slow going. The trackers had to double back a few times when they lost the trail and would have to find where they'd gone wrong. It all took time.

The day was hot and the slow pace irritated Sergeant Junu. Sweat soaked through his bandage and it was soon wet and pink with his own blood. While the trackers were once again trying to find the enemy tracks, he pulled the sopping bandage off. The wound stung as the stagnant air and his own sweat touched the gash. He gingerly touched it and his fingers came away bloody. He could feel his swollen cheek stretching the stitches. It felt as though they'd break, and his flesh would split.

He poured water over the bandage and squeezed it out, trying to clean and dry it as best he could. The wad of cloth looked dirty and was still tinged pink. He motioned a nearby private to help him reapply it and he could tell by the soldier's repellant reaction, that the wound didn't look good. The soldier placed his rifle on the ground to help the sergeant and Junu couldn't help asking, "How does it look?"

The young private lowered his eyes and nodded. "It looks fine, Sergeant." He bowed his head as he said it.

Sergeant Junu shook his head, "You're lying, Private." The soldier kept his eyes down and Junu shook his head. "No matter. There are far more, injured far worse."

He waved the private away and strode forward to find Junior Sergeant Hirosuku. "This is too slow! The renegades will be long gone at this rate."

Hirosuku kept his disdain for the man out of his gaze. "The men we're tracking are skilled at hiding their tracks. If we rush, we'll likely lose the trail."

"It appears we're heading south mostly. They're probably heading toward Mariveles. How far is it?"

Hirosuku shrugged, "I estimate fifteen-kilometers."

"I can still hear road traffic, we're not far from it. It appears they are simply paralleling it."

"That's my assessment too, Sergeant."

Junu's mouth turned downward. "You must hurry your men along, Sergeant. This pace is unacceptable. Their path hasn't veered much one way or another."

Hirosuku didn't like being told how to run his squad, particularly by this sadistic son-of-a-whore, but he nodded, "Yes, Sergeant."

He split his men up, sending one tracker around and ahead in the hopes of picking up the trail and allowing the men further back to move up, if he did. The danger, of course, was the lead element might blunder into the renegades and be ambushed. If that happened and he lost even a single man, he'd be sure Sergeant Junu didn't make it out of the jungle.

The leapfrog method worked well, and the reconnaissance squad increased their pace. At sundown, they found where the enemy had bivouacked beside a small creek. There were only a few minutes of light left and Sergeant Hirosuku was pleased that they were only a day behind their prey. He ordered, "We'll stop here for the night."

Sergeant Junu stepped forward, his bandage soaked red by the seeping wound. His eyes were bloodshot and his cheek was bulging. Hirosuku thought he could see it pulsing in the low light. "Why are we stopping?" asked Junu.

"We cannot track them at night. We have found where they spent the day. We are not far behind and will most likely catch up with them tomorrow while they rest."

"But they will be traveling tonight and get even farther away."

Hirosuku shook his head. "They are probably already at their destination, wherever that may be. If it's Mariveles, then they are surely there, since it's only a few kilometers away. If they were trying to get off the peninsula, they're heading the wrong direction. They are close but bumbling into them at night would be a good way to die. Besides, my men can't track what they can't see."

The vein on Junu's forehead was pulsing, but the throbbing from his cheek was even more intense. He wanted to order them to continue, but Hirosuku seemed to know what he was doing and he did feel tired. He swallowed his anger and gave a curt nod. "Have one of your men assist me with my wound. I need the bandage cleaned and reapplied."

Hirosuku nodded. "Of course, Sergeant."

The sun had set and Tarkington had the guides leading them back toward the village. They were mostly out of water. The guides didn't know of anywhere other than the creek they'd stayed near the night day before to refill, so they moved in that direction.

It was never a good idea to retrace steps already taken, so they moved north, then angled back toward their bivouac site, hoping to hit the creek further upstream. Tarkington would rather have taken a more direct route to the village, but the lack of water would be taxing and he felt there was minimal risk of running into trouble. The risk of losing men to dehydration was far greater.

The jungle was thicker during the first part of their trek, but when they started moving west, toward the creek, things thinned out. Even though it was dark, he could see they moved through a forest of pine trees, whose presence in the jungle always struck him as odd. He wondered if the relative sparseness was due to logging, or if it was that way naturally. He'd probably be able to tell once it was light. He shook his head, he must be getting tired; his mind was wandering.

He focused, knowing that if he was feeling the effects, the rest of them would be too. He considered stopping for a rest but rejected the idea, knowing most of them were out of water and stopping would only delay quenching their thirst.

He moved forward and touched Winkleman's arm. He slowed and listened while Tarkington spoke. "Make sure the men are sharp. No mistakes, we're almost to water and a break." He was guessing, but he thought they must be. Winkleman nodded and quickened his pace, passing the message along.

Ten minutes later the line suddenly stopped. Tarkington saw Winkleman crouch, holding up his fist. Tarkington immediately passed the signal and went to a knee, pointing his rifle into the darkness. He realized the night sounds were not as vibrant as normal. How long had that been going on, he wondered? He cursed himself for once again dropping his guard, despite his own warnings.

Long minutes passed. He knew not to move, something was going on and he trusted the guides, particularly his scouts. They'd inform him when it was appropriate to move and not before.

He thought, not for the first time, how exposed they were. They were a guerrilla unit now, operating without any backing from the US military. If they got into trouble there'd be no one they could call, no support whatsoever. It was a lonely and terrifying feeling, but one which he'd need to get accustomed to, for it was the new normal.

Finally, he saw movement in front of Winkleman. Someone was passing info along. Tarkington moved forward until he was beside his sergeant. He saw the worried look on Henry's face, as he whispered, "Japs. In our old bivouac."

Tarkington realized two things instantly: they were not in a good position to attack, and they were being followed.

Tarkington's stress level was high. They'd nearly bumbled into the Japanese bivouac. Only the keen senses of the scouts and guides had kept them from being discovered. They broke away, moving back the way they'd come. It was slow and excruciating, but finally they were far enough away to reconvene and talk things over.

Tarkington rallied them around him in a tight circle. He kept his voice low. "We're being followed. Not sure how, but they're onto us. It can't be a coincidence that they're spending the night in the same spot." He looked from man to man, they were nodding their heads. "They're obviously skilled. We'll be more careful from here on out, but I don't want to risk them following our tracks back to the village." He looked at their haggard faces. "We have to take them out." An uneasy silence and Tarkington continued. "We have the advantage. We know their route and can set up an ambush. I'm open to suggestions, but I think that little valley we went through the other day would be a good spot." He looked to the men who were nodding in agreement. "Okay, here's what we'll do. First, we get water. Then we retrace our steps and set up the ambush. I figure it's three-kilometers, we can get there and set up before dawn, easily. Any questions? Suggestions?" Eduardo translated for the other Filipinos. When no one spoke, Tarkington nodded, "Okay, let's move to the water and be on our way."

They moved with more caution but were soon at the creek and silently drinking and filling canteens. With their thirst satiated, they passed around food and ate what they had, saving the last bit for the next day's march. Tarkington hoped they'd find food on the Japanese, assuming the ambush was effective. If it wasn't, their food situation wouldn't matter.

Eduardo explained to the Filipino guides where they wanted to set up the ambush and they nodded and quickly moved off. After the water, the men were rejuvenated and moved well making very little noise.

It took an hour and a half to move the three-kilometers. The sky was clear, and the half-moon rose lighting up the jungle with gray light. They were careful to stay well off their original path, the one the Japanese would follow.

The original path led toward a game trail which cut through the base of two opposing, lightly-jungled hills. They'd come to the area two days before and, although it would have been much easier to pass through the four-hundred-yard-long cut, they'd chosen to go over the hills. It was too obvious a spot for an ambush and they'd all agreed to go around. Tarkington figured the Japanese would also veer away from the cut and follow their tracks into the jungle. The area in front of the game trail was open, without much cover. They'd move up the hill and set their ambush so they'd have a height advantage and clear fields of fire.

They went up the left hill, well away from their original trail and crossed to the right hill, well beyond where the valley ended. They were careful to cover their tracks.

They moved three-quarters of the way down the hill and when they could see the wide-open area in the moonlight, began digging foxholes.

Tarkington spread the nine men out in an upside-down L shape, with the base of the L at the top and the rest moving down the hill, ending a couple of yards onto the flat. He wished he had a machine gun, but all they had were Springfields, a couple of Japanese Arisakas, and four grenades. Each man had plenty of extra ammunition, hopefully enough to kill all the Japanese.

The men worked hard, digging and concealing their fighting holes. Two-hours later, with dawn an hour away, Tarkington did a final inspection. His foxhole was up the hill and closest to the valley. His sharpshooter, PFC Henry, was in the hole beside him. Eduardo and the guides were next. The rest of holes moved down the hill at fifteen-yard intervals, ending with Stollman and Skinner sharing a hole with all the grenades. Now all they had to do was wait.

6

Sergeant Hirosuku had the men up well before dawn, eating, drinking water and shitting. By the time the jungle lightened with the sunrise, they were ready to go.

He addressed the impatient Sergeant Junu. "It is light enough to begin, Sergeant." The man's face was even more swollen and his bandage was soaked through again. His men had helped him clean and reapply the bandage, but the wound looked awful and Hirosuku was sure it was infected. Junu's left eye was nearly shut from the swelling, and the left side of his mouth turned up awkwardly and unnaturally, giving him a macabre look as though he were grinning. "Your wound does not look good, Sergeant. If you wish, I can have a few of my men escort you back to a field hospital."

Sergeant Junu shook his head and uttered, "No. I'm fine and have my orders." Hirosuku bowed slightly and Junu continued. "Carry on. We'll find them today, I can feel it."

They'd found where the trail started again the evening before, so they quickly reacquired it and continued tracking. The tracks no longer headed in a southerly direction, but east. Like the day before, Hirosuku had his men split up, with one group moving twenty-meters ahead searching for signs, while the rest stayed back and followed the known trail. Like the day before, they made good time. The path didn't diverge much.

Sergeant Junu asked, "What is east of us? Where are they going?"

Hirosuku answered, "Not much. The gulf of course, but I'm surprised they're no longer heading toward Mariveles. Perhaps they are circumnavigating and coming from behind." Junu didn't respond just shrugged and mumbled something under his breath. Hirosuku could tell the man was in excruciating pain. "Be sure to drink plenty of water, Sergeant. That wound is..."

"Stop," barked Junu, spraying blood-spackled spit with his words. "Worry about finding the renegades."

Hirosuku's jaw rippled as he ground his teeth. He wanted to punch the surly bastard's wound and watch his eyes bug out, but instead he simply bowed slightly and turned away.

The men made good time and by late morning they were three kilometers from the bivouac sight. They came to a clearing. There were two hills which nearly intersected creating a small valley at the far end. The lead element stopped before entering the clearing, awaiting instructions from Sergeant Hirosuku.

Hirosuku didn't like it. They'd be exposed as they crossed, which was why his experienced squad hadn't entered. The fighting was officially over on Luzon, but they were following a group who didn't seem to have got the word or were taking things into their own hands.

Sergeant Junu stopped beside him and growled. "What are you waiting for? Let's move out."

Hirosuku pointed. "We'll go around, make sure the other side doesn't hold any surprises."

The vein on Junu's forehead popped out and he sputtered. "No more delays. You're too cautious, there's nothing to fear. They couldn't possibly know we're tracking them, so there won't be any surprises."

Hirosuku's lips creased in silence. He shook his head, but before he could speak, Junu sputtered, "I've let you lead because this is your squad, but I'm senior. I'm taking command." He pointed at the tracker who'd been out front, "I'm ordering you to advance and pick up the trail. It probably goes through that gap." The private glanced at Sergeant Hirosuku and Junu nearly burst his stitches. "Move, Private!" Against his better judgement, Hirosuku gave him a slight nod.

As Junu noted, there was an obvious game trail leading through the gap, but the forward element didn't see any tracks leading that way. Hirosuku stood at the edge of the clearing, he didn't like the look of the valley and decided the men they were tracking hadn't either and had chosen to go over the hill. It's exactly what he would've done. Using the game trail would be easier, but it was also a perfect place for an ambush.

The lead element motioned that they'd found the trail leading up the hill, just as he'd suspected. His thirteen-man squad, including Sergeant Junu, moved to the signaling tracker, crossed the open ground and began up the slope.

Sergeant Hirosuku stopped suddenly, pulling the submachine gun off his shoulder. His men noticed and stopped too looking side-to-side. Sergeant Junu was beside him and looked annoyed. "What the hell's the matter now?" Hirosuku shushed him and Junu's eyes nearly bugged out of his head as he seethed, "Don't you dare quiet me you piece of..."

The sudden crashing sound of rifle fire stopped his tirade. Bullets thumped into flesh and the air filled with puffs of red-tinged mist. Sergeant Hirosuku dove to the ground and yelled, "Cover," but it was too late for many of his men. He could see at least four down, unmoving. Others were calling out, writhing in pain trying to crawl away from the killing ground.

He crawled forward to the prone body of Private Husu and shook him, but there was no response. He looked beyond him and saw winking flashes and smoke a little way up the hill. A bullet snapped near his ear and he ducked. He felt Husu's body lurch with another impact. He realized there was firing from the left side too.

He lifted his Type-100 submachine and aimed left, firing a short burst at a puff of smoke. He saw an object flying toward him. It looked like a rock, but his brain quickly deduced it was far more dangerous. "Grenade!" he yelled. He ducked behind the dead soldier and waited.

An instant later the ground shook with an explosion, then another and another. Dirt and debris rained down on him and he lay with one hand gripping his weapon, the other over his cloth cap.

The firing continued and he knew he had to get his men out of this killing ground before it was too late. Behind him was open ground, they'd be cut to pieces long before they made it to the far side. Their only chance was a headlong charge. He heard rifles returning fire, so he knew some of his men were still alive and fighting. He yelled at the top of his lungs. "Left! Move left. Now!"

He got to his knees. The air was still thick with smoke and dust from the grenades. He saw four other men also getting to their feet. He stood the rest of the way and fired from the hip as he ran toward the puffs of smoke. He screamed a battle cry, trying to encourage his men. From the corner of his eye, he saw one of them fall face-first.

He ran straight at the enemy position. He could see two smoking barrels and veered toward them. The barrel to the right belched smoke and flame and he heard a terrible impact as another of his soldiers dropped like a sack of rice, his scream cut short along with his life.

The nearest barrel swung his way. He was closing the distance but knew he wouldn't make it. He fired wildly as he ran. The enemy rifle barrel looked immense and suddenly it spewed fire and Hirosuku felt his chest cave in as though struck with a mallet.

The force took his breath away and suddenly nothing worked. He fell, not able to arrest his fall, his arms suddenly useless. The last thing that flashed through his mind before darkness enveloped him, was his hope that Sergeant Junu was dead too.

The ambush worked perfectly. Tarkington had his rifle at his shoulder, the dull ache from the kick muted by the adrenaline coursing through him.

The initial onslaught had dropped most of the Japanese and the grenades had nearly finished the job. The brave assault by the four remaining soldiers — charging directly at the line — had failed and all four were piled in a line where they'd been shot. Tarkington hadn't dared fire upon them for fear of hitting his own men, but they'd run right at Skinner and Stollman, who had calmly dispatched them with accurate, controlled fire.

The clearing was littered with bodies and smoking craters. There were a few wounded, but most were motionless. Tarkington pushed himself out of the hole. He looked at the brass casings littering the bottom. He didn't remember reloading, but he obviously had at least once.

PFC Henry got out of his hole and keeping his rifle ready, drawled, "Don't get killed by one of the wounded. You know how they are."

Tarkington nodded, remembering the way Sergeant Flynn had died while searching the dead. He descended the hill, keeping his own rifle ready. He was relieved to see all his squad members moving from their holes toward the grisly killing ground.

Skinner was attaching his bayonet to the end of his rifle. He went to the first writhing Japanese soldier. He was face down and his legs moved as though trying to crawl away. The back of his uniform shirt was red and glistening with fresh blood from multiple holes, yet he continued to live. Skinner thrust his bayonet into his back, severing his spine, as though dispatching a wounded deer. He extracted the blade and moved to the next man, the resolve on his face never wavering.

Tarkington saw Winkleman wiping his brow and reloading his rifle. "Wink, everyone accounted for?" Winkleman nodded. "Good, let's get their guns and ammo. Also check their packs for food."

PFC Stollman scowled, "Jap food?"

"Better than no food," chided Raker.

Each Japanese soldier was run through with a bayonet unless they were obviously dead. They'd learned from hard experience. Henry approached a soldier who was mostly beneath a grenade-shredded body. He kept his rifle aimed at the man underneath, kicked the obviously dead soldier off and stepped back. The man he exposed had stripes on his arms and a nasty wound on his cheek. The bandage, which had presumably been covering it, was hanging by the coagulated scab. The stitches in the wound were torn and the fleshy cheek tissue was oozing pus. The sergeant's chest rose and fell but he appeared to be unconscious.

"Found a live one over here. A sergeant." Suddenly the man's hand pulled a pistol from behind his back. Henry was ready for it, he stepped forward and kicked, sending the pistol flying. He stepped onto the sergeant's arm with all his weight and stuck the barrel of his Springfield against the seeping cheek wound. The sergeant whimpered in pain.

"Wouldn't try that again, Tojo," he smirked, then spit a stream of tobacco juice into his face.

Tarkington strode over to Henry, beating Skinner there in time to keep him from skewering the sergeant. "Hold up a minute." Skinner scowled and moved his bloody bayonet closer to the soldier's face, dripping gore onto his nose. The rest of the men were busily going through the packs and pockets of the other soldiers, collecting ammunition, weapons and food. Tarkington didn't know if they were far enough away from the road to escape notice, so he didn't want to linger. The short intense firefight would probably bring curious troops.

He leaned over the sergeant and asked. "You speak English?" The Japanese sergeant didn't answer. The gash on his face looked as though it would explode at any moment, and Tarkington wondered how he'd gotten it. It was obviously not from the ambush. The stitches and bloody dressing were proof of that.

Skinner pushed the tip of his bayonet closer, touching the sergeant's nose. "Answer the man."

The enemy sergeant's eyes seethed with hatred and Tarkington could tell Skinner wanted to slice him open. He tapped Skinner's shoulder, "Help the others. We have to be out of here in five minutes." Skinner reluctantly pulled the bayonet back and walked off. Tarkington watched him go and noticed one of the Filipinos leaning over a dead soldier near his head, carving something with his knife. He'd seen other Filipinos take ears as trophies and shook his head. It was a repulsive practice, but it also put the fear of God into the enemy, which was never a bad thing.

"Get him up," he said to Henry.

Henry stepped back and indicated with his rifle barrel that he should stand. The sergeant understood and wobbled to his feet. His front was splattered with blood and white, nondescript chunks of tissue. It looked like parts from the soldier in front, who'd taken most of the grenade blast. It was a wonder the sergeant had managed to remain unscathed.

Tarkington conferred with Sergeant Winkleman who'd come up beside him. "What d'you think we should do with him?"

Winkleman shrugged. "If we let him go, he'll go straight to his buddies and he knows our unit makeup and strength. I can't see how we can let him go. Can you?"

"Yeah, guess you're right. He can't really help us one way or another." He pulled his sword from the scabbard. "Save some ammo and quieter this way."

The sergeant's eyes went wide and he held up his hands and uttered broken English. "Please, no kill."

Tarkington shook his head, "Not sure I've ever known a Jap to beg for mercy. Speak English, yes?"

"A — a little, yes."

"You wanna live you're gonna answer my questions or I'll cut you in half." He held up the sword and looked at him with hard eyes. "Understand?" He sliced the sword back and forth, it cut the air with a crisp swishing sound.

"No kill. I talk."

Tarkington looked at the others, they were finished pilfering the bodies. Each man carried an extra weapon slung over their shoulder and their pockets were flush with clips. He wondered what kind of grub they'd found. Probably rice balls, but food was food.

He redirected his gaze to the wobbling sergeant. "How'd you pick up our trail?"

The sergeant looked at him in confusion, as though he didn't understand, but Tarkington had a feeling he was bluffing. "Well, he doesn't know English enough to help us." He stepped forward and reared the sword back to slash his head from his shoulders.

The sergeant's face blanched white and he held up his hands. "Old man. Old man in village." He pointed back northwest. "He give you up for bags of rice."

Eduardo translated for the Filipino guides and they all looked incensed. "Makapili," hissed Eduardo.

Winkleman's mouth turned down, "Maka — what?" he asked.

"Makapili," repeated Eduardo. "Help the enemy. Filipino help Japs — Makapili. We should kill them. Disgrace our country."

The Japanese sergeant pointed at his swollen face. "I kill them. Old woman shot me." He grinned as though they were friends with a common enemy.

Tarkington remembered what he'd seen on the road yesterday. The Japanese officer ordering the murder of a defenseless GI. He remembered the tortured look on the GI's face, how he'd died in agony as his guts spilled and he bled out. He remembered how they'd left his body to rot and be picked apart by the jungle animals and insects. Using the handle of his sword, he smashed it into the sergeant's wound. The sound was like popping an overripe cantaloupe. Blood sprayed Tarkington's face, and the Japanese sergeant couldn't contain his scream. He dropped to his knees clutching his face.

Tarkington looked around, it was time to go. He lifted the sword and brought it down hard, slicing through bone and muscle, sending the sergeant's head rolling from his body. Tarkington stepped away then wiped the sword on the convulsing man's back until it was clean. He sheathed it with a satisfying 'snick' sound.

Winkleman looked on with disgust. He took a deep breath and blew it out slow. Tarkington stopped in front of him. "What? Spill it."

Winkleman shook his head. "Nothing. Just that, well you told him you wouldn't kill him if he answered your question."

Tarkington looked him in the eye and nodded. "I know I did, but we can't take him with us and like you said, he'd give us away."

"I know. It — it just doesn't seem right somehow."

Tarkington's face darkened and he put his finger to Winkleman's nose. "This is a different war we're in now." He raised his voice so the others could hear, "If we hope to survive, we have to be as brutal as they are," he pointed his thumb at the decapitated sergeant. He turned his attention to Henry. "You got more of those playing cards?" Henry reached into his back pocket and pulled one out. "Let's let 'em know who they're dealing with." Henry nodded and tucked the playing card with the words 'Tark's Ticks' scrawled on the front, into the sergeant's bloody shirt collar.

7

Captain Gima walked among the festering bodies of the reconnaissance squad, lined up on stretchers, ready to be moved to the road and transported for proper burial.

Captain Husukima had summoned him when he'd been told about the massacre and the playing card which had been left on the decapitated body of his senior sergeant. He'd known Captain Gima for years and knew the story of the Tark's Ticks playing cards. He knew Gima had a personal vendetta against the group of Americans.

Captain Gima pulled out the card he carried from his lapel pocket and compared it with the one pulled off the sergeant. Captain Husukima's jaw rippled and he spoke with barely contained rage. "These barbarians must be found and killed."

Gima nodded and surveyed the ambush site. It was well chosen, assuring maximum damage to whoever was in the small clearing. The holes the enemy had fired from were well concealed and provided excellent cover. As soon as the reconnaissance patrol entered the clearing, they'd sealed their fate.

Gima left the sergeant's body and stood beside Sergeant Hirosuku's blood-smeared corpse. His cause of death was obvious, a bullet to the center of the chest. Gima knelt beside him. "I knew this man. He was smart, a good soldier. A veteran of countless battles. It was unlike him to enter this clearing without first checking for an ambush. He knows better."

Husukima shrugged. "Perhaps he let his guard down since the opposition surrendered. He wasn't expecting an attack."

Gima shook his head. "Unlikely. He was a professional in pursuit of a renegade force. He should've expected an ambush."

"Regardless, he led his men into it and paid for his failure with their lives and his own."

Gima stood and rubbed his chin, glancing back at the decapitated body. "He held the senior rank."

Husukima bristled, "Sergeant Junu was also a veteran." Husukima knew his surly sergeant had a reputation for excessive brutality. He'd been with Husukima throughout the China campaign and he'd seen the man do things which would give a lesser man nightmares. "It makes no difference. They are all dead. The important thing is to track down and kill these, *Tark's Ticks*."

"Yes, I quite agree. Have your men found an exit trail?"

Husukima's men had been searching for a sign telling them which way the renegades had gone, but after three-hours had still come up with nothing. Husukima shook his head. "They are skilled. My men have found nothing."

Captain Gima nodded. "I will take over the search. I have another reconnaissance squad with excellent trackers. You can get back to your duties now."

Husukima braced and bowed. Gima outranked him, gaining his promotion a month before his own. He bristled, knowing Gima was dismissing him as though he were more of a hindrance. "Keep me informed of developments." Gima hardened his eyes, not liking his tone, but Husukima continued. "These criminals decapitated my sergeant. I want justice as much as you do."

Captain Gima nodded. "I'll keep you informed, Captain. Carry on." He turned away without another word. He needed to get his men here as soon as possible while the trail was fresh. He had no doubt his trackers would be able to pick up the trail if Husukima's blundering men hadn't already tainted it. He looked to the sky, it was still clear, although a thunderstorm could erupt in these parts almost without warning and wash away any traces. He mumbled to himself. "*Tark's Ticks.* I'll find you."

After the ambush, Tarkington's squad moved north. One of the Filipino guides led while the other stayed behind with Eduardo covering their tracks. They spent extra time making sure they left minimal signs of their passing. The squad they'd killed in the clearing had tracked them easily, despite their natural tendency towards stealth. Knowing the Japanese had men capable of following a difficult track through jungle made them extra careful. They were confident this time that their trail would be nearly impossible to follow. Their survival, and that of the villagers who sheltered them, relied upon it.

Being careful made the trek back slower, but they'd pilfered plenty of food and the skilled Filipino hunters were able to supplement the rice balls with the occasional killed prey.

They traveled both day and night, only taking a few hours during the hottest time of day, to rest. On the third day, they came close to the village, which had held the Japanese, noting it was once again abandoned. They finally returned over the mountain and dropped into the relative safety of the hidden valley.

As they descended the far side of the mountain slope, they were suddenly surrounded by armed Filipinos. They froze. An electrified instant of terror was replaced with merriment, as the Filipinos smiled and lowered their weapons, smiling, slapping their backs and welcoming them home. Tarkington hadn't had a clue they were there until they stepped from the jungle. He leaned toward Henry and asked, "Did you know they were there?" Henry grinned, not giving anything away.

They were ushered into the village as conquering heroes. The success of their mission was evident by the captured Japanese weapons and the withered ears hanging from the guide's necks like medals. The village elder sent a group of young men trotting off into the jungle. Eduardo explained, they were going to make sure no one followed.

Tarkington was exhausted, but he went immediately to PFC Vick's hootch. Stollman was already there telling Vick all about the ambush. He stopped when Tarkington entered. Vick was standing, clearly eager to hear the news. Tarkington reached his hand out and Vick shook it briskly. "How you feeling, Vick?"

Vick touched where he'd been shot and nodded. "Good. I really am. I'm ready to get back in the game."

Tarkington smiled and nodded. "Well, that's the best news I've heard in a while. Stolly gets lovesick out there without you around."

Stollman shook his head, sending his longish red hair flinging side-to-side. "Don't know about that, Tark. Hard to tear him away from you sometimes particularly when you're snuggling."

Vick shook his head. "On second thought, I'm not feeling too well. You two will have to snuggle. I'm out."

Stollman and Tarkington laughed. Tarkington added, "It'll be good to have you back." Vick nodded. Fatigue overcame him, "I'm bushed." He pointed at Stollman. "Get some rest, Stolly."

"Yes, Sergeant," Stollman answered.

Tarkington turned to leave and Vick said, "Those kids you sent back are a real pain in the ass."

Tarkington turned back with an eyebrow raised. "How d'you mean?"

"They're constantly pestering me. Wanting to hear about the action I've seen, asking about tactics, how to do this, how to do that. Annoying as hell."

Tarkington nodded. "They're young but wanna fight. You think they will?"

Vick turned serious and nodded. "Yeah. I've no doubt. I've heard some of their stories, most lost family to the Nips. They've been through a lot. They'll do whatever it takes to dish out some revenge."

Tarkington slept hard for ten straight hours. When he woke, he was disoriented and momentarily wondered where the hell he was. It all came flooding back though and he swung his legs off the raised sleeping platform and looked at his boots.

They were ragged, with multiple holes. The leather flaps were frayed and barely hanging on. They were on their last legs and that was fine with him. He'd discussed it with Henry and they agreed the Japanese trackers were probably successful because they recognized the boot print of a GI.

It was time to go native, making themselves indistinguishable from their Filipino friends. Of course, there was nothing they could do about their skin tone. However, they'd been on the island so long, most — except the fair-skinned, red-headed Stollman — were deeply tanned, and at first glance could pass for natives if they were dressed correctly. Stollman would have to wear long sleeves and keep his hair under wraps, but he did that anyway.

Tarkington's body ached and he moved from side-to-side, stretching. He examined his body, it was full of micro-cuts and abrasions from countless hours of arduous travel through a hostile, thorny jungle.

He remembered the first time he'd patrolled the jungles of Luzon, before the Japanese attack in December. He'd been far worse off. The insects had been the issue then. They were still there, they still bit him, but he barely noticed them anymore.

He thought about the POWs he'd seen on road. He doubted they had anywhere near as good a night's sleep. He doubted if they'd slept at all, in fact. How many more would die today? How many were bayoneted yesterday? Was it the Japanese intention to kill them all? Was the march north simply a way to kill them off and pass it off as something other than criminal? He shook his head, whatever, he wouldn't feel sorry for his predicament and he'd kill as many Japanese as he could before they finally caught up with him.

He stepped from his hut. It was early morning and he momentarily felt guilty; the villagers were scurrying around, busy with the day-to-day work of living. He saw a group of women coming out of the jungle with large bundles of firewood balanced on their heads. At the other end of the village, men worked herding goats and pigs from one enclosed area to another. An old man and woman stooped on their front porch hacking at roots and loading a basket with the succulent sections. He felt like a slouch. He didn't see any of his men, nor the Filipino kids from the military academy.

His stomach growled as he smelled meat cooking, or perhaps it was the smoke from the smoker. His attention shifted to the sounds of distant shouting, followed by answering shouts in unison. It brought back distant memories of boot camp.

It was coming from deeper in the jungle, beyond the far end of the village. His curiosity piqued, he walked in that direction, nodding his head at Filipinos who smiled back. One passing young man handed him a long, thick chunk of smoked meat. He chattered away, smiling the entire time and Tarkington took the food and bowed, nodding his thanks.

He continued walking and bit off a chunk. He was surprised at the sweet, savory taste. He was used to rather bland, salty meat, but this was something else altogether. He glanced back at the boy who'd given it to him. He was still watching him and Tarkington made an 'mmm' sound and rubbed his belly. The boy nodded emphatically and skipped away, chattering to no one in particular.

The sound of military-style drills became more obvious the closer he got to the edge of the village. He entered the jungle, following a well-used trail. He was in his bare feet, but the ground was smooth and easy to walk on.

He followed the trail for fifty-yards before it opened to a good-sized clearing. He stopped and continued chewing the delicious meat. The Filipinos from the academy were lined up facing Sergeant Winkleman. PFC Vick and Stollman were on either side keeping their eyes on the cadets. They were in perfect order, their backs straight and their long rifles on their shoulders.

Stollman walked back inspecting the men closest to him. He stopped and leaned into a cadet and yelled in his face, "Straighten up soldier! Shoulders back." He adjusted his stance to his liking then moved down the line.

Tarkington had to stifle a laugh. The unruly-haired, rarely-in-proper-uniform, PFC Stollman extolling how to stand at attention was comical in its irony. He moved back a few steps wanting to see more before giving away his presence.

They took the cadets through some basic marching drills. It was obvious they were old hands, probably the only thing they did consistently at the academy. Then they took them through a bayonet drill. They put their rifles down and exchanged them for sticks of comparable size and weight.

Vick got them in order, each cadet facing off against another, while Sergeant Winkleman watched with his arms crossed. Vick held up his hand then dropped it. The cadets on the right attacked while the others parried and defended. Tarkington ate the rest of his sweet meat and wiped his mouth with the back of his hand. "Well I'll be damned," he muttered to himself.

He nearly yelled out when Henry spoke up right behind him. "Vick's done a good job," he drawled.

"Dammit, Henry. Don't sneak up like that." Henry just gazed at him with a bemused look on his face. Tarkington nodded, "He hasn't been idle while we were gone." The bayonet drill switched, now the attackers became the defenders. "They definitely have some training under their belts. But damn, they still seem like kids to me."

Henry agreed, "I think the oldest one's sixteen and the youngest is fourteen."

"We're talking about putting eighth-graders into combat against veteran soldiers."

"When you put it like that — but these kids'll fight regardless. If you say they can't join us, they'll do it on their own and get killed. We can at least help them stay alive longer."

Tarkington shook his head a sadness overcoming him. "Yeah, I know."

He stepped out from the shadows and walked toward the training ground. Winkleman saw him and barked, "Recover."

The cadets were breathing hard and some were holding bruised arms, but they stopped parrying and thrusting and stood at attention as Tarkington walked to the front and stood beside Winkleman. Vick and Stollman joined them. "You've been busy, Vick."

"Well, they were driving me crazy, so 'idle hands' and all that. Figured I'd see what they could do and one thing led to another. I've been putting them through PT every morning too." He crossed his arms over his chest, "They work hard."

"Who's in command?" asked Tarkington.

Vick pointed at the boy to the front right. "Angelo is the oldest and had the highest rank at their school."

"Speak English?"

Vick nodded. "Yeah, they all do. Some even better than Eduardo."

Tarkington strode forward and stood in front of the boy. He recognized him from the week before but couldn't recall his name. His chin was held high and his gaze steady. Tarkington put his fists on his hips and asked, "What's your name?"

"Angelo Fernandez, Sergeant."

"You're the honorary Lieutenant?"

"My honorary rank at the Academy was Lieutenant. Yes Sergeant."

Tarkington leaned into him. He was a foot taller than the boy. "Well now you're in the real world, son. Your new rank is sergeant. Pick a man you trust to be your second in command." The boy hesitated and Tarkington barked, "Now!"

Angelo glanced sideways and called out, "Anthony Trujillo."

A boy a couple of spaces away stepped forward and Tarkington strode his way and faced him, looking him up and down. He was skinny but taller than Angelo. He looked petrified to be called out. "Your new rank is sergeant. You will take orders from Sergeant Fernandez, who is your superior and your squad leader. Understood, Sergeant Trujillo?"

"Sir, yes sir!" he yelled in a high-pitched voice.

"Don't call me sir. I work for a living, dammit." The boy looked momentarily confused, trying to understand what he meant. "Call me Sergeant, or even better, Staff Sergeant."

"Y — Yes Staff Sergeant."

Tarkington focused his attention back to Angelo. "Break your men into two teams. You'll take orders from any one of us," he indicated the GIs, "and you'll pass those orders along to Trujillo, who will lead your second team. Got it?"

"Yes, Staff Sergeant," answered Angelo.

Tarkington raised his voice so they could all hear. "You're no longer at the academy. This is not a game. We are being hunted by the Japanese. We are alone. There's no support, no one we can call for help. If you are captured, you'll be tortured." He stopped, letting that sink in. "Some of you will die. Probably most of you." He put his hands behind his back and paced, then stopped and faced them again, raising his voice "This is your chance to leave. If you aren't fully committed, you should go now and save us a lot of trouble. There's no shame in it. No one expects you to fight. You can sit this out and hopefully the war will pass this island by and you can get on with your lives."

The only sound was the chittering of insects and the rustling of long grass blowing with the warm breeze. A full minute passed and no one stepped forward. "Very well." He continued, "You will follow orders without question. We will be fighting as guerrillas. Hit and run tactics. The *only* chance you have of survival is listening and following orders. Is that clear?"

There was a resounding, "Yes Staff Sergeant."

Tarkington nodded and lifted his chin, looking them over slowly. Their young eyes stared back at him, sparkling with exuberance. He was sure they were dreaming of glorious battles. He knew reality would dim their exuberance, he only hoped they'd survive long enough to understand that.

8

They spent the next three weeks training. The cadets had a good understanding of military basics from their time at the academy, so the training went smoothly. They were taught ambush, hand-to-hand fighting and bayonet drills. An obstacle course was constructed and all the men, including the GIs, went through it at least once a day. It became a competition and soon the young cadets were able to beat the GIs' times.

Tarkington knew the day was coming when they'd need to make their presence known. The ambush was weeks ago and Tarkington had no illusions the Japanese were still actively looking for them, but he couldn't stay in the safety of the village forever. He felt they had to do something, fight back and make the Japanese pay.

The one and only radio in the village made it sound as though the Japanese were conquering the entire world with ease. The heavy propaganda was coming from the city of Manila. The voice was Filipino, and Tarkington was sure she only transmitted what she was told to transmit. He wondered what the real news was but understood he may never know.

The one thing he did know: the US military had ceased to exist on Luzon and Corregidor. But what about elsewhere? Was MacArthur in Australia, or had it fallen too? He wanted, and needed, more information if he hoped to be successful in this guerrilla war.

He called a meeting. They gathered in the hall. Tarkington and the rest of the GIs looked like natives. They wore hand-made sandals, ragged shorts, and long-sleeved shirts rolled up halfway. When they were outside, they wore wide-brimmed straw hats, favored by farmers to keep the sun off. Their skin was dark but it would take little more than a concentrated glance to know they weren't native, mostly because of their facial hair, which they worked to keep trimmed.

The village elder was sitting in the chair at the head of the long table and Tarkington spoke to him. "Vindigo, may I speak?" he asked. Vindigo nodded and Tarkington addressed the room. "Men, I think it's time we re-entered the war. It's time to venture out and see what's going on outside this valley. It's been three weeks since the ambush. I know the Nips haven't forgotten about us, but the hunters say things have died down substantially." Eduardo whispered to the hunters and they smiled and nodded. "We don't have enough ammunition to mount a large assault. The easiest way to resupply is to kill Japs and take their weapons and ammo, but that's dangerous and time-consuming. What we need is to find an ammo dump.

"Vindigo and I sent out village scouts a week ago and they found one that's lightly defended and somewhat close, about ten-kilometers from here." He pulled out a paper map of the area. It was left over from another era, but the general shape of the Bataan Peninsula was accurate. "Our little valley is here and the ammo dump's here." He placed his finger along the main road leading to Mariveles. "We can leave tonight and be there by tomorrow night." He looked around the room, "We can be back here day after tomorrow."

The cadets murmured excitedly. They'd been training hard and were eager to prove themselves.

Tarkington was happy to see the way the cadets moved through the jungle. Most of them were city boys, growing up in and around Manila, but their young minds and bodies had adjusted to the jungle easily. He only brought half of them, not wanting to bring an overly large force. With his GIs, guides and cadets, they numbered sixteen.

The second team of cadets, led by Sergeant Trujillo, were disappointed to be left behind, but he assured them they'd get their chance and reminded them about following orders. They were to work with the villagers doing chores and hunting in order to continue earning their right to stay there. It wasn't glamorous, but necessary.

They'd all become decent at shooting the small bows favored by the village hunters. Henry took such a liking to them that he had one slung over his back in case he needed to kill silently from a distance. He wasn't as good as the Filipinos but he could hold his own and they respected how quickly he picked it up. Henry admitted he'd used bow and arrow plenty of times back home on the bayou.

The main road was off to their left and it was mostly quiet. A few trucks trundled by — their headlights shining bright — not at all nervous about air strikes. There hadn't been sounds of combat for a long time. Before Corregidor fell, a month after the surrender of Bataan, there was a near constant thunder from the thousands of artillery shells fired from the tip of Bataan at Corregidor. Now, with Corregidor and the mouth of Manila Bay open to the Japanese, the night was relatively quiet.

Despite the lack of Japanese, it took most of the night to move the ten-kilometers. They took it slow, using the time to familiarize themselves with each other. They'd trained hard together over the past few weeks, but no amount of training could prepare them for the real thing.

Joshua, the lead Filipino guide whispered into Eduardo's ear and he passed it along to Tarkington and Winkleman. "Joshua say ammo dump close."

Tarkington nodded and signaled the cadets to stay put and watch their backs. Stollman stayed with them, the rest moved up with the sergeants.

Moving slow and steady they crawled to the edge of the jungle and peered into a small abandoned village. There was a dim light hanging from a post and it shone on an area surrounded by fencing. Within the fencing were wooden crates. They were stacked two-high and five-deep.

Near the front gate, two bored looking guards paced slowly, smoking cigarettes and talking in low murmurs. After a couple of minutes, they walked in opposite directions following the fence-line, angling back toward the darkness. The far wall wasn't fenced. It butted up against a sheer rock wall. When the guards met the rock, they'd mosey on back, eventually meeting at the front again, where they'd speak, smoke, then repeat the process.

They watched them for ten minutes, noting there was very little variation to their pattern, and they seemed to be alone. Tarkington wondered if their relief was nearby, but Joshua, who'd found the ammo dump, assured him there were only two guards who would be relieved in the morning by more troops from another town a kilometer away. Tarkington assumed the small cache of ammo was too small to waste a lot of manpower defending. After tonight, that would probably change.

Tarkington signaled them to move further back into the jungle. Once they were all gathered, he laid out the plan. Skinner and Raker would go around to the back of the fence where they'd observed the guards turning around. Joshua, Tuan and Henry would use their bows. Eduardo translated to Tuan and Joshua. They smiled broadly. Once everyone knew their assignments it was time to put the plan into motion.

Henry, Tuan and Joshua slithered right, stopping at the closest point where the guards came together near the front. Raker and Skinner split up and worked their way through the jungle until they were in position near the rock wall. Tarkington strained to see either one of them, but they may as well have been invisible.

Now they'd wait. The guards were at the front chatting quietly puffing their cigarettes. Soon they turned away from each other and started walking. Tarkington watched the red glow of the cigarette on the right. When the guard entered the darkness near the rock wall, the cherry-red glow suddenly dropped and sparked as it hit the ground. It remained there, motionless. Tarkington didn't see or hear anything, but knew Skinner had been successful, or there would've been a commotion. He relaxed his grip on the submachine gun.

The guard on the left stopped at the wall and turned. His pace was slow, just as it had been every other time they'd watched him make the circuit. Tarkington easily tracked his progress by the burning tip of his cigarette.

Tarkington heard the creaking of bows being pulled back and imagined the three archers aiming and straining to keep the tension. He hoped Raker wasn't advancing or he might be hit if one of the archers missed.

The second guard stopped at the normal spot, stamped his cigarette beneath his boot and looked for his comrade to appear around the corner. Suddenly his chest seemed to sprout branches as three arrows slammed into him and buried deep. He stumbled and stared at the protrusions as though confused by them, then his face changed and he screamed. It was cut off an instant later when Raker ran up behind him, covered his mouth and jammed his knife into his neck, severing his spine. He held the convulsing body for a few seconds, then slowly lowered it to the ground. No one moved while they listened for a reaction.

Silent minutes passed, and when nothing happened, Tarkington signaled the GIs to move forward. Stollman ran forward and slammed the chain keeping the fence door locked with the butt of his Springfield. Tarkington grimaced, hoping the rifle's safety was on. A misfire would not be optimum at this point. The chain broke on the second hit and the GIs streamed into the ammo dump. Tarkington looked behind, making sure the cadets were still watching their backs. Satisfied, he stood and trotted to the enclosure.

The crates were nailed shut and the GIs pried them open with their knives. The lids came off with loud squeaks, which grated on Tarkington like fingernails down a chalkboard.

Tarkington had his captured Type-100 submachine gun at port arms, ready to fire. He pried his eyes from the darkness when he heard Stollman give a low whistle. "Jackpot," he said. He was holding up a Japanese grenade. He grinned and stuffed as many as he could fit into his satchel.

Vick opened a box and hissed, "Ammo. Lots of ammo." He stuffed clips into his satchel until it was nearly bursting then trotted off toward the jungle. He waved as he entered, and two cadets sprinted across and started filling their satchels. Soon everyone had full satchels of ammunition and grenades.

Winkleman had been working on a crate near the back and he came trotting around the corner like he'd stolen the keys to the city. He held a Type-96 light machine-gun. "Look what I found. Can I keep her, Dad?" he joked.

Tarkington grinned. "Are there more of those?"

Winkleman nodded, "Plenty of those banana magazines too."

"Take it to the tree-line and tell Stolly to come get one. It's not his BAR, but close enough. You come back too and grab as much ammo as you can, those six-point-fives are good for the Arisakas too."

They finished pilfering the ammo dump three-hours before dawn. They dragged the dead soldiers into the enclosure and hid them between boxes and tried to replace the crate lids to make it look like they'd never been there. The more confusion they sowed the longer it would take the Japanese to begin searching for them.

On the way back, they opted to stick to the road, or at least the side of the road. They were heavily weighted down with their loot and needed to get as far from the ammo dump as possible and didn't have time to cover their tracks. Tarkington figured the road was well-traveled, so another set of sandaled foot prints would go unnoticed and be impossible to distinguish from any other foot traffic.

The grinding sound of an engine soon forced them into the jungle. They quickly hid and watched the bright lights of a small jeep with a mounted machine-gun and a larger troop truck full of Japanese soldiers holding onto the sides, drive past.

Once it was safe to talk, Tarkington said, "They're moving fast. Wonder if they're reacting to us?"

Winkleman nodded in the darkness. "There's a good chance. Haven't seen much traffic and what we *have* seen isn't in that much of a hurry."

They got back to the side of the road and Tarkington ordered them to move faster. Soon they were trotting along at an easy jogging pace. Their loaded packs and satchels bounced and rubbed painfully but their sense of urgency kept them moving.

After fifteen minutes the procession stopped and Joshua signaled they needed to move off the road and enter the jungle. The line of men followed him into the darkness doing their best not to make an obvious track. Tarkington wasn't too worried; the Japanese would have to scout every inch of the road and would still be lucky to find their exit point.

He felt better when the sky suddenly opened and they were hit with a heavy rain. It pounded them and the instantly muddy conditions slowed their progress. Rainwater dripped off his nose in a near-constant stream. The rain altered the jungle's look and feel and Tarkington felt lost. If Joshua hadn't been along, he doubted he'd have found his way back.

After a few miserable hours, they finally made their way into the valley and the village. They took the captured weapons directly to the main hall and spread them out on the long table, showing off their bounty. The two light machine guns caught Vindigo's eye and he chuckled through a toothless grin. He hefted the formidable weapon and pretended to fire it, making stuttering shooting sounds, which sounded an awful lot like farts. The men watched in stunned silence for a few seconds, then the stress of the past few days fell away and they laughed uncontrollably.

The final count was two Type-96 light machine guns with twenty full banana-shaped magazines, forty-five grenades, six Arisaka rifles and two boxes of 6.5mm ammunition, which was interchangeable between the light machine guns and rifles.

Tarkington looked the loot over and nodded his approval. "Not a bad night's work," he said, slapping Winkleman's shoulder.

Winkleman nodded, "At least now we can get the cadets used to firing their weapons."

"Yes, but it's still not a lot of ammunition. Wouldn't even come close to taking us through an extended fight."

Winkleman acknowledged that, "No, but it's a good start. Wish we coulda taken it all."

Tarkington sighed and rubbed his chin. "I was thinking about that. How hard would it be to get a hold of a truck? There's still plenty of old trucks driven around by farmers and whatnot. Pretty soon, it'll be business as usual around here. The odd truck driven by a local could go unnoticed and might give us an advantage. I'll have Eduardo ask Vindigo about that. He must know someone willing to help. Someone loyal."

The rain continued to hammer outside. Sheets of water came off the roof cutting deep rivulets into the dirt and creating tiny rivers in the ground, all running toward the creek.

Tarkington found Eduardo loading empty magazines with 6.5mm bullets. "This rain's intense. Is it the start of the rainy season?"

Eduardo shrugged, "A little early. June is normal start."

"Well, June's next week."

Eduardo smiled and nodded. "Yes, rain starts next week."

Tarkington smiled. "Okay. Gives me an idea." He motioned for Eduardo to follow and they went to Vindigo who was still looking over the weapons. "Vindigo," the elder looked up. "What happens to the creek once the rainy season starts?"

Eduardo asked and translated the answer. "He says it floods and gets big. Dangerous."

"Is there a bridge?" Eduardo asked and Vindigo shook his head. "So, they're stuck over here when that happens?"

Eduardo translated. "Yes. Wait until river small. Plenty to hunt on this side." He pointed west. "Trails to the West lead to other valleys."

Tarkington smiled and nodded. "Wink, come over here." Winkleman put the other Type-96 down and came over. "Let the men know, we're gonna build a bridge over the creek this week."

Winkleman looked at him sideways. "A bridge?"

"Yep, a temporary bridge, something we can put into place and take apart when it's not in use."

Winkleman's mouth turned down. "None of us are engineers."

"Doesn't need to be pretty, just functional a couple of times. Hell, even just a few stout logs."

"All right, Tark." He hesitated, "Can I ask why?"

"It'll be our escape route during the rainy season. We've both been through their rainy season, most everything shuts down, but I wanna use it against the Japs. They won't expect it. They won't be able to track us and we've got the perfect egress back here."

Winkleman rubbed his chin, thinking about it. "There's a reason everything shuts down, Tark. The whole place becomes a mud-pit. Nothing can move."

"Yep, we'll have to learn to fight through it. I think we can do some real damage though and when the dry season arrives, we'll hunker down and reassess."

With the help of the villagers, trees were cut down and mules helped haul them to a point upstream from the village where the creek went through a rocky, deep canyon. The villagers said the water would rise to the brim, but they'd never seen it actually go over the top. The bridge would need to span the forty-foot gap. Getting the timbers in place proved difficult. Finally, a system of ropes slung over overhanging trees was used to place the felled timber into place.

It took four days of hard work but the result was a rudimentary crossing point. Tarkington stood on the village side and looked it over. Winkleman and Eduardo were on the other side. Winkleman yelled, "Come on across, Tark. Break its cherry."

Tarkington nodded and stepped onto the notched trees which were side by side. They'd cut off the tops so the thickest parts were the walking platforms. With great effort, they'd placed the trees so the bases were on opposite sides of the canyon, making the overall width more even.

Tarkington stepped across with his arms out for balance. Once over the deepest point in the canyon, he slowed. He didn't have a big problem with heights but the lack of handrails made him hold his breath as he crossed the crux point. Soon he was across and was greeted by cheers from the villagers and GIs. He smiled and wiped the sweat off his brow. "Let's put a rope across for balance. Once it starts raining, it'll be slick as snot out there."

"We can do that easily," chimed Winkleman.

Tarkington looked back over the span. "Only if it doesn't interfere with the mechanism."

Winkleman pointed to the taut ropes attached to the severely bent trees on the village side and traversing down to wrap around the timbers near his feet. Then he pointed across the canyon. "Shouldn't be an issue. Once the lines to the trees are cut, they'll lift this edge and pull it back across the channel. I don't think the support line will get in the way of anything. We can cut it and it'll fall into the creek. If the Japs investigate, they won't see much, the bridge will be pulled back and this'll look like any other part of the jungle."

"It'll be a bitch getting the bridge back in place."

"Yeah, but with the ropes and those long poles, they'll be able to push it back across." He shrugged, "At least, that's the theory. Doubt the trees will last too long though, eventually they'll snap. It should work at least once though, which is one more than I hope we'll need."

Tarkington nodded, "Amen. If it all works out, the Nips'll never get near this spot."

9

With the bridge construction done, the men rested, waiting for the rainy season to start. June 1st came and went without a drop. Tarkington asked Eduardo and he shrugged, "Late. Tomorrow."

Sure enough, the evening was streaked with dark clouds and the air had a thick, wet feeling. The rain started at 1600.

Tarkington called the men into the main hall and they sat around with their rifles. Stollman had one of the Type-96 light machine guns beside him. He'd fired it a few times and was happy with its operation. It was about the same weight as his beloved BAR but held thirty-rounds versus twenty. The magazine sprouted from the top and curved, but the sights were unhindered and he liked them better than the BAR sights. He also liked the handle, which allowed him to carry it like he was carrying a suitcase.

With the rain coming down in sheets, the air in the main hall felt stuffy but at least the well-built building didn't leak, so as long as the doors and windows were open it was a tolerable space to stay dry.

After eating a feast of various meats and tubers combined into a stew, Tarkington stood and addressed them. The cadets stuck together forming their own group in the back of the room. "With the start of the rainy season, it's time to go out and hit the enemy." The GIs remained stoic and the cadets could barely contain their glee. They murmured among themselves until Tarkington glared and Sergeant Fernandez shushed them with a harsh look. "We'll leave in the morning. I don't think there's any reason to work at night in this weather. The Japs'll hopefully be holed up, no reason for them to be out and about, but we'll see. This'll be an extended trip. A reconnaissance mostly. If we come across a target we think we can hit without being caught, we'll do it." He looked the men over. The GIs knew what the next few days held and were unreadable; the cadets looked as though tomorrow was Christmas morning. "Any questions?"

When there were none, he turned to the village elder, "Vindigo, are you willing to lend us Joshua and Tuan?" Vindigo didn't need Eduardo to translate, he simply nodded his assent.

They left before light the next morning and by dawn were beside the main road leading to Mariveles. Instead of heading that way, though, they followed the road north. The rains continued on-and-off all day. One minute it was clear, the next, raining so hard they could hardly see their hands in front of their faces.

The road was hard pack, but the intermittent hammering rain was starting to have an impact. In low spots the water pooled and seeped, making large muddy puddles.

At one such spot, they came upon a stuck Japanese troop truck. They heard the revving engine long before they saw the truck and crept forward for a closer look.

The Japanese soldiers were out, trying to rock it back and forth to get it out of the hole. Finally, they were successful, and the truck lurched out, got back onto the hard-pack road and stopped. The undercarriage dripped chunks of mud. The filthy soldiers got back into the truck and Tarkington and his men watched it trundle away around the corner.

He looked at Winkleman, "You thinking what I'm thinking?"

Winkleman smiled and nodded. "Can't think of a better spot to hit them."

A half-hour later, they were set. Tarkington split his twenty-man force.

Most were with him on the west side of the road and the rest were on the other side, past the mud hole. He mixed the GIs with the cadets.

The plan was simple, the men on his side would initiate the attack when the Japanese stopped or slowed to deal with the mud-hole. If the initial ambush didn't kill them all and they moved to the east side of the road for cover, the second group, consisting of Winkleman, Skinner and six cadets, would hit them from the flank.

The rain continued to sweep the area in dark sheets. Despite the warm, muggy air, sitting perfectly still in the rain made them cold. The cadets couldn't keep from shivering. The GIs and Filipinos were cold too, but they did a better job of ignoring it.

Two miserable hours passed before they heard the rumbling of engines. Out of the dark sheets of rain, a column of ten trucks, led by a covered armored car came around the corner. The ambushers were invisible in the jungle, their painted faces and dark skin perfectly camouflaged. Tarkington looked to Henry and slowly shook his head. Henry passed the signal to the others, there were too many. They'd let this convoy pass unmolested.

The armored car stopped at the dip in the road and a soldier with stripes on his arms, stepped out and strode to the puddle. He tested the mud and nearly slipped. He stepped back toward the car and waved.

The passenger side door opened and Tarkington heard the sergeant yelling. The passenger yelled an order back and disappeared into the shelter of the car. The sergeant scurried past the car and pounded on the side of the first troop truck, barking orders. Japanese soldiers emptied out of the back and hustled forward. Most carried their rifles, but a few carried long, two-by-six boards between them. While the riflemen watched, the boards were laid across the mud-hole, creating a makeshift bridge. More boards were brought until the hole was nearly covered.

Cadet Sergeant Anthony Trujillo watched the Japanese soldiers work while he stroked his Arisaka rifle's trigger-guard. He was well-hidden alongside the road beyond the puddle. Winkleman was beside him, staying perfectly still. Trujillo had a perfect view of the Japanese soldiers as they worked.

His heart pounded in his ears making them hot. He wondered if perhaps they were steaming as the rain splashed them. The Japanese were close, so close he knew he couldn't miss if only he'd get a signal to attack, but the order was clear: hold fire. He knew there were too many trucks for them to take on, but he itched to fire, to kill the men who had taken everything from him. Instead, he calmed his breathing. He'd follow orders. He hoped the others would too.

He slowly looked toward the other cadets. He couldn't see them and for a moment he felt a rush of panic. Had they left him alone? He turned his body more and he felt tension at his midsection as his belt pulled against his rifle. He ignored it and continued to rotate. When he heard the rifle shot, he spun back, angry at whoever had fired until he realized his rifle barrel was smoking.

The nearest Japanese soldier looked up from the hole and their eyes met. For an instant, time stood still, then all hell broke loose.

The Japanese soldier screamed a warning. It was cut off with the sudden sound of Stollman's light machine gun, which was quickly joined by rifles and Tarkington's submachine gun. Japanese soldiers crumpled where they stood, the sodden air bright with bloody mist. The soldiers in the hole lay down, trying to make themselves as small as possible.

Sergeant Trujillo was mortified at his accidental discharge but was determined to make up for it or die trying. He aimed and fired toward the hole, but Winkleman squeezed his shoulder and yelled, "You'll hit our guys. Cease fire, dammit!"

The one-sided battle continued. The nearest trucks were riddled and more soldier's fell. The armored car's windscreen shattered and imploded, appearing to spark and glow with bullet hits. Trujillo pointed at the hole and yelled, "Japs!"

Winkleman saw a helmeted head poke up. He pulled one of the captured Japanese grenades off his belt, pulled the cotter-style pin and pushed the copper top. Even over the machine gun fire, he heard the internal click. He threw it at the hole, careful not to throw it too far and spray his own men with shrapnel. It bounced on the near-side lip, then rolled out of sight into the hole. There was an explosion, followed by screaming. Skinner lobbed another from his position to the right. It flew high overhead and exploded in midair, only feet above the hole, spraying the surviving occupants with shrapnel.

Skinner broke from cover and ran, his rifle at hip-level. Winkleman shoved Trujillo, pushing him to follow. The young sergeant sprang up and followed Skinner, eager to do his part.

Skinner got to the edge of the hole, fired, worked the bolt and fired again and again until his clip was empty. He dropped into the hole to get out of the line of fire and reloaded. He scooted along the boards, climbing over shredded, bleeding bodies until he was at the far lip. He crawled up the side in time to see the rest of the squad from the other side of the road, coming out of cover and moving toward the end of the long line of trucks firing all the way. The hammering sound of Stollman's LMG bullets smashing against the metal and wood bodies of the trucks was constant.

He turned when Sergeant Trujillo was suddenly beside him with wide eyes. Skinner scowled and kept his barrel trained forward, covering the squad's advance. He expected to hear more gunfire, but instead it quickly dropped off. He was confused; if those trucks were full of troops, they'd face stiff resistance.

He looked behind and saw Winkleman moving his portion of the squad forward, keeping to the cover of the jungle. He must be expecting the same thing — a strong response — but it wasn't happening. The firing was diminishing, not increasing.

Skinner waited until Winkleman and the rest were abreast of his position. He growled at the young Filipino, "Cover me." The young man nodded and positioned himself on the lip, his rifle propped ready to cover his advance.

Skinner got to his feet and ran in a crouch to the front of the riddled and smoking armored car. He rose, sweeping his barrel over the dead bodies. The inside looked like something from a haunted house. The upholstery was dripping with blood, brains and tissue. No one was alive.

He moved to the first truck's front tire. There was a shot so close that the smoke from the barrel surrounded his sandals. He lunged onto his side and fired at a shape beneath the truck. The soldier was working the bolt to fire again, but his body shuddered with the impact of Skinner's shot and he screamed. Skinner worked the bolt and fired point-blank into the soldier's chest. The Japanese flopped onto his back and gasped for air like a dying fish. His eyes glassed over and the tension seeped from his body.

Skinner chambered another round and got to his feet. Yelling caught his attention. He looked up in time to see another soldier, two trucks down the line, crouched near the front tire aiming his rifle at him. Skinner knew he'd be too late and braced for the impact. A shot came from behind and he felt a bullet whip past him. The Japanese soldier took the bullet in the shoulder and fell backward, his shot going wide. Winkleman rose from cover and fired his Type-38 rifle, ending the threat.

Skinner looked behind and saw the young cadet's smoking barrel, then glanced at Winkleman and saw the concern etched on his face, despite the camouflage. Skinner smiled and nodded that he was fine. He stood and looked back at Trujillo still in the hole. He waved him forward and waited until he was beside him. "Nice shot," he said. The Filipino's smile was ear-to-ear.

They stayed on the road, moving from truck to truck, checking each one for survivors. The main force had swept the trucks from the other side and killed the passengers and the drivers who'd been desperately trying to back their vehicles out of the kill zone. Thankfully, the only truck holding troops was the first one.

When they got to the last truck, they reformed with the rest of the squad. Henry and Raker had gone down the road a hundred yards to watch for more traffic. Winkleman sent two cadets the other way with explicit instructions to bust ass back to them if they spotted or heard anyone coming. They nodded and took off with the speed and eagerness only seen in the young.

Tarkington asked, "You guys okay? From the sounds of it, we must've missed one or two."

Skinner held up two fingers. "You missed two. We," he looked back at Sgt. Trujillo, Winkleman and the others, "Took care of 'em."

Trujillo's grin vanished when he saw Sergeant Fernandez coming his way with fire in his eyes. He went right up to Trujillo and barked in Tagalog. Trujillo lowered his gaze. Fernandez slapped the side of his face hard. Winkleman stepped forward and before Fernandez could slap him again, clutched his arm and held it. He shook his head. "He made a mistake. You can deal with it later. Now's not the time."

Fernandez's seething eyes bore into Winkleman and he tried to break free, but he held firm, his gaze expressionless. Winkleman released his grip and Fernandez looked hard at Trujillo one last time before rejoining Tarkington and the others. Winkleman slapped Trujillo's shoulder, "I saw what happened. Be more careful next time. Nice shot, by the way. Saved Skinner's butt."

Trujillo looked up at him, the corners of his eyes glistened, but he quickly looked away. "I was stupid. No excuse. He's right to punish me."

Skinner chimed in, "You'll have plenty of time for that shit later."

With the ambush over and everyone accounted for, they circled around Tarkington at the last truck. The rain continued to beat down, in more of a constant rhythm now.

Tarkington spoke. "Looks like we got ourselves a bunch of trucks full of ammunition and supplies. Unfortunately, we can't take them all. We'll take the two that aren't as shot up, load 'em up with what we want and burn the rest. This is a busy road, so we need to work fast."

He looked at his watch, it was starting to succumb to the wet circumstances but for now the hands continued to tick. "We leave in twenty minutes. We've got men out on either side but if the Japs come, we leave and fade into the jungle. If we get split up, we meet back at the bridge site near the village." He looked around at the nodding men. "Okay, let's get to it."

Like a huddle at a football game, the group hustled away moving to each truck in turn. They decided the sixth and seventh trucks were the most roadworthy. Each truck was already half-filled with various useful items and they stacked more on top until there was just enough room for the squad members.

The trucks which weren't shot up too badly but were staying behind, were used to push the damaged ones out of the way. The last vehicle to be moved was the riddled armored car. The vehicles were off the road at odd angles and looked abandoned and sad. From the bottom seam of the armored car's back door, blood dripped and mixed with the rainwater.

With the two stolen trucks loaded, the question of how to burn the others was broached. Winkleman unscrewed one of the gas caps and sniffed. "Gasoline. They'll burn. Soak rags and stuff 'em into the tanks. We'll light a few in the center as we leave, they're close enough, they might all go up when the ammo goes."

Ten minutes later, two of the middle trucks had gas-soaked cloths stuffed into their open gas caps. Henry and Raker stayed back, waiting for the stolen trucks to cross the covered mud-hole. Before attempting it, the cadets pulled the Japanese bodies out of the way. They held their breath, hoping the trucks would make it and when they did, a muted cheer went up. Henry and Raker lit the makeshift wicks with Zippo lighters and took off running.

The men in the back of the last truck helped them up while driving slowly. Once up, Henry pounded on the side, and the truck accelerated away quickly, closing the gap with the lead truck.

Skinner and Winkleman were the drivers and they drove faster than was prudent for the wet conditions, but getting off the road without being spotted was paramount, and they didn't want to be caught in the coming blast. They punched out the spider-webbed windscreens so they could see and the wind and rain whipped their faces.

They'd gone a mile when there was a low rumble behind them. Henry and Raker grinned and looked back but they were too far away and the rain too thick, to see the results of their work. The rumbling continued and increased as more ammunition cooked off.

Tarkington was in the lead truck. He heard the rumbling explosions and smiled at PFC Vick and Stollman. Stollman had his LMG pointed out of the shattered front screen, the bipod resting on the hood in case they met any Japanese. They all squinted through the rain drops.

Vick, nearest the door asked, "Where to now, Tark?"

"To the abandoned village." He paused, a memory suddenly flashing through his head. For an instant he relived Lt. Smoker's body being riddled by a Japanese heavy machine-gun. Vick noticed the pause and saw the momentary pained look on Tarkington's face and surmised it was probably the same village where they'd lost half the platoon a few months before.

Tarkington recovered and continued, "Hopefully this rain'll cover our tracks. We can hide the trucks, unload the loot and either take it back to the village or bury it somewhere for later use. It'd be great to have the trucks too. Never know when we'll need 'em."

Vick asked, "How much farther? Being on this road gives me the creeps."

Tarkington shrugged, "Dunno, be looking for it on the right. It's the same one we pass when we come out of the valley. You know, the one that held the Japs on our first patrol."

A few minutes later, Skinner raced around a corner and slammed on the brakes. The truck slewed sideways and he expertly corrected, keeping the truck upright and on the road.

Winkleman slowed slightly for the corner, not trusting his driving skills as much. He came around the corner and saw the lead truck sliding wildly. Winkleman watched the Filipino cadets in the back holding on with death-grips to the metal slats holding up the canvas top. He hoped no one was crushed by falling boxes.

Skinner got control and the truck stopped nose-to-nose with a Japanese military sedan. The hood was much lower and the Japanese driver's face was only feet away, gripping the steering wheel with both hands. There was an officer in the passenger seat, he hadn't been paying attention and when his driver slammed on the brakes he'd been pushed forward into the dashboard and ended up partially on the floor.

He came up spluttering and yelling but stopped when he saw the color leave his driver's face and his jaw drop. The officer looked up and saw the massive truck grill only inches from his own. His eyes widened when he saw the immense barrel of a machine gun aimed at his forehead and the camouflaged American face grinning behind it.

He jolted from his momentary trance and clutched at his side trying to bring his sidearm up. He'd just cleared the barrel from his holster when Stollman squeezed the trigger and fired eight rounds. The bullets had a devastating effect. The Japanese writhed and blood splashed the windscreen before it shattered and collapsed in a thousand pieces of glass.

The intense noise of gunfire, followed by the sudden quiet of the rain and the hissing barrel of the LMG, was surreal. Tarkington cursed, "Dammit, Stolly. You nearly blew my damned eardrums out."

Stollman shrugged, "He went for his sidearm."

Tarkington yelled at Vick, "Get out and check on 'em. See if the car's still usable. We're close to the village, we can bring it with us."

Vick got out and nearly ran into Eduardo who'd come from the back and had his rifle up and ready. Tarkington saw him. "Everyone okay back there?" Eduardo dropped his barrel and nodded. Tarkington ordered, "Help Vick get the bodies to the back seat. If the car's okay, we'll take 'em with us, see if they've got anything useful."

Vick opened the driver-side door, his rifle ready, but it was obvious the Japanese were dead. The engine wasn't running — the clutch had lost engagement as the driver died, killing the engine — but it still clicked and hissed as it cooled.

He pulled out the driver and let him fall onto the road with a wet slap. Blood mixed with rainwater, streaming toward the edge of the road. Vick wiped the seat with his wet sleeve, sat down and evaluated the vehicle. He depressed the clutch and turned the key, revving the engine. He leaned out the side window and called. "It's good."

Henry and Raker joined them. They opened the back door, lifted the driver's body and hefted him into the back seat. Eduardo opened the passenger door on the other side and stuffed the dead officer into the back seat on top of the driver, then sat down despite the blood and gore. He smiled at Tarkington and gave him a thumbs up. Henry and Raker trotted back to the rear truck and soon they were moving again, following the sedan to the abandoned village.

10

Captain Gima stood in the rain with his fists on his hips looking at the burning carnage of trucks and bodies. He'd been called when a search of the ambush site produced a playing card with the words, 'Tark's Ticks' scrawled across it. Gima had put out a notice that he wanted to be informed if such a thing was found.

There hadn't been any resistance in the Bataan Peninsula region since the troops were ambushed southeast of here, three weeks ago. There'd been a few incidents in and around Manila, but those bits of resistance had been ill-conceived and squashed quickly and easily with excessive force.

This ambush was something else altogether. Taking on a ten-truck convoy in the middle of the day, meant they had plenty of men, weapons and ammunition. There'd been only one truck carrying troops, the rest supplies, but he doubted the attackers would've known that. They'd taken on what could have been a full company. *Or had they known?* He shook his head, there was no way. Filipinos, even those who collaborated, were not allowed near staging areas like the one this convoy came from. The only other possibility was a traitor and the idea of that was simply ridiculous.

The hard-pack road was succumbing to the incessant rain. His boots were covered in mud and the tracks from his own vehicles showed troughs in areas where the road dipped. Another week of this and vehicular movement would be severely limited.

Indeed, the rain had clearly played a major role in the ambush. The Americans knew the trucks would have to stop and deal with the deep mud-hole, providing them with troops in the open and bunched up. The rain was also their salvation, there was no way to track them, as their prints had washed away minutes after they left them.

Lieutenant Gunu approached, braced and snapped off a crisp salute. Gima scowled, but instead of reprimanding the young man for saluting in a combat zone, he returned it quickly. "Sir, there are two trucks missing from the convoy."

Gima nodded. "Interesting. It seems the Americans decided to take more than they could carry. Have you heard back from Captain Husukima?"

The lieutenant shook his head. "No sir. He left Mariveles yesterday but never reported in. He and his driver haven't been seen or heard from, sir."

The edges of Gima's mouth turned down and he shook his head. Captain Husukima and his company were in charge of this region and the fact that he'd been on the road around the same time as this ambush took place, did not bode well for his wellbeing. "Collect the dead. Get them back to Mariveles and continue searching for Captain Husukima." He glanced up at the rain, letting it splash his face and run down his cheeks. He sighed. "I fear he may have suffered the same fate as these men, Lieutenant."

"Yes sir. We'll keep looking." He bowed and turned away to follow Captain Gima's orders.

Gima considered his next career move. The war was going well and he wanted to join the frontlines and fight to push the Imperialists out of the region. His dream of leading his company onto the shores of Australia was closer to being a reality than it ever had been before, but he'd also vowed to avenge the deaths of his men by these American gangsters who called themselves, 'Tark's Ticks'. He had hoped they'd faded away, but the burned-out hulks of trucks and rain-soaked, bloated bodies, told him otherwise. His jaw rippled and he murmured to himself, "I'm coming for you, Tarkington."

Major Bill 'Zeke' Hanscom woke from a fitful sleep. It was dark and he surmised it must be early morning. He looked around, remembering he was in a monastery in the bustling city of Manila. Something had shaken him from sleep. He looked to the door and saw the dim silhouette of a monk standing there in his red robes. Even in the dimness, his eyes seemed to glow.

Zeke rubbed the sleep from his eyes. He didn't speak, he knew there would be no answer, as brother Mathew had taken a vow of silence. He also knew, he wouldn't have disturbed him, unless something was wrong.

He swung his legs and placed his feet on the hard-wood floor. He stood and wrapped his diminutive frame in the red robe of a monk, tucking and wrapping until it was snug and comfortable. His head was shaved, just like the other monks, and his naturally dark features and small stature allowed him to fit in almost seamlessly.

Months before, when it was obvious Luzon would fall, he'd been ordered by MacArthur himself to take two trusted soldiers, leave the intelligence segment of I Corps, and install themselves as anonymous monks in Manila.

They'd taken two long-range radios with plenty of extra batteries and with the help of Filipino soldiers, made the dangerous crossing from the Bataan Peninsula across Manila Bay and into the occupied city of Manila. He, Staff Sergeant Miller and Sergeant Gonzalez had been escorted to the monastery, where they'd been ever since.

So far, the monastery and the monks within it had been left alone. The Japanese had insisted on searching the ancient building when they first took the city, but they hadn't returned since.

Hanscom, Miller and Gonzalez had watched from afar as the Japanese finally broke through the defenses on Bataan and forced the surrender of thousands of GIs and Filipinos. The doomed island of Corregidor soon followed and the feeling of utter abandonment and despair was hard to shake off.

Hanscom and his men were well-hidden, they looked like the other monks, however they didn't speak the language fluently. They worked on that daily, being tutored by Sinjin, the weathered and ageless leader of the monastery. They'd improved dramatically but were still not good enough to pass muster if interrogated by one of the hated Makapili collaborators.

In order to avoid this inevitability, Sinjin had allowed them to take a mock vow of silence. They could talk among themselves and with Sinjin during lessons, but not to any of the other monks. Hopefully, if the Japanese returned, they'd respect their vow of silence.

Hanscom knew he was putting the monastery and everyone in it in extreme danger. If they were discovered to be harboring Americans, the Japanese wouldn't hesitate to kill every one of them and burn the building to the ground, probably with them inside.

So far, they hadn't achieved anything which warranted the risk. They monitored the radio on the proper frequency at the designated time each night, but they'd received no orders. It was frustrating and made them feel abandoned and forgotten. Hanscom had considered using the radio to reach out and remind someone that they were still there, but the danger of the Japanese intercepting the signal was too great.

Now he followed Brother Mathew through the candle-lit hallways. The monk led him to a stout wooden door leading to Brother Sinjin's room. Mathew opened it outward and the calming scent of incense combined with candle wax wafted over him. Mathew indicated he should enter and when he crossed the threshold the door shut softly behind him, leaving him alone with the meditating Sinjin.

He took a few steps forward, his bare feet making barely a sound. He waited. He knew it could be seconds or hours. He closed his eyes, readying his mind for what could be a long wait. He and his men had become accomplished at meditation. Being surrounded by it day in and day out, and seeing the amazing things it allowed the monks to do, it was inevitable. Hanscom also noticed it made time slip by much faster, or slower, depending on what you were trying for.

He opened his eyes when he heard Sinjin's soft voice. The headmaster of the monastery had moved the thirty-feet separating them without even a whisper of sound. His voice was thin as paper and clear as a bell. "There is news of an attack on Bataan. A group calling themselves, 'Tark's Ticks,' destroyed a convoy of trucks carrying ammunition."

Hanscom hid his shock and nodded, considering. "Tark's Ticks," he repeated as though testing the phrase. "Rather repulsive."

"What is a, 'tick'?" Sinjin asked.

Hanscom remembered pulling countless ticks from his dog after hunting Valley Quail in California. The thought of their gray, blood-bloated bodies made him shiver slightly. "A bug which feeds on the blood of animals. They start out tiny but can increase their body size remarkably when filled with the blood of their host. Then they drop off and lay eggs, I think. Disgusting things."

Sinjin nodded, "Ah, Garapata," he said using the Tagalog word. "This sounds like an American unit."

Hanscom nodded, rubbing his chin absently in thought. "Yes, you're right. I've never heard of them though. We're not in the habit of naming our military units in such a manner."

"I was told they left playing cards with 'Tark's Ticks' written across the front on one of the dead Japanese."

"That's brutal. And stupid," said Hanscom. Sinjin looked at him with raised eyebrows. Hanscom explained, "If they're caught, they'll know everything they've done. It's like leaving a trail. There'll be no mercy if they're caught."

Sinjin nodded. "The Japanese are not merciful people. Perhaps it is worth the risk for the cohesiveness of belonging to a recognized group. And it can cause fear in the enemy."

"Hmm, perhaps you're right. Thank you for the information." He bowed slightly.

Sinjin said, "Do not despair. Your mission here will matter. It's only a question of time."

He put his hands together and bowed deeply to Sinjin. "I know you're right, Sinjin. We must learn patience." Sinjin nodded and bowed back and Hanscom left the room and closed the doors behind him. He was alone, so he muttered to himself, "Certainly in the right place for that."

There were too many weapons and boxes of ammunition to carry to the village all at once. They wanted to cart it all there, but it would take many trips and would be tough in the muddy conditions. Tuan and Joshua conferred away from the group and finally Tuan broke away.

Tarkington saw him leave and asked Eduardo, "Where's he going?"

Eduardo shrugged, "To the village?" he guessed.

Tarkington figured he was going to get help transporting the supplies and forgot about him. "Let's bury what we can't carry."

The ground was spongy and easy to dig in, but the incessant rain filled the holes quickly, making the effort futile. They opted instead to drag the extra supplies into the jungle and camouflage them as best they could. The vehicles were driven as far as possible into the jungle and camouflaged well away from the supplies.

Just as they were finishing, Tuan returned. Tarkington saw him speak with Joshua, then wave Eduardo over. They spoke animatedly and soon the three strode to Tarkington and Eduardo smiled and said, "There is another trail to the village. Easier for moving weapons. Not as steep."

Tarkington squinted and asked, "Why are they just telling us about it now?"

Eduardo answered, "Secret way. Few outsiders know about. Keeps them safe."

Tarkington nodded, "Well, I guess better late than never. Where is it?"

"They take us when ready."

Tarkington directed his men to load more into their packs and stuff their pockets full, assuring them the new route would be easier. The majority of the weapons would stay behind and they'd make runs back and forth as needed.

The secret route was so well-hidden, Tarkington doubted he could've found it even if he had known the approximate location. Tuan went to a boulder surrounded by a small moat of clear spring water. He stepped into the pool and pushed into the lush vegetation growing on the rock and hanging into the water. He seemed to disappear into the face of the rock. It seemed as though the rock had swallowed him. Tarkington stepped into the pool, pushed tentatively into the vegetation and slipped into some sort of cavern. It was dry and dark and he put his hands out in front to keep from walking into a wall. After a few yards, there was a turn and the cavern lightened up. He could see streaks of daylight ahead through more thick foliage. Tuan stood on the other side, holding the curtain of plants back like he was backstage at a play.

Tarkington stepped through the curtain and the beauty of the canyon ahead took his breath away. There was a trail, which wound through sheer cliff walls covered in green moss and purple and pink flowers. The moss was so thick it absorbed most of the rainwater, leaving the trail damp, but not yet muddy. He let out a long whistle and soon the others were standing beside him, gaping too.

Eduardo said, "Trail long but not steep."

Tarkington marveled, "It's the most beautiful place I've ever seen."

The trail made traveling with the extra weight much easier. The incredible beauty of the place made them forget their loads and soon they were at the bridge. They were met by warriors stepping from the jungle, some wielding rifles, others bows, and were escorted the rest of the way to the village.

Vindigo and his warriors were ecstatic with the new weapons. Once again, the weapons and ammo were laid out in the hall and the villagers walked by like bidders at a silent auction. The three Type-92 heavy machine guns got the most interest.

Over the next few days, Tarkington and his men helped the Filipinos set up defensive positions along the ridgeline overlooking the hidden valley. They dug concealed foxholes and trenches and would place the two Type-92 heavy machine guns there when the time was right. The third would be kept in reserve.

The Filipinos and Americans figured out the intricacies of their operation through trial and error and their general knowledge of firearms. More trips down the hill followed until there was enough ammunition for each machine gun to inflict heavy damage.

They'd also captured a crate of Japanese knee mortars along with two crates of 50mm ammunition. These took longer to figure out — the Japanese characters impossible to decipher — but eventually they got the hang of them too. The Filipino cadets delighted in competing against one another, trying to hit more and more difficult targets, and were soon proficient in their use and able to teach the GIs some of the finer points. The ingenious and deadly launchers would certainly come in handy when the time came to use them.

Tarkington hoped they could keep the village from being discovered, but doubted it was possible. If they kept attacking, the Japanese would eventually sweep the whole area, and they'd find the secluded valley, especially once the rainy season ended. The crummy weather kept the Japanese Air Force grounded, at least for the time being, or they probably would've already been discovered.

Having the heavy machine guns and the knee mortars would allow them to mount a stalwart defense, which would give the residents a chance to melt into the jungle and valleys to the West. He hated the thought, he'd come to think of the Filipinos as family, but the reality was they were at war and crappy things happened in war.

A week after the ambush, the men were fully rested and antsy to go back out. The ecstasy of hitting hard and getting away with it was intoxicating and addictive. The cadets were particularly eager, since many felt they hadn't played a large role yet and wanted to put their new weapons to the test.

Tarkington didn't want to go out without a plan. He called a meeting and soon the cadets, GIs and Filipinos were gathered in the hall. Vindigo was there as he was for every meeting, whether it involved him directly or not.

Tarkington stood and addressed the twenty-plus men. "We lucked out. The ambush could've easily gone bad. If the trucks had been full of troops," he paused and found Sergeant Trujillo's face. Trujillo immediately turned away in embarrassment. "There'd be far fewer of us here right now. But the fates smiled on us and it turned out to be the best haul of weapons, ammo and food, we could've hoped for." He motioned to Vindigo. "The town now has the means to defend itself if the Nips ever find this place. I'm as eager to get back out there as everyone else, however I don't want to risk it until we have a clear target." He let that sink in, then continued, "We have plenty of weapons and ammo now. What we need is a worthy target. Something that can make a difference. So, this is what we're gonna do." He leaned onto the table with both hands. "My squad of GI's will go out and find a worthy target. A small force has a better chance of staying hidden than does a large one wandering around with no destination. We'll leave tomorrow morning. While we're gone, I want your men," he pointed at Staff Sergeant Fernandez, "To stay here and defend this village until we come back with a target." Fernandez's jaw clenched and he stood, obviously not happy. "You have a question, Fernandez?" he asked icily.

Fernandez gave a curt nod and in his adolescent voice, said, "Yes, Staff Sergeant Tarkington." He licked his lips. "How long will you be gone?"

Tarkington shrugged. "We'll take enough food for four days. That should be enough time to find something worth hitting. Any other questions?" He scanned the room.

Fernandez wasn't finished. "I propose I take my men in the opposite direction and search for targets. That way we'll cover more ground."

Tarkington noticed Henry was staring hard at the cadet. Tarkington shook his head and focused on Fernandez. "No. It doubles our chance of discovery and I want you here in case the Japs show up. The defense of this village is vital and relies on your men manning the machine guns on the ridge."

"But..."

Fernandez tried to continue but Tarkington yelled, "That's final, Sergeant!" Fernandez seethed, sending daggers. "Sit down," Tarkington finished. He waited, and after a few uncomfortable seconds, the young Filipino sat and crossed his arms. "We leave at 0300. Pack accordingly. I don't plan on contact, but bring plenty of ammo, just in case. Dismissed." As the men stood and made their way to the door, Tarkington called out, "Fernandez." The young man stopped and looked his way. "Stay here a minute." Fernandez kept his chin high and nodded his assent.

Once the soldiers were gone, all that remained were Tarkington, Fernandez and Vindigo. Tarkington remained beside Vindigo at the head of the table and addressed Fernandez. "I agreed to take you and your cadets in because you said you would behave like soldiers. Your outburst —" he paused then continued, "tells me you're not keeping up your end of the bargain."

Fernandez grimaced, his anger evident. "We are not children. We can..."

Again, Tarkington interrupted, his voice loud and menacing, "Then stop *acting* like children!" The outburst echoed around the hall and Fernandez went silent. He looked down at the table, momentarily cowed. Tarkington softened his voice, but the ice was still evident. "I have to be able to trust you. If I hear you went off on your own, you're done. In fact, if you put this village in danger in any way, I'll consider you an enemy." He leaned onto his hands and stared at the top of Fernandez's head until he finally looked up. "I will *hunt you down*. Understand?" Fernandez knew the crazed American wasn't kidding. He gulped, nodded and mumbled beneath his breath. Tarkington cocked his head, "What was that? I couldn't hear you."

Fernandez straightened and faced Tarkington, raising his chin and finding his pride. "I said, I understand, Staff Sergeant Tarkington."

Tarkington nodded, "Excellent. Dismissed." Fernandez did a perfect about-face and marched out of the room.

The two older men watched him go and when he was out of sight, Tarkington asked, "What do you think, Vindigo?"

Vindigo considered, never one to speak before he was ready. "Young man. Full of pride and courage. He'll listen." He added as an afterthought, "For now."

"I hope he lives long enough to figure things out, for his and the other cadets' sakes."

11

Sergeant Gonzalez broke away from a meditation session and made his way slowly through the quiet halls of the Monastery. He had decided that whoever had built the place had either been a genius, or completely insane. It had taken many weeks before Gonzalez, Miller and Hanscom felt comfortable finding their way through the labyrinthine hallways to the doorway which led up the long stairs to the tiny room just beneath the attic.

Gonzalez stood in front of the small door, looked around to be certain he wasn't observed, pulled out the key hanging from around his neck, inserted it into the ancient keyhole and unlatched the door. He quickly stepped inside, pulled the door shut behind him and locked it. He wasn't worried about being seen and reported to the Japanese by another monk, but habit dictated his fieldcraft, and even after many months of boredom, that meant stealth.

He jogged up the wooden stairs and was panting slightly when he came to another door. This one wasn't locked and he pushed it inward and stepped into a tiny room. It had a desk, a rickety chair, a radio and a small window, which looked out over Manila Bay. Going to the window and admiring the view was always the first thing he did. Not only was it beautiful, it was also a perfect vantage point to observe the comings and goings of the Imperial Japanese Navy. HQ had never asked them to report their movements but they kept detailed reports just in case.

They monitored the radio from 1400 to 1500 every day, the designated time they'd set up before leaving I Corps those many months before. Every day since arriving in April, one of the three sat in the chair and jotted down what the Japanese Navy were up to that day.

At exactly 1400, Gonzalez turned the radio on and listened. Despite being disappointed for months on end, there was always a glimmer of hope that perhaps this would be the day they rejoined the war effort.

He listened intently for five minutes before scooting the chair closer to the window and counting how many ships and what kind were in the harbor today. He checked the list from the day before, it was Major Hanscom's handwriting. Nothing much had happened. There was still a Japanese destroyer anchored out near Cavite. It had limped in nearly a month before spewing smoke. They'd inquired about the name but no one seemed to know.

His thoughts were suddenly ripped from his observations as he heard first static, then a chirping coming from the radio. He nearly knocked the chair over in his haste to bring it back to the table.

He licked his lips and had his pencil poised over paper, ready to write down the coded message. When it didn't come right away, he thought perhaps he'd imagined it, as though he were wishing it to be true. Then another bit of static. He touched the frequency knob, making sure it was set correctly. Then there was a voice, distant and scratchy but an American voice, nonetheless. "Victor, Victor, this is Papabear. Do you read me? Over."

Gonzalez could hardly contain himself. He took a deep breath, depressed the send button and tried to sound as calm and cool as possible. "Papabear, this is Victor. I read you loud and clear. Over."

There was a pause then the voice again. "Good to hear you're well, Victor. Standby for traffic. Over."

"Good to hear your voice, Papabear. Ready for traffic. Over."

"Roger. Traffic follows: Alpha, six, seventeen, Lima. The Otter and the Waiter are an odd pair. Talk to Heather and there will be Lentils. Break six-one-five. How copy? Over."

"Copy all." He read the numbers and nonsense phrases back and it was confirmed.

"Message read back correct. Out." The radio went silent and Sergeant Gonzalez stared at it as if it were a magical device which had just come to life and might do so again. He still had fortyfive minutes before 1500 hours. He wanted to run down the stairs and tell the major, but missing another transmission would be dereliction of duty. In the meantime, he would work on deciphering the message.

Twenty minutes later he'd matched the numbers and letters from the phrase book in sequence. When he read the message, he whistled and shook his head. "Now we're gonna get busy."

Major Hanscom was overjoyed that they'd finally received a message from Papabear. He had really been starting to wonder if they'd been forgotten. Sergeant Gonzalez had done his best to contain himself as he did a quick-walk through the dimly lit halls, nearly blowing out multiple candles as he passed.

When Hanscom saw him, he knew he'd heard from command. Gonzalez stepped beside him and wanted to blurt out what had happened, but they were surrounded by monks, who all knew they'd taken a vow of silence. They were facing another line of monks who were chanting and swinging incense side-to-side.

Normally, Hanscom enjoyed the ritual, but now he wanted it to end so he could talk with his sergeant in private. He could feel Gonzalez was ready to burst at the seams.

The ritual finally ended and the monks dispersed with bows and smiles. Zeke and Gonzalez turned and left the hall and walked as slow as the rest until they got to their shared room. Inside, Staff Sergeant Miller looked up and immediately got to his feet sensing the excitement. Before the door shut, he blurted, "You heard something?"

Hanscom finished closing the door, scowling and bringing his finger to his lips. When it was closed he addressed Miller. "Dammit, Sergeant. We're supposed to be tight-lipped, remember?"

"Sorry sir, but dammit, something has happened. Look at Gonzalez! He's about to do a backflip, he's so excited."

Gonzalez handed the slip of paper to Major Hanscom. "It happened. They finally got in contact. I was sitting there watching the harbor when there was static, then a chirp and then a voice. An actual American voice. Papabear." He told it as though it was the most exciting experience of his life.

Miller smiled and nodded. It took a lot to make him smile and Gonzalez wasn't sure he remembered ever seeing him do so. Gonzalez thought he was the most tight-lipped soldier he'd ever come across. He was also the first man he'd turn to if their situation required violent decisive action.

Miller watched Major Hanscom. "What's it say, Zeke?"

Hanscom summarized. "They want to know if there have been atrocities and what kind of resistance, if any, is occurring." He looked at his sergeants. "Could they have heard about the prisoner march from Mariveles? I wouldn't see how."

Miller shook his head. "I saw it for myself at the train station in San Fernando. Those guys were barely hanging on. It's for real all right."

Hanscom nodded. "And I've just heard about a possible American resistance cell across the bay on the peninsula. Sinjin heard about some group that leaves calling cards on dead Japs, 'Tark's Ticks'."

Miller scowled and repeated the name as though it left a bad taste, "Tark's Ticks. Sounds like a bunch of cowboys."

Gonzalez chimed in, "There's been a few incidents around here, but nothing organized. Those guys organized?"

"Sinjin said they hit a good-sized truck convoy and made off with a lot of weapons and ammo. They killed a bunch of Japs and burned the vehicles."

Miller asked, "In this weather?"

Gonzalez nodded, "Makes some sense. The weather keeps the Japs from reacting quickly. The roads are a muddy mess."

Hanscom added, "And makes 'em harder to track I'd guess."

Miller nodded, "I guess every advantage counts when you're fighting as a guerrilla. You gonna tell command about them?"

Hanscom equivocated, "I'll confirm the atrocities but I'll need to contact these Tark's Ticks yahoos before I pass that along." Miller and Gonzalez looked at their commander expectantly. Hanscom looked from one to the other, "Me and Miller will check 'em out."

Gonzalez's shoulders slumped but he quickly recovered and nodded. Hanscom put his hand on his shoulder. "Don't worry Gonzo. I have a feeling there'll be enough action over the next few months to satisfy all our cravings."

He put the message over a candle and it blackened then flamed and he dropped it onto the hardwood floor, stomped on it and twisted, turning it to dust. "I'll send the message to Papabear tomorrow, see if there's anything else they want. We'll leave the next morning. Dig up our pistols and let Dominic know we'll need a guide. I'll let Sinjin know."

"Yes, sir," They chimed in unison.

The next evening, Zeke manned the radio, along with the two sergeants. They didn't transmit during the same time as they'd received the day before. In the message from command, a transmit timeframe was relayed and now they transmitted at exactly 1820 hours. They kept it short, lessening the chance of the signal being picked up by the wrong people. Now that the connection had been established, the messages would be short and straight to the point.

The second radio was stuffed in a corner, covered with a tarp. If the radio chatter continued, they'd take it to another part of the city and use it on and off to throw off the Japanese who'd undoubtedly be trying to triangulate their position. For now, it seemed overly cautious, but they were here for the long haul and eventually the Japanese would organize themselves enough to actively hunt for spies.

There were no new requests or questions from command, so they went back to their room. Gonzalez stayed near the door, making sure no one came in unexpectedly while Miller and the major changed out of their monk clothes and into their Filipino civilian clothes.

They cleaned their service pistols, 1911 Colt .45s and stuffed two extra magazines into their small packs. They were stuffed into the bottom of the packs inside a small compartment. If searched, the hard pieces would seem like a part of the structure of the pack, at least that was the hope.

When they were packed and ready, they slid into bed and tried to sleep. It would probably be the last time they'd see their beds for at least a couple of days.

Major Hanscom arose at 0300 hours and had to jostle Miller awake. Hanscom wasn't sure he'd slept at all, but Miller had the ability to sleep any time he put his head down. It was a skill both Hanscom and Gonzalez envied.

Gonzalez, who hadn't slept either, helped them with their gear, it wasn't much. The last thing they wanted was to stand out from other Filipino civilians, so their packs held just enough food for a day, as though they weren't traveling anywhere out of the ordinary.

The Japanese had been in power for a number of months but were just starting to enforce the rules they'd posted all over the city and one of those rules was no traveling further than back and forth to work. The civilian refugees from the battle were either back at their villages, staying with relatives, or dead.

They ate a cold breakfast of meat and rice. There weren't many monks out and about this time of day, but Sinjin was there to see them off. He bowed deeply, clutched their hands and said a prayer for safe travels. Hanscom gripped Gonzalez's hand. "Hold down the fort. I expect we'll be out a week, but I wouldn't start to worry until two weeks. The radio's our lifeline, so stay vigilant."

Gonzalez nodded, "Of course, sir. Good luck." He gripped Miller's hand and they stepped out into the muggy night. The rain had stopped, leaving the streets steaming and muddy. Gonzalez felt an empty pit in his stomach as he closed the door and turned to face Sinjin.

Sinjin bowed his head slightly and said, "You will see them again."

Gonzalez bowed back, "I sure hope you're right."

Colonel Hideko Takashima was called to the communications room at 1825 hours. The intercepted transmission the evening before had gotten his attention and he'd told Lieutenant Aki, the junior counter-intelligence officer in charge of communications, to call him no matter the hour if the signal was received again.

He burst into the radio room and Lt. Aki braced and saluted. Takashima saluted back. "Another transmission?"

"Hai sir. It ended minutes ago."

"Did you get a fix? A location?"

He stayed braced and shook his head. "No, sir. It was too short, but it was the same transmission style. I'm confident it emanated from the same location as yesterday."

Takashima nodded. "And you're sure it is somewhere within the city?"

He nodded, "Hai. The incoming signal was weak but the outgoing signal very strong, just like the one before."

Takashima glanced at his gold wristwatch, a parting gift from his wife. "The time is different than yesterday. That will make it more difficult to pin down." Lt. Aki nodded. "I want you to spread the men out north and south of the city. I want them monitoring all the time, ready to move at the first hint of a transmission. We should have the location pinned down in a matter of days, weeks if we're unlucky." Lieutenant Aki's face blanched and he looked at his feet.

Takashima knew what the problem would be but asked anyway. "What is wrong, Lieutenant?"

Aki's eyes raised and he bowed slightly. "We only have one of the units at our disposal, sir."

Takashima's lips pursed to a thin line. "Colonel Nakata?" the colonel asked. Lieutenant Aki looked as uncomfortable as a junior officer could look. He wanted no part of the feud between the two intelligence branch colonels. He nodded and looked down again.

Colonel Nakata led the feared but favored Kempeitai, the secret police of the Empire. Colonel Takashima led the Army Intelligence unit. They had the same basic goals, to keep order and hunt down sedition, but they had vastly different approaches.

Nakata used fear and intimidation, Takashima, information and craft work. Takashima was the chief of police for a good-sized city before he turned his skills to the Army. He thought of Nakata and his henchmen as amateur thugs. He had to stomach them though, for they were the darlings of the Emperor.

Takashima swallowed his anger and nodded. There was no use yelling at the lieutenant, it was not his fault and he couldn't have prevented it even if he'd tried. "Then start with the north. I'll see what I can do about finding another unit. Manila is full of natives who don't like us. It could be a breeding ground for a resistance movement if we don't put a stop to it immediately." Lieutenant Aki was relieved to have his orders. He saluted and went to the radio intent on carrying them out.

Takashima left the stifling hot radio room and clenched his fists in anger. He wondered where Nakata had the three other portable units. The man could have split them up, leaving him two, but instead took three, assuring the job of tracking illegal transmissions would be nearly impossible. Was that his game: trying to make him look incompetent by taking the very tools he needed to do his job? Didn't the fool understand they were fighting a common enemy?

Talking sense to the man made no difference. It was as though he were a stone that could not be deterred from its path down the hill once it got going. The only reason he even had a job was his single-minded dedication to hunting down anyone that needed hunting. He'd torture, rape, or maim anyone he thought would help him find his prey. He'd even gone after a second cousin to a soldier who'd been outed as speaking against the war in China. He went so far as to cripple the poor man, even though the soldier was already behind bars.

The second cousin told him he barely knew the soldier, only having met him once when they were six. That didn't matter to Aki, the unfortunate man finally confessed. It was the only thing that would make the pain stop. He was hung alongside his cousin a week later.

Colonel Takashima would have to be careful. He wasn't afraid of the man, in fact, he relished a one-on-one duel. He was sure he'd win. Takashima was in excellent shape and was a master of hand-to-hand combat. He had no doubt he could best the blocky, out-of-shape Kempeitai colonel in an even match.

He was also confident in his intellectual prowess. Before the war, Nakata was considered dim-witted and was only promoted when the more militant regime took power and saw in him, a kindred, brutal, spirit. A man who would do the secret police's bidding, no questions asked. He'd proven himself countless times, his body count of his own people, in the hundreds. Nakata might be a bully and a dullard, but he had friends in high places who could make Takashima's life difficult.

12

The mixed squad of GIs and Filipinos left the village during an intense downpour hours before dawn. The creek, had been steadily climbing its banks but so far had not gone over, leaving the squad a viable crossing point. If the rain continued, they'd probably have to return over the bridge.

At sunrise the rain slackened and the day brightened somewhat, however the thick layers of cloud didn't allow for full sunlight. The temperature was still high with the added pleasure of one hundred percent humidity. Despite this, though, Tarkington felt himself shiver as they hunched in the jungle overlooking the main road. It was a sloppy mess, and the one short convoy they saw, of two trucks and a car, made deep cuts into the mud. They had to keep moving or risk sinking and being stuck.

It would have been an easy thing to attack the convoy, but they already had plenty of supplies. Their mission was to find targets which would make a difference to the war effort. Hitting random convoys was detrimental to the Japanese war machine, but the more times they did such things the more chance of being caught or followed back to the village. Tarkington thought if he was going to risk his men's lives and those of the Filipinos, he wanted it to be worth the risk.

After seeing the trouble the convoy had on the muddy road, Tarkington decided then and there not to use the captured trucks until after the rainy season. They'd stay hidden for the time being. Hopefully they wouldn't rust away.

After ten minutes watching the road without seeing more traffic, they crossed into the less dense jungle on the other side. Tarkington looked back at their tracks and muttered to Sergeant Winkleman, "Tracks are almost gone already. This rain's both a blessing and a curse."

They gathered across the road and conferred. "San Fernando's about fifty-kilometers. The train station there is worth a look. I'll bet the Japs are using it more now that the rainy season's here. It might be a viable target, slow 'em down a bit. We'll move to the coast. It'll be easier to move and we'll be able to see if there's any vulnerable shipping too."

The men nodded. Tarkington hadn't told Vindigo or anyone else in the village of his planned route. It wasn't because he didn't trust them, it was more to keep the villagers clueless in case the Japanese came while they were gone. They couldn't tell them where they'd gone if they didn't know.

Eduardo passed the information onto the two Filipino guides. Tuan and Joshua nodded emphatically, pleased to know where they would be leading them. They moved off in a single-file line with the Filipinos out front, followed closely by Raker and Henry, then the rest.

Tarkington carried the submachine gun, the others had rifles and four grenades each. Tarkington had convinced Stollman to leave his new love, the Type-96 light machine gun, behind. It was heavy and if they needed its considerable firepower, they'd be in deep shit as the plan was to avoid contact.

The jungle was a dripping mess. The ground was soft, sometimes muddy and it was an odd sensation for the GIs to be wearing sandals in such adverse conditions. The mud seeped over their feet and squished between their toes. After the initial discomfort, feeling the elements soon became second nature and helped them move silently as though more connected. They were no longer foreign soldiers on foreign soil, but creatures of the jungle — an integral and deadly part of its varied lifeforms.

The Filipinos led them quickly through the interior. At Tarkington's direction, they avoided villages, both occupied and abandoned, despite the Filipinos wanting to show themselves and possibly be given respite from the near constant rain. After skirting one such village, the procession stopped and Eduardo signaled Tarkington forward.

Eduardo motioned to Tuan and Joshua. "They have relatives in the next village and want to stop there for the night."

"Relatives?"

Eduardo nodded. "They say the village is safe. They hate the Japanese. No *Makapili*." He said the last word with dripping hatred.

Tarkington nodded and glanced at his men. They were wet and the mud traveled up their bare legs past their knees. Most of their faces were splattered with a light layer of mud streaked with sweat and rainwater. They'd made good time, barely stopping to rest, except when someone needed a piss break. Letting the men sleep out of the elements would be a good reward for the hard day.

He took a deep breath and let it out slow. "What d'you think, Wink? Should we risk it?"

Winkleman shrugged. His eyes looked tired, but he'd do whatever he thought was right, not based on his own personal comforts. "Being under-cover and eating a hot meal would be nice. But it's a risk, no matter how small."

It wasn't an answer because it was ultimately up to Tarkington. He nodded to Eduardo. "Have them go in by themselves first. Don't mention us. If things are the way they remember them, then we'll come in later."

Eduardo nodded and passed the information along. The guide's smiles were broad, the prospect of seeing friends and staying dry and warm for the night made them almost giddy.

They watched them enter the quiet village. Each hut had lazy wisps of smoke snaking from the center pipes, but other than that, there was no sign of activity. The squad spread out in a defensive formation, their weapons facing outward. Tarkington sat beside a thick tree. He could only see a tiny sliver of the village through the dripping branches and leaves. The two guides were nowhere in sight.

He opened his bag and pulled out a strip of dried meat and tore off a sizable chunk. The salty taste made his mouth dry and he chased the meat with a slug of tepid water from his canteen. His combat belt, holding his sword, ammo and canteen, was the only thing that might identify him as an

American soldier, but many native Filipinos wore the same belts — minus the ammo and canteen — due to their overall utility. He wasn't planning on anyone giving him close inspection, particularly the Japanese, so he wasn't overly worried about the canteen.

He screwed the lid back on and clipped it to the belt. There was movement and noise and he instinctively clutched his submachine gun, bringing the barrel up. He saw Tuan and Joshua enter the jungle, smiling. They hadn't been gone as long as he thought they'd be.

Tarkington lowered the muzzle, looking forward to being somewhere dry where he could give the weapon a good cleaning. So far, it had performed wonderfully in the inclement weather, but no weapon was impervious to the effects of rain and mud for long.

Eduardo talked with the excited guides. He listened, nodded, then staying in a crouch, moved to Tarkington. "They say village is safe."

"Pretty quick assessment." Eduardo's mouth turned down and he gave a slight shrug. Tarkington got to his feet and sought out Henry. "What d'you think, Henry? Got any sense of danger?"

Henry considered and scowled but shook his head. "Not really. But this rain dulls my senses a little."

Tarkington looked surprised. "Really? Thought you were always sharp as a tack." Henry grinned and Tarkington realized he was joking. Tarkington sighed. "Well you're no help."

He waved the men forward and followed the Filipinos into the clearing. The feeling of open space after being cloistered in the jungle made him feel vulnerable. His head was on a swivel watching for danger. Villagers came out of huts and stood on their covered porches and watched them materialize from the jungle. Tarkington thought they must look like near-drowned rats.

Tuan and Joshua led them to the largest of the huts. It sat six-feet off the ground, supported by multiple struts. Tarkington wondered if it was for flooding or status purposes. They ascended the steps and were suddenly out of the rain. Tarkington looked up at the overhang and blew out a long breath of relief.

A man was standing in the darkness of the doorway. Tarkington hadn't noticed him at first, but when he smiled and reached a hand out, Tarkington shook it. "Thank you letting us stay." He said in broken Tagalog.

He'd been trying to learn the language for a long time and could say half phrases here and there. Since being surrounded by the language daily, everyone's Tagalog had improved.

The man smiled and Tarkington realized if he was the village leader, he was much younger than most. In English, he said, "You are most welcome." He stepped aside and motioned they should enter. "We haven't seen Americans since the surrender," he added as the men filled the deck and followed Tarkington inside one-by-one.

"No doubt," said Tarkington.

The village leader's name was Sampson. He was roughly the same age as Tuan and Joshua. They were not related but knew each other from markets where both sets of parents traded goods before the war. Now they were grown men, important hunters and warriors, and Sampson was the village leader, despite his young age.

Sampson made the men comfortable, giving them dry, clean clothes while their own were washed and hung over fires to dry. Food was prepared, the occasion of visiting Americans enough to make it a feast.

While stuffing themselves with wild boar, snake, monkey and other exotic meats, Tarkington leaned toward Sampson who was sitting on a rug beside him. He had to raise his voice to make himself heard over the many other animated conversations. "Thank you for your hospitality. I hope you haven't stretched your food too far."

Sampson flicked his hand as though shunning a pesky fly. "It is nothing. We are good at storing food."

Tarkington bit into a savory, dripping piece of meat and around a mouthful asked, "You are not the oldest man here. How is it you are the village elder?"

Conversation around them dropped and the effect made its way around the room, until there was near silence. Joshua and Tuan looked around in confusion until Eduardo beside them translated, then their faces fell and they stared.

Tarkington was stunned by the response and placed the piece of meat on the plate and swallowed down his mouthful with an audible gulp. Once able to talk, he said, "I'm sorry. I didn't mean to offend. It's just that in every other village I've ever been in, the elder is the eldest. I meant no disrespect."

Tarkington saw a flash of anger in Sampson's eyes which was quickly replaced with a smile, but it didn't quite travel all the way to his eyes. He extended his arms encouraging them to continue eating. "It's okay. It's okay." The circle relaxed somewhat and the men continued talking and eating, although somewhat guardedly.

Sampson leaned closer to Tarkington and said, "You are correct. It *is* unusual." He pointed to an old man to his right. "That is my father, Benjamin. He is the village elder by age. He passed the village elder status to me, his only son."

Tarkington nodded, but knew there must be more to the story. He'd never heard of such a thing and the odd reaction, almost of fear, made him think perhaps the transition of power had been less than smooth.

Sampson finished eating and his plate and bowl were whisked away by a woman who kept her head down as though she were serving a king in the olden days. Tarkington pushed his own plate away and another woman appeared and took it away. "Thanks," Tarkington muttered and he caught the woman's quick glance before she was gone.

Sampson leaned toward Tarkington. "We thought all Americans surrendered."

Tarkington nodded. "We weren't with the main group when the surrender happened. The final orders I received were to continue the fight as guerillas."

He nodded, "So you *do* continue to fight? Are you the group that attacked the convoy?"

Tarkington didn't like the direct question and answered. "We continue to follow our orders."

Sampson's face darkened with the evasive answer. He continued, "I only ask because I heard there were many weapons and ammo taken. You must have a large stockpile."

Tarkington glanced at Winkleman to his right. He was leaning in, taking a keen interest in the conversation. Tarkington answered, "We have plenty of weapons and ammunition. Yes."

Sampson nodded and smiled. "Perhaps so much that you'd be able to give us some."

Tarkington looked Sampson in the eye. "Are you resisting the Japanese? Are you fighting?"

Sampson shrugged. "It's impossible to resist without weapons and ammunition. We have resisted in small ways. Hiding food from them, sabotaging vehicles cutting communication wires."

Tarkington nodded. "A dangerous game to play."

"We would do more if we had weapons."

Tarkington rubbed his chin, considering. "Are you suggesting an alliance?"

Sampson moved his head side-to-side, as though equivocating. "We are Filipino, you are American. America has abandoned us to the Japanese. It is now our responsibility to fight them."

Tarkington furrowed his brow. He didn't like how the conversation was going. "America has not abandoned the Philippines." He tapped his chest and indicated the other GIs with a sweep of his arm. "We are still fighting. The might of the United States won't let this invasion stand."

Sampson shook his head. "America fought and failed. You and your band are outside your commander's orders. They surrendered. You fight illegally."

Tarkington's face darkened and he stared hard at Sampson. His voice had an edge of barely contained rage. "Illegal? My country and *your* country have been attacked. There is nothing illegal about our resistance. We will fight them until they're defeated or we're dead." He got to his feet. "End of story."

Sampson stood quickly and faced him. "You will take us to your weapons cache or..." All conversation stopped and the GIs stiffened. Sampson had insisted their rifles be left beside the door as they entered.

Now there were two lanky villagers with old Springfield rifles guarding them.

Tarkington took it all in. "Or what?" he asked venomously.

"Or we'll force you to do so." Tarkington noticed the .38 caliber pistol in Sampson's right hand. He realized he must have had it hidden beneath the pillow he sat on.

Joshua and Tuan looked wholly dismayed and asked Eduardo to translate. He did so quickly and the two stood and faced their friend. They spoke quickly and Sampson waved the pistol around, barked something in Tagalog and they stopped. He glared at the two men. Eduardo spoke, "He told them to..."

Sampson aimed the pistol at Eduardo face. Tarkington saw his finger move to the trigger. He reacted instantly, clutching Sampson's outstretched arm, ruining his aim, while at the same time tackling him to the ground. The pistol fired once before Tarkington wrestled it from his hand and aimed it at Sampson's head.

Winkleman pulled his sidearm, the 1911 .45 caliber, searching for more threats. Henry moved quick and silent as a snake and when the guards raised their rifles, Henry was already behind them, holding his own pistol to the nearest guard's head and they both froze in place.

Eduardo called out, "He's hit."

All eyes went to him Eduardo gripping Tuan's shoulder. Tuan was leaned forward, his head on the ground as though praying. The back of his head glistened with wetness and bits of gray matter and skull dotted his black hair. Eduardo pulled his shoulders back and the neat hole in the center of his forehead left little doubt he was dead. His eyes were still open, but the life was gone.

Joshua stared in disbelief at his best friend and a low growl built from deep within him and soon he wailed.

Tarkington placed the barrel against Sampson's head, wanting nothing more than to pull the trigger and avenge Tuan's death. But he knew if he did, they wouldn't leave the village without a hard fight.

Raker and Skinner were up with Henry. They got to their rifles and were ready to rock and roll. Henry kicked the guard behind the knee while holding his hair and the man dropped to his knees. Skinner did the same with the second man and hissed in his ear. "Move you die." The barrel of his Type-38 rifle firmly against the back of his head. The rest of the squad was up covering the stunned Filipinos with their recovered weapons.

Tarkington kept the .38 caliber pistol aimed at Sampson's head while he got to his feet. Sampson stayed down, his hands up, never taking his eyes from Tarkington's. "Get up," Tarkington growled. He moved behind him. "Slow."

Sampson kept his hands up and got to his feet, glancing at the dead body across the way. "I didn't mean to kill Tuan. It was your fault, you made me fire."

Tarkington waited until Sampson was standing. He pressed the barrel against the back of his head. "You son-of-a-bitch. *You* killed him. You pulled the gun. You were going to shoot Eduardo." He looked around the circle at the villager's faces. "What the hell's the matter with you? We have a common enemy. Why attack us? We're on your side, for chrissakes." There was no answer and the villagers were unable to hold his withering gaze.

Tarkington ordered Sampson's hands and feet tied. He sat him on a bench in the center of the room. Stollman and Vick stood on either side of him holding their weapons ready. The villagers were cowed by the night's deadly events and Tarkington thought they seemed more embarrassed than anything else.

The rest of the squad were on the outside of the circle holding their rifles ready. Tuan's body was wrapped in a blanket and Joshua stood over him with his head down and his rifle slung over his shoulder, weeping softly. The villagers had been searched and any weapons taken and placed in a pile. There weren't many, mostly knives and a couple more .38 caliber pistols.

With the situation in hand, Tarkington went to Winkleman who was standing beside Henry. He addressed them both in a low whisper. "I'm at a loss, I have no idea what to do here."

Henry spoke in his slow, considered southern twang, "I've seen it before.

Different factions emerging with the same goal but going at each other's throats to be the leaders."

Tarkington was always surprised with Henry's experiences. He was no older than him but seemed to have insights into a lifetime's worth of living. "Yeah? Where?"

"Believe it or not, my little hometown had two...well, I guess you'd call 'em gangs. The common goal was survival, really. It was mostly subsistence down there, but there were hunting and fishing boundaries. If one group got in the way of the other, or crossed a boundary," he shrugged, "Well, there'd be trouble."

"Like killing?"

"Nah, that never happened. More like getting the shit kicked out of ya. And once that happened it would escalate. Completely counter-productive to the overall goal."

"So, any suggestions?"

Winkleman looked to Henry and he finally tilted his head and gave a slight grin. "Right now, we're in their territory. We didn't know it, but now we do, so we should leave."

Tarkington pursed his lips. "Not sure how I feel about that. I mean what if they rat us out to the Japs? Or ambush us?"

Henry shook his head. "Not how it works. At least in my experience. I guess the game wardens and cops were the enemy in my case but bringing them in was never even considered. Everyone knew once you did that, we'd all suffer."

Winkleman asked, "What about the ambush part?"

Henry shrugged, "Don't seem like they've got a lot of weapons to do something like that. The whole reason they tried to take us was to get weapons."

Tarkington nodded. "Okay. We'll keep 'em in here tonight and take shifts watching them. We'll release 'em in the morning. At least we'll be dry for once."

13

Major Hanscom, Staff Sergeant Miller and their Filipino scout Dominic, made their way out of Manila looking like any other Filipino workers leaving the city for a day of manual labor. They kept their heads down and avoided other groups. Dominic would do the talking if it came to it. The Americans could hold their own with the language, but it would be obvious they weren't native.

There was a roadblock leading out of the city. The Japanese guards wore ponchos and looked miserable standing in the mud and rain. They stood to the side and watched the workers with disinterest. They didn't stop anyone, but simply walking past their glowering faces spiked Hanscom's heart rate.

Once past, Hanscom whispered to Miller, "Doubt their lax behavior will last long. Once they're firmly established, moving around will be harder."

Miller nodded and whispered back "No doubt. Once the rainy season's over, things'll change."

Dominic led them west along dirt roads, and the group dwindled as more and more people peeled off onto splinter roads. Soon they were nearly alone. The sun was warm on their backs when they made it to the water of Manila Bay. The four other Filipinos who'd stayed with them, moved off to a small boat and loaded nets and buoys, then pushed off with practiced ease. They didn't give Dominic's group a second glance.

Once they were alone, Dominic pointed at the dim outline across the bay. "That is the Peninsula, you remember coming across no doubt, but we are not crossing." He pointed north. "We'll use the boat to travel into the western arm of the Pampanga River. We can move upstream toward San Fernando. It will get us close and we'll avoid any more roadblocks."

Miller looked at the motorless boat and scowled. "That's a long way to row."

Dominic smiled and walked along the mucky beach then followed a small cut where a muddy stream emptied into the bay. He motioned them to follow and they trotted to catch up. He led them up the creek forty-yards and pulled back thick foliage revealing a plank of wood and something bulky covered by a gunny sack. He pulled the sack away to reveal an old outboard engine and a steel tank of gas, painted green and brown "We will not be rowing."

Hanscom saw a few other boats already on the water, none had outboard motors. He asked, "Won't we stand out with an engine?"

Dominic shrugged. "Before the invasion, most had engines but gas and oil are hard to get now. We conserved, they did not. Also, we will be far from other boats as we move north."

Once the engine was mounted and connected to the gas tank, Dominic waved them inside and he pulled the starter cord. It took three pulls before the engine purred to life and they moved away from the shallows to deeper water. The ten-horsepower motor wasn't fast, but it kept them moving steadily and didn't attract the attention that a more powerful engine might.

They ate up the miles, the land sixty-yards to their right was mostly empty, but the occasional person they did see, barely gave them a passing glance.

Hanscom kicked the ten-gallon fuel tank. "That gonna get us back too?" he asked.

Dominic shook his head. "More gas up the river."

Hanscom knew there were Filipino resistance elements in Manila, and he knew Dominic was a part of it all, but he didn't know the extent of their preparations. "Did you stow the engine and gas yourself?"

Dominic gave him a curious look as though wondering how much he should tell him. He shook his head. "No. When it was obvious the Japanese would take Luzon, me and," he hesitated, trying to find the correct words. "My friends knew gasoline and oil would be hard to come by so we hid as much as we could find. This is my own engine but there are others hidden around the bay. We share the fuel and only use them in emergencies. It is the communist way."

Hanscom raised his eyebrows, nodded and continued, "You offered us your assistance when we first went to the monastery, but you didn't tell us there were others."

Dominic smiled, "There are others. Of course. Communism is the will of the people. There are many of us."

Hanscom exchanged a look with Miller, then shook his head. "We were bellyaching about being left out of the war and all along there's a resistance cell right under our noses setting the groundwork for the future."

Miller shrugged, "We didn't have orders."

Hanscom tilted his head back and forth, equivocating. "I need to change the way I'm thinking about this whole thing."

Miller asked, "What d'you mean?"

"We coulda been getting ready. Doing stuff like Dominic, stockpiling and finding friends with similar goals. Instead, I moped around waiting for orders." He looked off toward the West. "We're on our own. I — *we* need to take the initiative, be more proactive."

Miller smiled and nodded his agreement. "You're right, Zeke. Getting out like this is good. We've been shut in the monastery like a bunch of ostriches with our heads in the sand." Dominic's smile faded, as he did not understand the reference. Miller waved it away, "Never mind, Dom. Just know we'd like to know more about your group and be more involved." He looked at Major Hanscom hoping he hadn't overstepped his boundaries, but Hanscom nodded. The look of determination obvious on his face.

"You are American. Capitalists not Communists."

Hanscom asked, "Is that a problem?"

Dominic grinned, "Not yet."

Two days had passed since the tragic killing of Tuan at the hands of Sampson. Eduardo assured Tarkington that he knew this area well, so he ordered Joshua to take his friend's body back to his village for a proper burial and to tell Vindigo to be vigilant in case Henry's assessment of Sampson's readiness and resolve were incorrect. They helped Joshua truss the body in a poncho and he slung the weight over his shoulder easily enough, assuring them that he'd be fine by himself.

True to his word, Eduardo steered them clear of other villages and pockets of population. They'd seen two Japanese patrols and easily avoided them. The closest patrol passed beneath them as they hid on a low ridge, only forty-yards away. The Japanese were off the road, using a muddy game-trail. It was tempting to attack the bedraggled patrol, but Tarkington didn't want to draw attention, so they let them pass.

Now they were moving along the same road which had been used to march the American and Filipino prisoners north. All signs of the brutal march were gone, the rain having scoured the footprints and blood away. If there had been any more bodies left along the side of the road, the jungle had long since reclaimed them.

It was midday and Tarkington wanted to give the men a rest. They'd started marching three hours before dawn and staying sharp while slogging through the wet conditions was becoming difficult. He figured if he was tired, they were tired.

He found a wide point in the road and mumbled to Winkleman. "Let's get off the road and take a break." Winkleman nodded and passed the order along. The men moved like tired automatons.

The rain stopped, the sun poked from behind a cloud and steam immediately filled the area with a thick, stifling fog. The respite from the rain was welcome. The GIs took off packs, rummaged for food, then sat upon them, keeping their butts out of the mud and their rifles close at hand.

Tarkington checked in with each man. They were hardened soldiers. Their sinewy muscles belied their power. These men had gone through hell and back and their futures were likely to be full of more hardship and pain, yet morale was high. They knew their jobs backwards and forwards and Tarkington didn't think he could've asked for better men.

He moved off to relieve himself in the jungle. As he found a likely spot and did his business, he looked off through the trees in a daze, until something glinted and caught his eye. He focused on the spot, there was something there, something out of place. He brought his submachine gun up and moved a few feet to see better, forcing himself to breathe slowly.

He stood up straight when he realized there was no danger. He stepped into a little clearing. There were mounds of rock, marked with crude wooden crosses at their heads. Sitting on top of each mound was whatever the soldier had had on them when they died. There were torn boots, sunfaded hats, empty and battered canteens, and on a few, hanging from crosses, were the unmistakable outlines of US dog-tags. He'd seen the glinting of the dog-tags as the sun caught them.

He counted twenty individual graves, lined up neatly. He doubted the Japanese had done this. He went to the nearest grave with dog-tags on it. He rubbed the dirt and grime from the letters and read the words: Herbert T. Gladstone. Next of kin was Thomas R. Gladstone and he hailed from Portland, Oregon.

Tarkington mused about the next of kin, Mr. Thomas Gladstone. The agony he must be feeling, not knowing if his son was dead or alive. Would he even know he'd been captured? What would he think if he knew his son had most likely been murdered while on a forced march along a sunsoaked dirt road in the Philippines? Would he ever know the truth? Would he go through the rest of his life wondering? Of course, he didn't know the soldier, but he figured he must've been young since the listed next of kin wasn't a wife.

He looked at the boots: the toes curled, and the sole separated from the leather in spots. The leather was thin, and he wondered how many arduous miles of torment they'd seen. He noticed movement behind him and turned to see the rest of his men staring at the mini graveyard. Those wearing hats took them off in respect and simply stared.

Tarkington stood and Eduardo came up beside him. Tarkington gulped back a growing lump in his throat. "Your people buried them, no doubt. Putting our soldiers to rest."

Eduardo nodded and pointed across the way. "And our own." Tarkington noticed the different items on the last row of graves. Instead of dog-tags, necklaces and various trinkets of remembrance hung from these crosses. These were people buried by those who knew them: wives, husbands, mothers, fathers, sons, daughters and friends.

Tarkington nodded. "We owe your people a great debt."

Eduardo shook his head. "No." He paused and finally said, "You owe us vengeance."

They continued moving north. Overall, the road was much straighter than the Bagac-Mariveles Road, but this section was winding, steep and had many switchbacks. Tarkington doubted any motorized vehicles could make it down the roads in their slippery condition. They were forced to keep to the sides, the center too slippery even for walking.

When they finally topped out, they stopped to catch their breath and Tarkington reminded them to drink. In the wet conditions it was easy to forget, making the risk of dehydration even more pronounced.

Eduardo walked back to Tarkington. Tarkington noticed he wasn't out of breath and his slight limp, from the bullet wound months before, was virtually gone. Eduardo pointed at an old road signpost, but whatever signs once hung there were gone. "Sign is gone, but I think we are close to San Grif. We will see it once we move down the other side."

"San Grif? Anything there?" asked Tarkington.

"Before the war, it was a large truck refueling depot. The Japanese might be using it as such again."

"Why here? Seems like we're in the middle of nowhere."

"It is halfway between Mariveles bay and San Fernando's railroads. A stop-off point in case repairs were needed. Also, fuel."

That piqued Tarkington's interest. "A fuel depot? Now that would be a worthy target. Can we get a look at it without being seen?"

Eduardo looked around and shrugged. "There are steep hills west. We could see into town from there."

"Good, take us there."

Eduardo nodded and took them further up the road. Evening was setting in and the building clouds promised another deluge of rain. Eduardo slowed and looked left as though searching. They were on a flat stretch which was obviously the top of the pass, but certainly not the top of the ridge. Winkleman pointed to the knife edged ridge on the left. "Are we trying to get up there?"

Eduardo nodded. "There is trail somewhere nearby. I hear about it." Ten minutes later, Eduardo found what he was looking for. He beamed as he pulled back the heavily sodden fronds and branches. Beyond was a green-walled trail. "This it."

Tarkington nodded. "Let's get in there before dark, looks like it might get pretty damned narrow and steep."

They walked along the trail until it was apparent going farther would mean moving along the cliff's knife edge. There was a little clearing, which looked like it might've been a good spot for a picnic before the war. The rain started in earnest as they settled into their chosen night lager. They had four canvas covers between them. They sent one with Raker, who had first watch, and the rest were spread out and connected to create a dry area for sleeping. It worked marginally well. The rain lasted an hour then lifted, leaving the ground spongy and the men cold.

No one slept well. Sleep came in precious snippets and by morning, none of them felt rested. It wasn't unusual, in fact, it was accepted as the norm, and they'd all learned to deal with the constant fatigue while on patrol. They could sleep once back in the safety of the village.

As dawn broke, they ate a paltry breakfast of dried meat and rice. When it was light enough to see the trail, they settled into a line with Eduardo and Henry at the front and moved carefully along the trail. Soon they were walking along a sheer ridgeline. The slopes to either side were steep and full of lush greenery. The trail was slick, and one misstep would send a person to certain death.

Eduardo stopped after half a mile. They were at the highest point of the trail. Below there was a thick layer of fog, hugging the ground. It looked like a white carpet thick enough to walk across. The trail was a little wider here, enough for three abreast. Tarkington moved carefully to Eduardo's side. He was sitting on the cliff edge, his feet dangling over a thousand feet of nearly vertical green.

Tarkington sat beside him, his butt scooted back a bit. "Quite a fall from here."

Eduardo nodded, "Don't fall, Tark."

"Not planning to." He pointed at the layer of fog. "So, San Grif is down there in that soup?"

Eduardo nodded. "I think so. It must be. Unless I'm lost."

"Hope the fog thins out." Winkleman came up beside them and Tarkington said, "Town's down there somewhere."

Winkleman rubbed his forehead. "Glad to be sitting down. I'm not too good with heights."

Tarkington looked him over and noticed he was white as a sheet and as far from the edge as he could get. "You okay?" Winkleman blew out a long breath, but looked queasy. "Take Raker with you and head back to our night lager. Cover our rear from there."

"I'm okay, Tark. Just kinda dizzy."

Tarkington pushed his shoulder. "I mean it. Get to more solid ground. I need someone down there anyway, might as well be you. You look like you're about to lose it."

Winkleman couldn't take his eyes off the swirling fog hundreds of feet below. He finally shook his head and nodded. "Yeah, okay. You're right. I'm not doing well."

"Raker," Tarkington yelled. PFC Raker trotted down the trail as though he were on a flat stretch in Kansas and stopped behind the three of them. "Take ol' Wink here back to our lager and cover our rear."

Raker nodded and slapped Winkleman's back. He jolted and gripped the ground. "Sure thing, Tark." He stood and stepped over Winkleman, who was low to the ground. "Come on, Wink." Winkleman stood on shaky legs and willed himself to follow. "Hold onto my shoulders if you want, long as you don't get too close. I know how you west coast boys are," Raker joked but Winkleman ignored him and concentrated on his next step. They moved off, Raker's voice trailing away into the greenery, "This isn't that high. My father's an iron worker on those big sky-scraper projects. Now, *that's* high..." his voice trailed off as they disappeared out of sight.

The fog dissipated an hour later and the town of San Grif spread out below them. They were two ridges back from the town. There was another — much lower and wider ridge overlooking the town. From their height they could see over it and could see every foot of San Grif.

Despite being a thousand feet up and at least a quarter mile away, they felt exposed on the knife-ridge, so they got on their bellies. Tarkington gave a low whistle. "That's a lot of Jap trucks." He pointed to the near side, "And look at those containers. Gotta be fuel. If we hit those, this whole place goes up." He squinted, "Wish I had a pair of binoculars. I can't get a good idea on defenses. I see people moving around but can't tell if they're Japs or just villagers." He pointed to the closer ridge. "What about that ridge? Is there a trail?"

Eduardo shrugged. "I don't know."

"Well, guess there's only one way to know for sure. Traffic's non-existent. If we're careful, I think we can get down there in daylight." He looked at Henry who nodded his agreement.

Three hours later they were on the lower hill overlooking San Grif. They followed game trails, weaving through the low scrub greenery. They had good cover from below and moving through the brush was relatively easy. The edge of San Grif was only a couple of hundred feet away, so they pushed forward until they found a good observation point. The men spread out in a defensive half-circle. Tarkington had the nub of a pencil and was sketching the base as best he could on a piece of paper he'd brought along for just such an occasion. There were guards, but not enough to dissuade him from an attack. He wondered about such light defenses but chalked it up to the Japs feeling safe.

They left the area when the sun was tilting toward evening. Tarkington was pleased with the information. He tucked the sketch into his shirt pocket along with the pencil and once they were back on the road and out of sight of San Grif, he conferred with the men. "I think we found our next target." The men nodded. They all looked tired. "We'll head back and start prepping. It'll be a big operation and we'll need the cadets' help. Anyone have any concerns?"

Vick said, "Looks like we could do some real damage, but we're a long way from the village."

Tarkington nodded. "We can work out the specifics back at the village, but you're right. We'll be out here at least a night after we hit them. I think we can disappear in these hills though."

14

The trip back to the village took less time than the trip out. Tarkington was happy to see the cadets manning the foxholes they'd dug at the top of the ridge. Of course, he didn't see the local Filipinos until they stepped from the jungle behind them, in the perfect position for an ambush. They escorted them into the village and that night they feasted and were asleep soon after. Being dry, warm and relatively safe was the perfect recipe for sleep.

The next morning, Tarkington woke up refreshed and invigorated with purpose. The more he thought about the attack, the more certain he became about their ability to pull it off.

After breakfast he asked to see Vindigo and soon he was in the hall sitting at the long table facing the village elder who sat at the head as usual. "Do you know this Sampson, the leader of the village to the East?"

Vindigo scowled. "I do, but I know his father better. It was news to me that Sampson is their leader. Last I heard, Benjamin was in charge. Not good news."

"Sampson's a hothead." Vindigo pulled his head back, not understanding the term. "He's aggressive. Young and dumb."

He smiled. "Yes. Young and dumb," he laughed uproariously. "I like that," he said after catching his breath.

"Are you concerned with the village's safety? He seems unpredictable."

"Joshua told me what happened. We lost Tuan, a great tragedy. His mother and father will mourn his passing for years." He looked down remembering the boy. He'd watched him grow up from an infant. "We will all mourn his passing." He brought his chin up. "Joshua said it was accidental?"

Tarkington moved his head back and forth, considering. "Yes and no. He drew a pistol, which was no accident. He intended to take us prisoner and steal the weapons we have buried. The gun went off when I jumped him. He was about to kill Eduardo, but instead shot Tuan, who was beside him."

Vindigo scowled and he stroked his chin. "He was going to shoot Eduardo?"

Tarkington shrugged. "I think so. I was right beside him, I saw his eyes, saw him putting his finger to the trigger. It's why I jumped him."

"Why didn't you kill him?"

"I figured if I'd done that, we'd have had to fight our way out. They don't have many weapons, so we didn't feel they were an immediate threat, when we left."

Vindigo nodded. "A good choice. Having heard this, I think they are more of a threat than I first thought."

"Can you reach out to Benjamin?"

"I would like to know why he is not in charge. It is highly unusual and only done when the elder becomes too old to perform the duties of an elder."

Tarkington pursed his lips. "He seems as healthy as you or I." He shook his head. "I don't like it. If Sampson's a threat, he might hit while we're out with half your force."

"Hmm. Yes, I see what you mean. I will send a message."

⸻

The next day was spent planning the attack. The cadets were excited, and Sergeant Fernandez knew the depot they were targeting from before the war. He didn't know the Japanese had taken it over, but once he saw the layout, he realized they'd kept it much the same way it had always been. "I was in a training convoy. We were on a field trip and used the depot to refuel. We drove right up to the fuel containers and they filled us directly from them. It will be easy to get close and destroy them. I wonder why they were left for the Japanese to capture?"

Tarkington shook his head. "In the chaos of those first few days, a lot of things didn't get done that should've gotten done." He pointed at the sand table they'd made of the depot and refocused them on the task at hand. "There's no need to get close, though. We can use the knee mortars and simply launch grenades at them from the ridge." He pointed at the low ridge they'd been on, "Here," then pointed at the line representing the road leading out. "Your cadets will stay on the road and give us covering fire while we retreat off the ridge."

Fernandez bristled and he said, "My men have been practicing with the knee mortars. We are better at..."

"Dammit!" Tarkington's sudden curse stopped the lead cadet from finishing. "This is the way we're doing it." He smacked the sand table nearly sending the various pieces flying.

Fernandez swallowed, closed his eyes and nodded. "Yes, Staff Sergeant Tarkington. We will do our duty."

"If you don't, we'll be exposed. You have to put down a base of fire to keep the Jap's attention off us." He pointed to an area near where the road and the ridge met. "This area is about thirty-yards of open ground. If the Japs are awake, they could cut us down as we cross. It's *imperative* your men give us covering fire." He stared hard at Fernandez.

Fernandez gave one brisk nod. "We will not fail, Staff Sergeant Tarkington."

"Okay. One more day getting ready here. We'll leave day after tomorrow. Clear?" There were nods all round. Tarkington straightened. His GIs dispersed but the cadets stayed. Tarkington didn't like their formality but he'd come to expect it, "You're dismissed." He shook his head as he watched them leave the hall nearly in lock-step marching order. "For chrissakes," he muttered.

They slept well and the next day prepared for the attack. Men went down the hill to the hidden weapons depot. They brought back rifle ammunition, grenades and shells for the knee mortars. The ammo was dispersed to all of them, the 50mm rounds for the knee mortars, given to Vick, Stollman and Skinner.

Tarkington had his belt full of magazines for his submachine gun and four grenades hooked to his combat harness. His weapon was clean, his knife razor sharp and his sword hanging at his side. The ancient weapon didn't seem to ever need sharpening, even if he'd had the proper tools to do so.

They kept their packs light, not expecting to be out longer than three days. One day to get to the ridge and two to get back. If they were pursued and unable to break away, they'd head inland and hopefully lose them in the many hills and valleys surrounding San Grif. If not, they'd have to fight their way out.

That evening, Vindigo called them to join him for a final meal in the hall. The men were well-rested after their two days out of the rain. They ate well and when their bellies were full and the men laid about in various positions of repose, Vindigo motioned Tarkington to his side.

He sat beside the elderly chief and smiled. "Thank you for another proper send-off."

Vindigo nodded. "The men need good food to fight well." He paused and Tarkington thought perhaps he just wanted to engage in small talk, but he soon continued. "My messenger came back from Benjamin's village an hour before the feast." Tarkington looked at him with surprise wondering how he'd missed his return. Vindigo grinned. "He came in while you were at the training ground." Then Vindigo scowled and shook his head. "Not good news. Benjamin is dead."

Tarkington was stunned. "Dead? How?"

"The messenger was told, he died in his sleep. From old age, apparently."

Tarkington shook his head. "I saw him just the other day. He didn't seem sick. He's not even that old."

Vindigo nodded and stroked his chin. Sadness crept into his eyes and

Tarkington remembered Benjamin had been a good friend. "I think his death is suspicious," Vindigo stated bluntly.

Tarkington nodded his agreement. "We'll call off our attack. Sampson might attack us any day."

Vindigo shook his head once hard. "No. I can't imagine the villagers agreeing to such nonsense, but If they come, we will have enough men to stop them. We will set up the Japanese machine guns. They will be manned until your return. I will send out scouts. If they attempt to approach, we will have plenty of time. We can fire the mortar grenades and stop them with machine guns. Besides, the creek is near flood and won't be crossable."

Tarkington didn't like it but nodded. "If we run into Sampson what do you think *our* response should be?"

"If you see Sampson, he is no doubt searching for the weapons cache. I do not want to battle them though. We have a common enemy in the Japanese, there's no need to fight among ourselves."

"Agreed. But if Sampson is willing to kill his own father, he may be willing to kill other Filipinos." He looked down at the wood slats of the floor and kicked at a knot of wood. "I don't trust him."

"What time will you leave?"

"0300. I don't like leaving here during daylight. Too easy to be spotted and compromise your village."

They ventured from the village, making their way over the bridge, up the slope and down toward the abandoned village. The morning was dry for a change and despite the darkness, they made good time.

They got to the road, it was still a muddy mess. They didn't notice any fresh truck tracks.

By noon, they were at the top of the pass. They hadn't encountered Japanese patrols and saw very few locals. The ones they did see showed little interest, keeping their heads down, minding their own business, trying to stay dry.

They moved past the entrance to the trail leading to the knife-edged ridge. There was no sign of their prints from four days before. The rain was miserable but vital to their invisibility.

As they neared the crest, they slowed their pace, knowing San Grif was a half-mile further along. They crested the road and saw the town in the distance. A thin layer of mist hung over it and it looked abandoned, but as far as they knew there was still at least half a platoon of Imperial Japanese soldiers there.

They moved to the right of the road until they were out of sight from the town. Tarkington gathered the cadets together and spoke in a low tone. "This is where you'll set up. There's plenty of cover. When we hit them, you'll know." He pointed to the road. "That's when you'll move there and give us covering fire." He pointed to the low ridge to the left of the road, "That's where we'll be coming from. It's wide open. We'll be exposed, so you *have* to be ready to cover us."

Fernandez nodded, hiding his anger at being told again what he already knew. "Yes, Staff Sergeant Tarkington," he uttered.

Tarkington moved across the road. Winkleman slapped Fernandez's shoulder. "Once you earn his trust, he'll ease up on you." Fernandez gave him a curt nod and Winkleman took up the rear, following the rest of the GIs across the open space and into the low scrub of the ridge.

They moved silently along the same game trail they'd used before until they were looking down upon the fuel depot. Now that they were closer, they could see Japanese troops milling around. There seemed to be a heavier concentration near a building in the center of town, which Tarkington guessed was their barracks.

The fuel containers were an easy knee mortar shot from their position. PFC Vick, Skinner and Stollman had the weapons out and were calibrating the tubes' angle and placing the 50mm grenades onto the tubes to what they hoped were the proper depths. How far down the tube dictated how far the grenade flew. Firing from above the target made some of it guesswork.

Each had three more shells laid out beside them. It was probably overkill, but none of them were experts with the weapons and they wanted to be sure to have enough ammo in case they needed to hit the fuel containers more than once. If their initial strike was successful, they'd use the extra rounds to cover their withdrawal, keeping a few in case they needed them later.

They hemmed and hawed among themselves about shell placement until they finally decided they were ready. Vick nodded to Winkleman, who was overseeing them, and he nodded to Tarkington. The other GIs were spread out ten-yards apart, their rifles off safety and ready to fire.

Tarkington raised his hand, looking over the target. The townsfolk seemed lazy, riding out the rainy season indoors, only venturing outside if there was a need. The few Filipinos he saw were on their porches, whiling the hours away. He could see two Japanese guards hunkered near the fuel containers, using them for cover against the rain, which had started falling lightly. He hoped there weren't any Filipino civilians nearby. He felt the nausea of coming combat and swallowed against a dry throat, then dropped his hand.

There were near simultaneous thumps of firing knee mortars. The explosive projectiles arced through the air almost gracefully. Tarkington saw the arcs were wrong, they'd hit beyond the target. His suspicions were confirmed a moment later. There were three muted explosions, twenty-yards too far, exploding harmlessly in the street beyond. The reaction from the Japanese guards was slow. They stepped away from the containers and looked around in confusion. Neither of them unslung their rifles.

The GIs were already inserting a second round of grenades, not as far down the tube this time and by the time they fired, the Japanese guards were more alert. They heard the pops and spun toward the ridge, pointing and yammering excitedly.

This time, the grenade's trajectories looked better and Tarkington knew they were on target. Vick's grenade arced toward the forward fuel container and the other two towards the one to the left. Vick's grenade impacted the curved side and exploded, sending hot shards of metal into the container. Gasoline erupted from the side, spilling out like a leaking bathtub but there wasn't an explosion.

The other two grenades impacted the second container two-seconds apart. The first grenade ripped a hole and the second blew up near the spewing gas, igniting it. There was a whoosh as the flames traveled into the container then an earsplitting explosion. A fireball, reaching a hundred feet

into the sky sucked the oxygen from the air and created a breeze which
rustled the cover noticeably. The first container followed soon after. The
hundreds of gallons of already-spilled fuel ignited and spread out,
engulfing the two Japanese guards who were already dead from flying
shards of metal. Their bodies turned to ash in an instant.

The GIs hunkered and watched, mesmerized by the destruction. They
could feel the heat and the plants around them were suddenly dry. Nearby
structures and trucks caught fire and soon there were more explosions as
gas tanks ignited.

Tarkington snapped them out of their trance. He stood and yelled,
"Let's go!" He sprinted along the trail, the others following in his footsteps.
More explosions ripped through San Grif and Tarkington hoped the locals
wouldn't get caught up in the growing conflagration but knew they probably would.

They got to the end of the ridge. The next thirty-yards were wide open.
Tarkington knew he had nothing to worry about. The Japanese would be
too preoccupied trying to stay alive. He ran, happy to see the cadets in the
middle of the road, right where he told them to be. They had their rifles to
their shoulders and were firing at distant targets. Tarkington yelled, "Cease
fire. You'll only tip 'em off."

Fernandez nodded and repeated the command, "Cease fire, cease fire."
The random shots stopped and soon they were all on their feet and trotting
down the back of the hill, away from the spectacle of San Grif.

After fifteen minutes of running, they were beyond the switchbacks.
Tarkington figured they were far enough away and stopped them. They
were all breathing hard, but they hunkered and formed a tight defensive
circle. He looked back and saw the huge black cloud darkening the sky.
"Holy shit. That went up way more than I expected."

The GIs were nodding their agreement. "Never seen anything like it,"
remarked Vick.

Winkleman watched the black cloud, "Hope that fire's not spreading
through town."

Guilt flooded through Tarkington's gut. "Dammit, I know. I didn't think
it'd spread like that, especially this time of year."

Eduardo shook his head. "Fire will go out. Too wet."

"I sure as hell hope you're right," muttered Tarkington. He was sure at least some local houses had been destroyed he just hoped the entire town wasn't wiped out.

Henry called out. "Something's coming. I hear engines."

The rain had ceased for the time being and, sure enough, there was the distant sound of engines coming from the direction they were heading. Tarkington ordered, "Cover. Take cover." The men scattered to the right of the road and were soon invisible in the low scrub and greenery.

The sound increased as the vehicles approached. There was one struggling truck, followed by a black sedan. The tires sank into the mud and the vehicles slid around the slight turn, but they were making headway.

When they were past, Tarkington stepped from the jungle and looked the way they'd gone. "There's no way that could be a reaction force. Too soon; the nearest town's too far away. It must be a scheduled delivery or something."

Winkleman shook his head, "I didn't see many troops, just a few to help load or offload supplies, I'd bet."

Tarkington added, "There's no way they'll make it up that steep grade to the top. They'll slide all over. Wonder what they're thinking?"

Winkleman shrugged and looked at the sky. "Taking advantage of the rain stopping?"

"Still a mud-bowl out here." He bit his lower lip and decided. "Let's see what they're up to."

15

The cadets led them back the way they'd come along the road, keeping to the side in case they came across the Japanese vehicles. The deep tire tracks through the mud were easy to follow.

There was still a black pall of smoke rising into sky, meeting and mixing with the overcast clouds. Tarkington worried it meant more of the town was burning.

When they got to the beginning of the grade, they were surprised to see the tire tracks leading up the slope, as though they'd had no problem with the mud. Henry hunched down, observing the tracks closely. Tarkington stood beside him, his submachine gun at the ready. Henry shook his head, "It's weird, there are all sorts of slip marks back there, but here, where you'd think they'd be slipping, the tread marks are solid. It's like they were pulled up or something."

Tarkington nodded, "Some kind of winch system maybe."

Henry nodded, "I didn't notice a winch on the front of either one of those vehicles, but I also wasn't looking for something like that. It would make sense though."

Tarkington waved them back into cover. "We'll keep out of sight and follow their track. I wanna see about the town too."

They moved up the steep grade, slipping on the mud but making headway. Their theory of the winches was confirmed when they noticed the tire tracks taking odd turns here and there as the angles of pull were corrected. They also found the trees they had used. The newly-scarred bark was obvious, now that they knew what to look for.

Just before reaching the top of the grade, Winkleman caught up with Tarkington and asked, "What's the point of this, Tark? I mean we should be miles away from here. This wasn't the plan."

Tarkington took a deep breath and let it out slow, pointing to the still-thick, black smoke. "I need to see the damage." He looked at his feet, "If the town's gone, I — well I don't know what I'll do. I just need to know."

Eduardo appeared from the jungle and trotted up to the two sergeants. "Truck is at top of road. Close by," he whispered.

Tarkington nodded and waved the others further into the brambles. They advanced slowly until he could see the truck and sedan, idling side by side on top of the pass. There were Japanese pointing and gesturing wildly toward the town. Two soldiers were facing a larger group and Tarkington surmised that the two were from the town, filling the newcomers in on what had transpired.

After a few minutes, two soldiers were left behind with the truck and sedan while the rest went down the hill. Once the main force was out of sight, the two soldiers sat on the hood of the truck and watched the smoke curl into the sky.

Tarkington still couldn't see what was happening over the crest, so he slowly pushed forward until he could. The sight took his breath away and he immediately felt weak-kneed and nauseous.

The town was indeed still burning. He could see figures of men, women and children desperately trying to put out the flames by throwing wholly inadequate buckets of water. He marveled at the destruction. The gasoline-fueled fire burned hot, immediately drying out and igniting the wood and thatch structures. He saw Japanese troops among the townspeople, fighting the conflagration threatening to destroy the entire town.

The day darkened more, and he looked up and saw an ominous storm cloud overhead. It was the first time he was happy to know what was coming. The first rain drops were huge and heavy and the drops hitting his wide-brimmed hat made loud smacks. He noticed the two Japanese soldiers sitting on the hood, look up and immediately hustle off to take refuge inside the vehicles.

Sergeant Fernandez came up beside Tarkington. "I will take my men and kill those soldiers while they're inside the trucks. We can drive and save time."

Tarkington watched the world turn to water. The rain was heavy, cutting visibility to a few feet. Water came off the brim of his hat in a near constant curtain. He knew the fire would be out in a matter of minutes, but he also knew most of San Grif was already ash. He imagined the newly-homeless occupants scrambling for cover, their homes suddenly and violently ripped from them. He shook his head. "No more killing today, Sergeant," he had to raise his voice to be heard over the rain. Fernandez was about to protests but Tarkington simply turned away and moved back down the hill.

Captain Gima stood in what remained of the town of San Grif. Though it had burned three days before and been doused with heavy rain, the area still reeked of smoke.

He pointed to the low ridge overlooking the town. "And that is where you found the card?"

Lieutenant Amano nodded. He was nervous to be in Captain Gima's presence. Amano was newly arrived on the island but had heard of Gima's battlefield heroics and his decision to stay on the island to hunt down the American resistance unit known as, *Tark's Ticks*.

He and his platoon had been too busy fighting fires and moving fuel trucks and containers out of harm's way to even begin looking for the perpetrators. Indeed, if a few of his men hadn't described seeing the arcing grenades, he might not even have known it had been an attack. For all he knew, the old fuel containers could have leaked and one of the nearby soldiers lit a cigarette at the wrong time.

He was sure the image of the two blackened, withered shapes near the containers would haunt him for the rest of his life. It was all that remained of the two soldiers who'd been on duty that day. But once the fires were out, he'd sent a patrol to the ridge and they'd come back with the sodden playing card. The writing was smeared and impossible to read.

Captain Gima held it up to the sky and turned it in his hand. "It is damaged and unreadable, but it must be them. Any tracks? Any sign of them?"

Lieutenant Amano shook his head. "The rain which put the fire out was the heaviest we've seen yet. It washed all signs away. He pointed to another lieutenant directing the cleanup of charred timbers nearby. "Lieutenant Tashiro arrived an hour after the attack. He came from the South and didn't report any enemy sightings."

"That doesn't surprise me. If they went that way, which would make the most sense, they wouldn't allow themselves to be caught in the open. These are skilled and ruthless terrorists."

Amano gulped. "I've heard they eat parts of the men they kill." He looked embarrassed and lowered his head as soon as the words left his mouth. He silently berated himself for voicing such a ridiculous rumor.

Gima didn't scold him though. "They have captured the imaginations of the men. By leaving these cards," he tapped the growing pile in his lapel pocket, "They sow fear and with fear comes rumors and lies. I can assure you, though, they are just men. Men that bleed and die, the same as you and I." He looked around at the soldiers milling about. There was also a handful of villagers standing around as though dazed. Their houses were gone and he wondered what it must feel like to suddenly have nothing. "How many soldiers do you have here?"

Amano gulped but answered immediately. "I have eighteen men. I lost four dead and two wounded."

Gima nodded. "I will need to borrow your men, Lieutenant. I want them loaded and ready for a three-day march. We leave in an hour. I will take them south and scour every inch for any sign of them." Amano blanched but nodded and saluted. He turned to a nearby sergeant and passed the order along.

Captain Gima closed his eyes thinking about what he'd given up to remain on Luzon. Most of his beloved company was sent forward without him. They were on transports being sent to bolster units in the Solomon

Islands. One platoon remained with him, but they were stationed south, twenty-kilometers from San Grif.

He'd traveled with his driver, Private Hano, and Sergeant Uchida. Bringing the whole platoon here wasn't feasible. Even with just the small military jeep, they'd had trouble getting here. Getting the big trucks here would've put them back days and he was already behind. He hadn't gotten word of the playing card until two days after the attack.

He was sure Tark's Ticks were long gone, but he had to do something. The quicker he found and killed every man associated with Tark's Ticks, the sooner he'd be back with his company. He knew every day that went by, made that possibility less and less possible.

When Lieutenant Amano's platoon was braced in front of him, he put his hands behind his back and slowly walked up and down their ranks. Troops put on garrison duty were not the cream of the crop and these men were no exception. They looked more like a platoon of clerks than Imperial Japanese Army soldiers. But despite their outward appearance, he knew each man would follow his orders to the letter and without question.

He addressed them with a raised voice. "We will be hunting a group of American terrorists. The same savages that burned half this town down, killing your friends and comrades. The next few days will be hard, but you are soldiers of the Emperor and I know you will make me proud. All I ask of you, is everything you have. If we find this murdering band of Yankees, we'll kill them where they stand." He stopped pacing and squared his shoulders to them. "Understood?"

A less than rousing, "Hai."

He nodded and looked at his watch. The inside of the face was foggy with condensation, but the hands still worked. "We leave at 1000 hours. Dismissed."

Lieutenant Amano barked at them to disperse and they hustled off to finish packing for what was sure to be a miserable and frightening foray into the wild.

Captain Gima and Lieutenant Amano sat in the back of the covered jeep and waited for the bedraggled platoon to catch up. Private Hano, the driver, stared straight ahead concentrating on keeping his eyes open. Sergeant Uchida in the front seat never seemed to tire. He kept his head on a swivel, his rifle ready for anything. This was the second day of their fruitless search and the constant rain was getting to all of them.

The inside of the jeep was hot and muggy. The windows fogged when they were shut making the inside a sauna, but if they were opened even a crack, the incessant rain found its way inside.

"Your men are performing admirably, Lieutenant." Amano nodded his thanks and when it was obvious he wasn't going to speak, Gima continued. "Have any of them seen combat?"

Amano shook his head. "Not until the other day, sir." He stammered, "But — well we didn't really know we were in combat. We never saw the enemy or even fired a shot."

Gima nodded, thinking whoever put this timid officer in the rear echelon was a smart man indeed. Physically, Lieutenant Amano appeared strong and fit, but when you talked to him, his shyness was painful and Gima wondered how he commanded at all. It was not the way of an effective officer. Enlisted men would obey orders if they were clear, concise and delivered with absolute confidence. Gima doubted Lt. Amano could order lunch with authority.

Gima smiled, "Sometimes that is how combat goes. Your platoon took casualties. Even the timidest of soldiers will yearn for revenge after something like that. It is up to you to show them the enemy so they may kill them and avenge their comrades."

Amano's voice was low and barely decipherable, "Yes, sir."

Out of the fogged back window, Gima saw the platoon coming around the corner. A few soldiers were on the road while the rest were in the jungle, searching vainly for tracks. Gima opened the squeaky side-door and stepped out, immediately feeling better despite the rain coming down in sheets.

He lowered his head and spoke to Lt. Amano. "Here they come." He saw Platoon Sergeant Ono walking along the edge of the road. He was the only soldier who really earned the title. Gima wondered what the wizened old sergeant had done to get assigned to such a group of docile, rear-echelon soldiers. He raised his voice to the NCO walking near the ditch. "Find anything, Sergeant?"

Sergeant Ono straightened his back and barked back. "No, sir. The rain has done a number on any tracks they might have left."

Gima frowned, it was unusual for an NCO to give more than a yes-or-no answer. This was probably why the sergeant wasn't in a front-line unit. He'd probably upset someone one too many times. "Okay, Sergeant." He pointed. "There's a village up ahead. We'll allow our Filipino subjects the honor of housing us for the night."

Sergeant Ono licked his lips and gave him a crooked smile. "Yes, sir. The men could use a rest."

There it is again, thought Gima. The lurid smile the sergeant gave him made his skin crawl and he leaned into the car and asked Lt. Amano. "Did Sergeant Ono spend time in China?"

A brief flash of fear crossed Amano's face and he nodded quickly. "Y — Yes. He *has* seen combat, sir."

Gima's frown grew. Lt. Amano was obviously afraid of his own grizzled platoon sergeant. He shook his head. *How did this man ever become an officer?* He decided he'd investigate Lt. Amano's past. He had no doubt he'd find some powerful person behind his commission. There was no way he could've become an officer on his own merit. Gima liked to know who he was dealing with if at all possible.

The village was less than a kilometer off the main road. It wasn't visible, but Gima knew where it was from his previous travels. He'd visited as many villages as possible in his search for information on Tark's Ticks. He recalled the village elder of this village was named, Benjamin. It was a small village full of back-country Filipinos. He didn't remember much else about it. All the villages and towns he'd visited were basically the same. He was used to the underlying hatred the locals tried to hide behind their fake smiles.

As the jeep turned off the main road and made its way down the much narrower road to the village, Gima asked, "Have you much interaction with locals, Lieutenant?"

Lieutenant Amano shrugged. "I spoke with San Grif residents, sir."

Gima pursed his lips. "San Grif will seem like a major city compared with these outlying villages. The residents are subsistence farmers and hunters mostly, but that doesn't mean they aren't dangerous. Keep your guard up, they consider us invaders."

Amano nodded, "Yes, sir." He looked over his shoulder at the road behind, "Should we wait for the platoon, sir?"

Gima scowled and shook his head. "No. They won't attack us in daylight. They are cowardly and would only strike if they were positive they could get away with it. They know they'd be wiped out." He paused then continued, "The elder's name is Benjamin as I recall." Amano nodded.

The jeep slowed as it came to the junction of the road with the entrance to the village. Most of the huts were meters off the ground, propped on stilts. There was one building which was much longer than the others and Gima tapped his driver's shoulder and pointed, "Take us there." Private Hano nodded and turned the wheel, doing his best to avoid the huge puddles which looked more like mini ponds. Hano picked the highest point he could and parked in front of the building.

Sergeant Uchida stepped out, brandishing his rifle. Satisfied that the curious villagers didn't pose an immediate threat, he opened the back door and Gima and Amano stepped out.

From the front of the long building a young man stepped out and smiled in greeting. He spoke Tagalog and when there was no response, switched to English. "Hello. Welcome." He extended his arms in greeting and stepped aside inviting them inside. "Come in. Dry inside."

Captain Gima looked around. There were a few villagers here and there, but he knew most would avoid the Japanese and keep out of sight. The two officers mounted the steps and stood on the porch in front of the young man. Gima had one hand on the pommel of his sheathed sword. "Where is Benjamin," he asked in English, "the village elder?"

A shadow passed over the man's face and his smile faded. He looked at the floor and shook his head sadly. "Benjamin, my father," he paused and raised his eyes, "died. Only a few weeks ago. Sad." His smile returned and he tapped his muscular chest. "I am Sampson. I was the village leader even before my father's passing. He gave me the honor."

Gima looked surprised but nodded. "I met your father." There was no need to say more, a Filipino's life didn't mean a thing to him. "I am Captain Gima and this is Lieutenant Amano." He pointed as the rest of the platoon sauntered into the village. They looked miserable and their eyes darted around, taking in the village. Platoon Sergeant Ono grinned and waved to a cluster of three young Filipino girls. They were quickly whisked inside by their mother. "We require food and shelter for the night."

Sampson bowed slightly, knowing it wasn't a request but a demand. "Of course. There are empty huts. Small but dry. We shall feast."

16

Captain Gima and Lieutenant Amano sat cross-legged in the great hall and ate the offered food. It wasn't a feast, as Sampson promised, but that was to be expected. He leaned toward Lt. Amano, who was scraping the last bits of rice and pork from the bottom of a bowl. "A feast for them perhaps. Villages like this one survive by hunting and raising whatever farm animals they can. They must raise enough food for themselves *and* for us." Lt. Amano gave him a confused look and Gima continued. "Once a week they are required to give half their food to our troops. It was once a month, but that gave them too much time to hide what they had. I'm sure they still hide most of it, but if we find them actively deceiving us, they pay a heavy price."

A Filipino girl, who looked to be in her early teens, came through with a pitcher of water and poured. When she got to Sergeant Ono, he grinned and clutched her leg as she poured. Once his cup was filled, he continued stroking her and his hungry look left little doubt what he had in mind. She stood stock-still, until he finally slapped her ass and let her go about her business.

Captain Gima watched Lt. Amano during this lewd behavior. Amano did his best to pretend he hadn't seen it, but Gima knew he had and was simply too afraid of the platoon sergeant to do anything about it. Gima scraped the bottom of his bowl and set it down in front of him. "If you don't do something about your platoon sergeant, he'll rape that girl."

Lieutenant Amano nearly dropped his bowl. He stammered, "W — What did you say, sir?"

Gima's jaw tightened. "Don't play dumb with me, Lieutenant. You heard me and you saw what he did. You know what he'll do later. There are some in this Army that allow such things, even encourage it." He looked Amano squarely in the eye. "I am *not* one of them. Get control of your platoon sergeant."

Amano glanced over at the sergeant who was still leering at the girl. He gave a curt nod, "Yessir."

Gima ignored Lt. Amano and focused his attention on Sampson sitting to his right. He spoke in English. "What happened to your father? How did he die?"

Sampson answered, "Died in his sleep. He old man."

Gima tilted his head, "I remember him as healthy." He grinned, "But I don't know how to judge your people. You age prematurely."

Sampson let the insult roll off without acknowledging. "Older than he looked." He took a sip of water.

Gima asked, "Have you seen any resistance fighters?"

Sampson almost blew the water across the room but managed to swallow and shake his head. "No. No resistance here."

Gima smiled. "There was an attack on San Grif. Did you hear of it?"

Sampson had heard about it only hours after it occurred, but he didn't know if he should let on. He shook his head. "No. San Grif far away."

"Yes, I suppose it is. Still, I'm surprised. News seems to travel fast from village to village."

There was an uncomfortably long pause and Sampson finally filled it in. "I heard of a fire in San Grif. Not attack, but fire."

Gima frowned, shook his head and sighed. "It was not an accident. The town was attacked and nearly burned to the ground." He spread his hands out to the room, "Men from this platoon died. We are hunting them. Any news of the attackers would mean a great deal to a small village like yours." He let that sink in, while Sampson took another long sip of water. Gima reached into his lapel and showed Sampson a playing card. "Have you heard of, *Tark's Ticks*?" The last two words fell off his tongue like turned milk.

Again, Sampson nearly spat his water across the room. He swallowed, wiped his mouth and shook his head. "Tick tock? What?"

Gima shook his head, "No, not, 'tick tock'...*Tark's Ticks*," he repeated, having pronunciation problems of his own. "They are American GIs. Criminals, fighting despite their Army's surrender."

Sampson shook his head too emphatically. "I don't know these men."

Gima smiled. "Very well. I'm sure you would tell me if you did. It would be bad if I found out otherwise." He stared at the young Filipino until his eyes finally dropped to the floor.

Once the Japanese officers were done eating, they were escorted to an abandoned hut. There were two raised beds covered with thin sheets. Lt. Amano sat upon the furthest bed and tested the sturdiness with a shake. It rattled but held together. The room was dingy, but the roof didn't leak. Being out of the rain was all they really cared about.

Once they were alone, Gima paced in front of the door. "Sampson knows something about the Americans. He is not a good liar, even in English, I can tell he is hiding something."

Lt. Amano, who didn't know English at all hadn't followed the dinner conversation between his officer and Sampson. "Do you want my men to arrest him, sir?"

Gima stroked his chin but shook his head. "No. These Filipinos are proud people. But I don't believe Sampson is an honorable man. He says his father died of old age, but I remember him being quite healthy and not as old as many others I've seen. I wonder if he had something to do with his death."

Amano was stunned at the accusation. "Killing his own father?"

"Some men are driven this way. To us it seems ridiculous, he wields power over a tiny village in the middle of nowhere, but it is the pinnacle of power here and that is sometimes all that matters." He shrugged, "It is all relative."

"But killing his father is extreme."

"Yes. And that extremism might be something we can leverage. He's a young man yearning for power. We'll see what happens to his memory once I offer him more power than he can imagine."

Sampson paced back and forth in the great hall wondering what he should do about the Japanese in his village. He'd wanted to make a difference in the struggle against the invaders and this was the perfect opportunity to do so. There was a light platoon here, his men could wait until they were mostly asleep, silently kill the guards and dispatch the rest of them at their leisure. They would suddenly be rich in weapons and could inflict even more damage, perhaps even more than Tark's Ticks.

The mere thought of the night they stayed in his village made him angry. The buffoon American Sergeant had tackled him and made him shoot and kill Tuan, a longtime friend. *And they blamed me.* Claiming he was about to shoot that displaced scum from Manila, Eduardo. His smug face made him want to, but he only meant to scare him. He closed his eyes. Deep down, he knew he had wanted to wipe the smugness off his face with a bullet, but he'd denied it vehemently to anyone who'd listen.

If they'd just offered to share their weapon's cache, none of it would've happened. Weren't they fighting a common foe? But they were selfish and chose to hoard their bounty and the result was an accidental shooting.

He'd considered sending men to follow the group. They'd eventually lead them to the weapons cache and then he could pilfer it for himself. Then *he'd* have the power in the region. Then *he'd* be the fearsome resistance leader, rather than the Americans. After all, they'd had their chance and failed. Now it was the Filipino's time to fight. But the Americans had always been an arrogant people and refused to truly share power. Even during the battle of Bataan, the Americans were in charge. Things might've turned out differently if the Filipinos were allowed to fight without their overbearing rules and orders.

His right-hand man, Deputy Hingi, sat with his legs crossed, watching him pace. Hingi was always calm and always seemed to know what was best. He'd been the one who suggested his father should consider ceding power to his more energetic son. He convinced Benjamin that during these tumultuous times, with invaders roaming free, a young warrior was needed to start an effective resistance. Benjamin had eventually agreed.

After the accidental shooting that killed Tuan, Benjamin had tried to take back his seat as village elder and leader. Hingi had been the one to suggest and instigate silencing his father once and for all. 'For the greater good of the country,' he'd implored.

Sampson stopped pacing and faced him. "What do you say, Hingi? Should I attack the Japanese and take their weapons? It would be an easy thing."

Deputy Hingi stroked his chin and pondered the question. "It would be an easy thing, I agree, *and* you'd acquire weapons which would help our cause." Sampson nodded, pleased he'd come to the same conclusion as the older and wiser Deputy. But Hingi continued. "However, it would mean abandoning the village. It would be difficult to hide such a large killing. Perhaps the captain has radioed their location for the night. If they fail to return, they'd surely come looking and would burn the village with us in it, even if they found no trace." He shook his head and looked at the floor. "You know how barbaric they are."

Sampson's smile faded, he nodded and continued to pace, trying to look as smart as his Deputy. "Yes, I thought of that, and thought we could perhaps," he hesitated as he was coming up with an idea on the fly, "Perhaps we would join with Vindigo's village." He warmed to the idea. "Make a stronger village by combining the two."

Hingi scowled and shook his head slightly. "I doubt many would follow you. You are not a king. This is their home. It is *your* home. You are the village leader. If you did as you say and joined Vindigo, he would not share power. You'd become as common as me." He stood and shook his head. "You are a true leader and your village needs you to be their leader."

"Hmm, yes." He thought through Hingi's words, "I will let them live and find another way to get weapons."

Hingi looked hard at the floor and kneaded his chin as though thinking hard. He put up his finger as though coming to a momentous conclusion.

"There is another way. A way to keep your power and make a difference in this war."

Sampson's interest was piqued, "Yes, what is it?"

Hingi smiled inside, this boy was so easily manipulated, much more so than his father. "You have something the Japanese captain wants very badly...information."

James Torres cursed the predicament he'd put himself into. His mother was ill and unable to assist in the clean-up after the visiting Japanese were fed. He'd volunteered to take her place. He'd been behind the great hall, beneath the back window busily scraping dishes when he heard the unmistakable voice of the village leader, Sampson, and his wretched Deputy Hingi, speaking.

At first, he tried to ignore them, but soon he couldn't keep himself from eavesdropping and, by the time he'd heard more than he wanted to, he realized he had a terrible decision to make. At one point during the evil conversation, it was all James could do to keep himself from launching into the room and thrashing Hingi and his forked tongue.

Since becoming the village leader, his one-time friend, Sampson, had changed and not for the better. At first, James thought it normal; Sampson was suddenly responsible for the welfare of the whole village. But the village had existed for hundreds of years, it could take care of itself. When Sampson's father died in his sleep, suspicions flew, and James noticed Sampson staying in the great hall and taking advice from Deputy Hingi more and more.

The initial shock of Benjamin's death swept through the village like a dark cloud. He'd been a beloved man. He was kind and didn't treat his leadership responsibility as cumbersome or even too important. There was very little to do really. The main role of the village elder mainly consisted of being a judge when someone brought a complaint against another, which happened perhaps once a year. With Sampson, it had been altogether different. He had his hand in almost everything and Hingi was always nearby spouting poison.

But this was different. What he'd just heard would undoubtedly tear the village apart. How could Sampson even consider doing what Hingi suggested? It was madness and would surely end in his own destruction and probably the towns too. Unlike many other villages, they'd survived the Japanese onslaught. That would change if Sampson continued on this course.

Normally, James would've confronted his long-time friend and tried to convince him not to listen to Hingi, but since the Tuan killing, Sampson had become unpredictable and dangerous. James swallowed against a dry throat, thinking about the image of Tuan face-down, a dark exit-wound hole in the back of his head. He didn't want to suffer the same fate. He made his decision.

James stood in front of Vindigo, trying to keep his knees from shaking. He didn't know why, but he'd always been afraid of the elder leader. He'd been met on the surprisingly difficult-to-find trail leading to the village by two sentries. He knew them both and they lowered their rifles when they recognized him. They'd questioned what he was doing this far from home at this early hour.

He'd left his village, telling his mother he was going to visit a friend in another village. She'd questioned the timing, but he'd left before she could press the issue. He walked for most of the night and, when he was escorted to the village, he insisted on seeing Vindigo right away, despite the early hour.

Now he stood before him and Vindigo asked, "What are you doing here, James?"

"Sorry to disturb you, sir, but I have disturbing news." He paused and Vindigo nodded and leaned forward in his chair. "There's a Japanese platoon in our town. They took shelter from the rain. We fed them and put them up for the night. After they went to their beds, I overheard Sampson speaking with Deputy Hingi…"

Vindigo scowled and reared his head back in revulsion and interrupted. "*Deputy* Hingi? He has a rank now? That man is monkey shit."

James couldn't help smiling. He nodded and continued. "Yes sir. He is always at Sampson's side. Sampson wanted to kill the Japanese and take their weapons but Hingi convinced him a better way was to give up your village."

He paused as Vindigo's jaw rippled in anger. Vindigo growled, "Go on."

James felt suddenly nauseous but continued. "He — he is going to give up *Tark's Ticks*. The — the Japanese officer asked him specifically if he knew where they were. Sampson didn't tell him at first but plans to give them away."

Vindigo reared back and sputtered, "But — but why? What does he hope to gain? He'll be a collaborator. The villagers won't allow that to happen, they'd be hated forever."

"Hingi said they'd negotiate with the Japanese and in exchange for the information, they'd give him..." he stopped and licked his lips not wanting to see Vindigo even angrier than he already was.

Vindigo leaned forward, the chair creaking beneath him. "Give him what?" he hissed.

"This village. He'd take over the town and be the leader of both."

"Ridiculous. He'd have his throat cut in the middle of the night."

James continued, "And he'd have access to the weapons cache he says you have hidden."

Vindigo leaned back and shook his head slowly. "He wants to play both sides then. He'll take up arms against the Japanese once he has access to the cache, is that it?"

"That is what they talked about, yes. They'd keep the weapons cache a secret, move it in case someone told the Japanese the location and take up resistance against the Japanese. Hingi said they'd never suspect them since they'd be considered collaborators."

Vindigo looked toward the dark doorway to his left and raised his voice and spoke in broken English. "Did you hear? Understand?"

James watched two men emerge from the darkness. One was Filipino, he recognized him from the night Tuan was killed. He remembered his name was, Eduardo. The other was Sergeant Tarkington, the leader of Tark's Ticks. James' eyes bugged out. It was like seeing a legend come alive.

The tall American nodded and said, "Eduardo translated, I think I got the gist of it, yes."

Vindigo focused on James again. "When would this happen?"

James shrugged. "I don't know for sure, but the Japanese are planning on leaving this morning. They are searching for *Tark's Ticks*. There was an attack on San Grif and they are searching for their trail. I think he'll tell them before they leave."

Eduardo translated and Tarkington addressed Vindigo. "They could be here this evening."

Vindigo nodded, "They would not be able to get into the village. The river is swollen, the ground is muddy. We could hold them off until the dry season."

Tarkington studied Vindigo's strong features. "Yes, but then your village would be overrun and everyone inside killed. They'd burn it to the ground and hunt down anyone that escaped."

Vindigo stood and strode to the American. He put his gnarled hand on his shoulder. "It was always going to be this way. When I took you in, there was no other way it could end. Even without Sampson's treachery."

Tarkington pursed his lips and nodded. His eyes went to slits and James thought he looked as dangerous as a viper. "The Nips don't know we know they're coming. There's only one route they can take. We'll make 'em pay for every yard, then we'll cross the river and drop the bridge."

17

Captain Gima slept fitfully on and off. He finally got up hours before dawn and paced, thinking how he'd extract the information from Sampson. The young Filipino would be easy to manipulate, but he would need to be careful not to upset his inflated sense of importance. He'd have to make him feel like an equal partner. A man of prestige and power. In other words, he'd have to lie.

With a firm plan in mind, Gima sat on the edge of his bed and pulled his high leather boots on. The suppleness had long since turned hard. The combination of excessive heat and constant wetness wreaked havoc on all fabrics. He'd buffed the boots as well as he could, but he knew his first step into the mud would eclipse his efforts instantly. It wasn't about keeping his boots clean though, it was about calming the mind with a menial chore. It was about process and a satisfying result.

Lieutenant Amano was also awake and dressing. Gima knew he'd slept well by the soft snores he'd listened to all night. Yet another sign of his lack of combat experience. Most of the combat veterans he knew woke up occasionally with bad dreams, oftentimes screaming. It was only the sociopaths and the rear-echelon troops that didn't have bad dreams. He thought Sergeant Ono was probably in the former category.

Gima was surprised when he noticed one of the villagers stepping onto the steps. In the dim light of pre-dawn, he could see it was Sampson's lackey. He was older than Sampson and Gima remembered how, during the evening meal, how he'd quietly stood by taking everything in. Without even realizing it, Gima's subconscious had put the man down as being mildly dangerous.

Gima stood and approached the doorway, his hand resting on the pommel of his sword. The guard outside had his Arisaka rifle up and angled toward the villager, the bayonet steel glistening in the low-light. Gima stepped from the hut and said, "At ease, Private." The guard immediately straightened his stance, put his rifle on his shoulder and stared straight ahead.

Gima stepped to the edge of the porch. In English he said, "Yes?"

The villager lowered his gaze, put his right hand in front of his waist and bowed as though addressing a king. "Captain Gima. The Mayor would like a word with you at your convenience."

Gima studied the man's lowered head. Despite the misplaced royal theatrics, he sensed the man was intelligent. "What is your name?"

The villager straightened and raised his eyes but didn't quite meet his gaze. "Deputy Hingi, sir."

Gima's mouth turned down. "Deputy?" he asked. Hingi simply nodded, but Gima could see the anger his derisive tone caused. *This man is full of himself.* He looked back inside the hut. Lt. Amano was on his feet and stretching the sleep from his muscles. He ordered, "Roust the men, Lieutenant. I don't want to stay in this dung-heap longer than I have to."

"Yes, sir," he snapped back.

Gima smiled and gestured for Hingi to lead the way. Hingi turned and Gima followed close behind. He stepped off the last step and felt his boots sink into the mud, erasing his buffing efforts. He looked up, noticing the rain had stopped for the moment. His uniform would remain dry, at least for the time being.

The day was brightening allowing Gima to evaluate Deputy Hingi better. He was short and dark and looked much like any of the other natives, but he walked with purpose and held himself with some esteem. He wondered if the man had some education past the elementary school level. The American influence had instilled the value of education in the

populace and no doubt there were many decent schools of higher education. But, for the most part, the Philippines was still a relatively uneducated
country.

Hingi led him to the same building they'd eaten in the night before.
Hingi mounted the steps, stopped on the porch and gestured toward the
door. "He is inside, sir."

Gima looked behind him, there were a few villagers about. Across the
way he saw soldiers emerging from huts and moving around the back to
take leaks. He doubted he was in any danger, but years of living in hostile
countries had taught him never to let his guard down and he wasn't about
to start now. He strode past Hingi, his hand still on the pommel of his
sword.

It took a moment for his eyes to adjust to the darker room. He saw
Sampson standing in the center of the room. Sampson gestured to a chair,
and in English, said, "Good morning, Captain. A seat, sir?"

Gima shook his head. "I would rather stand." He purposely left off the
Mayor title. *Mayor indeed.* The man had little more power than any of the
village inhabitants. He seemed to think he was some sort of royalty and
wondered if it was the sycophant Hingi's influence. It would be amusing, if
it weren't so pathetic. He looked at his watch. "What is it? I would like to be
on my way as soon as possible." Of course, he had no intention of leaving
before grilling the young man about what he knew about Tark's Ticks.

Sampson smiled and nodded, "Of course. I have news which I feel
would benefit your search for the Americans you seek."

Gima's head snapped up and the intensity of his gaze made Sampson
look away. This man was going to make this even easier than he thought. "If
you know something you should tell me right now." His voice was filled
with icy resolve.

Sampson looked beyond Gima, looking for help from his lackey. He
stammered, "I — I would want something in return."

Gima squared his shoulders and took a step toward Sampson, the grip
on his sword tightening. "Your life will be enough."

The color drained from Sampson's dark face and his lower lip trembled.
He opened his mouth, but nothing came out. Gima gave him an evil grin
and he thought the boy might lose his bowels. "I — I want..."

"You want what? If you don't give me the information, I'll have Sergeant Ono work on you until you do. I'm not here to play games."

A diminutive voice behind him, reminded him that Hingi was there. "Sir, if I may?"

Relief flooded Sampson's face and Gima slowly turned toward Hingi. "Yes? What is it?"

Hingi looked past Gima and his eyes showed pity towards his leader. "We know where they are. We will show you. We only hoped to be thought of in good stead with the Japanese."

"Tell me now and I won't have you both tortured and killed."

Sampson finally got his nerve back. "They — they are in a village. A day's walk. The village is hard to find."

Gima smiled despite wanting to continue to instill fear, but this was his first positive step toward finding and killing the American gangsters and avenging his men. This was the first step in getting off this cursed island and getting back into the war. "You will take me there, now," his voice was low and dangerous, and Sampson gulped and nodded, then looked at the floor.

It didn't take long for Vindigo to roust his men and prepare them to move out of the valley. They were excited about the coming battle and even more excited to know they would be hitting the Japanese from terrain they were intimately familiar with.

Tarkington figured the Japanese force would get to the area near dusk. He had no idea how many soldiers would be coming. James described a smallish platoon, but the Japanese might bring more men. If he was assaulting an unknown village, he'd want more than a platoon.

When they had their gear sorted and ready to go, Tarkington called the GIs, Filipinos and cadets to the center of the village. The sky was partially overcast and it hadn't rained yet that morning. Steam rose from the ground, making it look like the hot-springs he'd seen while visiting Yellowstone as a kid, just about fifty-degrees warmer and one hundred percent more humidity.

He looked around the group. They were mixed evenly. Despite the differences in skin color, backgrounds, and age, they were mixed as though they'd known each other their entire lives. He could feel the excitement and nervousness coming off them. They were all warriors and the coming battle made them almost giddy.

He held up his hands, quieting them. "As you all know, the enemy is most likely on their way here. We don't know how many are coming, but we're reasonably sure they have no idea we know they're coming." He waited for Eduardo to translate to the Filipino villagers, then continued. "If they move fast, they'll be here this evening. If they wait for reinforcements or move slowly, they'll be here in the morning.

"Vindigo and I have come up with a good plan. We'll have help carrying extra ammunition and weapons from the ammo cache to various points along the Jap routes." He nodded toward the women and children ready to move out with them. "We'll hit them early, starting at the abandoned village, then fade back to the next position and hit them again. We have two more ambush sites beyond that. We'll leave men at each, ready to give covering fire. After each ambush the next will be bigger and so on until the last one. By then, they'll be cautious and perhaps even beaten.

"You villagers know these spots well. It will be up to you to help the others less familiar with the terrain. At each ambush site, there will be at least four of you leading us back to the next ambush site. It will probably be dark, so make sure you don't lose anybody."

He waited for Eduardo to translate and looked around the group making sure everyone was understanding the mission. They all nodded and focused back onto him. He continued. "After the last site, we'll fall back to the ridge. If they follow, we'll cut them down with the heavy machine guns while our main force retreats across the bridge. Once everyone's across, we'll pull the bridge and thumb our nose at any survivors."

When Eduardo got to that last part, there was raucous laughter as GIs and Filipinos alike put thumbs to noses and practiced the mocking gesture.

Sampson and Hingi stayed inside the great hall after Captain Gima left to ready his men. Sampson rubbed his temples and rocked back and forth on the floor, repeating over and over, "What have I done? What have I done?"

At first Hingi consoled him, telling him he had no choice but to tell Gima, but when the young man continued to spiral into debilitating self-pity, he grew angry. He stepped in front of him and grabbed his shoulders and shook him. "Snap out of it, man. What's done is done. Now's the time to make the most of it, not sit here like a pathetic slug until you're squashed. Now's the time for leadership, to take control and lead the men confidently."

Sampson shook off his grip and got to his feet. His eyes were slits and he stared hard at Hingi. "Lead the men? I'm to lead Filipino against Filipino? Most will not do it. They have friends there. *I* have friends there. This is madness. What was I thinking?" He stopped shaking and acting like a wild animal in a trap. His vision focused he straightened his back and he came to a decision. "I will attack *them*." He licked his lips and his eyes widened as the plan came to him. "The men will be given weapons. Surely the Japanese wouldn't allow us to lead them without weapons. Once we're armed and in the jungle, we'll attack." He pointed at Hingi who was staring at him in astonishment. "Tell the young men to meet me inside here. You keep the captain and lieutenant occupied. I only need a few minutes."

Hingi started to protest but Sampson seethed at him, "Do it, now." He stepped forward, withdrawing the .38 pistol and aiming it at his chest. "Do it or die, Deputy."

Hingi put up his hands in surrender and backed away in mock defeat. He'd never seen Sampson so sure of anything since he suggested he should be the village leader. Except the spark in his eye now was even more intense. It was the look of a warrior ready to fight and die if necessary.

Hingi kept backing away, the pistol muzzle never wavering. When he got to the edge of the doorway, he turned away and hustled out of sight. He took a deep breath. He'd do Sampson's bidding; he'd send the men to him and he'd tell them of his inane plan.

He smiled to himself. The original plan was falling apart and being replaced with an even better one. Of course, when his future grandchildren were asking him how he'd become the village leader, he'd tell them it had been his plan all along. He'd be considered a genius.

Captain Gima left the meeting with Sampson and went straight back to his hut and yelled, "Lieutenant Amano, front and center!"

Amano shot out of the hut and stood at rigid attention. "At your service, sir."

"Assemble the men. We leave as soon as possible. Get it done, then return here and I'll fill you in. We can brief the NCOs while we march."

Minutes later Amano was again at attention and after he heard what Captain Gima learned, the color drained from his face and he thought he might pass out. Gima looked annoyed at the response. "What is wrong? This is the best news I've received in months."

Amano shook his head quickly, trying to shake off the fear he felt climbing from his gut to his throat. "N — Nothing sir. Nothing's wrong."

"Then why do you look as though you'll be sick?"

Amano had no idea how to respond but he stammered, "J — just excited, sir."

Gima leaned back and laughed uproariously. When he recovered, he shook his head, "Good one, Lieutenant. You're not excited, you're petrified. But don't be, this will be easy. We'll be attacking an unsuspecting town, not even frontline soldiers, but criminals."

"*Tark's Ticks*, sir?" he asked.

"Yes, *Tark's Ticks,*" he said, with dripping hatred.

"Would — would it be," Amano stopped unsure if he should proceed. He clamped his mouth shut tight.

Gima looked at him, "Finish what you started to say. 'Would it be' what?"

"Do we have enough men, sir?" He blurted it out rapidly.

Gima considered. He paced and stroked his chin, then stopped in front of the lieutenant and nodded. "I understand your concern. It's valid. Your men are not combat troops, but garrison troops." He looked his subordinate in the eye and said, "I'll radio HQ and order the rest of my platoon to join us. The roads are not good for travel, but they should arrive a half day behind us. Just in time for mop-up operations. Will that ease your mind, Lieutenant?"

Amano swallowed, gave a quick nod and murmured, "Yes, sir."

There was a rap at the doorway and the guard saluted and said, "Sir, there is a Filipino here to see you."

Gima looked behind him and saw Deputy Hingi looking backwards as though not wanting to be seen. Gima nodded, "Let him enter." The guard stepped aside and Hingi hustled in obviously relieved. "What is it, *Deputy?*"

Hingi kept his eyes down and his voice low, "Sir, there's been a development I think you should be aware of..."

18

Captain Gima and Lieutenant Amano rode in the back of the car while Platoon Sergeant Ono and the driver, Private Hano rode in front. Gima invited Ono to join them, rather than his own Sergeant Uchida.

Ono was on edge, not sure what was in store for him. His plan to have his way with a village girl the evening before hadn't worked out and he was bitter that his pissant lieutenant had chosen last night to grow a pair of testicles. He'd considered sneaking into a hut late at night anyway, and he would have if Captain Gima weren't around.

Ono knew Gima was a straight-arrow combat veteran, a tough son-of-a-bitch, who wouldn't hesitate to execute him on the spot if he were found forcing himself on a hapless Filipino. He sat in the front passenger seat of the car, happy to be out of the rain, but nervous as to why he was there.

Private Hano kept a slow driving pace, keeping the marching platoon members within sight. Since they weren't off in the jungle searching for tracks, they moved much quicker.

Around noon, Private Hano looked up from the engine dials and stated, "Sir, we're low on fuel."

Captain Gima ordered, "Pull over. Fill the tank and we'll let the troops rest for fifteen minutes. Help the private, Sergeant."

Ono nodded, "Yes, sir." He stepped out, shouldered his rifle and met Private Hano at the back where the spare gas tanks were attached. He pulled out a cigarette, an American brand and felt his pockets for a lighter, finally finding one.

Hano lifted one of the spare tanks and gave the sergeant a look. Ono lit the cigarette, the smoke making him squint. "You got a problem, Private?" He spat a stray piece of tobacco off his tongue and when Hano didn't answer, added, "I asked you a question, soldier."

Hano put the gas tank down and faced the sergeant. "No problem, Platoon Sergeant."

Ono looked at the two officers still inside the jeep, discussing something. He lowered his voice. "I'm not going to help you, if that's what you're upset about. Your captain can sit on his sword for all I care."

Hano's face darkened. He had the utmost respect for Captain Gima and this lecherous piece-of-shit sergeant was a flea in comparison. "I'm going to open the fuel tank and put the gas in. Please step away with your cigarette." Ono blew a plume of smoke into Hano's face but didn't move. Hano didn't open the fuel tank. He glared at Ono who ignored him taking another puff. "I can't follow the captain's order until you take a step back, Platoon Sergeant." He raised his voice, hoping Gima would hear.

Ono took the cigarette out of his mouth and allowed the smoke to filter out through his nose. It rose slowly and wreathed his face, lingering. When he spoke, the smoke blew out as though the outside temperature was freezing rather than hot and muggy. "Fill the tank, Private," he hissed.

Private Hano braced, looked straight ahead and barked, "I will not put the officers' lives at risk, Sergeant."

Ono heard scuffling and the vehicle jostled as both officers moved to exit. Ono shot daggers with his eyes. "You'll pay for this you little cockroach."

The two officers approached from either side, Gima near Ono and Amano near the driver. Gima looked the sergeant up and down but didn't say anything, waiting for Ono's commanding officer to deal with him.

Finally, Lt. Amano asked, "What is going on here, Sergeant?"

He pointed at Private Hano who was still facing forward at attention.

"The private won't fill the tank, *sir*." The way he said 'sir' was enough to make Gima's blood boil, but he kept his mouth shut. The lieutenant needed to get this sergeant under control.

"Why won't you fill the tank, Private?" asked Amano.

"Sir, Platoon Sergeant Ono's cigarette risks lighting the fuel on fire and I didn't want to risk it while you were both inside the vehicle, sir."

Amano looked at the scowling sergeant, the cigarette hanging limply from his lips, the ash pile at the tip growing by the second. Amano gulped at the hard look Ono was giving him. He shut his eyes and shifted from foot to foot, then finally ordered, "Either — either step away from the vehicle or put out the cigarette, Platoon Sergeant."

Ono took the cigarette out of his mouth and looked at the glowing tip but didn't make a move. Gima had enough. Quick as a viper, he grasped the hand holding the cigarette, twisted Ono's arm behind his back and pushed him against the back of the vehicle. He pushed Ono's arm high up his back and he grunted in agony as his shoulder threatened to pop out of joint. Gima took the cigarette and held it up to Ono's face. The tip still glowed with color and heat. Ono's eyes widened and reflected the glow. Gima held it there, leaned forward and hissed into his ear, "I've had enough of your insubordination, *Sergeant*." Ono's eyes narrowed slightly and Gima pushed his arm higher, eliciting a whimper.

Ono gave a quick nod and beads of sweat rolled off his forehead. "Yes, sir," he uttered. "Yes, sir," he repeated louder.

Gima released his arm and the sergeant let out a gasp of air. He shook out his arm and clutched his shoulder. Gima still held the cigarette. Ono faced him, stuck his chest out and braced, his gaze looking past him. Gima flicked the nearly-consumed cigarette and it bounced off Ono's chest with a spark and fell to the wet ground. Ono didn't flinch.

Gima looked at Hano and nodded once, "Fill the tank, Private." Hano stifled a smile, quickly unscrewing the gas tank lid and transferring the fuel. The glug-glug was the only sound. Gima looked at Lieutenant Amano, his relief obvious. "If he gets out of line again, you have my permission to shoot him," he said loud enough for everyone to hear.

Lieutenant Amano blanched at the thought but gave a curt nod, "Yes, sir. Thank you, sir."

It continued to rain, but nothing like the heavy storms they'd seen over the past week. The road and jungle steamed making for poor visibility. If they'd still been battling the Americans and Filipinos, Gima would have moved much slower, fearing an ambush. He kept the platoon moving quickly though, wanting to get near the village before dark.

He looked back at the platoon. The soldiers looked tired and worn despite having rested the previous night. The twenty strong men of the village looked much fresher. Gima had given them eleven rifles between them. He'd ordered Japanese soldiers with sidearms to use them instead and made a show of handing out the rifles to the villagers. The others had pistols, mostly small caliber .38s and a few had small bows and arrows.

Sampson had looked particularly delighted when he received his rifle. Gima made sure the Type-38 bolt action rifles had five rounds already loaded. He told them that was all they could spare and made sure each villager knew how to use the safety and how to fire, without actually trying them out.

Sampson came sauntering up to the vehicle, his rifle slung over his shoulder. Gima rolled the window down partway and Sampson pointed, "There's an abandoned village ahead. From there we will move west. We'll be in jungle all the way to Vindigo's village."

Gima nodded. "I'll send most of my men forward to sweep it, you stay and cover the rear. Then you'll lead us into the jungle."

Sampson's smile couldn't get any wider. He nodded, "Yes. Good."

Gima ordered Hano to pull the vehicle to the side and park. Sergeant Ono had been a model soldier since the incident hours before. He hadn't uttered a word.

Once parked, they all stepped out and stood around the vehicle as the rest of the men caught up. The Filipinos stepped aside allowing the Japanese soldiers to pass by. The officers stayed behind along with Hano and Sergeant Uchida. Amano sent Platoon Sergeant Ono forward to help clear the village.

Amano couldn't stop looking at the smiling Filipinos. Gima nudged him in the ribs, "Eyes front, Lieutenant." Amano nodded and did his best not to stare.

With the Japanese soldiers in front, Captain Gima motioned for the Filipinos to follow. Sampson smiled, nodded and took his rifle off his shoulder and led his men forward. The officers followed, and Gima nonchalantly unsnapped the holster cover of his pistol.

The abandoned village had a large central area and the soldiers entered it with their rifles ready, led by Platoon Sergeant Ono. The Filipinos trotted forward and closed the gap and when the soldiers were nearing the huts, Sampson yelled, "Now!"

The eleven soldiers with rifles aimed at the soldier's backs and pulled the triggers, but nothing happened. There was a smattering of pistol shots, but no one was closer than thirty-yards and not a single bullet found their marks.

The Filipinos all looked at their weapons as though they'd never seen them before. They yanked back bolts, seeing the brass still in place and tried again, but now the Japanese soldiers were turned and holding their rifles at their shoulders, but they held their fire.

One of the Filipinos with a pistol aimed and tried again. Before he could squeeze the trigger, three soldiers fired and Gima watched his back explode as all three bullets lanced through him. He dropped face-first into the mud, his blood mixing with rainwater.

The rest of the Filipinos stopped struggling with their rifles, seeing the angry muzzles leveled at their chests and their deadly effects. None of the bow and arrow holders had time to fire and they held them at their sides and looked from muzzle to muzzle in panic. Sampson backed away, all color drained from his face. He threw his rifle to the ground.

Gima stepped toward him, his sword out and leveled and Sampson felt the point touch his back. "Not another step, my friend."

Sampson put his hands up and slowly turned to face Gima. The sword never moved and was now ready to eviscerate the young man with a swipe. "How? How did you know?"

Gima looked beyond his shoulder, "You should never trust anyone."

Sampson looked over his shoulder and saw Deputy Hingi striding toward him, his facial expression flat. Sampson's face darkened and he seethed, "You! You — you betrayed me."

Hingi lifted his chin slightly and stopped beside him, "You are a fool. I saved the village from certain destruction."

Sampson sprang at him, gripping Hingi by the throat and riding him to the mud, squeezing with every ounce of his power. Hingi gripped the stronger man's wrists, trying to pry him off, but it was no use. He looked desperately at Gima for help, but the captain stood there with his sword in hand, watching as though viewing an interesting sumo match.

Sampson continued to squeeze and Hingi's face turned purple, his eyes went bloodshot and his tongue poked from his mouth as though he'd swallowed a fat, pink worm. A high-pitched wheeze escaped Hingi's throat and Sampson squeezed harder until Hingi's larynx crunched. Hingi's eyes rolled to back of his head and his face went slack, a stream of bloody saliva coming from the corner of his mouth.

Sampson lifted Hingi's head and smacked it hard against the mud, then released him. Hingi's head flopped to the side, his neck at an unnatural angle. Sampson had to pry Hingi's dead fingers from around his wrists. He stood on shaky legs and faced Captain Gima and his glimmering sword. The only sound was the rain. Sampson lifted his chin, read to die.

Gima shook his head. "You will not die so easily as your *deputy*." He switched to Japanese and raised his voice, "Platoon Sergeant Ono."

Ono ran forward and braced. "Yes, sir."

"Disarm them. Then line up the men who took rifles and execute them."

Ono couldn't keep the smile from creeping across his face. "Yes, sir." He barked orders to the soldiers and they disarmed the Filipinos with brutal efficiency.

Gima watched, pleased with the welcome change which had come over the garrison platoon. They'd been subjected to a lot over the past few days and were taking their frustrations out on the men who only minutes before thought they were going to shoot them in the back.

One Filipino hesitated to give his pistol up, the private reacted instantly and smashed the butt of his rifle into the man's face, knocking him to the ground. The villager clutched his face, blood spurting between his fingers as he rolled side-to-side in the mud, moaning. The private cursed him and kicked the forgotten pistol away from his hand then stomped him in the gut and stepped back.

Sampson watched his fellow Filipinos being disarmed and beaten. His shoulders slumped and he shook with the realization that he'd failed them. Without looking at him, he asked Gima, "How? The rifles?"

Gima smiled, "It was a simple thing to dismantle the rounds and take the gunpowder out."

"What will you do with us?" Sampson asked barely above a whisper.

Gima pointed. The men who'd held rifles were grouped together in front of a hut with a sagging front deck and one-by-one were forced to turn away then pushed to their knees. When one resisted, Ono slashed the back of his knee with his bayonet. The man went down screaming, clutching his slashed knee.

Sampson could only watch in cold horror as the Japanese unloaded the faulty ammo from the rifles and inserted live ammunition one at a time. The sound of bolts slamming forward and snicking to the side gave the action a desperate finality. The Filipinos faced the jungle. They looked at the ground in front of them and Sampson could see a few shaking as they cried. "Don't do this. Kill me. I'm responsible."

Gima nudged Lt. Amano and ordered him, "Give the order."

Amano strode forward obviously loathing what he had to do. He stood beside his men who were holding their rifles at port arms. Lieutenant Amano looked back at Gima who didn't change his hard expression.

Amano raised his hand. "Ready, aim..." he hesitated as his men raised their rifles and took aim at the crouched Filipinos. He dropped his hand, "Fire!" A ripple of fire and the Filipinos slumped forward onto their faces. A few were obviously still alive and Amano, who looked like he might be sick, ordered, "Finish them, Sergeant."

Ono unslung his rifle, delight in his eyes. He fired a shot into each of their heads, whether they were already dead or not.

When it was done, Amano strode back to Gima. Gima could see the timid officer's eyes had changed; hardened. The reality of war's ugliness had finally found its way into him and now he would be changed forever. Hopefully, Gima thought, for the better.

He turned to the shaking, pathetic Sampson. He looked as though he'd aged twenty years over the past few minutes. "Now you will take us the rest of the way to the village."

———

The GIs, along with two Filipinos from the village and four cadets, were spread out along the only real pathway through the jungle leading west from the abandoned village. It was unlikely the enemy knew about the secret back-way path. It was a closely guarded secret and Vindigo was sure Benjamin didn't know about it, which meant his son didn't either. But, just to be safe, there were guards posted along the cliff ledges.

Tarkington stiffened, seeing a shape in the jungle, but relaxed when he recognized Raker and Henry. He'd sent them to the abandoned village hours before, to be his early warning system.

Henry hunkered beside him and Winkleman leaned in close to listen. "They're just coming into the village. A platoon of Japs and about twenty Filipinos. Most armed with rifles. I recognized Sampson among 'em."

Tarkington shook his head in disappointment. Having fought beside Filipinos, he had the utmost respect for their loyalty and bravery. Knowing there were traitors, or 'Makapili,' as they called themselves, reminded Tarkington that every culture had the occasional bad apple. Sampson, apparently was one of them, but the tragedy was, he was leading other Filipinos down the same treacherous path. How had he convinced so many to take up arms against their own countrymen? It seemed impossible.

Tarkington asked, "So about forty men altogether?" Henry nodded and moved across the trail from him. Tarkington wasn't worried about the size of the force, he didn't plan on taking them on in a fair fight. He'd hit them hard, then fade back to the next line and do it all over again. By the time the enemy hit the third ambush, he figured they'd be whittled down pretty good and possibly destroyed.

Now, they would wait. He could feel the wet, soggy ground pulling him deeper and he welcomed it. The lower he was immersed, the less likely he'd be seen. It was wet and miserable, but he was used to it and had even come to relish the close contact with Mother Earth. It centered him and put his mind at ease.

He perked his ears up when he heard a smattering of muffled shots. His men were all accounted for, the shots weren't aimed their way. He briefly wondered if they'd missed a well-hidden villager on their sweep but discounted the notion. If there'd been anyone there, they would've known about it long before.

He looked across the trail and could just make out Henry's camouflaged face staring back at him. He gave Tarkington a half shrug and Tarkington focused his attention back down the trail. A minute passed and again there was firing, this time three shots in quick, almost simultaneous succession.

Tarkington's curiosity was piqued but he knew it would be folly to leave cover and investigate. Perhaps it was some kind of ploy to draw them out. He shook his head, that wouldn't make any sense, they were too far from the village and why risk giving up the advantage of surprise they thought they had.

Long minutes passed and Tarkington wondered whether the shots meant something else. Perhaps they'd called off the search. He still was not inclined to investigate, but the thoughts racing through his mind tormented him. What if they knew they were there and were even now flanking them? He was letting his imagination get the better of him. Even if they'd somehow sniffed out the ambush, they wouldn't be able to sneak past the Filipinos guarding their flanks, this was their backyard.

Another, much louder and close together discharge of weapons deepened the mystery. The following series of single shots made it seem as though they were taking target practice. It reminded him of the range during basic training.

Finally, after another thirty minutes, there was movement in the jungle directly in front. Tarkington almost felt relieved. He didn't know what the shooting was about, but now it didn't matter because the enemy was coming into the kill zone.

The lead man looked familiar, he wasn't Japanese but Filipino. In the evening light, he saw it was the village leader, Sampson and he wasn't armed. He saw more Filipinos behind him and none of them were armed either. Henry said they'd been armed. *What the hell's going on?* They walked with their heads down, taking no pains to be stealthy. They looked as though they were on a forced march.

It didn't matter, they'd be the first to die. Behind them, he saw Japanese soldiers. They were being a little more careful but had to walk fast to keep up with the Filipinos. It seemed to Tarkington that they were watching the Filipinos more than the surrounding area, almost as though they thought they'd try to escape. But escape what? They were collaborators.

Tarkington was near the middle of the ambushers and when Sampson was adjacent to him, Tarkington fired a short burst from his submachine gun at the first Japanese soldier. The rest of his men opened fire, cutting a swath of death. Men fell where they stood or were knocked backwards with bullet impacts. Out of the corner of his eye, he saw Sampson's body fall unnaturally.

Tarkington continued to fire in short bursts, aiming carefully, watching his targets fall one after another. His weapon clicked on empty. Without a word, he swapped magazines, got to his feet and dashed back toward the rear, breaking contact. He could hear the rest of his men running all around him. Finally, after they'd gone thirty-yards, there was return fire.

The enemy were shooting at shadows. They were beyond the slight crest of the hill and out of danger, being led by the Filipinos to the next ambush site.

He followed Joshua down the short slope then up the other side and over another small ridge. By the time they finally got to the next site, Tarkington was breathing hard. His legs ached, but he couldn't keep the smile off his face when he saw all his men filtering in. Winkleman did a quick headcount. "All accounted for, Tark," he whispered. There was still the occasional muffled shot from the ambush site, but they were wasting their ammo.

Tarkington nodded, and signaled for the men to spread out and fill in the gaps. In front of each scraped-out depression, there were two grenades and two fresh clips. Tarkington had his own stockpile of magazines for his submachine gun. So far everything was going as planned.

He settled into his hole and got control of his breathing. This site was much less jungle covered, but they had the advantage of height and would use that to hurl grenades down upon the enemy. After the initial explosions, his riflemen would snipe, then join the rest of them back at the next ambush site. Once again, it became a waiting game.

19

Captain Gima lifted his head out of the mud, his chin dripping with dirty water. Off to his right, Lieutenant Amano was curled up in a ball, whimpering like a child. Platoon Sergeant Ono was fifteen-meters ahead, firing his rifle as quickly as he could work the bolt, but there was no return fire. Gima yelled, "Cease fire!" Ono and the few soldiers brave enough to fight back stopped firing into the empty jungle.

A pall of silence descended on them along with the mist, then the moans of wounded filled the air. Gima yelled, "Get your men up and moving, Lieutenant." When there was no response, he reached out and clutched the back of Amano's shirt and pulled him. Gima got to his feet and stood over him. "Move up, now," he ordered.

Amano saw the rage in his eyes and for a brief moment he feared him more than the ambushers. He got to his feet and stammered, "Move up. Move up. Set up a perimeter."

Soldiers stumbled to their feet, looking around in fear and aimed their rifles haphazardly. Ono got to his feet but stayed low, his rifle at his shoulder, sweeping side to side. He took a few steps forward and barked, "Cover one another and move up thirty-meters. Find the wounded."

There were no more shots, the only sign of enemy the lingering smoke from their rifles. Soon the chaos of the ambush wore off, but the fear remained. The platoon was spread out protecting their flanks while a few soldiers with medical kits worked on the wounded.

Gima got the report from Lt. Amano. He looked as though he might throw up as he said, "We — we lost seven dead." He swallowed the bile threatening to come up. He'd seen some of the dead and wounded and the blood and gore sickened him. Men he'd led had died in battle and the weight of the responsibility felt physical. "Four wounded." He looked down and shook his head. "Two won't make it unless they get to a hospital."

Captain Gima shook his head. "Dammit. The Filipinos led us right into an ambush."

Amano looked up quickly and his eyes narrowed. "You think they led us on purpose?"

Gima shrugged, "I doubt it, Sampson's body is over there along with a few others. I didn't think him suicidal."

Amano nodded, "We found five dead Filipinos including Sampson." He did a quick calculation in his head. "There's no sign of the other two."

Gima nodded and pursed his lips. "We won't find them. They can disappear like ghosts in the jungle. We'll sweep their village when this is over and round them up. They won't get away with their double-crossing treachery."

Amano looked at his men. They were low, their rifles pointing outward. There seemed to be far fewer of them than there used to be. The light was fading, and Amano figured they had another two hours before it was completely dark. "What do we do now, sir?"

It was a question Gima had been pondering for the past few minutes. He weighed the pros and cons of continuing. Without the Filipinos, he couldn't be sure he'd find the village, particularly at night. Hingi had given him a good idea where to find it, but he'd be searching blind without a guide.

His warrior instinct told him to attack without let-up, stopping to lick his wounds was against the fiber of his being, but there was something else bothering him. The ambush had been too perfect, too well timed, too well executed. Somehow, they'd known they were coming.

He finally answered. "We collect our dead and wounded and retreat back to the abandoned village and wait for the rest of my platoon to arrive. I expect them soon, before nightfall. In the morning, we'll advance slow and if the enemy is still lingering, we'll make them pay."

Amano nodded, his relief obvious. "What of the Filipino bodies?"

Gima scowled, "Let them rot like the animals they are."

It appeared the harried run up the hill had been for nothing. Tarkington and the rest were ready for the second ambush, but after two hours the sun set and the jungle faded to darkness. There was no sign of pursuit. The jungle sounds were normal. Tarkington knew they'd killed or wounded many, but he doubted they'd put a big enough dent in their numbers to make them give up.

He'd sent Filipino scouts into the darkness to be sure the Japanese weren't trying to get around them and they'd returned telling him the surrounding jungle was devoid of Japanese. There were, however, five dead Filipinos at the scene of the ambush, but the Japanese force was nowhere to be found.

Tarkington was disturbed by the news. He asked Eduardo, "Does it seem odd the Japs would leave the Filipino bodies behind? I mean, I know they don't like Filipinos, but they were helping them. Doesn't seem like a good way to keep them helping."

Eduardo agreed. "That *is* odd. Maybe something to do with the shots we heard before the ambush?"

Tarkington lifted his eyebrows. "Yes, perhaps you're right. That was weird."

Eduardo took it a step further. "Maybe that is why they don't come. They don't have guides to show them the way."

"There's no way we killed all the Filipinos, there were only five bodies. I saw Sampson go down. Maybe losing their leader was enough for them."

Eduardo looked serious. "I can't believe Filipinos are willing to attack their countrymen. Sampson had a large force..." he stopped and shook his head, trying to picture it. "Is unimaginable to me."

"Nothing surprises me anymore when it comes to human nature," Tarkington stated.

Eduardo shook his head, not able to let it go so easily. "My country is a series of islands, but it is *one* country. We are colony for centuries and now five years from independence. I know it is hard to understand. You come from a huge country, America, but we are more..." he paused trying to come up with the correct word.

"Patriotic?" Tarkington offered.

Eduardo nodded, "Yes. Nation pride is everything. We share a common struggle. It brings us together even though kilometers of ocean between islands."

"Yes, I see what you mean. Seeing fellow countrymen turn against you must be hard. I can't imagine coming across an American siding with the Japs."

Eduardo nodded his head slightly. "I think something else happen. It is unimaginable."

"Well, perhaps we'll find out more tomorrow."

Gima was pleased to see his platoon arrive in the abandoned village, despite the late hour. He'd expected them earlier but Platoon Sergeant Sakai, explained there were many deep mud-pits they were forced to negotiate. The men were tired and dirty but ready for a fight.

The veteran soldiers brought extra ammunition and food, but also renewed energy and hope to the bedraggled and battered garrison soldiers. The supplies were divided up evenly and the additional food helped everyone's morale.

Platoon Sergeant Sakai was visibly upset to be handing their provisions over to the bedraggled garrison soldiers. Gima had been through many campaigns with the salty old soldier and they shared a mutual respect. He was the closest thing to a friend Gima had with any enlisted man, or officer for that matter.

He slapped Sakai's shoulder when he saw him grating his teeth. "I know they're garrison troops, but they've performed their duties well these past few days. A few hours ago, they had their first real taste of combat. They are still green but deserve respect."

Sakai nodded. He'd never question an order, but he didn't have to always like them. He pointed, "I've heard about Platoon Sergeant Ono." He paused as he watched him sauntering off with a box of ammunition. "I thought he was dead."

Gima leaned close and said, "We aren't that lucky."

Sakai looked at his commander with surprise, such levity was unusual from any JIA officer. Gima was different though, a soldier's officer. Sakai nodded and smiled. "I heard he was an ass, but tough."

"I'd agree with that. I had to put him in his place yesterday. He's behaved since, but I'd watch him."

"Yes, sir. And what of Lieutenant Amano, sir?"

"He's coming around, Sergeant. The morning will be challenging for us all."

"Are there more troops coming, sir?"

"I radioed the situation to command. They asked if I needed more men." He stared off into the night and finally shook his head. "I told them no. I think we have enough now."

An hour before light, the Japanese left the relative safety of the village and moved west into the jungle. They stayed to the right side of the trail they were ambushed on and came upon the site from the side an hour later. If there was another ambush, which would have been poor tactics, he would've taken them from the flank. All they found, though were the rotting corpses of the five Filipinos.

The terrain alongside the trail was harder to move through, but they also moved slower knowing there were hostiles nearby. Gima didn't care how tough the terrain was, he was determined to sniff out an ambush before it could be sprung and if that meant a slow advance, then so be it.

His point man, Corporal Sada, was one of the best in the business. When his company was split up, Gima insisted on keeping Sada, knowing his abilities as a point man were unsurpassed, probably in the whole division. He had the utmost confidence in his ability to *not* walk into an ambush. And, as an added bonus, he was incredibly skilled at hand-to-hand combat. Like most of the men in the platoon, he was the cream of the crop from the company. *With these men*, Gima thought, *I cannot fail.*

The terrain opened up and they moved a little faster. Sada stopped at the edge of a small clearing. In the gray morning light, Gima could see the expansive vibrant green covered mountains rising all around. Most were knife-edged and cut crazy angles through the land. The dark clouds over-head promised heavy rain any second.

He wished for a moment, he'd stopped Sampson from strangling Hingi, he could have used his guidance. The path forward was uncertain and looking beyond, he couldn't fathom which slicing valley the village was tucked into. So far, they hadn't come across anything which was much more than a game-trail. He knew the general direction from the crude map Hingi had scraped into the ground, but looking now, he wondered. He seemed to be leading his men into endless, impassable mountains.

He was crouched beside Sada and whispered, "The ridge ahead. Perhaps we can see more from there."

Sada nodded slowly and pointed to the left then made a hooking motion. His raspy voice always startled Gima and he remembered it was a souvenir from a botched surgery when he was a boy. "I'll move that way and check it out."

Gima nodded. "Take Private Nitta and Otake with you. I'll wait for your signal." Sada gave a slight bow and signaled the eager young privates to follow. They were the youngest in the platoon but Gima had seen them march and fight for days on end without ever losing their step or high morale. They were also excellent marksmen with their Type-38 rifles.

Tarkington conferred with his men around midnight, asking for their input about the coming day. He'd laid out his concerns that instead of coming headlong into them, the Japanese had either fled, or more likely, would be coming at them with more men and more caution, in the morning.

They'd discussed all possibilities and after an hour, decided to stay put and confront them from this spot, sticking to the original plan. They took two-hour watch shifts, but none of them slept.

With daylight came heavier rain. It had rained on and off all night but only lightly. In comparison to what they were used to, it was almost pleasant. The morning, however was a different story. It held off for a while, but eventually the dark cloud overhead unleashed a torrent and swept them with waves of rainwater, forcing them to leave their shallow foxholes, which quickly turned to swimming pools.

Tarkington was sitting beside Henry, trying to keep his wide-brimmed hat centered, keeping most of the rain off his shoulders at least. He had his submachine gun tucked close to his chest in an effort to keep it dry too. He'd need to give the weapon a good cleaning once he was back in the village.

They shared the thick trunk of a tree, which also helped lessen the deluge. Visibility was cut to a few feet. Finally, after fifteen minutes, the rain stopped as though someone had turned off a spigot.

Tarkington shook his head, "This place never ceases to amaze me." Mists formed almost as though by magic, oozing from the ground and rising slowly, like a sluggish sea-monster with countless tendrils.

The view down the hill to the next low ridge was suddenly crystal clear and Tarkington froze, focusing. Henry noticed his body stiffen and looked down the hill following his gaze, knowing better than to ask.

Tarkington didn't know what he'd seen, but something had caught his eye, something out of place. Over the long months living in the jungle, he'd learned to listen to his inner voice and trust his instincts. Like a wild animal, he was attuned to the rhythms of the jungle and something was off.

He shifted his gaze and concentrated on a bush to the left of where he thought he'd seen something, allowing his superior peripheral vision to work. There it was again, and this time he felt Henry stiffen, he'd seen it too.

The rest of the men either saw it or felt the change because everyone's concentration was centered on the ridge below. No one moved a muscle, even though they were well-hidden behind a thick copse of trees and shrubs. It would take a keen eye to see them even if they were jumping around waving their arms.

Tarkington squinted and saw a blur of color slightly off from the vibrant green of the ridge. Though it was at least two hundred yards distant, he saw the outline of what could only be a man, a soldier. He saw a quick movement, like a hand waving, or perhaps someone tripping and catching himself, whatever, he had the figure pinpointed.

The slope in front was steep but easily climbable. There was even a discernible trail winding up in a series of cutbacks. The low shrubs and clumps of trees allowed anyone coming up, decent cover. To either side the cover was better, but they'd have to negotiate steep ridges which looked slippery and endlessly time-consuming to get around. The slope was a natural funnel, leading directly toward their waiting ambush.

This was the normal route to the village. But, despite that, the route was by no means obvious. If the villagers didn't have outsiders with them, they took the secret trail, which meant there wasn't an obvious path to follow here. Indeed, it seemed more like a game trail until you were on it, then you'd notice the sandal tracks of other people. The fact that the Japanese were beneath them, proved they didn't know about the secret trail and someone had tipped them off about the villages' location.

Tarkington hissed to Henry, "Here we go."

The rain finally stopped and Gima pulled himself from beneath the natural cover of the jungle. Lt. Amano looked as miserable as a drowned cat. Gima's men were stoic, their faces unreadable, knowing there was nothing to do but wait it out.

This kind of rain was like a timeout, both sides unable to move or fight. Gima shook his head and cursed himself: *don't get complacent or make assumptions.* He was facing a skilled enemy. Despite losing many soldiers the day before, none of his men had even glimpsed their enemy. The only sound had been the cracks of rifles, snapping bullets, dying soldiers and Filipinos.

He glanced up the hill, wondering how much progress his lead scout made in the deluge. It had started minutes after the three of them disappeared up the left side of the clearing. It looked like a good spot for another ambush and he hoped they hadn't walked into it during the rain. He doubted he'd have been able to hear the shots.

Finally, the rain subsided, allowing him to see up the slope. He strained to see but it seemed Sada and the others had been consumed by the rain and jungle.

A moment later, he breathed a sigh of relief seeing Corporal Sada poke his head out from a thick layer of brambles and wave. Gima waved back and Sada dropped down quickly, becoming one with his surroundings again. Gima nodded to Sergeant Sakai, who stepped forward, rainwater dripping off his chin. Gima pointed up the hill, the way up the low ridge was open.

Gima thought perhaps Tark's Ticks had retreated, not wanting to stick around for an alerted enemy. He hoped not, these hills and valleys were endless and could hide an entire civilization. He didn't relish sifting through their intricacies. He craved a quick, decisive and deadly clash, then he could leave this place with a clear conscience.

Despite how easy it looked to move up the center of the open-faced ridge, he directed his men to take the same route the scouts had taken. He left nothing to chance. The route proved safe. It would be more difficult, and would take longer, but all he had was time.

Half an hour later and breathing hard, he finally hunched beside Corporal Sada, who looked worried. Gima understood why. The ridge they were on was small and there was a bit of a downslope before the next slope started up. It was covered with thick mist and looked like an even more obvious ambush spot than this one.

The slope was longer and for the first time he could see a trail between wispy arms of mist. Multiple switchbacks told him the trail was used by humans. That wasn't the worrisome part though. The slope started wide and funneled down to maybe twenty-meters wide at the top, which was covered in thick brush, trees and boulders. It was a perfect ambush spot and there didn't look to be any way around it. The cover leading up to it didn't look terrible, but men firing down upon them from concealed protected positions would have a huge advantage.

He whispered for Sergeant Sakai to bring him his binoculars. He hefted the heavy, German-made binoculars and scanned the ridge, but the darkness inside the thick jungle was impenetrable. He had the distinct feeling he was being watched though, and knew by the tense looks of his men, that they felt the same.

He dropped the binoculars, letting them swing heavily from his neck. He took in a breath, blew it out slow and wiped his brow. He looked to Lt. Amano. He looked tired and scared, but that was nothing new.

In another time, he could've called on air support or possibly an .artillery barrage, but the low clouds made air support impossible and there were no artillery units left on the island. As far as he knew, they'd all been moved to Corregidor to protect the entrance to Manila Bay.

"Sergeant Sakai," he whispered. Sakai scooted beside him, ready to do his bidding. "You get the feeling we're being watched?" Sakai nodded, keeping his gaze up the slope. "Me too. No doubt from up there." He looked at the high green cliffs surrounding the slope to either side. "There's no way around unless we had climbing gear, and even then it would take a week."

The silence grew and finally Sergeant Sakai asked, "What are your orders, sir?"

Captain Gima squinted and finally nodded, "We go up the hill, but here's how we'll do it."

Tarkington was on his belly. He could occasionally see movement on the low ridge, far below. The Japanese weren't trying to hide. They either didn't think they were being observed or realized they were too far away for effective rifle fire. He yearned for the old days when he could've called in an artillery strike, but those days were long gone.

It was difficult to discern how many soldiers there were. He'd see movement, then nothing, then more movement. If the Japanese decided to come, they'd have to make their way down the short slope to the base of this one. They'd be able to do so without exposing themselves too much, but it didn't really matter. They'd be out of range until they were at the base of this slope and then they'd have decent cover until they were about halfway up. That was where the real killing would begin.

Minutes passed before he finally saw men emerging like ants from the ridge. They moved down the short slope, not rushing but not being careful either. Tarkington leaned toward Henry and muttered, "Looks like a reinforced platoon at least."

Henry nodded his agreement and drawled, "I count thirty-eight men but I might've counted one or two twice."

The Japanese made it to the bottom of the slope. They were within rifle range, but not easy rifle range. Tarkington thought things over. Yesterday he'd intended to let them get close and roll grenades down upon their heads, but that was when he thought they'd be charging headlong up the slope giving chase. They hadn't done that, instead reacting with caution. Perhaps he should engage them earlier. The ridge he sat upon was an obvious ambush spot. The Japanese officer would see that immediately. He'd shown caution and restraint so far and there was no reason to believe he'd suddenly throw caution to the wind. He must assume they were up here waiting. *What would I do?*

The sudden staccato of a heavy Nambu machine gun left little doubt what the Japanese had in mind. Tracer fire ripped up the hill from the right side of the slope. Bullets whizzed through the thick foliage, smacking tree trunks and zinging off boulders.

Tarkington knew his GIs would simply hunker down, but he yelled for the benefit of the cadets. "Stay down and hold fire. He's probing us. Hold your fire." There was a brief pause, then another long burst swept from right to left, chewing up the ground near the edge of the ridge.

Tarkington lifted his head and saw the Japanese soldiers climbing the slope. They were split evenly: half on the left, half on the right. They weren't running but moving steadily. He had a decision to make. They were coming as if they knew they were there. The way they kept their intervals and covered their movements, bounding from cover to cover, told him they wouldn't make the mistake of bunching up, even if he *didn't* return fire.

He nodded, deciding he'd have done the same thing if the roles were reversed. If the officer was wrong and the ridge was empty, then he was only out a few hundred rounds of machine gun ammo. If he was right, he could overrun the position.

Tarkington called, "Wink. Get the sharpshooters and knee mortars in position. They want a fight, we'll give it to 'em." He tapped Henry's shoulder. He was aiming down the muzzle of his trusty Springfield rifle, adjusting the sight picture, waiting for the order. "You think you can hit that machine gunner?"

Henry spat and shook his head. "He's well concealed. It'd be a waste of ammo."

"Okay, fire at will." Henry's body settled into the mud and grass and his breathing steadied. The bark of his rifle made Tarkington jump, but he saw his target far down the hill drop out of sight and the lingering red mist left little doubt. "Nice shot."

There was rippling fire up and down the line and a few more Japanese slumped, but most dove for cover. Flashes and puffs of white smoke erupted from down-slope and soon leaves were tearing from branches overhead and falling onto their backs. The heavy thumping of bullets impacting mud kept their heads down.

Tarkington knew he had little chance of hitting anything at this range with his submachine gun, so he kept his head just high enough to call out targets for Henry. "Downslope ten yards and to the right of the last one. Behind the downed tree. He'll pop his head up near the center, he's reloading."

Henry found the tree and adjusted, placing the sight just above the tree and in the center of its length. Bullets continued to snap overhead, but he was unfazed, his heart rate slow and steady, along with his breathing.

Tarkington said, "There. He's up."

Henry opened both eyes and saw the shape to the right a few feet. He adjusted and saw the plume of smoke as the soldier fired. He waited a fraction of a second for the air to clear. The soldier was off his sights, working the bolt action. Henry squeezed the trigger and the soldier's head snapped back and he fell out of sight.

"He's down."

Tarkington heard the thump of a knee mortar. He looked left and saw Sergeant Fernandez on his knees with the funny looking knee mortar arm anchored into the ground. He'd fired it with a low angle, eyeballing it rather than using the built-in measurements, which would have had him arcing it more. Tarkington almost yelled at him to use it correctly but stopped himself when he saw the grenade explode near the furthest forward soldier on the right and send him flying sideways.

Another thump from Tarkington's right and he saw another 50mm grenade arcing toward the group to the left. The grenade exploded between two soldiers who'd just gotten to their feet to bound forward. The front man was blown onto his face and the other fell backwards.

The machine gun fire from the Nambu increased along with the volume of rifle fire and the men ducked and rode it out for a few seconds before rising and continuing the fight. Tarkington yelled, "Fernandez!" The young cadet looked his way, the smile on his face unforgettable. "Nice shooting. Can you hit the machine gunner?"

He poked his head up to get a better look then quickly ducked again, seeing the smoke near the bottom of the slope and marking the general area. More of the cadets were launching their grenades. He shrugged and called out, making himself heard over the rippling gunfire, "Perhaps. It's a long shot but firing from above like this..." he smiled. "I'll try."

Tarkington nodded and called back. "Give him two shots, then concentrate on the troops."

More pops as more knee mortars were fired by the cadets. Their accuracy was astonishing, and Tarkington realized how truly skilled they were with them. He watched Fernandez adjusting the angle of the tube. Fernandez poked his head up one last time for a final check.

His head snapped back unnaturally, and the back of his skull came apart as gray matter and blood sprayed the cadet behind him. Tarkington watched in horror as he fell to the side, the smile forever frozen on his face. A smile which would haunt him for the rest of his days.

"No!" he yelled in anguish reaching for him.

Henry came off his sights. He saw Tarkington reaching toward Fernandez' smoking half skull. Tarkington seemed to be frozen in place, his lower lip quivering, his eyes wide and staring. "Tark! Tark snap out of it!" he yelled but no response. "Wink!" he barked.

Winkleman took a break from firing, his ears ringing. The unusual call from the lead scout, made him look up. Henry was pointing. Tarkington was on his knees reaching out like a mummy, staring at something. He seemed to be frozen in place. He followed his gaze and saw the lump, which had been Sergeant Fernandez a moment before. "Shit," he cursed. He low-crawled the fifteen yards as bullets snapped overhead.

He got to Tarkington's side and slapped his leg. "Tark! Tark! Wake the fuck up!" He got to his knees and was about to slap his face when there was an explosion. He was hurled forward onto Tarkington. Dirt and dust rained down on them.

Stollman yelled, "We're in range of their damned knee mortars!"

Winkleman assessed the situation and gave the order that needed to be made. "Fall back! Fall back!"

Instantly the men went to their bellies and pushed themselves backwards. The explosion seemed to knock Tarkington from his trance, and he followed Winkleman's urging.

Once they'd gone fifteen yards backwards they were completely out of sight from the slope below and they got to their knees. More explosions rocked the ridgeline, sending dirt and bits of wood and branches flying. They trotted backwards until they were completely out of danger. The sound of battle became distant, even though it was just over the ridge.

The cadet who'd been behind Fernandez, cradled his body awkwardly, tears streaking down his cheeks. Tarkington went to him and took the body. He looked down at the dirty, smiling face, the neat hole on the ridge of his nose the only thing out of place. He slung him over his shoulder, then looked at Winkleman, his voice wavering but back in charge. "You know what to do." Winkleman nodded and Tarkington addressed the others, "Let's get out of here."

Winkleman, Stolly and Vick stayed behind, watching the others melt into the jungle. The chaos on the ridge continued for another few minutes but finally died down when there was no return fire.

The three of them crawled forward until they were feet from the cliff edge. Bullets still whizzed and snapped overhead, but the knee mortar barrage had stopped, at least for the moment. They each pulled three grenades from their satchels and placed them within easy reach. They could hear yelling as the Japanese soldiers bounded forward. They were close and would be coming over the top in seconds.

Winkleman nodded, and hissed, "Now." They each activated a captured Japanese grenade and hurled them over the lip in high arcs. They didn't wait to hear the airburst explosions before activating and throwing the second and third in quick succession.

The explosions were muted, exploding over the lip of the ridge, but the yelling and screaming told them they were effective. They ran after the others as the ridge erupted with more slicing bullets and thumping explosions.

20

Major Hanscom was delighted with the small boat's progress up the sliver of the Pampanga River. Dominic had steered the boat through endless inlets and turns finally entering the river mouth. Hanscom was quite sure he'd never be able to find his way back. One inlet looked much the same as any other, but Dominic knew them like the back of his hand and was never in doubt.

Once out of the sometimes-shallow estuary and into the main river, their way became obvious. The ten-horsepower motor chugged against the lazy flow of the river and they made slow but steady progress. There were more people along the river and they passed many small villages and endless dikes, interlacing and connecting rice fields. None of the villagers paid much attention to them, though

The water route was by no means the quickest way to San Fernando, but they hadn't seen a single Japanese soldier, which made it worth the extra time. Taking the road meant passing through many checkpoints and their luck would only hold out so long.

Dominic steered the boat toward shore and Major Hanscom gave him a questioning look. Dominic said, "More gas."

Hanscom noticed a small dock sticking out from the bank. It was old and sagging and looked abandoned. As they approached, Miller and

Hanscom tensed seeing armed Filipinos stepping from behind the brush along the bank and advancing toward them. Dominic whispered, "Friends," and gave them a wave. One man waved back. Two of the six walked out on the dock and slung their rifles, while the others watched them. Hanscom exchanged a glance with Miller.

Dominic cut the motor and the boat drifted expertly alongside the dock. It was secured with short ropes and a quick conversation in Tagalog ensued. Hanscom's limited grasp of the language told him it was small talk between acquaintances. The exchange of gas cans was made. Dominic indicated they should move to the dock and he handed them their packs.

Hanscom and Miller stepped out. Hanscom was relieved to stretch his legs before the next leg of the journey. He extended his hand and introductions were made all around.

The Filipinos were young, but he could tell by their hard eyes that they were warriors. An older man stepped from behind a house, which had seen better days. He had a Japanese Arisaka rifle slung over his shoulder, which meant he'd either stolen it, or killed someone to get it. His face was a mask. He stepped up to the taller Americans and extended his hand. In near perfect English he said, "Welcome Major Hanscom. I'm Major Nieto."

Hanscom was startled but he grasped the offered hand and shook it. "Pleased to meet you Major Nieto. Have we met?"

Nieto shook his head. "Not personally. I know you from your dossier."

"My dossier? How could you have that?"

Nieto's lips turned up slightly, in what passed for a smile, Hanscom supposed. "It's my business to know who operates within my country, particularly Manila. After all, it's my zone of operation."

Hanscom gave a sideways glance at Dominic who stared back knowingly. "Well, I feel at something of a disadvantage. This is Staff Sergeant Miller."

Nieto nodded toward the enlisted man then shrugged. "I've been wanting to meet you, Major. We have a lot to discuss. Please follow me."

Hanscom looked back at Dominic who was still in the little boat. Dominic waved, pulled the engine to life and turned away from the dock, motoring downstream and disappearing in the mist-covered river. Sergeant Miller's eyes darkened at the sudden change in plans.

Major Hanscom stated, "I thought Dom was taking us all the way to San Fernando."

Major Nieto nodded and indicated they should continue following him. "Yes, but things have changed. Come with me. I will explain everything that's happened."

Hanscom and Miller were surrounded by the band of Filipino fighters and escorted through the dingy town. They weren't sure if they were under their protection, or under their thumb.

Hanscom pictured where he'd stuffed his pistol in the pack, knowing he wouldn't have enough time to get it if everything fell apart. He eyed Miller, whose steady, calm gaze belied the nerves he figured he must be feeling. He was thankful to have the stalwart warrior at his side. He knew he could trust both his sergeants, but Miller was always calm and cool in situations like this. He thrived on them.

There was nothing he could do at the moment except follow Major Nieto and hope he wasn't walking to his own execution.

Hanscom observed the town, noticing how the townspeople didn't necessarily avoid them, but they didn't greet them either. He had the distinct feeling that Major Nieto and his men were outsiders and weren't altogether welcome.

They entered a single-story building near the center of town. It looked like any other building, shabby and pieced together with various combinations of wood, mud and thatch. The inside was clean though and occupying the center was a table with benches.

Major Nieto said, "Please, sit down. You must be hungry and thirsty."

Hanscom's stomach growled at the mention of food and he suddenly realized he was hungry. He took off his wide-brimmed hat exposing his shaved head and sat on the bench. Miller took the seat on the other side of the table. "Thank you. Yes, we are hungry."

Nieto barked off quick orders in Tagalog and one of the young men hustled out the door. Nieto unslung his rifle and rested it against a beam near the head of the table. He took his hat off and sat heavily, letting out a

sigh and running his hand through his short-cropped hair. "This is a particularly heavy rainy season."

Hanscom nodded, "It's only my second one, but it does seem more
intense than last year."

"They are always heavy, but this one is heavier than most."

"Your English is excellent. Where did you learn it?"

Nieto squinted and Hanscom wondered if he'd slighted him somehow.
Finally, Nieto answered. "From the nuns at the orphanage where I spent my
formative years."

"So, you're a Catholic?"

He shook his head. "No. I never took to it. Too much guilt. Besides
there's no room for religion in a communist society."

Major Hanscom chose his words, "I knew there were communists here,
but I had no idea they were so..." he paused gauging the man. "Organized."

The edges of Nieto's mouth turned upward slightly. "Since the outbreak
of war, we have more freedom. I know that sounds strange, but the government — both ours and yours — kept close tabs on us. With the Japanese
invasion, that changed overnight."

Hanscom knew the rising threat of communism in the Philippines was
a topic of concern for the United States before the war. The country was
only five years away from independence. The US didn't want to give up
power only to see it turn into a communist country whose goals were inher-
ently opposed. But Hanscom didn't know of any overt, or even covert,
efforts to shut it down.

Hanscom folded his hands together on the top of the table and leaned
forward. "I hope we can put our political differences behind us and focus
on the Japanese threat to both our countries' freedoms."

"Of course, we have a common goal. It is why we cut your journey to
San Fernando short." Hanscom nodded and gave the stoic Filipino his
undivided attention. Nieto continued, "There's something happening on
the Bataan Peninsula which we need to discuss."

"Yes? What's happened?" He noticed Miller leaning forward too,
waiting for the answer.

Nieto looked from Miller to Hanscom. "Have you heard of a group
calling themselves '*Tark's Ticks*?'"

Hanscom looked at Miller, not able to keep the surprise off his face. Nieto raised an eyebrow already knowing the answer. Hanscom nodded, "We heard something about them right before we left. What about them?"

"They're a rogue American squad harassing the Japanese. They hit a large convoy, taking many weapons and vehicles which are still at large. They ambushed the pursuit team, killing them all and left their calling card."

"Calling card?"

"Yes, they leave playing cards with 'Tark's Ticks' written on them." Nieto stood and paced. Hanscom and Miller watched him closely. He finally stopped and leaned on the table. "Yesterday they hit a fueling station in the town of San Grif and nearly burned the entire village to the ground." He looked at each man, then continued. "Civilians died and many more lost what little they had. This type of attack will turn the population against us. This will make our struggle harder." He raised his voice and slammed his hand flat against the table with a sharp crack. "You must order this renegade band to stop operations before they kill more civilians."

Hanscom stood and faced the irate major. He wanted to remind him that the only way they'd ever get their country back would be with the might of the United States and her allies, but he reigned in his anger when he saw the slight shake of Sergeant Miller's head, warning him to tread carefully. "This is obviously news to us. We have no contact with them. As I said, we only just heard about them two days ago."

"You are an American officer. They are American soldiers. They must obey a direct order from you, or face court-martial."

"Yes, of course, assuming their commander doesn't outrank me."

"They are led by an NCO. A Staff Sergeant Tarkington."

Hanscom was stunned. "You have a lot of information, Major. It would help us both if we shared our resources and information."

Nieto dismissed it with a wave of his hand. "You have no resources. I have a strong network and you have a long-range radio to your countrymen who are battling just to survive. We will not wait around to be saved. We will take our country back with the strength of the people."

Hanscom leaned back, crossed his arms and threw caution to the wind. "That may be the case right *now*. But make no mistake, Major; the only way you take back your country is by kicking the Nips off first. An *uprising,*" he paused, "will only get a lot of your fighters and probably a lot of innocent civilians, killed. Eventually you're going to need us, and how you do things right now," he slapped his hand down, matching the crack of Nieto's. "Will make a huge difference."

Nieto's eyes narrowed and he leaned forward and sputtered, "Are you threatening me, Major?"

Hanscom shook his head and scrunched his mouth, "Nah. I'm just giving you a suggested path forward. Your decisions today will have lasting impacts on your outcomes tomorrow, that's all."

Nieto's face went neutral again and it looked as though it took all his willpower to do it. He cocked his head to the side and again his mouth upturned into a smile which didn't quite reach his eyes. "You will order *Tark's Ticks* to stand down?" he asked.

"Can you get us in contact with them?"

"They don't have a radio that we know of. The village we suspect they are operating out of is nearly impossible to find unless you're a local." He nodded, "But I will get you there. I'll send you tomorrow. One of my fighters knows the region and may be able to get the word out."

Hanscom nodded, "I have orders to investigate any resistance units and to make recommendations. I also have orders to confirm or deny Jap atrocities toward POWs. It's why we were heading to San Fernando. You must have news of such things?"

Nieto nodded. "Of course. Most of the POWs are northwest at a camp outside the town of Cabantuan." His eyes went even darker, "They were force-marched in the blazing sun, without adequate food or water. Many died on the march. Atrocity?" He nodded, "Probably by Western standards, but they are Japanese, a cruel people. I expect such treatment."

"Any idea how many died?"

He shook his head quickly. "No. But the road is littered with dead, both Americans and Filipinos."

Hanscom and Miller were roused a few hours before the sun rose, given a breakfast of rice and foul-smelling fish and hurried out the door and into the silent town. In the center of the road, four Filipinos wearing wide-brimmed hats and well-used shirts and shorts, stood with rifles slung over their shoulders.

The communist leader, Nieto, had left soon after their meeting the night before. Major Hanscom had replayed their conversation over and over in his head as he'd laid on his bunk. He didn't mean for it to become confrontational, but the brazen man had pushed him beyond what he could take sitting down.

Discussing it with Miller late into the night, they concluded that no real damage was done. They figured the man probably respected someone willing to stand up for their country rather than rolling over. In the end it didn't matter: they were on their own, many hundreds of miles from any overseeing US military officials. If they survived this war, they'd be happy to answer for any wrong decisions.

They strode up to the four shadowy figures. The Filipinos parted, faced them and one of them stepped forward with his hand extended. He had a genuine smile on his face. "I am Ignacio." He pointed to the others, "This is Rueben, and Taran." They each nodded as their names were called and Hanscom tried hard to memorize and match their faces with their names, but it was difficult in the darkness.

He touched his chest, "Major Hanscom and Staff Sergeant Miller, pleased to meet you. Which one of you knows the area we're going?"

Ignacio touched his chest. "I have been to the town we seek. It was when I was a boy." Hanscom thought he looked like a boy now. Ignacio continued. "Rueben and Taran know a little English. I can translate if needed."

Hanscom nodded, "Okay, let's get a move on."

They left the town behind them walking along the dark, deserted main road. The rain had stopped for the moment and the night was not as stifling or muggy. It was almost pleasant.

When the town was well behind them, Hanscom moved out of the single file line, moved to the front and walked beside Ignacio. He pointed at the rifle on his shoulder. "Aren't you worried about Jap patrols?"

He shook his head. "They do not patrol here. They are still concentrated in Manila. There are soldiers stationed on the peninsula too, but not here. Not yet. When we get to the peninsula, we'll be more careful."

Hanscom nodded, still wondering why they felt the need to show off their rifles. If there was no threat, what was the point? "We have pistols in our packs. Should we get them out? Is there danger here?"

Ignacio shrugged, "Yes there is danger. Not from Japanese, but other Filipinos."

Hanscom furrowed his brow wanting more information. "Other Filipinos?"

"Yes, other groups."

"You mean other factions of resistance fighters?" Ignacio nodded. "Has there been violence?"

Ignacio's lips pressed together as though remembering a personal memory. "No killing, but beatings. The next town won't join us even though they are communists too. Their leader is not a true communist. He only craves power."

"Will there be trouble?"

Ignacio shrugged, "Good idea to have your pistols out. But we'll slip through. They are lazy."

An hour of walking without seeing another soul, led them to the edge of another town. Hanscom and Miller had their pistols tucked into their waistbands but didn't have rounds chambered. The feeling of an early morning jaunt disappeared and Hanscom could feel the Filipinos tensing up with each step toward the town. There were no lights on, but the outlines of buildings were clear against the night sky. To Hanscom and Miller it looked identical to the town they'd just left.

Ignacio whispered, "We walk straight through. No stopping." He repeated the command to the two Filipinos, who nodded and shifted their rifles on their shoulders. Hanscom exchanged a glance with Miller.

Walking down the main street of a potentially hostile town in the wee hours of the morning, was a harrowing experience and a great way to get shot. Hanscom's head was on a swivel, imagining armed communists in every darkened window. The familiar, faint smell of human excrement wafted over him and he ignored it. It was a common smell, the sewage systems were still rudimentary by western standards and the overflowing water levels that came with the rainy season, didn't help.

They were nearly to the end of town when dark figures strode out from open doorways to the left. Ignacio's step faltered for an instant, but he kept walking, trying to ignore the growing presence.

When they were abreast of the figures, a gravelly voice called out in English. "Stop."

Ignacio didn't stop but answered with rapid-fire Tagalog. Hanscom heard him use Major Nieto's name. From the shadows more talking and this time anger was evident. Ignacio didn't respond but quickened his pace slightly. The gravelly voice came again, followed immediately with a gunshot and a bright muzzle flash, aimed into the sky.

Hanscom and Miller crouched and had their pistols out. Ignacio and the others stopped and had their rifles off their shoulders standing still as stones. Hanscom and Miller stood slowly. Ignacio said something, his voice menacingly slow now.

The tension was building. The shot brought out more figures from doorways and soon the way was blocked behind them too. In the darkness Hanscom could see the outlines of brandished weapons of all sorts. Some had rifles, others machetes and he even saw a few shovels and axes.

Miller mumbled to Hanscom, "This isn't good."

Hanscom couldn't believe the situation. Anger rose, he ground his teeth and stepped toward whoever'd fired the shot. He was short but broader than most Filipinos, his American-ness unmistakable when he wanted to show it. "Who's in charge here?" he demanded, striding straight up to the group. He put his pistol back in his waistband and placed his hands on his hips as though scolding school children.

A figure stepped out from the group, holding a smoking rifle. He spoke in broken English, "I in charge. Major Reyes my name. You in my town."

Hanscom felt Miller on his left side and slightly back. He hoped he hadn't put his pistol away. Hanscom extended his hand. "I'm Major Hanscom." The Filipino looked at his hand with disdain. Hanscom withdrew it. "There's no reason for hostility, Major. We aren't Japanese. We aren't your enemy. We need to pass through your town. We are on a United States Army mission."

Reyes looked confused and one of his men stepped forward and whispered in his ear, obviously translating. When he understood, he leaned back and laughed uproariously. Hanscom was ready to tear his throat out, but he internalized his rage and waited.

Reyes finally recovered, shook his head, mimicking the words, "United States Army." His face grew serious. "Gone. Lose war. No army here, only us." He smacked his chest.

Hanscom shook his head. Had the US lost so much credibility in such a short time, or was it just the communists wanting them to fail? He touched his own chest and smiled. "The Army is still here. *We're* still here," he indicated Miller.

Reyes listened to the translation and shook his head but moved on. "Where you go? What *mission?*" he butchered the last word.

Hanscom didn't fancy telling this blowhard anything about their mission, so he lied. "We're looking to organize resistance groups like yours. To integrate them in order to mount an effective campaign against the Japanese." He paused to let the translator catch up. Ignacio stepped forward to protest, but Hanscom looked over his shoulder and even in the low light, Ignacio could see the clear signal to stand down. Hanscom continued. "We have a common enemy. It's madness to fight among ourselves. This isn't about politics, it's about defeating the Japanese. That is the first and most important step."

Reyes listened and shrugged. "Japan will fail. Communists win." He spoke to his translator who translated to Hanscom. "It's only a matter of time. Only communism will win. It is the will of the people."

"Tell him, that's politics. We need to win the war first."

Reyes considered then nodded and spoke to his translator. "The major says, we will help you fight the war. He will send three men with your group, to give you safe passage through our territory."

Ignacio couldn't be restrained, "*Your territory?* Your territory doesn't extend beyond the borders of this town. We don't need your protection or permission."

Sergeant Miller moved fast knowing what was coming. He pulled his pistol, chambered a round and put it against Reyes's forehead. Nieto's warriors had their rifles leveled too. Reyes's men reacted slower bringing their rifles to bear on Miller's head.

Hanscom was stunned at the escalation, but he also knew it was the right call. There was too much hatred between these seemingly-identical groups. He pulled his own pistol but didn't chamber a round. He said, "We are leaving your town. You will do nothing to stop us."

It was translated and Reyes spat his reply. "No leave. You die."

Hanscom shook his head slowly and gave him a tsk, tsk, as though dealing with a child. "We're taking you, *Major*." Quick as a viper, Miller stepped behind Reyes, rested the muzzle against his temple and at the same time pulled his arm and lifted it painfully up the small of his back. He spun the stunned leader so that he was facing his men's rifle muzzles and walked backwards until he was beside Hanscom.

Hanscom raised his voice. "We won't hurt him as long as you don't try to stop us. We'll release him once we're safely away." The translator hissed the words angrily to his compatriots. They all looked ready to spit fire, but Reyes barked something and they looked at one another and lowered their rifles. "Good choice, Major," Hanscom said. "Now, let's be on our way."

21

By midday the five of them were well away from Reyes and his small town. They'd kept the surly communist with them for four kilometers then stopped off the road to see if there was pursuit. When they deemed there wasn't, they untied Reyes's hands and let him go. Ignacio wanted to kill him, insisting he was a detriment to the communist ideal and certainly a nuisance to Major Nieto. Inwardly, Hanscom agreed, but he couldn't bring himself to allow it. He hadn't fallen *that far* from the decency tree.

They'd waited until Reyes was out of sight, then cut overland, heading in a more westerly direction. Hopefully, Reyes would still think they were heading north. They had no doubt he'd send men to search for them, but in the vastness of the peaks and valleys, they'd have little chance of finding them.

The morning's intrigue was a memory and the more immediate need to hide from roving Japanese patrols became paramount. It still hadn't rained, although there were some nasty black clouds building in the distance. The lull brought out more traffic and twice they had to hide in the jungle as Japanese supply convoys trundled past.

The last convoy caught Hanscom's eye. He noticed a large contingent of soldiers manning mounted machine guns almost as if they expected to be attacked. He'd seen plenty of Japanese troops since the countries' capitulation, but none were acting the way these men did. He pointed it out to Miller, "Think it's because of *Tark's Ticks*?"

Miller shrugged, "Could be. San Grif, the town that was attacked, isn't too far from here. Maybe they're shaken up from that."

Ignacio heard them talking and added, "The peninsula always has a bigger patrol presence, but I agree. The guards looked like they expected to be attacked."

Now that they were out of rival faction territory, the Filipinos dismantled their rifles and carefully stowed them in oily rags in their small packs. Hanscom and Miller stowed their pistols, hoping they wouldn't need them again.

By evening they were still far from their destination. Ignacio walked beside Hanscom. "We will stay in a village up ahead. I know them. They won't ask questions."

"How far are we from San Grif?"

Ignacio equivocated. "Perhaps ten-kilometers due east."

"So, these folks will have some idea about the attack?"

Ignacio nodded, "They have friends and acquaintances there. Yes."

They entered the village without fanfare. The inhabitants were taking advantage of the rain lull and it was a hive of activity. One roof had three men on top, adding thatch where it must have been leaking. Other villagers were in the nearby woods. Upon closer inspection, Hanscom realized they were collecting small snails which writhed at the bottom of their baskets. Everyone was outside and everyone looked happy for the break.

Their entry into town didn't change that. In fact, Hanscom felt as though they saw strange men enter their town every day. Miller and Hanscom looked like Filipinos at first glance, but their American-ness was obvious upon closer inspection. But here, the locals didn't seem to care. He felt as though he'd gone back in time, before the Japanese invasion, when the Filipino people were genuinely happy to see Americans. He wondered if it was always like this on the peninsula or if it was simply a result of the break in the weather. No matter, it was refreshing.

Ignacio waved at people and they waved back as though he were a resi-
dent. Hanscom asked, "Is this your hometown?"

Ignacio shook his head. "I'm from Manila, but my father sent me here
most holidays to stay with my cousin's family." He directed them toward a
nondescript thatch, mud and wood hut. "They live here."

A woman came out of the door at that moment with an old broom and
began sweeping the dirt off the porch. She looked up when she noticed the
men approaching and immediately dropped the broom, put her hand to
her bosom and exclaimed, "Iggy." She poked her head inside and yelled.
"Iggy's here!"

Two middle school-aged children launched out the door and hugged
their older cousin. Ignacio smiled and patted and stroked their heads as
they held tight. "Hello cousins." He smiled at the woman who stood beam-
ing. "Hello, Auntie Mim." He broke free and hugged his aunt. "It's good to
see you." He looked beyond her, "Where's Jim?"

Her smile faded a little and she waved her hand west, "He's helping in
San Grif. I expect him home tomorrow."

Ignacio swept his hand back to the others. "Those two are Taran and
Reuben and those two are Major Hanscom and Sergeant Miller."

They all took their hats off in greeting. Aunt Mim smiled, "Hello. Americans or British?"

Hanscom stepped forward, "American, ma'am."

Her smile broadened. "I thought you'd all left. It's good to see you here."

Hanscom smiled back, thankful to find a friendly face. "Thank you,
ma'am. There's still a few of us around. But it's probably best to keep that to
yourself."

She glanced around the town, no one was taking any obvious notice of
the re-union. She waved them inside. "Come in, come in. You look tired."

Soon they were all crammed into the small but comfortably dry house.
Despite their insistence that they had their own food, she cooked enough
rice for them all and served them each a steaming cup of tea.

The sun set and soon they were sitting around the hut comfortably full.
Hanscom complimented her, "Your English is very good Mrs. Mim."

The two young boys laughed uncontrollably, and she tittered and
laughed too. "That's just what Iggy calls me. Mahilum is my name. Iggy

couldn't pronounce it when he was little. Shortened it to Mim. Always been such a smart young man," she teased.

More laughter from the others and Ignacio launched off the floor and tackled his nearest cousin who squealed in delight. The other dropped his bowl and threw himself onto the pile. They rolled around like bear cubs and laughter filled the room. Finally, Ignacio pinned both of his cousins and stepped off their chests. He held up his hands as though he'd just won the heavyweight boxing title. "I can still best you both," he chided.

Hanscom shook his head. The man who'd wanted to kill Reyes in cold blood just a few hours ago was still barely more than a child. He leaned over to the tsk, tsk-ing Aunt Mim and asked. "Your husband is at San Grif you said?"

She nodded, continuing to watch the boys' antics. "Yes, to help after the fires."

"Do you know much about that? What the cause was?"

She reared back and looked at him as though he'd grown another head. "Of course. It was you Americans who started it. *Tark's Ticks*," she said the last words with reverence and slight fear. "You don't know?"

Hanscom nodded. "I'd heard, but I wasn't sure. Do you know much about them? *Tark's Ticks*, I mean?"

"I'd have thought *you* would." He shrugged and she pursed her lips and continued. "They're a deadly squad of American supermen. They're ghosts, killing Japanese, taking ears as trophies and leaving the death's head calling card like avenging angels. The Japanese fear them and I would too if they were after me." Her voice changed and her eyes sparkled. "But they're not after us, no they're out for Japanese blood."

"But didn't they cause the fire in San Grif. Didn't civilians lose their lives?"

She nodded matter-of-factly. "Of course. It's war. Civilians always suffer ten times more than soldiers. It's always the way."

Hanscom nodded and noticed Miller leaning in, listening. "So, the townspeople of San Grif aren't mad or seeking revenge against *Tark's Ticks*?"

"Goodness, no." She clutched her chest as though the mere thought would give her a heart attack. She leaned in and in a lower, more conspiratorial voice, said, "We love *Tark's Ticks*. They are good at killing Japanese."

Hanscom and Miller exchanged glances. Hanscom asked, "Is it safe to go to San Grif? I mean for someone like me and Sergeant Miller?"

"You're obviously foreigners but you made it here without trouble. It's no different going to San Grif. There are many Japanese in the town, though. Be best to observe from afar."

Hanscom looked at Miller, "Be worth a look, don't you think?"

Miller nodded. "Be good to see effects of the attack. Might learn something about Staff Sergeant Tarkington and his men."

The next morning, they were up early saying their thanks and goodbyes. The boys were sad to see their older cousin leave but Ignacio promised to return and told them they should try to get stronger, so he'd have more of a challenge next time.

Once out of town, they moved slow, careful not to accidentally run into a Japanese roadblock or patrol. They knew a group of young Filipino men would attract attention.

If they were stopped, all bets were off. There was no way Hanscom and Miller could pass for Filipinos for long. If there was any doubt, one word would give them away as non-local, and without the fake vow of silence which protected them to some degree at the monastery, they'd be as good as dead.

They moved their pistols from the bottom of their packs to the top, so if they were stopped, they'd at least have a fighting chance to inflict some damage. The Filipinos would have no chance to put their rifles together, so if they were discovered, the plan was to run like hell and hope to lose them in the jungle. It was a terrible plan and in the back of Hanscom's mind, he knew the pistol's main function would be ending his own life before capture.

The reality was, if captured, he'd be tortured. He had no grand illusions that he could withstand it for long and keep silent about everything he knew about the monastery, the various resistance groups, and the many people like Aunt Mim who'd helped them along the way. It would be their death sentence, so he'd decided long ago that capture wasn't an option. Taking his own life was against every fiber of his being. He had no idea if he'd be brave enough to do it and he prayed he'd never have to find out.

It started raining and for the first time Hanscom welcomed it. The rains shut down movement, particularly Japanese movement. It was a steady rain, not the violent deluges they'd seen, but just enough to keep them wet and the roads muddy.

The road they were on was not a main thoroughfare, but a small track heading east to west. It climbed and descended peaks and valleys, cutting a straight path through. The Filipinos were in front, staying vigilant despite the rain.

Ignacio was in the lead. He suddenly stopped and motioned them to get off the road. They'd done so a few times during the day already and each time there'd been good reason. They didn't hesitate and scurried into the brush to find cover. Hanscom pulled his pack off and stuck his hand into the top flap, feeling his 1911 colt .45. It gave him a sense of reassurance, a connection to the past.

Around the corner, Hanscom heard sloppy footsteps then he saw the outline of people walking. He could tell right away they were villagers but it was better to stay hidden and keep their whereabouts secret as much as possible. You never knew if a villager might be working for the Japanese.

This time, though, Ignacio stepped out suddenly and gave the civilians a start. He didn't give them time to get upset. He opened his arms and rushed forward. "Uncle Jim. It's me, Iggy."

Jim's face went from startled to angry, to thrilled within seconds. He embraced his nephew, slapping his back. Ignacio pushed himself away, acknowledging the others watching the reunion. He spoke Tagalog and gestured and motioned, obviously explaining what he was doing there. He pointed toward the jungle and Hanscom, Miller and the rest broke cover. There was more murmuring among them and introductions were made.

Hanscom didn't like their presence being paraded around like they were waving a sign and said to Ignacio, "We need to keep moving. I want to see the town before dark."

Ignacio nodded and slapped his uncle's shoulder. They hugged again and soon the villagers were around the next corner and out of sight. "That was my Uncle Jim," he stated again.

Hanscom nodded, "I know. You introduced us. Look, I don't think it's a good idea to let every Tom, Dick and Harry we meet know about us."

"Tom, Dick and Harry?" He shook his head, "That was Efrin, Jose and Joriz."

Miller guffawed and Hanscom shook his head. "Look, the Japs have a handsome bounty out for American heads. The fewer people know we're out here, the better. Okay?"

Ignacio nodded but still had a confused look on his face. "My uncle would never tell the Japanese. He is family."

Hanscom put up his hands and nodded, "I know, I know, but who knows about the others?"

"The others are from the same village. They won't tell."

"Alright, alright, just try to keep us out of the limelight. How far is San Grif?"

He pointed at the next ridge. "Just over the ridge. It opens to a valley and San Grif is at the bottom. We'll leave the road soon and go through the jungle. We can see the town from the ridge."

An hour later they were perched on a ridge overlooking San Grif. They were far enough away not to be noticed. The rain was still steady, but not as heavy and the visibility was decent. It was obvious what had happened. Across from where they crouched, they could see what remained of three large metal gas containers.

Most of the metal was gone, but the concrete bases held what was left... jagged pieces of blackened metal. The remaining bowl-shaped containers were filled with rainwater and Hanscom bet there was a layer of gas on top. The condition of the containers told him the power of the explosions. He figured the tops of the containers must have flown hundreds of feet into the air and probably rained chunks of burning metal in every direction, not to mention thousands of gallons of fuel. No wonder half the town burned. It must've been one hell of a scene.

Miller gave a low whistle. "The tanks must've been full. There's almost nothing left of 'em."

Hanscom pointed out the Japanese soldiers. Some were working, but most were directing Filipinos in the clean-up crews. Instead of helping them rebuild houses, they were making them clean up the fuel depot area. Even days after the attack, San Grif still looked like a hellscape. Hanscom squinted and pointed at the low ridge line behind the gas containers. "Think they fired from there?"

Miller nodded, "That'd make sense. How'd they ignite 'em though? That's a long grenade throw."

"Yeah, you're right. Maybe they snuck in close."

Miller gave one shake of his head. "I'd sure like to meet these guys. This depot is *gone*. Japs'd be stupid to put it back up, too exposed and open to attack."

Hanscom agreed. "It's strategically placed, but yeah, doubt they'll do that again. The more attacks the harder things are going to get for these guys."

Miller nodded, "Especially when the rainy season ends. Something like this won't go unpunished. The Japs'll hunt 'em down."

Hanscom looked in each direction, north and south. The ridge he suspected they'd attacked from was on the southwest of town. It would make sense if they retreated that way. "Which way is the hidden village from here?" he asked Ignacio.

Ignacio pointed left. "South about a day's walk from here during normal times. Two days with the Japs."

"Well, I've seen enough. Will you be able to find it?"

Ignacio tilted his head back and forth, "It was a long time ago, but I remember the general area." He shrugged, "We'll see."

22

From San Grif, Ignacio led them south. They kept to the road but had Taran scouting back and Rueben forward. If anything came, they'd warn them. The Filipinos weren't worried, if they were seen alone, the Japanese wouldn't give them a second look, but everyone together might garner some attention, especially so close to San Grif.

The rain continued, and the few civilians they did see, kept their heads down. The roads were muddy but showed signs of vehicle traffic. It appeared the Japanese were still trying to use them. Some of the tracks looked fresh.

They pushed hard, wanting to take advantage of the mostly empty roads while the rain continued. They ate and drank while walking and by the time Ignacio stopped, it was nearly dark, and they'd made good headway.

"We are close. I thought it would take longer. We will stop for the night and have tomorrow to search."

It was welcome news to Hanscom, his feet were aching and he had multiple rub spots from the simple sandals he wore. Open sores didn't heal well in the wet conditions.

They moved off the road and found raised ground which wasn't as muddy and spongy as the surrounding area. Ignacio knew of another nearby village, but Hanscom didn't think it a good idea to be seen in the area, so they opted to rough-it. Despite the wet conditions, Hanscom was dog-tired and slept well beneath his small canvas poncho.

He awoke with a start when he felt a hand on his shoulder. He opened his eyes seeing Ignacio smiling down on him, holding a cup of something hot and steaming. "Tea," Ignacio offered and Hanscom sat up, feeling as though every muscle in his body had been stretched, and pounded with a hammer.

He took the tea, "Thank you. You built a fire?"

Ignacio nodded, "Small, no smoke."

Hanscom sipped the tea, it was weak but tasted wonderful. He was embarrassed to see it was light. He'd slept hard and even though his body ached, he knew his reserves had been replenished. "You should have woken me earlier."

Ignacio shrugged, "There's no hurry."

Miller came and sat beside him. "Good morning, Zeke."

Hanscom took another sip. "You get some of this?"

Miller nodded, "Hours ago, yes."

"Can't believe I slept that long. Feel like a damned teenager."

Miller said, "While you were out, Iggy and I took a look around. He's pretty sure we're close, as far as he can remember. We came across a village a couple of kilometers up the road. Looks abandoned. He remembers it when it was lived in. Said he remembers passing through it on the way to the hidden village. Kinda like a gateway. Remembers his father speaking with the head-man, getting directions."

"You sure it's abandoned?"

"Well, we didn't go inside, but the huts are falling down and there aren't any animals or anything like that. There's a few burned-out Army trucks shoved to the side of the road, but nothing recent."

Hanscom nodded, "Might be a good place to spend the night, if we don't find the village today."

Once Hanscom had eaten and done his daily duties, they left the camp and moved toward the village.

The Filipinos had their rifles reassembled and slung over their shoulders. It was a risk; an armed Filipino was strictly against Japanese rules. If spotted, they'd be considered resistance fighters and attacked on sight. But they hadn't been spotted yet and the added security the rifles provided, particularly in this area, was worth the risk. Hanscom and Miller had their pistols tucked into their waist bands, loaded and ready.

Ignacio led them along the same route he'd taken Miller on earlier and after an hour of bushwhacking, they found themselves at the edge of the abandoned village. There was no movement, but they sat and watched for a few minutes to be sure. Hanscom thought the village was probably once a nice place to live. It was close to the main road, yet far off enough not to attract too much attention. There were gentle terraced hillsides, which still looked intact, suggesting that the village was probably abandoned because of the Japanese invasion. He wondered where the villagers had gone. Would they return to work the terraced rice fields? Seemed an awful waste, if not.

Before entering, Hanscom suggested sending a sentry out to watch the road. If there were visitors, unwanted or otherwise, they'd most likely come from that direction. Ignacio agreed and sent Taran off to keep watch near the road. Satisfied that they wouldn't be surprised, they moved into the village.

Ignacio walked slowly past each building trying to remember boyhood memories of the place. Hanscom followed him, while Miller and Rueben went hut to hut, just in case someone was hiding.

They eventually joined them and Miller shook his head, "There's no one here. Things are in pretty decent shape still. Most of the floors are dry with a few exceptions, but I'll bet this place was occupied before the Japs landed." He shrugged, "Wouldn't be a bad place to spend the night if you wanna get outta the rain."

Hanscom nodded, "Was thinking the same thing."

Ignacio walked to the center of the village and sat down. Hanscom could tell the young man was frustrated. He hunched beside him. "Having trouble remembering?"

Ignacio pointed at a hut to the right. "I'm almost sure that was the hut my father and the village elder spoke in, but," he shook his head, "I'm not sure where we went from there."

"Would it be helpful if we did a walk around the perimeter? We might find a trail or something."

Ignacio nodded and got to his feet in a quick fluid motion. Hanscom stood and both his stiff knees popped and protested. He ignored it as best he could, but he was reminded that he wasn't a young man anymore. This walking for days on end through the jungle was taking a toll.

Ignacio pointed to the southernmost section and said, "Let's start from that end. I have an idea the trail goes south then west."

They called Taran back and moved off, pushing their way into the brush on the edge of the village. Normally this area was probably cut back and kept clear but the quick-growing jungle plants filled in the area thicker than before and they were forced to push through. The foliage lessened once they were thirty yards in.

Within minutes they came across an old, overgrown trail leading south. Ignacio shook his head, "I don't know if this is the way."

Hanscom shrugged, "Let's follow it and find out."

The jungle was encroaching heavily on the trail, but they were able to follow it easily. It meandered and wound up and through hills and valleys. They were cautious, not wanting to stumble onto a Japanese patrol. Hours later they were many kilometers from the village. They stopped and filled canteens from a stream. The water was a little cloudy with silt from the high flows of the rainy season, so they sat and let it settle to the bottom of their canteens. Hanscom asked, "Does this seem right? It doesn't seem to be leading us toward any kind of valley and it's still heading south."

Ignacio knit his brow and answered, "I think it should've veered west by now."

Hanscom pursed his lips and asked, "Should we keep going or head back to the village?"

Ignacio looked pained to say it, "I — I think this is wrong. I've wasted our time."

Miller shook his head, "We've still got time to get back and find another trail before dark."

Ignacio nodded, "Yes, we should head back. We can move faster now that we know it's safe."

They retraced their steps back to the village in silence. Ignacio was obviously embarrassed to have led them astray. He kept up a fast pace trying to make up for lost time. The rain continued on-and-off and their outgoing tracks were still there but fading. They were soaked from brushing past wet leaves and the exertion and warm air kept them sweating.

When they deemed they were close to the village, Hanscom pushed Miller forward. "Slow Ignacio down." Miller trotted forward and finally caught up to him. Ignacio was annoyed but understood the need for caution.

They regrouped and approached the village slowly. Miller whispered to Hanscom, "Something feels off."

Hanscom nodded, agreeing. He signaled a halt and they hunched and conferred on the trail. Hanscom whispered, "Something's different."

Ignacio looked annoyed, wanting to get on with the search, but Taran spoke into his ear and Ignacio's gaze changed from annoyed to cautious in an instant. He whispered, "Taran feels it too."

They moved slowly up to the buffer of thick foliage and stopped to listen. The rain increased and the drips and slaps of raindrops hitting leaves and puddles was all they could hear at first. Then there was a hint of something else. A human voice, barely discernible but everyone heard it and hunkered lower. There were more voices, some louder. Hanscom recognized the harsh tones. "Japs," he whispered.

They froze in place unsure what to do. Minutes passed and Hanscom was about to move them off the trail in case they were being tracked. He nearly pissed himself at the sound of gunshots.

They dove to the muddy ground. Hanscom and Miller pulled their pistols and quickly chambered rounds. They expected more shooting and charging Japanese, but instead there was nothing. Then another volley of shots. Hanscom brought his pistol up and the muddy muzzle wavered as he aimed into the thick brush, but nothing came.

Ignacio looked back at him, his eyes panicked, ready to bolt. Hanscom put his finger to his mouth, urging him to remain quiet. Ignacio licked his lips and nodded. He turned back to the threat. There was talking and yelling and Hanscom recognized Japanese *and* Tagalog. Ignacio looked back again, the panic replaced with confusion, he'd heard it too.

Hanscom needed to know what was happening. He signaled Miller to push forward. Miller nodded and slithered past him on his belly, the sticky mud making slurping sounds. The mud made it difficult to get good purchase with his sandaled feet, so he veered off the trail and pushed into the thick foliage. Ignacio followed and Hanscom pushed to the edge and watched them move slowly.

He continued to hear voices. Miller and Ignacio were difficult to see now. He looked to his right where Taran and Reuben were still as stones. He held up a hand for them to stay put and they nodded, happy to do so. He pushed forward and realized the thirty yard thicket was easier to traverse at ground level. He followed Miller's and Ignacio's track and soon came upon the soles of their sandals, side-by-side. He scooted up beside Miller and froze.

They were ten yards back from the edge of the village and peering between two thatch huts into the center of the village. There were Japanese soldiers aiming rifles at Filipinos. Some of the Filipinos held rifles, some bows and small pistols. Near the back of the group, a Filipino had his hands wrapped around another Filipino's neck. He slammed his head down, released his grip and pulled himself off the motionless man. Even from forty yards, it was obvious the man was dead, his extended tongue and oddly-angled neck, left little doubt.

The relief of realizing they weren't the target of the gunfire made Hanscom feel better about his chances, but the mystery unraveling in front of him was maddening. *What the hell is going on?* At first glance, it looked like a confrontation between Filipino resistance fighters and Japanese soldiers, but something else was happening. Why were they in the middle of the village? Surely, they wouldn't attack the Japanese in the open, and why had one Filipino strangled another?

The mystery grew as they watched the Japanese separate eleven Filipinos from the others and march them to the edge of the village, almost directly in front of where they watched. Hanscom had to remind himself to breathe, worrying they were close enough to hear his heartbeat. They watched in silent fascination as the Filipino who'd strangled the other, was imploring the Japanese officer. It occurred to Hanscom that they seemed to know each other. Miller turned his head, catching Hanscom's attention, and mouthed, 'what-the-hell'.

Hanscom had no answer but watched in horror at what was obviously about to happen. The eleven Filipinos were forced to kneel and the soldiers behind them held rifles at port arms. Another officer approached, a junior officer. He held up his hand and uttered quick orders. Rifles were raised and aimed at the defenseless Filipino's backs.

Miller reached out and squeezed Ignacio's arm hard enough for him to look over in anger. Miller shook his head with a stern look, the message obvious: don't do anything stupid.

The order was given, the hand went down, and the rifles barked in unison. The kneeling men flopped forward. The junior officer turned away from the slaughter and Hanscom could see the disgust on his face at what he'd just done, but it didn't lessen Hanscom's hatred of the man. Words were uttered and an NCO with a pinched face stepped forward and put an additional shot into each of their heads, silencing moans.

Miller continued to clutch Ignacio's arm, making sure he didn't react. Hanscom looked over Miller's back and saw the anguished look on the young man's face. It was heartbreaking, but he knew if they'd tried to stop it, they'd be dead too. He glanced behind but couldn't see Taran or Reuben. He figured they must be pulling their hair out with worry. He hoped they had the sense to stay put.

What followed was even more bizarre. The Japanese forced the remaining Filipinos at gunpoint to move west into the jungle.

They stayed in cover until they were sure everyone was gone, and only then did Hanscom speak. "What the hell just happened, Sergeant?"

Miller shook his head slowly. "I have no idea, Zeke."

Once they were sure the Japanese were gone, they moved back and explained the situation to Taran and Reuben. The relief on their faces as they emerged from the brush was obvious. Hanscom figured they were moments away from bolting.

They huddled together and Hanscom whispered, "I don't know what's going on, but they seem to know where they're going." He focused on Ignacio, "You said the village is west of here and that's the way they're headed. Wonder if they're going there?"

Miller nodded, "It would make sense. Perhaps they're forcing the Filipinos to show them the way. Maybe they tried to resist and that's what led to the executions."

Hanscom nodded, "None of it is good news. Means they know where Tark's Ticks are holed up, and they've got hostages."

Miller said, "We've gotta warn 'em."

Ignacio joined in, "I may not remember perfectly, but I only remember one entrance to the village. I don't think we can get in front of them."

"Do you remember how far from here it was? Even an estimate?" Hanscom asked.

Ignacio nodded, "I remember we left in the morning and walked at least half the day. The trail was narrow and beautiful. I remember it was a big secret and my father felt honored to be entrusted with it."

Hanscom considered, "I don't think we have any other choice — we've gotta follow 'em."

They checked rifles and pistols and moved around the edge of the village, carefully. The tracks of so many men were easy to find. They followed and soon were on a muddy trail. There were sandaled tracks but also the distinct notched toe of a Japanese infantryman's boot.

They moved slowly, careful not to catch up with the Japanese rearguard. The trail moved through sparse jungle, weaving in and out of small trees and brush, but headed generally west.

The sudden crashing of gunfire sent them sprawling to the ground, scrambling for cover. The occasional bullet whipping through the jungle overhead kept them low, but the amount of gunfire didn't match up with the incoming fire. That, and the fact that the shooting was much farther away than it would've been if the Japanese were firing at them, led them to believe that, once again, they weren't the targets.

There was distant yelling ahead and more shooting but as quickly as it started, the intensity stopped. There were a few random shots but soon the jungle was quiet.

Hanscom exchanged a nervous glance with Miller. Once again, they had no idea what was happening. This confrontation was much more intense than the earlier one. There was still yelling, orders being barked, interspersed with the cries of men in pain.

Hanscom didn't like his location. If the Japanese moved back, they'd be directly in their path. He got to his feet, keeping low and signaled them to follow him to the right, off the obvious retreat path. They hustled into the thin jungle and it was all Hanscom could do not to break out in a sprint. He felt as though he'd be seen any second and shot. He felt fear creeping up from his gut. He hated the feeling, but it kept him moving, despite the burning in his legs.

Miller bolted ahead and finally stopped and crouched, breathing hard. Hanscom slid in beside him and turned back the way they'd come. He glimpsed the three Filipinos still crashing through the jungle full-tilt. He waved his arm to get their attention and Ignacio veered toward him, the others following close behind. They were soon all together, looking back the way they'd come.

Once Hanscom got control of his breathing, he strained to hear but there was no more shooting and he could no longer hear yelling or moaning. He concentrated on the area they'd just left, hoping they were far enough off the trail not to be seen. The silence was maddening. He had no idea what was going on and didn't like the feeling. Slow minutes passed and still nothing.

Hanscom heard a commotion from behind and turned to see Ignacio signaling him frantically. The look on his face wasn't fear, but excitement. He exchanged a glance with Miller and motioned for him to stay put. Miller nodded and continued watching the jungle.

Hanscom stayed low, moved to the still smiling and waving Ignacio. When he was beside him, he asked, "What is it?"

Ignacio punched his chest proudly. "I found the trail." He pointed behind him. "It's back here. Near those rocks."

Hanscom said, "Show me." Ignacio nodded and moved back toward two large boulders covered with bright green moss. Rainwater streamed from the moss forming a large puddle of clear water around the rock base. It looked like the puddle was most likely there all the time, like a natural spring.

Ignacio crouched in front of the boulders which leaned against each other but seemed to be joined by the moss. It looked like one solid mass of rock. Ignacio pointed, "It's here. When I saw this, I remembered."

Hanscom could only see a wall of moss. "I don't see it," Hanscom stated. Ignacio stepped into the spring, his muddied, sandaled feet dirtying the water. He moved to the rocks and pushed against the moss. It flexed and moved as though it were a curtain across a window. He pulled and lifted and the whole mossy front moved. Ignacio pointed beneath and Hanscom leaned down and looked beyond the mossy wall. Instead of solid rock, there was a dark passageway. He couldn't see more than a few feet, but there was no doubt it was a passageway. "Wow, that's amazing. Are you sure this is it?"

Ignacio nodded with vigor. "I have no doubt. I remember the moss doorway. I'd forgotten, but when I saw it the memory returned."

Soon they were all in front of the spring. Ignacio held the moss door aside as best he could and Hanscom led the way into the darkness, his pistol ready. The first few feet were lit by the daylight from the entrance, but once he rounded a corner, it was pitch black. He held his free hand out, feeling like a blind man in an unfamiliar room.

The ground was firm and there was a strong earthy smell. He had the feeling the ground here was dry, as though the recesses were well-protected even at the height of the rainy season.

He moved fifteen feet before he saw a tiny shaft of light coming through like a solid beam. He moved toward it like a moth to light, then turned and waited for Miller to catch up. He heard, rather than saw him and he whispered, "Up here." His voice seemed to be absorbed by the walls.

Once he saw Miller's faint outline, he moved forward, and the little shaft of light showed him that the ceiling was high enough to stand easily.

More light ahead and soon he came to the end of the natural tunnel. This end was also well-hidden by a cover of moss, however it wasn't as thick, allowing countless shafts of light to stream through.

Hanscom went to the edge of the moss and found a peephole to look through. The outside was wet and looked dismal. He was loathe to leave the dryness but pushed the moss curtain aside. It was heavy with wetness. His shoulders strained to keep the curtain open as he passed through, letting the heavy curtain flop back into place, once he had passed. He marveled at how it immediately hid the entrance through the rocks.

He felt exposed, and crouched, sweeping his pistol side-to-side. When he didn't see any threats, he took in the most beautiful canyon he'd ever seen. He was standing on a well-used trail. Ahead, he could see it winding toward an impossibly narrow canyon covered with almost fluorescent green moss and little dots of color from wildflowers growing directly out of the rock walls. The walls were incredibly steep and looked impossible to climb, even with ropes and climbing gear.

He heard Miller grunt as he pushed the moss curtain aside and stepped onto the trail. He looked around and gave an appreciative low whistle. "It's like we've stepped into another world."

Hanscom nodded his agreement. "It's beautiful."

Soon they were all out of the tunnel and gaping at the incredible beauty of the place. Ignacio's smile was ear-to-ear and he kept nodding. "I remember this place. I remember the flowers." He sniffed, "You can just get a hint from here."

Hanscom sniffed and nodded his agreement. "Wonderful. And this leads to the village?"

Ignacio nodded more vigorously and wiggled past them until he was in the lead. "There's only one way to go," he said pointing. He trotted ahead and the infectious beauty of the place had them all trotting along, despite their fatigue.

Soon they were in the tight confines of the canyon and just like Ignacio remembered, the walls were covered in fragrant pink, red and purple flowers. The place was downright magical and they felt like they were on a tropical sight-seeing expedition rather than a combat patrol.

That feeling disappeared when an arrow zinged into a thick root snaking along the trail like a massive boa constrictor. The thud and twang of the arrow burying itself was startling and they froze in place. The walls above them were suddenly filled with men aiming notched arrows and rifles down upon their heads. They'd walked right into an ambush.

There was a harsh voice from one of the men holding a rifle and Ignacio answered haltingly in Tagalog. A quick exchange and Ignacio turned to Hanscom and happily gave him the news, "They are from the village. We've found them."

23

The grenade attack on the ridge made the Japanese cautious and allowed enough time for Tarkington and his men to retreat up the final slope without harassment. The cadets manning the Type-92 heavy machine guns at the top of the ridge, were eager to unleash hell as soon as the Japanese were in sight.

They were alarmed to see their leader, Angelo Fernandez's body. Tarkington had refused help and carried the young man's body up the slope, draped over his back. He laid him on the ridge and looked down the slope. The low brush wouldn't provide much cover for the Japanese. He wondered how many were left.

He motioned to the body and addressed Cadet Trujillo. "You and the rest of the cadets take him back and tell Vindigo the Japs are coming and have men ready to drop the bridge." The cadets manning the machine guns looked sideways at him and Tarkington addressed them. "You stay on the guns, but the rest of you get back to the village." The two crews looked at one another with broad smiles.

They looked like children and for a moment Tarkington considered sending them back with their compatriots. Losing Fernandez, who was following his orders when he died, was tearing him up inside. The thought of losing more cadets was almost too debilitating to contemplate, but he knew they'd been trained on the heavy guns and were the best men for the job, even though they weren't old enough to shave. The image of Fernandez's head snapping back and falling, with that damned goofy grin frozen on his face, assaulted him and he had to shut his eyes and shake his head. "Dammit," he uttered under his breath.

Winkleman was beside him and saw his agony. He knew there was nothing he could say to make him feel better, so he simply put his hand on his shoulder and squeezed.

Tarkington opened his eyes and shook it off, grumbling something. He moved off behind the gun emplacements and ordered. "Okay Ticks, let's spread out and see if these sons-of-bitches wanna play some more." He glanced over his shoulder in time to see the retreating cadets — Fernandez's body between them — heading toward the village.

The rain continued in spurts: sometimes heavy, sometimes light, but always present. The cadets had dug water outlets leading from the foxholes and trenches out the back and downslope. The holes were by no means dry, but there was no standing water, which made them almost luxurious.

The machine guns were forty yards apart and the GIs filled in the gaps with their rifles and knee mortars. Tarkington ordered them to dig out the trenches. The work kept them occupied and warm and it was always best to be prepared, even though, if all went as planned, they'd be leaving the ridge soon after contact.

Tarkington checked on each machine gun emplacement reminding them that they weren't staying long and to be ready to break down the guns and sprint back to the bridge upon his order. He had Eduardo with him, and he repeated the orders in Tagalog to make sure they understood. He didn't want to lose any more men, particularly to anything as stupid as a misunderstanding. *I've already killed one man with my stupidity,* he berated himself.

Midday came and went and still the Japanese didn't come. Tarkington wondered if perhaps they'd lost too many men and had turned back. He was on his belly beside Henry, who was chewing on a piece of grass, watching the wood-line. He had his Springfield propped on a piece of wood. Tarkington wondered, not for the first time, how he could stay vigilant all the time.

Tarkington asked, "You think they'll come?"

Henry shrugged and spat the piece of well-chewed grass out. "Time'll tell."

Tarkington looked at his scratched and battered watch. He was amazed the thing still worked. "Been four-hours since the ridge battle." He looked to the sides of the slope, there was no way to get around them. This ridge was much like the other, only this one was wide all the way to the top — not as much of a funnel, but equally deadly to assault.

He wouldn't blame the Japanese commander if he'd decided to turn around and fight another day, he'd lost a lot of men over the past two engagements. But he knew, that wasn't how the Japanese thought. He'd seen them throw men at stout defenses, losing hundreds and doing the same thing the very next day. Losses didn't seem to have any effect on their commanders usually, but perhaps this commander was different. "Wonder if we killed the Jap head honcho? That might explain them not coming after us."

Henry nodded slowly, "Yeah, or maybe he's getting more..." He stopped and cocked his ear.

Tarkington noticed his lead scout suddenly go rigid. He hadn't heard anything but knew Henry didn't spook easily and when he did, it was worth heeding. A second later Tarkington heard a noise he hadn't heard since the Japanese general assault many months before...the whistling of incoming mortars. He yelled, "Incoming! Get down!"

He rolled into the trench, thankful he'd insisted they deepen them. Even though he was below ground-level, he felt exposed and wished he were deeper.

He listened to the increasing whistle of mortar shells then cringed as the shells exploded just in front and showered him with mud and debris. More were on the way and he knew the next batch would land directly on the ridge.

He curled into a ball and held his hat tight to his head, as though the thin-woven straw would stop shrapnel.

The shells landed and he felt the impacts in his bones as the ground shook. The muddy conditions dulled the sounds of the explosions and even dulled their effects, the soft ground allowing the shells to penetrate deeper before exploding.

More shells exploded and Tarkington felt the weight of mud across his back. He was glad for the extra protection but started to worry that he might be buried alive. He stayed down, letting the mud pile higher. More impacts landed behind the ridge, the Japanese gunners sweeping the entire area.

He took the opportunity to shimmy forward. Mud slid off his back and he continued forward, feeling the weight lessen. Finally, his head was out of the hole and he could see down the slope. He spat out dirt and mud and tried to see through the rain and debris still coming down. It took him a moment, but he saw shapes scrambling up the hill.

He yelled, "Japs coming up!" More whistling of incoming mortars and another round of shells landed on top of the ridge, making him push his face as far into the mud as possible. When the shells stopped, he pulled his dripping chin from the mud. Soldiers were still coming and were now ten feet closer.

He felt for the hardness of his submachine gun and found it near his right leg. He yanked and it pulled through the mud as though he were pulling it through taffy.

He wiped the mud off the top and stuck his finger into the barrel, trying to clear it. Before he could get his weapon ready to fire, he heard the loud thumping of both heavy machine guns. The crack of rifles joined and he was relieved to know that at least some men were still alive and able to defend themselves.

He leaned out and aimed his submachine gun, then quickly ducked when a bullet passed so close that he thought he glimpsed it. He scooted backwards a foot, wondering if he were in the sights of a sharpshooter.

The shelling stopped for the moment, so he rolled right taking himself out of the hole. He scooted forward and when he didn't get shot, fired a short burst at the dull green of an enemy soldier. He missed badly and forced himself to concentrate. He fired again and this time he saw his bullets impact the ground in front of the soldier and the Japanese soldier dropped out of sight, either hit or taking cover, he didn't know which.

He watched tracers slice down the hill, crisscrossing the slope from the two heavy machine guns. The cadets were firing long, then short bursts, laying down a withering and deadly wall of lead. Once again, he found himself impressed with the young Filipinos.

For the first time, he noticed what he figured was the same Japanese Nambu machine gun from the earlier attack firing up the hill. He couldn't see where it was coming from so he ignored it. He fired a burst at a lunging soldier. The soldier was crouched low and he saw at least two of his bullets hit his back. He dropped flat onto his face again.

He heard the whistling of more mortar shells over the intense volume of fire and yelled, "Incoming!" He rolled left and felt his body sinking into the safety of the hole. He shifted onto his stomach and curled into a ball, keeping his weapon close to his chest. The machine guns continued firing, despite mortar shells landing on the ridge.

He risked poking his head up. Despite the machine gun fire, the Japanese were advancing steadily under the cover of the mortar fire. He needed to get the men out of there before they got too close. If he waited too long, they'd be shot in the back as they retreated, but standing up in the middle of a mortar barrage was an excellent way to sprout holes.

He yelled, hoping to be heard over the din of combat. "We have to go! On my count everyone throws a grenade then we move out! Leave the machine guns!" He heard Henry relaying the message, so he knew at least a few would get it. The others would see what was happening and hopefully follow suit.

He pulled a mud-covered, Japanese grenade off his belt. He hoped it would work in the harsh conditions. He got to his knees, staying bent over as much as possible. He took a deep breath, pulled the cotter-pin, armed it with a hard slap and yelled, "Now!" at the same time hurling it as far as he could.

He clutched his submachine gun and pushed himself straight backwards, despite the whistling of more incoming mortar shells. He threw himself down the hill, immediately tangling his feet in undergrowth. He pitched forward and tumbled ten yards before he rolled to his feet again. He jammed his feet in, slipping in the mud and spun back toward the ridge he'd just abandoned. Men were running, falling and rolling as they tripped in their haste to escape. He had his submachine gun in his left hand and he waved frantically with his right, "Hurry up! Come on, move it! Move it!"

Men streamed past and he tried to count, but it was impossible. Explosions on the ridge sent him to his knees. He kept his submachine gun aimed, ready to shoot anyone coming over the top. He saw the machine gun crew on the right, laboring down the hill, one hauling the heavy machine gun, the other the tripod. "Leave that shit! Leave it!" he yelled but they either didn't hear him, or were ignoring him. He didn't see the other crew. He looked downslope, seeing GIs but no cadets.

Dammit, he cursed to himself. He couldn't leave them up there. He yelled to the struggling Filipinos hauling the machine gun, "Where are the others?"

They finally looked over at him as they passed and between labored breaths one uttered, "Gone. Dead. Direct hit."

Tarkington's jaw rippled as he clenched his teeth. "You sure?" he asked. He clutched the nearest cadet's arm, the one who'd spoken. He nodded, not able to speak.

His attention was drawn back to the ridge, it was filling with helmeted soldiers holding rifles with bayonets attached. He glanced down the hill, his men were halfway to the safety of the jungle. They weren't going to make it.

He aimed and fired a long burst, sweeping the ridge until his magazine ran out. Soldiers crumpled and spun away as his bullets impacted flesh. He ducked, swapped magazines and fired again. His target, a soldier getting on one knee to fire, pitched forward as three bullets tore into his chest and legs.

Rifles swung his way and he threw himself down as bullets snapped over him, some smacking into the mud near his head. He was exposed, with little cover. *This is it,* he thought. He cringed, waiting for the bullets which would tear him apart, but they didn't come. Instead, there was the thumping of grenades exploding on the ridge. He watched Japanese leap for cover, some hit by flying shrapnel.

He didn't wait for an invitation. He got to his feet and sprinted, taking huge strides down the hill. His speed overtook his ability to move his legs and with his last touch, he lunged forward, sending himself flying like a crazed circus attraction. His natural inclination to somersault saved him from breaking his neck and he rolled to his feet as though he'd planned it all along. Despite being the last to leave the slope, he was not the last to enter the jungle. Men he passed watched him literally fly by.

He crashed into the jungle. The cadets he'd sent away earlier were bracing knee mortars on the ground, firing up the ridge. He briefly noticed other faces he didn't recognize, Western faces.

With the Japanese taking cover on the ridge, they ran to the raging creek, followed it upstream and crossed the bridge. There were intermittent shots as the Japanese probed for them, but none were close.

"Everyone across?" Tarkington asked Winkleman.

He nodded, "Everyone that's coming."

Tarkington signaled the villagers holding machetes to the ropes, which were holding two trees' trunks down. They slashed them and sprang out of the way. One tree trunk extended upward, lifting the nearside of the bridge, but the one stretching across the creek snapped with a noise that was far more ominous than the Japanese mortars. The extra weight of the nearside tree pulling upward was too much for the strain on the other tree.

On the village side, the massive log was two feet off the ground and swinging slowly side-to-side, but the far-side was still firmly planted. The men saw the intact bridge and got to work trying to pull the log. If they could get it to move three feet, the end wouldn't be supported and would fall into the creek.

It was obvious after the first try that more men were needed. They dropped their weapons and put their backs into it. They were grunting and heaving, Stollman calling cadence, 'one-two-three-pullllll,' over-and-over. Inch-by-inch it moved closer.

Tarkington was pulling with everything he had, when he heard Henry yell, "Japs!" Henry's rifle cracked, he worked the bolt and fired again.

Over the din of the raging creek blasting through the tight canyon, Tarkington heard more shots, incoming. He felt the thud of bullets embedding in the wood. He saw flashes of green uniforms darting through the jungle. He didn't see many, but they kept up a steady stream of fire keeping them from moving the bridge.

"Stolly and Raker stay with me. Rest of you get your weapons and keep 'em off us."

Henry was on his belly, firing between two boulders. The rest of them spread out among the rocks, some fading back to fire from the cover of the trees. Soon the steady return fire slowed the Japanese. Tarkington yelled, "We need to push the log sideways. It's too heavy to pull."

The other two saw what he meant to do. They adjusted and put their shoulders into the log. It moved easily, still suspended by the rope. Once it had moved a couple of feet, Tarkington yelled to the nearest man, someone he didn't recognize. "You," the man's face was stark white. He pointed at himself as though to say, 'Me?' Tarkington strained to keep the log in place, sweat streamed off his nose and dripped onto the log. "Yes, you. Cut the damned rope. Now."

The man to his right, another unfamiliar face, fired his pistol then leaped over the other man. "I got it, Zeke." He moved fast. Pulling a sheathed knife from his belt, he slashed the rope and it snapped with a twang.

The log dropped and they sprawled over it as it suddenly dropped away. It was right on the edge of the cliffside, inches from crashing down, but not quite there. "Dammit," exclaimed Tarkington.

The man with the pistol said, "Just needs a little help." He put his shoulder into it and the others joined him. The log finally broke its bond to the land and the edge dropped into the churning creek. The stranger nearly went in right along with it, but Tarkington grabbed his shirt and pulled him back from the abyss. "Shit, thanks," he gasped once safely on the bank.

The log hesitated, then the current caught it and the water's immense power pulled it down further and soon yanked the far side off the bank and it plunged into the muddy water and disappeared. Seconds later it resurfaced and smashed into boulders, before finally wedging in the center of the stream, creating a fan of water which sprayed twenty feet over the top of the canyon walls.

The three of them gaped like children and Tarkington was reminded of he and his brother, Robert, spending entire afternoons throwing pieces of wood into rivers and watching them spin downstream. The sound of gunfire and the snapping of bullets overhead brought him back to reality.

He got on his belly and yelled, "Fall back! Fall back to the village!" He scooted backward, scooping up his submachine gun along the way. Once he was back twenty yards, the sound of the whitewater and the shooting lost intensity. He got to his feet, and staying in a crouch, hustled down the hill toward the village. Soon he was walking beside the two newcomers. "Who the hell are you two?"

The white-faced man had recovered and Tarkington saw he was older than the other. He gave a short grin and extended his hand, "Major Hanscom of the former I Corps Intelligence, and this here is Staff Sergeant Miller, also I Corps. You can call me Zeke, if you prefer."

Tarkington felt the ingrained urge to brace up and salute, but under the circumstances it seemed ridiculous, so he shook the major's offered hand, then shook Miller's. "I don't know where you came from, or how you got here, but..." he stopped in his tracks and put his hands on his hips. "How the hell, *did* you get here?"

Hanscom pointed to more men Tarkington didn't recognize — Filipinos. "That young man knew about this place. We happened upon the trail and were met by villagers guarding it. They brought us here a few hours ago. We heard the firefight and those young Filipino cadets insisted we give you a hand."

Tarkington nodded and kept walking. Hanscom kept looking back nervously. Tarkington shook his head, "They won't find a way across that creek until the water drops and that won't happen for a few more weeks." He wiped his brow, realizing he'd lost his hat somewhere along the way.

He looked around at the men making their way through the thin jungle. Every Filipino he saw had a smile and they were talking excitedly among themselves. The GIs looked tired but they smiled too. They'd dealt a heavy blow to the Japanese force and had gotten away with it.

He looked around and found Winkleman. "Wink," he called and Winkleman trotted up to him, eyeing the newcomers. "What's the..."

Winkleman cut him off, "Two Filipinos unaccounted for, but the other gun crew said they took a direct mortar hit. They're sure they're dead." He frowned, "We've got three wounded. One seriously." Tarkington looked around, not seeing anyone being helped along. Winkleman shrugged, "It's Yancy, one of the cadets. Took a bullet in the side, but refuses a stretcher." He pointed in the general direction. "Tough little bastards."

Tarkington nodded, then introduced Winkleman to their new arrivals. He didn't salute either, but shook their proffered hands. Tarkington saw cadet Trujillo and called to him. "Sergeant Trujillo, get Yancy a stretcher for chrissakes. He'll bleed out if he's not careful." Trujillo jumped at his name being barked, but nodded and sprang away, calling Yancy's name. Tarkington shook his head, "Welcome to the nut-house, gentlemen."

Captain Hanscom nodded and grinned, "And *Tark's Ticks*."

Tarkington looked at him in surprise and shook his head, mumbling to himself, "Great, just great."

24

Captain Gima looked over the bodies of his dead soldiers, hatred building in his soul. He and his remaining men had retreated away from the flooded creek to the relative safety of the jungle. The dead were lined up side-by-side. He walked by their booted feet, being sure to look at each man's contorted face.

He didn't have proof that the group who'd wreaked such havoc on his men, was Tark's Ticks, but he didn't doubt that's who he faced. Once again, they'd got lucky and got away, but this time he knew exactly where they were. He'd sent men up and down the cursed creek, searching for a way across. They returned, telling him they'd found nothing. In both directions the creek disappeared into craggy impassible canyons. The crossing the enemy had used was gone, whisked into the raging creek.

A full day had passed since the battle and as he looked the dead over, he came to a decision. "Lieutenant Amano," he barked.

Amano was sitting on a rock, rubbing his hand through his longish hair and thinking about all the letters he'd need to write. The burden of his men's deaths weighed upon him, pulling him deeper and deeper toward depression. He was not a hands-on commander and didn't even know some of their names. He'd never had to write letters to parents and wives, and was dreading the experience which might take days to finish.

He heard the now familiar bark of Captain Gima. He took a deep breath and blew it out slow, adjusted his officer's hat and walked along the muddy, spongy ground until he stood beside Captain Gima. "Lieutenant Amano, reporting sir."

Gima didn't look at him, keeping his gaze on the bodies. "Take Sergeant Ono and another from your platoon back the way we came. Take the car south and tell Colonel Ikada the situation. Tell him we've trapped a large resistance cell of Americans and require more men and ammunition." Amano was about to respond, but Gima continued. "Before you leave get the rest of your men looking for stout trees near the creek which can be felled to get us across."

Lt. Amano nodded, "I understand, sir." He couldn't keep the relief off his face. The thought of breaking away from this bloodbath made him want to smile.

Gima noticed and ground his teeth, then said, "We won't attack until you've returned with the required men and materials." He handed a sheet of rice paper to the suddenly deflated junior officer. "Give them this, it's a list of what we need." He slapped him on the back. "Hurry back, Lieutenant. I'll consider any delay an act of treason."

Lieutenant Amano blanched and went ramrod straight. "Yes, sir."

It had been four days since Staff Sergeant Miller and Captain Hanscom had departed the monastery. Sergeant Gonzalez had gotten word from Dominic upon his return, that he'd dropped Miller and Hanscom with the communist cell and that their mission had been changed by Major Nieto.

Gonzalez had never heard of Major Nieto and wasn't happy with the news, but there wasn't a damned thing he could do about it, so he carried on with his normal daily routines.

He was sitting in the radio room, it was 1430 and he hadn't heard anything from Papabear. He sat on the wooden stool and peered out the tiny window, scoping the new arrivals into Manila Bay with the well-worn binoculars. He jotted down his observations using the nub of the pencil. The little notebook was filled with entries and the writing got smaller and smaller as new information was entered, trying to extend the life of the scarce paper.

The radio suddenly squawked and there was a burst of static, which nearly made him fall off his chair. He scooted to the radio, flipped a page in the notebook and readied his pencil. An American voice broke through the static. "Victor, this is Papabear. How do you read? Over."

Gonzalez keyed the mic, "Papabear, this is Victor. I read you loud and clear. Over."

"Victor, Papabear. Instructions follow." There was a pause as though the speaker was passing the mic, or preparing to read a document. Numbers and nonsense phrases followed. It was a long transmission and by the time Gonzalez had it all down, his hand ached from using the tiny pencil.

With the sign-off — 'over' — Gonzalez keyed the mic one last time and read it back quickly. He didn't like how long they'd been transmitting and was relieved when Papabear finally signed off.

He pulled out the decoder book and matched phrases and numbers and, after two-hours, had the full decoded transcript in hand. With no one to report to, he simply stayed put and read it over carefully. He shook his head and made sure he'd done it correctly. When he was satisfied, he read it again and whistled. "They think we're miracle workers?" He shook his head.

He looked around the tiny room and sighed. He murmured to himself, "Well, guess this is the end of this." He pulled the battery out of the radio and placed it to the side, beside the secondary radio. He picked up the heavy hammer in the corner and slapped it onto his palm, testing its weight and durability. He stood over the radio and though every instinct in his body screamed against it, he slammed the hammer down over and over until the radio was left in pieces.

He tucked the battery into a fold of his robes and carried the second radio, still packed in the secure case, down the spiral staircase. He made sure there were no other monks in sight, hurried to his room, and shut and wedged the door with a shaped piece of wood.

He stowed the new radio beneath his bed, it wouldn't pass scrutiny but he didn't plan on having it there long. He hid the transcript and code book in a displaced brick in the wall, having to move his pistol and spare magazines to the side. Then he left the room and made his way to Brother Sinjin's chambers.

He stood in front of the huge double door and knocked. He heard Sinjin's papery voice and the doors opened. Gonzalez had met with Sinjin on multiple occasions but never in his own personal chambers. He stepped in, looking to the side, and when he didn't see anyone, wondered how the doors opened. He didn't ponder it long. Sinjin was standing facing him, his bright eyes staring unflinchingly into his own. Before Gonzalez could speak, Sinjin stated, "You will be leaving us."

Gonzalez looked confused, "How — ?" He stopped himself, knowing the answer would be even more mysterious. He nodded, "Yes. I have orders which I must deliver to Major Hanscom in person. I'll need Dominic, if that's possible."

Sinjin nodded, "Of course. I'll send for him when we're done here. Will you be returning?"

"I don't have orders to leave, so I assume we'll return, if you'll have us, that is."

Sinjin's gaze hardened, "I feel this will be our final meeting, but if the fates are wrong, you will always be welcome here. But I fear..." his voice trailed off and his eyes seemed to lose focus as though seeing something Gonzalez couldn't. He came back to this plane and continued, "No matter. We will always be friends with those who fight tyranny and evil."

Gonzalez nodded and gave a slight bow of respect. "Thank you, Master Sinjin. The message I received is quite specific with the timeline. I don't know if it's even possible, but the sooner I leave, the better."

Sinjin bowed, "I will send for Dominic right away. Meet in the foyer in fifteen minutes."

Colonel Takashima got an urgent call and was pulled out of a meeting to answer it. He was annoyed at leaving a meeting he'd instigated, one whose outcome would let him know once and for all his pecking order in the intelligence-gathering for the region.

He was head of Army Intelligence and in charge of the city of Manila.

The constant appropriations of funds and material away from his units by the head of the Kempeitai in the region, Colonel Nakata, had finally come to a head and was being addressed. Now he was called away urgently before the issue had been resolved.

He apologized, left the room and saw Lieutenant Aki standing there, looking nervous for disturbing his commander, but also excited. He braced, saluted, and Takashima saluted back, "This better be important, Lieutenant."

He bowed and handed him a paper. "We intercepted another message and we have a good idea where it came from. We had all our triangulation equipment nearby and the message was long. We have narrowed down the area to two city blocks, sir."

Takashima looked at the coordinates and nodded, "Excellent. This is perfect timing. Come into the room and give your report to General Kaya and Colonel Nakata."

The color left Lieutenant Aki's face but he managed to utter, "Yes, sir."

Without preamble, Takashima burst back through the ornate doors. Before the occupation, the building had housed the local government, now it was where the occupying forces planned and instigated their policies to keep the people in-line.

Takashima interrupted a conversation between General Kaya and Colonel Nakata with his quick entry. He sized them both up, knowing that whatever was being discussed was exactly why he didn't want to leave them alone. Colonel Nakata was a master manipulator, and despite his lower rank, Takashima had little doubt he'd send a veiled threat, backed by the Kempeitai, that Kaya should back him or either his career, or that of his family members, might suffer.

Takashima didn't hesitate and presented the flustered junior officer. "This is Lieutenant Aki. He's just intercepted a communique in Manila, using the triangulation radios we only just recently got back from Colonel Nakata."

All eyes were upon him and Lt. Aki nodded and bowed, clearly intimidated to be among the high-ranking officers. "Yes, that is correct." He looked at Colonel Takashima who gave him a slight nod to continue. Aki looked at the note he held, "We triangulated the transmission to a two-block radius in the center of Manila."

General Kaya looked pleased. He stepped to a wall with a large mounted map of the city. "Show me where."

Aki nodded, licked his thin lips and moved to the huge map. He looked at the coordinates and the tiny map he held and tried to correlate them. After a minute of impatient silence the heavily sweating lieutenant finally pointed to an area not too far from Manila Bay Harbor. "Here," he said, and used his pencil to draw a thin outline around the area.

All three officers moved forward and Colonel Takashima spoke up first. "Thank you, Lieutenant. Dismissed." Once the lieutenant was out of the room Takashima turned back to the map. "I know this area well. I'll have my men sweep it as soon as we're out of this meeting." He gave Colonel Nakata an imperious look then continued, "Of course we could have found them much earlier if Colonel Nakata hadn't *borrowed* half our units earlier when the previous transmission occurred." He hesitated wondering why Nakata wasn't squirming beneath his blatant attack. Was the man so stupid he didn't even know when he was bested...or was it something else?

General Kaya cleared his throat. "Excellent work, Colonel Takashima. Your men should be commended for a job well-done." The general looked him square in the eye and Takashima bowed his head slightly, glowing with success. The general continued. "Colonel Nakata will be taking over the investigation. He will sweep the area and round up this resistance cell."

Colonel Takashima's head shot up, and his eyes showed first confusion, then stark anger. He balled his fists, straightened his arms and sputtered, "I'm in charge of Manila. Army — Army Intelligence has jurisdiction here, not the *Kempeitai,* sir."

General Kaya nodded, his mouth turned down and he lifted his chin as he looked at him. "Yes, but that has changed. The city is now in the able hands of the Kempeitai and Colonel Nakata. They have more experience keeping tabs on groups of people. They have more resources and are better suited for it. Army Intelligence is for keeping tabs on the enemy."

"Aren't resistance cells the enemy, sir?"

General Kaya was not used to his orders being questioned by junior officers. His voice tightened and he said, "That will be all, Colonel. Turn over all intelligence to Colonel Nakata right away. You are dismissed."

Colonel Takashima had no choice but to swallow his pride, salute and spin on his heel. As he passed Colonel Nakata he hissed, "I'll make you pay for this, *Colonel.*"

Colonel Nakata smiled and said, "Excellent work, Colonel. I'll expect a full briefing from you within the hour." Takashima kept walking, muttered something unintelligible and left the room.

General Kaya said, "You might have trouble with him. Let me know if you do."

Nakata nodded and bowed. "He's a good officer. An *Army* officer. He's by the book. He won't like it, but he'll do it." He smiled but it didn't reach his eyes. "If I need your assistance, I'll be sure to ask for it, sir." *The day I need your help will be the day I die, you pissant little cockroach.*

After studying the section of the city where the transmission originated, he mashed his finger onto an area marked as a monastery. He looked at the junior officers surrounding him. They were all brutally accomplished Kempeitai officers with years of combined experience rounding up and doling out justice to those deemed to be threats to the cause. "Here is where we'll begin. We'll find our terrorists here. I'm sure of it."

Minutes later, they mounted black sedans and led a procession of three troop trucks, filled with Japanese soldiers, along the soaked streets of Manila. They splashed through deep potholes filled with muddy water and skidded and slid over muddy sections from overflowing creeks and ponds.

They finally arrived in front of the ancient monastery gates. Colonel Nakata stepped from the lead vehicle and stood in front of the locked gate. He'd visited here once before when they'd first entered the city. He remembered being made to wait while an old monk shuffled out and unlocked the gate with a huge steel key. He wasn't going to wait this time.

He nodded to the nearest officer, Lieutenant Jin. An order was given and two soldiers with long crowbars and one with a sledgehammer hopped out of the back of the first troop truck and hustled to the gate. They held their tools ready and Nakata nodded for them to continue.

Crowbars were inserted above and below the lock where the two parts of the door came together. The burly soldiers pulled hard. The ancient door screeched as metal bent backward and exposed the lock mechanism. Holding their crowbars steady, the soldier with the sledgehammer expertly lifted it to the sky then let the weight of the head work with his own strength. The sound was like a shotgun blast. The metal housing shattered and bent, destroying the locking mechanism at the same time. The soldiers pulled and the gate swung open easily.

At the same instant the lock was destroyed, the same old monk from months before came shuffling out the front door holding a key. He stopped when he saw his services were no longer needed. He stared at the gate as though he'd lost an old friend. Nakata had his Nambu pistol out. As he walked past him, he slammed it into the monk's face. The old man dropped to his knees holding his gushing nose. "You should be quicker next time, old man," hissed Nakata.

The other officers streamed past the bleeding monk, followed by a platoon of soldiers holding rifles with fixed bayonets. Colonel Nakata got to the huge, ornate front door and before he could pull it, it opened and there stood Master Sinjin with all the monks lined up behind him, their hands tucked in their sleeves and their shaved heads down. "Colonel Nakata," Sinjin said in Japanese giving him a partial bow.

Nakata sneered, "You remember my name? How quaint." His voice hardened, "Bring all your flock out and stand them in the courtyard while we search the monastery."

Sinjin stepped aside and motioned for the monks to file out. They shuffled past him, never raising their heads and soon were standing in neat rows in the courtyard facing back toward the monastery. Sinjin asked, "What are you searching for, Colonel?"

"Spies. American spies," he hissed.

Sinjin shook his head, "There are no Americans here, but you're welcome to search."

Nakata's jaw rippled and through gritted teeth, said, "I'm not asking for permission. You can make it easier on yourself by telling me where they are. I don't want to have to destroy anything of value."

"As I said, you won't find what you're looking for, so I've nothing to tell you."

"We'll see about that." He waved his pistol at the soldiers surrounding the monks. "Search the place. Don't leave a stone unturned."

For four hours, the monks stood in the courtyard in the rain while the soldiers tore their home apart. They weren't allowed to chant — the soldiers put an end to it by brutally beating the monk who'd started it — but they couldn't keep them from meditating and, despite standing for hours on end and being wet to their core, they didn't shiver or complain. Indeed, they looked as comfortable and composed as if they were inside, warm and dry.

Colonel Nakata finally stepped out of the front doors with a sneer on his face. It was something he practiced in the mirror and he'd perfected it. He walked up to Sinjin and thought he might have to slap his face to bring him from his meditation, but as he neared, Sinjin's sparkling eyes opened and he met the sneer with a small smile. "Did you find what you were looking for?"

Nakata nodded and stared into Sinjin's eyes. He lifted a half brick. "We found this in a tiny hidden room set off from the spiral staircase which leads to the tallest spire. The room was empty, but not as dusty or as full of spiderwebs as some of the other odd rooms we found." He looked behind him and pointed up the tower, "There's a tiny window which looks out over Manila Bay. The perfect vantage point to report ship movements. This," he hefted the half-brick, "Was in the wall, pushed in a little too hard, giving away the hiding place. It was empty of course, but there's no doubt it was recently used and emptied."

Sinjin's face didn't change, still the same half-smile and his eyes still sparkled. Nakata dropped his arm holding the brick and looked at the ground. He slowly brought his eyes up and in a low voice full of malice, said, "Tell me where they've gone and I won't burn this place to the ground with your flock inside."

Sinjin's expression still didn't change. Nakata's breathing increased and a vein coursing across his forehead pulsed. He brought the brick up and

smashed it down upon the top of Sinjin's head again and again, forcing him
to his knees. Blood sprayed and by the fourth blow, Sinjin's skull caved in
and he dropped to the ground. His body convulsed unnaturally as his
blood mixed with the mud of the country he loved.

Nakata finally stopped and looked at the monks, most still had their
heads down and were swaying slightly, mourning their leader's passing. He
yelled, "Where are they? Where did they go?" but no one responded or
even made a sound. Nakata pointed to the nearest monk. "Bring him
to me."

The nearest soldier walked behind the man and pushed him with his
rifle until he stood in front of Nakata. "Where did they go?" he asked. The
monk didn't respond but kept his head down and his hands tucked into his
red sleeves. "Kill him," Nakata ordered.

The soldier only hesitated for an instant before he lunged and buried
his bayonet into the monk's back, the tip poked out just below the sternum
and the monk stared at it, then slid off the blade and fell at Nakata's feet.
Blood spread quickly from his ruptured aorta. "Bring another." The next
monk stood beside the body of his brothers and Nakata asked the same
question. Again, there was no answer. Nakata signaled and the same soldier
thrust his bayonet into the man's back, yelling as he did so. The monk
looked Nakata in the eye, coughed blood into his face before his knees gave
out and fell beside Sinjin and the other monk.

Nakata was incensed. Bloody spittle dripped from his chin. He strode
forward, pushing his way violently past monks until he came upon a man
in the third row. He put the barrel of his pistol against his forehead and
pressed hard. "Where are the Americans?" he yelled in English. He
repeated it in his limited Tagalog and again in Japanese. When there was
no answer, he fired and the monk dropped as though he were hanging from
a line that had been cut. The man behind was covered in blood and brains
but he barely reacted as bits and pieces of his brother dripped off his
shaved head.

Nakata was shaking with anger but he knew killing more monks would
do nothing, they weren't going to tell him anything. He spit venom, "Burn
it. Burn it to the ground."

Filipinos from miles around came running when they heard the news that the ancient monastery was on fire. They came to help put the flames out but were kept away by the platoon of Japanese soldiers.

Soon, the soldiers were forced to move further away, the heat from the flames scorching their backs. The monks who'd called the sacred building home for most of their lives stood outside the gates and watched the flames reach toward the heavens. Some had streaks of tears down their cheeks, not for the monastery but for Sinjin and the others whose bodies smoldered and threatened to ignite in the heat.

25

A day after they'd crossed the creek, Tarkington watched the cadets bury Fernandez in a grave beside a meadow used for grazing animals. They chose his spot beneath a large tree. The plot of ground was relatively dry but they kept the grave shallow to avoid the seeping ground water.

The body was wrapped in a cloth shroud, his rifle inside with him. He was lowered into the hole carefully and the cadets stood around staring into the grave.

They looked to Tarkington and he realized they expected him to say a few words. He scowled, not knowing what to say. Winkleman punched his arm and Tarkington murmured, "Give me a minute, dammit." He took a deep breath, blew it out slow and raised his voice. "Sergeant Fernandez was a good man..." he hesitated and shook his head, "Hell, he was little more than a boy. But his courage and leadership, his dedication and his love of country and of his men was fiercer than any man I've ever known. He died too young, there's no doubt about that, but he'll always be remembered as a hero and a leader of men." He looked around at the cadets who were staring into the hole, one or two of their lips quivered and some shed tears, but most were stoic, doing their best to hide their grief, to act like men. "I don't know much religion, so someone else should do that bit."

Winkleman nodded, cleared his throat and said the words which would comment Fernandez's soul to eternity. When he was done, he nodded at the shovel bearers and they filled in the hole.

Tarkington turned away and Winkleman was beside him. "It wasn't your fault, you know." Tarkington didn't respond. "This kind of crap's what happens in war, Tark. Young men die."

Tarkington shook his head. "You and I both know it didn't need to happen. I ordered him to expose himself to fire on the off-chance he could hit that machine gunner. It was a fool's errand." He shook his head, remembering Fernandez's smile despite the hole in his head.

"You couldn't know what..."

Tarkington turned quickly to Winkleman and slapped his shoulder, turning him so they were face-to-face. "Don't try to make me feel better, Wink. I fucked up. I know it and I'll deal with it, but shut your damned mouth before I do it for you." Winkleman gave a quick nod and Tarkington pushed off, clutching the hilt of his sword.

Stollman and Vick, along with a few villagers were arrayed along the side of the creek, watching for enemy activity. Since the battle the day before, they hadn't seen any Japanese, but Tarkington doubted they'd just leave. He wanted to keep guard in case they figured out a way to get across.

Stollman was lying between two mossy boulders with his canvas poncho draped over him. Despite its many holes, it kept him relatively dry and trapped his body heat, keeping him warm despite not having moved for over three hours. He'd hauled the captured Japanese light machine gun out there with him. He knew it was overkill for the mission, but he wanted to get to know it, the way he used to know his BAR.

He had the bipod out, bracing the flared barrel. That, along with the thirty-round banana-shaped magazine coming off the top made the weapon look ominous and powerful. He'd fired a few hundred rounds, getting used to it, but he longed to fire at live targets. Many times over the past few days, he'd wished he had the Type-96 LMG, but had to settle for killing Japanese with his type-38 rifle.

He sighted down the barrel, making micro-adjustments, getting used to the prone position behind the weapon. His mind was wandering. The sound of hacking brought him out of his daydreams. He lifted his head, trying to see through the mists rising from the wet jungle. More hacking sounds and he decided it sounded like an axe against wood.

He pulled the poncho off his head and looked to the right, searching for Vick. He couldn't see him, but knew he was somewhere in the mist. He sneered thinking, *lazy bastard's probably asleep.* The sounds from the jungle continued, cementing his assumption of axe against wood. He still couldn't see anything except jungle and mist.

Half an hour later, he heard the groaning of bending, then breaking wood, followed by a crash as a large tree went down. He saw movement in the jungle caused by the tree's fall. He focused, looking for troops but only saw the shaking of nearby trees and bushes. He looked at the overhead cover and deemed it too thick for a knee mortar to bust through. He was sure that if it was more open, the cadets would be able to do some damage.

Vick was suddenly beside him, making him jump. "Dammit," he hissed. "Don't sneak up on me like that."

Vick whispered, "I didn't sneak, asshole. You're just deaf." They both scanned the jungle. "See anything?"

"Saw where the tree went down, but no Japs."

Vick nodded, "I'm gonna head back and tell Tark about this. There's only one thing I can think they'd be doing."

Stollman looked back at him and at the same time they said, "Bridge."

Vick smiled, nodded and slapped his shoulder. "I'll be back. I told Cirio I was going, so don't worry about them."

"Hope one of 'em sticks their head up," he caressed the LMG, "I'd love to use this beauty."

"Seems like you'll get your chance. I wouldn't bust her cherry before I get back though." With that, he hustled toward the village. Stollman watched until the mists enveloped him, then he refocused forward, scanning the jungle.

It didn't take long before Stollman heard scuffling behind him. He turned and waved when he saw Vick leading Tarkington. He saw others on the flanks moving forward slowly.

Vick and Tarkington lay beside Stollman. Tarkington asked, "Any more tree falls?"

Stollman shook his head, "No, but I heard voices, they're still out there."

Tarkington nodded, "I thought we might've whittled 'em down enough to turn 'em back. Wouldn't take much for them to fall a tree across the creek."

Vick whispered, "That's what we thought too. Don't know why they're falling trees that far back, though."

There was more scuffling behind them and soon Major Hanscom and Sergeant Miller were beside them too. "What've you got, Sergeant?" Hanscom asked.

Tarkington shrugged, "They're still out there and Stolly and Vick heard a tree being felled."

"Think they're building a bridge?"

"That or bunkers, but there's no reason for bunkers that I can see."

Stollman looked from the major to Tarkington and wondered if there was some kind of power struggle going on. The major obviously outranked Tarkington, but he was also new to the show. The major seemed like an okay guy, not the normal starched officer he was used to, but he decided then and there, if there was some kind of bullshit rank jockeying, he'd follow Tarkington, army regulations be damned. As far as he was concerned, they were no longer operating in the regular army, they were on their own and Tarkington hadn't steered them wrong yet.

Tarkington didn't hesitate to order, "If they come close," he pointed at a good-sized tree directly across from their position, "and start looking to cut trees that can span the creek, open fire. But I'd rather not get into a sniper battle."

Stollman nodded, "Got it, Tark."

Tarkington put his hand on Vick's shoulder. "Pass that along to the others and get them moved to areas with big trees across from them. I'll send more men up here with you. Those cadets are already itching for more action." He shook his head, "These bastards aren't gonna wait for the creek to drop."

Captain Gima didn't allow his whittled-down platoon to rest for long. The wounded were helped as much as possible, the more critical cases sent back on makeshift stretchers. There were two soldiers he doubted would make it in time to be saved, but there was hope for four others. The lightly wounded were patched up and allowed to rest, but would still be expected to fight when the time came.

He figured it would take two, perhaps three days before Lt. Amano returned with more men and supplies. He intended to make use of the time and be ready to cross the creek and attack the village as soon as possible. The creek was a formidable obstacle and he didn't have enough men or ammunition to continue the fight even if it was low enough to cross.

He crouched in the jungle, he could see the near edge of the creek but the far bank was obscured by the ever-present mist. He hadn't seen or heard the Americans since the battle the day before, but he was sure they were there, just out of sight.

He'd thought all day on how to cross the creek without exposing his men too much. There were a several trees close to the creek which would work for his purposes. The trick was to be able to cut them down near the bank without exposing his men to hostile fire while they did it. Of course, darkness would help, but he needed something more.

He glanced at Sgt. Uchida. "I want the men to cut down trees well back from the creek. Have them cut them into manageable lengths, say four-meter segments. They'll need to be light enough to be moved easily and lashed and stacked together once in place. Understood?"

"Hai," he bowed, then added. "We have no axes or saws, sir."

Gima scowled and looked hard at his sergeant. "They have entrenching tools and knives. I'm sure you'll be able to fashion some kind of cutting tool, Sergeant."

"Yes, sir," he turned and left.

Stollman was relieved of his position just as the light was fading from the sky. It had rained on and off but nothing heavy. The cadet who replaced him looked impossibly young. Stollman reminded him not to shoot unless they were trying to cut down trees near the creek. Of course, at night it would be hard to see what they were doing, but the sound would be easy to discern he hoped.

The rain started in earnest the moment he stepped into the village and he sprinted to get inside a hut before getting too wet. He ate, cleaned the LMG and slept for a few hours. Then it was his turn to relieve the cadet. There'd been no shots during the night, which was good news. He knew Raker, Henry and Skinner were out there on the line making sure the cadets didn't start shooting at shadows.

He and the other relief gathered in the early morning darkness and moved out. They all wore wide-brimmed hats and the GIs had their tattered ponchos, but the downpour made staying dry impossible.

Vick and Eduardo were beside him in the gloom as they sloshed through mud and pools of water. Once they were near the line, they stopped and Stollman murmured, "See you in a few hours, numb-nuts."

Out of the gloom, Vick answered, "Don't get your LMG pregnant."

Stollman wanted to quip back but nothing came to him, the miserable conditions seemed to dull his sharp wit. "Fuck you," was all he managed to come up with, but the dark shapes of the others were already out of sight and his voice was lost in the noise of the downpour.

He walked forward hoping he could find the cadet in the darkness. He found the boulder he had used as a marker and knew the cadet should be a few yards further along. He crouched, doubting he needed to, but old habits were hard to break and had kept him alive this long.

When he was sure he was close, he went lower and moved forward slowly. He saw the cadet's sandaled foot. He froze and listened for heavy breathing, hoping the kid wasn't asleep. When he didn't hear it, he tapped his foot. The cadet nearly jumped out of his skin. Stollman shushed him and slid in beside him. The ground was spongy and he felt the wetness soak his front. The cadet was shivering uncontrollably but he was wide awake. "You okay, Trujillo?" Stollman asked.

The lead cadet nodded, his lower lip shaking. "Just — just cold out here."

The air temperature rarely dipped below seventy-five degrees, but Stollman knew that laying there in the rain was cold, no matter how warm the air. He whispered to him, "Need to get you guys some of these." He touched his poncho, and Trujillo turned but couldn't see anything in the dark. Stollman asked, "You see or hear anything?"

Trujillo's shaky voice answered, "Yes. Wood cutting mostly. Not close though. At least, I don't think so."

Stollman nodded, "Guess we'll find out when the sun comes up. Get back to the village and warm up. You did good." Without another word Trujillo pushed himself to his feet and shuffled off into the darkness. Stollman slid into the spot, placed the LMG between the two rocks, and extended the bipod. He draped the poncho over himself, but he was already hopelessly soaked. He settled in and waited for the sun to rise.

Two hours later, it was light enough to see the edge of the creek, but the heavy rain kept him from seeing the other side. The ground was saturated, there were multiple rivulets of water coursing into his spot and pooling beneath him. His body warmed the water and he felt as though he were bathing in a tepid kiddie-pool. He wasn't cold yet but he felt he'd have to move soon if it didn't stop raining.

Finally, the cadence of raindrops on his poncho changed. It was slackening, then as though someone had hit a switch, the rain stopped. He sighed in relief and gazed over the flared barrel of the LMG. The after-rain mist was just starting to form and his view across the creek was momentarily unhindered. He tensed and pulled the LMG's stock tight to his shoulder. *What the hell is that?*

Across the creek and in front of a large tree, which would easily span the creek if cut down, was a neat stack of log segments stacked one on top of another. It was a few feet high and formed a low wall around the base of the big tree. It looked as though the Japanese tried to camouflage it but they'd failed. He knew right away what the Japanese had in mind.

He pivoted his sights, searching for any targets but didn't see anyone. They were either well-hidden or had faded back into the jungle after their night's work. *Tark's gonna wanna know about this.*

Captain Gima was pleased with the results of the night's work. The heavy rain had been both a blessing and a curse. It allowed his men to work without worrying about noise, while also keeping them hidden, but made the ground slippery and dangerous for tree cutting. The men had worked hard, their improvised axes making the job last three times longer than it would have if they'd had proper tools, but they persevered and were well on their way to putting his plan into place.

After the hard night's work, he let the men pull back to eat and sleep. Despite the heavy downpour, he'd heard many rumbling snores from hammocks and ponchos. The men were exhausted. They'd endured a lot of hardship over the past week and he was proud of them. Even the few remaining soldiers from Lt. Amano's platoon had risen to the occasion, proving to him once again the superiority of even the lowliest private in the Imperial Japanese Army.

He'd slept through most of the night's work, allowing Sergeant Uchida to oversee the project. He awoke before dawn and crept forward to see their work. There was still more to do, but he was pleased with their progress. Once the reinforcements arrived and a few more barricades erected, he'd be able to cross the creek and crush the enemy.

As soon as the men were rested and fed, Uchida put them back to work, hacking down more trees, well back from the creek-side. The wounded collected and cut vines to fashion into ropes, which were used to lash tree segments together. They dragged the cut segments as close as they dared, just out of sight of the men they knew would be waiting to shoot them. The business of pulling them forward, lashing them together and lifting them into place would be done at night. Hopefully the weather tonight would be as miserable as the night before.

Captain Gima was overseeing the wood cutting when he got word that Lieutenant Amano would be there with reinforcements soon. Captain Gima didn't show it, but he was beside himself with excitement. Amano had done what he had ordered and got it done faster than he thought possible.

An hour later, Lt. Amano reported in, "Reinforcements have arrived as ordered, sir," he stated, with more confidence than Gima had seen in the young man so far.

"Excellent work, Lieutenant. How did you get back here so quickly?"

"Command was already mobilizing to find out what had become of you and your men. We radioed from the car, and directed them how to find us. I requested everything you ordered, and they complied without question. They used troop trucks despite the muddy roads and made good time. Once we disembarked, we marched all night and into today. There're still more men coming, they are slowed by the supplies, which we loaded onto donkeys. I suspect they'll be a couple more hours, sir."

"Excellent, excellent." He looked the men over, they looked tired but far fresher than his men. He saw Platoon Sergeant Ono sitting on a rock, one of his boots off, rubbing his feet. "Sergeant," he barked, and Ono's eyes shot up and he stiffened. "Take ten men back up the hill to assist with the supplies."

Ono's mouth turned down but he knew better than to let his displeasure show to the by-the-book captain. "Yes, sir," he answered as he shoved his boot back on.

"Any problems with him?" Gima asked.

Amano shook his head, a slight smile on his face. "Not since you corrected him, sir."

"Good, good. Disperse the men, be back here in ten minutes and I'll show you how we're going to cross the creek and destroy the enemy tomorrow."

Amano snapped off a stiff salute and nodded, "Yes sir."

26

Tarkington, Winkleman, Miller and Hanscom crouched beside a couple of boulders listening to the sound of hacking and sawing. There was the occasional, unmistakable sound of a tree crashing to the ground. The noise was nearly constant, but despite Henry crawling as close as possible, the Japanese were working too far away to see. It didn't matter though, it was obvious what they were doing.

The sergeants and Hanscom were looking across the creek at the low wall which had been erected the night before. It was an ingenious, although obvious solution to the problem.

Tarkington shook his head and spat a stream of saliva. "If they stack them higher, those walls will keep their workers safe while they cut the trees down. Whoever this guy is, I think we must've pissed him off."

Hanscom nodded, "He does seem to have it in for you. Think they'll try to cross tonight?"

Tarkington nodded, "I think we have to assume so. Although he can't have a lot of men left. Who knows though, he could have gotten reinforcements." He concentrated on the little wall. It was two logs high and would need to be taller if it hoped to fully protect a tree cutter. The cutting and hacking sounds continued and Tarkington rubbed his stubbly chin. "The amount of cutting suggests this isn't the only place they're planning to do this."

Winkleman looked at the major seeing if he'd add to the conversation and when he didn't, chimed in, "I agree. We've already marked possible crossing points."

Tarkington nodded, then looked at the ground and sighed. "We've gotta move the villagers out of there. If the Japs get through, they'll be cut to pieces."

Hanscom asked, "Is there someplace for them to go? Seems pretty penned in to the west."

Tarkington nodded, "There are routes, but Vindigo says they're treacherous during the rainy season, often blocked by landslides. They use them to get to other valleys for hunting this time of year, but this rainy season's been worse than normal."

"Perhaps we should all retreat through them," Major Hanscom suggested.

Tarkington shook his head. "If they come tonight, there's no time. They'll find the trails and pursue us into a terrible situation. We'll be better off fighting them from prepared positions here while the villagers retreat. We'll slow 'em down, maybe even stop 'em cold. A lot of our ammunition and extra weapons are stowed near the abandoned village, but we have a lot stored here too. We'll set up the heavy MGs supported with the LMGs and those cadets are damned good with the knee mortars." He looked up, "Cover's a little thick but they can shoot 'em flat if need be and the secondary position is more open." He licked his lips seeing the situation coming together. He grasped Winkleman's arm, "You, Henry and Raker have the boys dig foxholes for the MGs, near the suspected crossing points. If we guess right, we can mow them down as they come across."

Winkleman nodded. "I'll get to it. Got about five-hours til dark."

Tarkington focused on Staff Sergeant Miller. Officially, they were the same rank but both Miller and Hanscom deferred to the man with the most experience. The leader of Tark's Ticks. "You know anything about booby traps?"

Miller's mouth turned down and he tilted his head side-to-side. "Some."

"We've got a lot of Jap grenades and even some mortar shells. Go back and have some of the cadets help you set up traps where we think the trees will fall. Dig holes with sharpened sticks at the bottom, whatever you can think of."

Miller gave him the thumbs up signal. "Will do, Sergeant."

He hustled off leaving only Hanscom and Tarkington. "Any other suggestions you can think of, sir?" Tarkington asked.

Hanscom looked at the surrounding jungle and pointed at some of the taller trees. "Be nice to have some sharp-shooters shooting down on the men behind the walls. Maybe these are high enough to get a good angle."

Tarkington gazed up and said, "Only problem, it's gonna be black out here tonight. They'd be shooting at sounds and once the Nips see their muzzle flashes..."

"Hmm, yes. I see your point." He looked overhead, "I know it's thick overhead, but we could still use the flare gun and shed some light."

"If we had any flare guns, I'd agree with you."

Hanscom looked at him quickly. "But you do. I saw one of the cadets with one. He has it tucked into his belt." He smirked, "I think he thinks it's some kind of large bore pistol."

Tarkington looked at him in amazement. "Well, if there's a gun, there's bound to be flare rounds for it."

Hanscom nodded. "I know what to look for, usually have different color tips."

"If you know Japanese you could read the boxes."

He shook his head, "Unfortunately, I don't."

Tarkington looked up at the trees and nodded, "Yeah, I think you're onto something."

With a defensive plan in mind, Tarkington went to speak with Vindigo. He found him in the great hall sharpening his long scimitar-shaped blade. He explained what he'd seen the Japanese doing and what he thought they had in mind. When he was finished, Vindigo nodded and said, "Good. Let them come. We will kill them."

Tarkington looked at the floor then back up at his old, dark eyes. "I think you should lead your people out of here. The sooner the better. We can hold them off while you escape to the western valleys."

Vindigo looked at him as though he'd lost his mind. "No, we will not abandon our village to them."

Tarkington was afraid he'd say that. "Well then — you and your warriors stay and fight — but the women and children should leave."

Vindigo's expression didn't change. "No. They would not go, even if I ordered them."

"But the only reason you're in this mess is because of us, because we're here. We've brought this upon you. I can't sit back and watch innocents slaughtered."

Vindigo stood and stepped forward, his deep inset eyes burning like embers of coal. "Then you should have a good plan for stopping them."

Tarkington knew it would be useless trying to convince Vindigo otherwise, so instead of wasting time he told Vindigo the plan. When he was done, he nodded his agreement. "We will kill many Japanese." He lifted his chin and puffed out his chest. "We have work to do before dark."

For the rest of the day, the weather was miserable. The rain was steady, making digging easy, but keeping the holes from flooding, difficult. The rain completely obscured them from view as they worked at the likely crossing points.

The sound of wood cutting continued and even seemed to increase. More trees fell. The din coming from the gloom made it seem as though they were across from a huge logging operation. It made them work harder, knowing they'd be dealing with what sounded like a large force.

By the time the sun set, and the gray day turned to darkness, the men were ready. Stollman sat on the edge of his foxhole, his LMG covered by his poncho, the bipods resting on slats of wood to keep them from sinking into the muck. Across from him, Vick tore at a strip of jerked meat and chewed with abandon.

Stollman whispered, "Japs can probably hear you chewing, for crying out loud."

The sounds of sawing and cutting diminished with nightfall. The relentless roar of the creek was ever-present, but the sudden drop-off from the Japanese was unsettling. "It's damned quiet all of a sudden. Think they're coming already?" Vick whispered, swallowing loudly.

"We'll know when they start hacking the tree across from us. There's no way to do that quietly. My money's on 'em coming tomorrow night though. They worked all day, might be tired."

"I'll put five bucks on that bet."

"Done."

Vick reached across and they shook on it. "Taking candy from a baby. Japs don't get tired, Stolly."

"We'll see."

A minute later, there was scuffling from behind and they heard Tarkington's voice, "Stolly, Vick, that you?"

"Yep," Vick answered.

Tarkington hunched. His face was barely visible in the ambient light. "Hear anything?"

Stollman shook his head, "Got real quiet over there." He gazed into the gloom. The only sound was the creek ripping past only yards ahead.

"Well, you know what to do if you hear 'em hacking that tree. Don't wait for a signal, just do it."

Vick pulled the flare pistol from his belt and rubbed the huge barrel, "Got plenty of flares, turn night into day."

Tarkington nodded and pointed to the right and left. "Remember, you've got MG support on either side. I expect 'em to hit us in the three spots I showed you earlier, but this middle one has the biggest tree. If they get it down, I expect most will surge across here." He gazed into the gloom, recalling how the terrain looked in daylight. Before moving off to the next hole he lowered his voice, "Now remember, don't stay here if they get across in numbers. You'll be in the way of the MGs."

Vick and Stollman nodded and Vick muttered, "Yep, got it, Tark."

Captain Gima was pleased with the work his men had achieved. Once the reinforcements arrived and settled, he put them to work. As requested, they'd brought plenty of axes and saws, which made the work go much faster.

The men who'd been hacking trees with entrenching tools were overjoyed to have the appropriate implements and took to the work with abandon. Their fatigue seemed to melt off them, the ease of using the appropriate tools giving them new vigor.

The constant rain and mist hid them from the other bank. He wondered what reaction, if any, all the noise was having on the Americans. If the Americans were still there, they couldn't fail to hear the commotion. In all likelihood, he'd cross and find an abandoned village and be back to square one. They were a guerrilla force, after all and fading into the jungle to the West would be the best way to continue the fight.

But, in the unlikely event they *were* still there, he pondered how he'd react to the noise if the roles were reversed. The obvious deduction would be a bridge being constructed. How would he combat a crossing? First, he'd find the narrowest, most obvious spot and set up his defenses to open fire when the troops were most vulnerable, during the bridge crossing.

He didn't have a clear idea how many men he was facing, but he doubted there were more than a handful of Americans. The rest were Filipinos, probably the great majority villagers without much military training. They'd obviously fought well so far, but he thought if he could get a sizable force across the creek at multiple points in the dark of night, there'd be no stopping him. They'd create panic and rout them. The battle could be over by the time the sun rose.

Lieutenant Amano came up beside him and reported. "All the tree segments have been cut and the vines for lashing them together are in place. We're ready to move forward and erect the walls on your order, sir."

Gima nodded. "The men have worked hard. Let them eat and rest for a couple of hours." He glanced at his watch, but could barely see the luminescent dials. "We'll move forward at midnight."

"Yes, sir. I'll inform the men."

Amano turned to go but before he took a step, Gima said, "We've lost a lot of men over the last few days."

There was a long pause, Amano waited for more. When there wasn't, he nodded, "Yes, sir."

"I doubt the Americans are waiting for us, but if they are, we'll lose more men."

Lt. Amano had never heard the captain be anything except confident and firm, but now he was hearing what he could only describe as weakness. He didn't know what to say. "Yes, sir. They will do their duty for the Emperor, sir." It was the standard, safe response.

"You've led your men well, Lieutenant. You've risen to the occasion, as they say." Amano was about to speak, but Gima cut in, his voice suddenly harsh and filled with hatred. "If *Tark's Ticks* are over there, I will expect no mercy. Kill everyone. Understood?"

Amano stiffened, "Understood, sir."

27

Tarkington went over and over what he might have missed in his preparations. He had little doubt that the Japanese would come that night. The increased tempo of work and the obvious change in the sounds of the hacking and sawing, told him the Japanese had gotten new tools and he inferred reinforcements had most likely brought them. Whoever the Japanese commander was, he was tenacious and pushed his men hard. He wouldn't wait for daylight or the following night. They'd come tonight.

He was in a foxhole thirty yards behind and twenty yards to the left of Stollman and Vick's position. One of the big machine guns was nearby, the crew manning it, two eager Filipino cadets. He could barely see the dark outline of the angry looking barrel in gloom.

Beyond them, were more cadets with rifles, knee mortars and plenty of ammunition. Winkleman and Eduardo were in their midst. Far to the right, another heavy machine gun manned by two more cadets. The village fighters were spread that way, along with Skinner and the remaining cadets.

Raker and Henry were in trees overlooking the scene with their Springfield rifles. They wouldn't be able to see targets until the flares were fired. The scouts had orders to fire only after the main force engaged, so their muzzle flashes wouldn't be as obvious. Major Hanscom and Staff Sergeant Miller were beside Tarkington.

The rain stopped at eleven PM, followed immediately with rising mist. The noise of the creek sounded louder and Tarkington wondered if it might spill its banks and flood them out of their foxholes. He hoped it would. It was the only thing which might keep the Japanese from coming.

The air was warm and he could feel his soaked clothes drying out from his own body heat. If the threat of imminent attack wasn't hanging over his head, the night would have been downright pleasant.

As the minutes ticked by, the mist thinned and he could see the occasional star through the jungle canopy. He didn't know what would be better for defending against an attack, rain or clear skies, each had advantages and disadvantages. Perhaps the Japanese commander would think the rain was better and would wait until it inevitably started again.

He gazed at his watch — midnight. He checked the two weapons in front of him in the foxhole. He'd use the rifle first, then the submachine gun if the fighting got close enough. Major Hanscom whispered, "Someone's coming."

Tarkington looked up and saw a dark figure making his way over in a crouch. It was one of the cadets from near Vick's hole. He stopped in front of Tarkington and he could see the young man's smile before he spoke. "Sounds near the tree. Creek is loud but heard voices and branches breaking."

"Any tree cutting?" he asked.

The cadet shook his head. "Stolly say no sawing or cutting, just sounds."

Tarkington looked at Major Hanscom. "Probably putting the rest of the wall up for protection." Hanscom nodded his agreement, but didn't answer. Tarkington wasn't looking for help, just thinking out loud. He licked his lips and touched the cadet's thin shoulder. "Tell him not to fire the flare until he hears them cutting the tree." The cadet nodded and scooted away. Tarkington said, "Don't want to give our positions away until I know they've got all their men bunched up."

Two more men reported in from other sections of the creek. So far, they'd guessed the crossing points correctly. After a half hour with no more reports, he decided they'd be coming across at the most likely spots they'd identified and not the other three they were watching. He tapped Miller, "Get out to the other spots and have them tighten up to the three crossing points then get back here." Miller stole a glance at Hanscom, clutched his rifle and nodded before trotting off into the night.

"Any time now," Tarkington said and blew out a long breath. Hanscom nodded.

At exactly midnight, Captain Gima gave the order for his lead elements to move to the three points of attack and lash together and erect the rest of the walls. It took an hour and a half before Lt. Amano reported back. "The walls are up, the trees have been prepped and the charges are set, sir."

Gima nodded. "Good. Move to your zone but keep the men well back until the charges go off." He unslung his rifle and looked at the sky. There were skittering clouds and he could see occasional stars. "Good weather for a night attack." He leveled his gaze at Lt. Amano. "When the trees go down, you know what to do." He looked at his watch, "The charges go off at exactly 0150." He looked from Amano to Sergeant Ono, who'd be leading the men across the northernmost crossing. "See you on the other side." They saluted and went to their assigned sections.

Gima felt the familiar adrenaline of coming combat. His senses tingled and his scalp itched with pinpricks of nervous sweat. He chambered a round and moved forward, Sergeant Uchida beside him. "I pray the Americans are waiting for us over there, Kenji."

Sergeant Uchida had not heard his commander call him by his first name for months. Not since just before the final attack against the stalwart American and Filipino lines. "Yes, Captain. We will crush them if they dare to stand and fight."

Soon they were stacked up behind the main force of Japanese soldiers crouched well back from the creek in the darkness. He tapped Uchida's shoulder. "Tell the men to set off the grenades at exactly 0150." They checked their watches against one another's, and Uchida moved forward, tapping men's shoulders as he passed.

The smell of newly cut wood mixed with the earthy smell of churned-up mud, made him think of other battles on other islands. He'd been at war for years, yet the thrill and anticipation of coming combat never faded. He looked at his watch…only five more minutes.

———

Time passed maddeningly slowly. There'd been no reports since the first one and Tarkington took that as a hopeful sign. Perhaps they were just getting things in place for a later attack. He'd be glad for more time to prepare, but in his gut, he knew the Japanese would come tonight.

The sudden shattering blast from across the creek confirmed his gut feeling. The sudden flash in the night momentarily confused him. He was expecting the sounds of hacking and sawing, not explosives. The rending, breaking sound of falling timber was unmistakable, then more explosions to the North and South. He realized in a flash — the Japanese weren't using saws and axes to bring down the trees but high explosives. He cursed himself for not thinking of it. The crashing of a large tree falling and smashing into the ground told him the method had been successful.

A pop from Vick and Stollman's hole and he saw a streaking flare smash into the overhead cover, bounce around crazily sending sparks in every direction, then hang up in the branches, burning furiously. The light was imperfect but it was enough to see across the creek.

Stollman fired a burst from the LMG. There was firing from the trees as Raker and Henry found targets. Another flare was shot, angled to the right, then another to the left a moment later.

The nearest heavy machine gun opened fire, the huge tongue of flame from the muzzle stealing Tarkington's night vision. He watched yellow tracer rounds lancing into the lashed together wood wall and it splintered but held.

From behind the wall, muzzle flashes erupted, and red and yellow tracer fire cut across the creek and sliced into the ground all around the dug-in heavy MG. The cadets ducked but kept up the fire. Tarkington yelled, "Short bursts! Don't burn the barrels, and don't shoot Vick and Stolly."

The second heavy MG to his right opened fire, the tracer rounds slamming into the southern wall. Tarkington was dismayed to see how well the explosives had worked. In the light from the flares, he could see at least two and from the volume of fire from the North, probably three trees down. The largest, in front of his position, had fallen at an angle, pointing it almost directly at Stollman's hole. They'd narrowly missed being crushed.

Miller yelled in his ear, "The MG won't be able to fire. Too close to Vick and Stolly."

Bullets whizzed and snapped through the brush and pinged off rocks making bizarre sounds. The flares caught in the trees lit up the scene just enough to see soldiers. Tarkington saw figures lunging onto the precarious felled tree in the center. There were large branches sticking out at odd angles, making it difficult for the Japanese to move quickly. One slip and they'd fall into the raging torrent just feet below them.

Tarkington sighted down his type-98 rifle and placed the open sights on a dark shape trying to push over a thick branch. The heavy pull of the trigger jerked the muzzle and his bullet missed the mark, but slammed into a soldier who'd just come around the corner of the wall. He saw the dark shape drop into the churning muddy water and disappear.

He worked the bolt and fired again, but his first target was already falling, hit with multiple bullets from Stollman's LMG. He didn't like how close the tree had landed to Stollman and Vick. He dropped the rifle and snatched up the submachine gun, yelling, "I'm going to get Stolly and Vick out of there."

Miller nodded, "I'm coming with you."

Tarkington leaped out of the muddy hole, his sandaled feet slipping, and he fell face-first into the mud. He struggled to his feet, Miller pulling on his shirt, and they took off running.

Tracer rounds flashed all around and Tarkington thought he could feel their heat, but he dove and slid to the lip of the foxhole without any new holes in his body. Vick nearly shot him in the face with the flare gun. "Jesus, Tark. What the hell you doing here?" Miller stopped a few feet back and fired his rifle then ducked down and worked the bolt action.

"Wait on the flare. Pull back, you're too close. The angle of the tree's all wrong for the MG. You're in the way."

Stolly nodded, fired off a long burst, then stood and hefted the LMG by the handle. Vick grabbed the grenade he'd left on the side of the foxhole, armed it and flung it as far as he could. It plopped near the far bank and exploded, sending mud, water and shrapnel in every direction. He clutched the back of the cadet's shirt who was still firing his rifle as quickly as he could work the bolt and pull the trigger. "Come on, dammit!" he yelled. The kid looked back and saw they were leaving. He nodded and lunged out of the back of the hole as though gravity had no effect on him. He turned and held out his hand to Vick who slapped it away. "Out of the way, kid."

Tarkington got off his knees and aimed at the dark figures on the log. He fired a short burst from his submachine gun, then ducked. The tree's branches and limbs blocked his view and he hoped that worked both ways. Bullets continued to snap through the branches, but most of the fire was directed at the heavy flashes of the MGs.

Tarkington glanced right. The sputtering flare was almost burned out, but he could see another tree down and the muzzle flashes of many weapons firing from the protection of another wall. To the North he also saw muzzle flashes but not near the intensity.

The heavy MG on the right side was hammering the wall, keeping the soldiers from crossing, but the cadets, villagers and Skinner's return fire volume was low and he wondered if they needed help. He tapped Miller's shoulder. "I'm gonna check on them," he pointed south.

Miller shook his head. "I'll go. You need to command." Without waiting for a response he took off running south.

"Dammit, he's gonna run right beneath the MG, he'll be cut to ribbons by friendly fire." Tarkington stood and took off running back the way he came, but angling toward the MG. The rest followed him and he waved them to continue to Major Hanscom's hole. "Up there," he shouted. "I'll warn the other MG." He glanced back and saw Stolly angling toward the center MG position, Vick and the cadet right on his ass.

Suddenly there was someone in front of him. The shape rose up like an apparition and he slid to a stop and brought up his weapon. "Easy, Tark. It's me, Henry."

Despite the chaos exploding all around, Henry's voice sounded almost bored. Tarkington took a moment to recover, then said, "Thought you were in a tree."

Henry glanced up, "I was, but that damned flare Vick shot ricocheted around and almost lit me on fire. I tagged a few of them before I left, but I was getting too exposed."

"Follow me." Tarkington took off running again, knowing Henry would be on his tail. They ran to the edge of the MG's foxhole then jumped in with the cadets. "Cease fire! Stop!" he barked and the MG went silent. The two cadets looked back at him with wide, questioning eyes. "Miller's moving across your front." He poked his head up but couldn't see him. "Give him a few minutes. Get more ammunition ready, give the barrel a break." Bullets smacked into the mud and sliced overhead. The rain hissed and sizzled on the red-hot barrel.

Henry lunged to the front edge of the foxhole and fired his rifle. Another flare erupted behind them and arced into the trees before hanging up in the branches. The firing immediately intensified up and down the line. Tarkington poked his head up and saw Miller running in a hunch toward the now actively firing southern line. He also saw Japanese soldiers on the southern log, nearly all the way across. Miller was out of harm's way. He tapped the gunner, "Open fire," he pointed at the enemy.

The cadet clutched the dual handles, lined up the barrel, ignoring the zipping sounds of bullets passing close and opened fire. The heavy roar and the long tongue of flame was impressive, and Tarkington watched the gunner adjust his aim until the angry tracer rounds were slicing into the men on the log. The gunner swept back and forth and soldiers were torn apart as the heavy rounds impacted their bodies and sent them sprawling into the raging creek.

"Keep pouring it on!" he yelled but the gunner didn't need encouragement, his eyes flashed with the intensity of a man possessed with blood lust.

Another flare overhead, this one— aimed their way to light up the southern attack point — burst overhead. It didn't get caught in the trees but sputtered to the ground quickly. In that short span, Tarkington saw there were Japanese soldiers on this side of the creek. "Shit," he said. "Japs made it across." Henry aimed and fired, seeing the threat at the same instant.

Tarkington sighted over his submachine gun and fired a two-round burst, his bullets kicking up dirt just behind a soldier lunging forward while firing from the hip. Muzzle flashes erupted from the line and the soldier went down hard, but there were more behind him. Tarkington sprayed them and knocked one man down. He briefly thought about Miller, he hoped he was hugging the ground, because he was right in their line of fire. "Careful of Miller," he shouted, but realized the sergeant was on his own. If the Japanese broke through they'd roll up their flanks fast, and his safety wouldn't matter.

Tarkington saw a group of enemy soldiers rise from near the creek side and run forward. Covering fire from the wall intensified, concentrating not on the MG but on the defenders to the front. He aimed and fired through the rest of his magazine. Soldiers fell but there were too many. Henry's rifle barked over and over. Tarkington was about to adjust the machine gunner's fire to the group when there was a series of explosions which lit up the charging Japanese. They were flung sideways into the jungle, the brief flashes of light showing missing limbs and spraying blood.

"What the hell was that?" asked Tarkington.

"Miller's booby traps. Was wondering if they'd set 'em off."

Despite the devastating effect on the charging soldiers, more men got across the creek and hunkered out of sight, taking shots at the defenders only yards away. Explosions erupted in the defensive line and Tarkington heard the screaming of wounded men and women. The wails hit him hard; he was losing people.

Suddenly Miller came lunging over the top of the hole and landed beside the gunner, who gave him a look as though he were an alien from outer space. Miller was breathing hard and even in the low light, Tarkington could see his face was streaked with blood, some streaming from an obvious head wound. "You okay, Miller?"

Miller shook his head, trying to catch his breath. "Jap — Japs are across."

Tarkington fired another short burst and glanced over at him, "No shit. You're hit." There were more explosions as Japanese soldiers hurled grenades into the line.

Miller touched his head-wound and winced but shook his head. "I'm fine. The Japs are pushing hard over there."

"You get to Skinner?"

Miller shook his head, "Too damned many. I couldn't get through. Fire coming from both directions."

Tarkington saw Henry take his eyes from his sights and glance at Miller, then Tarkington. Tarkington licked his lips and nodded. He loaded another magazine, pulled the bolt and said. "Stay here, Miller. Be ready to pull back with the MG crew. Henry and I are going for Skinner and the others. Cover us."

Miller nodded and tapped the gunner's shoulder. He paused and looked at him, clearly not liking the interruption. "Hit the wall when I say so." The gunner and loader both nodded their understanding.

Tarkington exchanged another look with Henry, "Ready?" Henry nodded and Tarkington hissed at Miller, "Now." The heavy MG opened fire on the soldiers behind the wall, and their fire diminished. Tarkington and Henry lunged from the hole and sprinted to the right, leaping and weaving over brush and rocks. The light from the flares was nearly nonexistent now but the flashes from muzzles and exploding grenades lit their paths for microseconds at a time and they made their way through the carnage and chaos.

The first hole they came to held two dead villagers. The smoking hole told them they were victims of a direct hit from a grenade. A few feet away were two bodies, helmeted Japanese soldiers. Henry saw movement, aimed and fired his rifle. The shot brought a call from someone in the next hole. "You alive over there?"

Tarkington recognized Skinner's voice. "That you, Skinny?"

"Tark? Hell yeah it's me." A sudden flurry of fire from the creek sent them scurrying to the bottom of the hole. Skinner yelled over the din of the incoming fire. "Couldn't keep 'em from coming across, Tark. Too damned many of 'em."

The heavy MG stopped firing and he heard Miller yell, "Reloading!"

"Damn bad timing," he yelled toward Skinner. "How many men you got left, Skinny?"

"Don't know for sure, but I know I lost at least four villagers and cadets with that last charge. Anyone make it from that hole?"

"No," Tarkington yelled. "They took a grenade."

"Then we're down by half." The fire subsided and Skinner yelled, "Here they come!"

Tarkington pulled a grenade from his harness, armed it and hurled it toward the creek without exposing himself. He followed it immediately with another.

The explosions rocked the advancing Japanese and lit up the area momentarily. He came up and sprayed bullets into shapes until his magazine dried up, then dropped back into the hole, "Reloading." His ammo pouch was getting lighter and he quickly assessed he had four more magazines. He swapped out the old for new and rose up again.

Henry fired point-blank into a soldier's midsection and the soldier's momentum carried him into the hole, his gut wound seeping intestines. Tarkington fired into the writhing soldier, ending his agony and collapsing his face.

Tarkington's ears were ringing and suddenly the battlefield went quiet as his mind shut out the noise. He fired into bodies and they fell at the edge of the hole making a grisly wall. Henry's face lit up with each muzzle flash and he wondered if he'd lose his best friend in the next few seconds. He hoped he'd die before he had to witness that.

From the periphery, voices cut through, but he couldn't decipher words. He kept firing and reloading until he felt someone hauling him out of the hole. He lost his grip on his submachine gun and he lost sight of it as it splashed into the mud and blood coating the bottom of the hole.

The force pulling him from the hole was strong and he had no chance to break free and retrieve the submachine gun. Suddenly his view was blocked by a face screaming at him. It was Skinner and his words were sinking in as though they were being shouted from a mountaintop, miles away. "Move your ass, Tark."

He focused and looked around for Henry in a panic. He saw him in front, running and shooting from the hip as fast as he could work the bolt. Tarkington desperately wanted a weapon. He felt the weight of the sword slapping against his side, reached for the handle and unsheathed it. Despite his sudden deafness, the sound of the sword leaving the scabbard was crystal clear. He ran after Skinner, Henry and the few remaining Filipinos.

A shape emerged from the gloom from his right and he turned to see a Japanese soldier running straight for Skinner's back, a long bayonet leading the way. The soldier was focused on skewering his prey and didn't notice Tarkington. With a mighty downward slash, Tarkington cleaved the man's head in half, the blade easily slicing through the soldier's helmet. The blade cut all the way to the top of his rib cage before Tarkington yanked it from his body; arterial blood sprayed as the body dropped and Tarkington stepped over it continuing his headlong sprint.

The tongue of flame coming from the heavy machine gun position directed their flight and soon they dove into the hole, Tarkington holding the blade close so he wouldn't skewer someone.

Henry immediately went to the lip of the hole and fired rounds into anything that moved. Tarkington watched the machine gun's tracer rounds shredding the log bridge, but there were many soldiers across, too many. "We've gotta fall back." He cupped his hands over his mouth and yelled, feeling his throat burning, "Fall back! Fall back to the next line." He hoped he wasn't too late.

28

Captain Gima was amazed at the ferocity of the defense. He had anticipated that no one would be there at all but, within seconds of blowing the trees, he knew he faced a hard battle. The intensity of incoming fire made him glad he'd used the time waiting for reinforcements to build the walls. If he'd simply dropped the trees without the extra protection, his men would have been mowed down, but the walls allowed his men to lay down suppressing fire, and acted as a protected staging area.

He didn't expect the heavy machine guns to be set up almost directly in front of where the biggest tree dropped. He received word that the northern tree had fallen at an angle and didn't quite reach across the creek. He adjusted his plan and sent the northern men south where the fire didn't sound as intense.

Over the din of battle, he yelled to Sergeant Uchida, "Stay here and keep their heads down. I'll go south to Lieutenant Amano." Uchida nodded and yelled at the men behind the wall to continue pouring fire across the creek. Gima hadn't sent more men across this section when he had realized that it was too exposed and the huge branches hindered the crossing too much. It was a costly lesson, the riddled bodies of soldiers caught in the branches attested to that.

Gima stayed low and ran, his rifle ready. Bullets snapped overhead, but most of the firing was directed at the river crossings. He was a lone soldier in the darkness and he figured he was hard to spot in the sputtering light from the damned flares. Those were another surprise, and he had no doubt they were Japanese flares from the captured trucks. Indeed, every bullet and weapon facing him had been manufactured in Japanese factories. The thought was maddening and he increased his speed, wanting to get into the fight and kill these savages as quickly as possible.

He slowed when he got to the south crossing. The intensity of fire had increased, and he saw yellow tracer from another heavy machine gun tearing up the felled tree and the men unlucky enough to be on it. He pushed forward until he was covered by the wall. It was shredded, and some of the vines holding it together were frayed and broken, but it held, and his men were cowering behind it. "Wait for the reload," he yelled.

Lieutenant Amano's face was streaked with sweat and blood but it was not his own. He heard Gima's familiar voice and found him in the dark. "Sir, that gun's tearing us up."

"Wait for the reload," he said again and Amano nodded. Bullets smacked into the wall and swept back and forth across the log finishing anyone still struggling across. Finally the gun stopped and there was only rifle fire. "Now!" he yelled and pushed the nearest man forward. "Go!"

The soldiers surged around the edge of the wall and mounted the log. Gima poked his head up and sighted his rifle across the creek aiming at the multiple muzzle flashes. He fired and yelled to the men around him, "Covering fire." He found Lt. Amano's eyes and yelled, "Go! Lead them across!"

Amano nodded and followed the men around the corner and onto the tree. The raging waters splashed up making the tree wet and slippery, but it was wide enough for two abreast and the branches didn't start until well past the opposite bank.

Gima rose and fired over and over, until his clip was empty, then ducked down reloading. He was up again, happy to see his men jumping off the tree and taking cover along the creek side. "That's the way. Now, go, go, go!" he yelled. He ducked back down as bullets from the big MG swept the log then raked the wall. There were gaps in the stacked logs and one man slumped to the ground with a grunt as a lucky bullet found a gap and exploded his heart as it passed through his body.

Gima pushed the body out of the way and got to the edge of the wall. He poked his head out and fired at the huge muzzle flash of the MG. Before pulling back, he saw Amano waving his arm, leading a group of soldiers forward. They were just meters from the enemy when there was a series of explosions all around and even above them. He watched in horror as the men were sent flying in all directions. The sight enraged him, and he lunged from cover, leaped onto the tree and sprinted across as though he were an Olympic sprinter. He made it, jumped off and was relieved to see a stream of soldiers following his example.

They joined him and pushed forward. The machine gun opened fire again and shredded the last few soldiers on the log, but now he had enough men across to rush the positions. He yelled, for grenades and soon there were explosions. He rose screaming and firing his rifle from the hip as he stepped over dead soldiers. He saw an enemy stand in his foxhole, and he had the passing realization that it was a female Filipino before he shot her in the face.

A grenade blast lifted him off his feet and he fell backwards, feeling hot needles of pain along his left side. He rolled on the ground thinking he'd die, but the pain told him he was still alive. Despite the all-consuming fire in his side, he rolled to his stomach and searched for his weapon, but it was gone. He tasted blood in his mouth and spit a gob onto the spongy ground.

The night sparked with flashes from grenades and the near constant muzzle flashes from both sides. He remembered his sidearm and went to draw it, but realized his belt, along with the holster, was gone. *Dammit,* he thought cursing his luck.

He tried to stand but the pain in his side roared and he swayed and fell over, landing on something soft. It was a soldier; his uniform was smoking and a small flame licked at his chin and lit up his face. Lieutenant Amano's dead eyes stared at him from his battered and bloody skull. The sight momentarily took Gima's strength and he had the urge to simply curl up and drift off to sleep.

The sound of battle and the yelling and cursing of his men fighting, killing and dying, snapped him from his stupor. He tore his eyes away but reached forward and slapped at the flame, extinguishing the disgusting licking tongue of heat.

He searched the area around Amano's body and found what he was looking for, a rifle. He stood on shaky legs. The battle had surged past him and he saw shapes in the darkness lit up with muzzle flashes. He saw men running — his men — and realized they were pursuing the enemy. The heavy din of the machine gun suddenly stopped. Had it been taken out, or were they pulling back? Only one way to find out. "Forward!" he yelled, "Kill them all!" There was a surge of yelling and renewed firing as the men responded to the familiar sound of their commander, in the heat of battle right beside them.

Tarkington urged the heavy machine gun crew to move faster. They were nearly to the secondary lines. He cringed, knowing most of the foxholes and trenches there were filled, not with soldiers, but women, children and old men. He'd protested vehemently, but Vindigo reminded him it was not his decision and every villager had been given the choice to fight or flee, and they'd all chosen to fight. It had broken his heart to watch young women hand their babies and children too young to fight, over to the oldest women, who would stay in the village and protect them for as long as possible. If the Japanese broke through, he had no doubt they wouldn't leave anyone alive.

He stopped, crouched and turned, holding his sword up. He realized what an inadequate weapon it was for the situation, but he still hadn't found a replacement weapon. There was a muzzle flash and he saw Raker's face lit up. Raker worked the bolt action, ran a few steps, turned and fired again. "Come on, Raker," Tarkington yelled. Raker complied and sprinted past, "Anyone else back there?"

Raker shook his head. "Only Japs," he answered breathlessly. He noticed the sword. "That all you got?" Tarkington nodded, keeping his eyes on the night. Raker reached into his belt and pulled out a 1911 colt .45 and handed it to him grip first. "Take this for chrissakes."

Tarkington stuck the sword in the ground and chambered a round in the .45. He pulled the sword and held it in his left hand as he aimed the pistol with his right. There was a muzzle flash, he gripped the pistol and fired. He almost dropped it, the kick, combined with the muddy grip, was not a good combination.

He turned and ran a few yards, passing Raker who fired again. Bullets continued to whiz overhead and slap the muddy ground, but the flares had burned out and they'd successfully pulled away from the Japanese, who were firing blindly but still in pursuit.

Finally, Tarkington noticed the terrain slanting up slightly. He knew the next defensive line was on top of the low ridge. "We're almost there," he urged. Raker grunted and ran past him. A series of muzzle flashes to the left caught Tarkington's attention and he aimed and fired twice. He doubted he'd hit anything — he was a notoriously bad shot with a pistol — but he figured the roar of the heavy caliber round might make them think twice.

Raker called to him, "Come on Tark, up here."

Bullets slicing near his head fueled his legs and he pumped up the small incline and nearly fell into a foxhole. He crouched and saw two figures looking up at him with wide eyes. Even in the darkness, he knew they were women. They aimed rifles into the night. He hesitated, swallowed then pointed, "Only Japs out there now." He didn't know if they understood, but they both nodded and pulled the rifle stocks to their shoulders, squinting over their sights.

Raker was to his right, motioning him over to another foxhole. "The MGs setting up here."

Tarkington ran to the hole, sheathed the sword and crouched. "Hurry it up. They'll be here soon." He looked down the low ridge trying to remember how the defensive line looked in daylight. There were muzzle flashes from rifles and pistols. "Where's the other MG?" he asked. Raker shrugged and Tarkington tapped his shoulder, "Help 'em set up, I need to find Vindigo."

He trotted along the line, coming to foxholes filled with scared but determined Filipino villagers: some men, some women, some very young. "Vindigo?" he asked and they pointed further down the line. The machine gun he'd left Raker with suddenly opened fire and he instinctively dropped to his belly and looked back. The massive muzzle flash was like a beacon for every Japanese soldier and the flashes of return fire told him he faced a large force. He hoped the women in the furthest hole had their heads down.

He got his feet beneath him and made it to the next hole, just as the second machine gun opened fire thirty yards away. The yellow tracers sliced into the night like something out of a Buck Rogers comic. *Guess that answers that,* he thought.

He was on his belly again, looking into a foxhole. A flare popped overhead and the thinner jungle canopy allowed it to arc and light up the area as it traversed the sky. He marked where it had come from, knowing that would be where he'd find Stollman and Vick. As if confirming, he saw the muzzle flash of the LMG.

A voice came from the gloom in the hole in front of him, "Hello Sergeant Tarkington."

"Vindigo!" He looked beyond him and saw the hole was more like a trench and was filled with Filipinos aiming rifles. Vindigo handed him a spare Arisaka rifle. "This will be better for you, I think."

Tarkington tucked the .45 into his belt, careful to put the safety on, and nodded, "Thanks." He took the rifle, chambered a round and turned his body toward the creek and the enemy. The flare was sputtering on its path to earth, lighting up shapes. He caught his breath as he realized the soldiers were getting close, using the cover of darkness to advance.

He aimed at a crawling shape but before he could fire, four Japanese heavy machine guns opened up and swept the line with lethal fire. Vindigo reached up and pulled him into the trench. He crumpled on the bottom and found himself looking at the stars. He realized it was the first time in at least a month, he'd seen a full sky of stars.

He struggled to his feet staying crouched as bullets smacked the wood barricades they'd erected in front of the line. Vindigo yelled over the din, "The men from the north crossing are near the other machine gun." He pointed that way. "The tree didn't cross, so they left and moved to center. The officer is with them."

Tarkington was glad to hear it. He hadn't heard from Hanscom, Eduardo, or Winkleman since the shooting started. "Where's Henry?" he asked. Vindigo shrugged his shoulders. Ice went up his spine. He'd lost contact with him during their headlong run from the first line. He shook it from his mind. He couldn't worry about one man.

Further along the line, there was the now-familiar sound of knee mortars firing. He lifted his head, bringing his rifle over the lip of the hole. He watched the launched 50mm grenades explode near the muzzle flashes of the heavy machine guns, but instead of silencing them, it seemed to fully wake a drowsy giant. The incoming yellow and red tracers looked thick enough to walk across.

He fired at a sprinting soldier, his bullet smashed into his shoulder, and he clutched the wound and fell forward. Tarkington worked the bolt and aimed at the soldier behind, but as he pulled the trigger, the flare extinguished and he had no idea if he'd hit anything but dirt.

The ground in front of him erupted with near misses, sending geysers of dirt and mud into his face. He called out as granules of dirt filled his eyes and he dropped into the bottom of the hole leaving his rifle on the lip. Vindigo was upon him instantly. "You hit?"

Tarkington gave his body an assessment and shook his head, "No. Dirt in my eyes." Vindigo unscrewed the lid of a canteen and dumped half of it over his head. Tarkington lifted his head, allowing the water to wash over his face and eyes. He immediately felt better, although he still had to squint and his eyes were watery and irritated. "Thanks," he muttered and gripped his rifle again.

The enemy machine guns settled into shorter bursts but they were effectively keeping their heads down while the Japanese soldiers continued to make progress. Tarkington poked his head up, aimed through blurry vision and fired. He noticed the machine gun to his right was no longer firing and he yelled, "Raker! You okay over there?"

Over the din of combat he heard him yell back. "Gun's jammed!"

Tarkington cursed, stood and yelled, "Flare right! Flare right!" then he yelled at the men in the trench. "Shift fire." He pointed right. "Cover the machine gun crew." Vindigo relayed the message in Tagalog and soon the fire from ten rifles pinned the Japanese from moving forward.

A flare burst overhead, arcing to the right. Tarkington sighted on a soldier's leg sticking out from behind a downed tree. He saw it move, so he fired and saw blood spurt as the leg was pulled into cover. He quickly chambered another round and searched for more exposed flesh. He saw movement behind a bush and fired into it twice. He dropped below the lip and reloaded then was back up.

The flare showed him just how close the Japanese had gotten. He knew that any second their machine guns would stop and they'd charge. He was reminded of previous battles unfolding the same way. He yelled, "Get ready!"

Seconds later, the Japanese machine guns stopped their steady stream of steel and a call went up, answered immediately with throaty yells and battle screams. Tarkington yelled, "Get that damned gun up, Raker!" The response was drowned out by the roar of screaming, charging Japanese soldiers.

Captain Gima was crawling forward alongside his men. Sergeant Uchida noticed his bloody side, but knew better than to remind his commander he was wounded. He decided he'd keep a close eye on him, it looked like he was losing a lot of blood. So far though, he was fighting the way he normally fought, like a cornered tiger.

Gima glanced back and saw Sergeant Uchida a few meters behind. Gima grimaced as pain shot up his side, but he gritted his teeth and pushed through the pain. Many of his men were suffering far worse than he was, he reminded himself. The steady hammering of his heavy machine guns was having an effect on the enemy fallback position, keeping them pinned down.

He was stunned there even was a fallback position. He had assumed that once they successfully pushed across the creek, the defenses would crumble, but instead they'd retreated at the last instant and now were now in a new defensive position. He wondered how long they'd been expecting this attack. They were far more prepared than he ever would have given them credit for. No matter, he thought, soon we'll be through them.

He continued coaxing his men forward. Despite the occasional flare which continued to vex them, he knew they were difficult to see in the darkness and the smoke of battle and the natural mist of the jungle helped. They were making good headway.

When he'd realized there was a second defensive line, he'd kept two squads in the rear to continue firing on the lines while the majority of the company crawled forward. The muzzle flashes would trick the enemy into believing they still had time.

The heavy machine guns on the low ridge continued to sweep the area, but their fire was mostly concentrated behind them, dueling with his own machine gun crews.

The enemy machine gun on the left side went quiet and he hoped the crew had been knocked out, but it was more likely a jammed gun or being reloaded. He evaluated whether the men were close enough for a charge. With the gun down, they'd have an excellent chance of success. He was about to order the charge when another flare burst directly overhead and many muzzle flashes sparked on the ridge. Bullets whizzed and zipped through the brambles and zinged off rocks. Perhaps they weren't as invisible as he had thought.

He looked back at Sergeant Uchida, who stared straight back at him. The loyal sergeant would follow him anywhere. Gima made his decision, it was now or never. He signaled him to halt the supporting machine guns. Uchida nodded and sent the signal back and after a few seconds the machine guns went silent.

He mustered his remaining strength and yelled, "Attack! Attack!" He pushed himself to his knees, his side sending shots of pain through his body, making him momentarily dizzy.

The roar of his men rising, screaming and charging, energized him and the dizziness passed. He aimed his rifle and fired at muzzle flashes, then got to his feet, screamed and plunged forward. He stepped over a soldier who looked to have stumbled, but the spray of blood told another tale.

His soldiers were sprinting, some stopping to fire then sprinting again. Some fell, but they were close, they would make it to the defensive line. They would roll over them and kill them all.

Suddenly the enemy machine gun, only meters to his right opened fire and the huge muzzle flash seemed to reach out and singe the charging soldier directly in front of the barrel. The eviscerated body fell forward and draped over the barrel and before the crew could put the gun back into action, his men were upon them and slashing bayonets into the gun crew.

From the corner of his eye he saw one of the defenders slashing and hacking at his men like a wild man. He was dressed like a peasant but he glimpsed his face in the flare of a muzzle flash and recognized the Western features of an American. *Tark's Ticks*, he seethed to himself.

He turned in that direction, bent on destroying him but slipped and fell and landed on the edge of another hole he hadn't noticed. His eyes widened when he saw two Filipino women. One was working the bolt action of a rifle, the other held a long scimitar-like blade. She screamed and thrust the blade directly at him. He knew he was about to die, there was nothing he could do.

He closed his eyes thinking of the irony of dying by the hand of a peasant woman. Instead of feeling the rusty blade entering his body, he felt himself jerked back violently and rolled away. Sergeant Uchida's action put himself in front of the blade and he grunted as it sliced into his guts and lodged in his spine.

Gima got to his feet and loomed over the cowering women. The one with the rifle fired and he felt intense heat pass through his already-injured left side. He grunted, but managed to level his rifle. The woman worked the bolt clumsily, knowing her life depended on it and the woman with the blade continued to try to yank it from Sergeant Uchida's spine. Neither succeeded. He fired, worked the bolt and fired again and again until his clip was empty. His face was splashed with their blood. The women's bodies crumpled to the bottom of the hole.

Tarkington fired his rifle as quickly as he could work the bolt. The Japanese were charging and they seemed to be rising up everywhere, but particularly on the right side, taking advantage of the jammed machine gun. There were soldiers in front of his hole but he continued firing to the right, seeing the immediate danger they posed. He reloaded and jumped out of the hole. He didn't have anything in mind other than to try to help the machine gun crew get back in the fight. Vindigo yelled his name but he ignored it and kept running, firing as he did. It was obvious that without the machine gun; the line would be overrun.

Just before he got there, the crew finally cleared the jam and he saw the cadet lean back on the handle and pull the trigger. A Japanese soldier, only feet away, took the full brunt. His midsection turned to mist, and his body slumped forward, and draped over the muzzle pulling the handles out of the cadet's hands. It was as though things were happening in slow motion.

He saw Raker lunge forward, trying to free the muzzle embedded in the soldier's guts. Then Japanese soldiers flooded over the top, slashing and lunging with bayonets. The gunner took two blades to the chest and he fell back, pulling the soldiers with him, their bayonets wedged in his ribs. The loader had his .38 caliber sidearm out and fired point-blank into the mass of bodies, but he was slashed with a bayonet and Tarkington saw his throat explode in gouts of blood as though a fire-hose had been holed.

Raker reared back and punched the nearest soldier in the face, then pulled his knife and slashed and hacked, keeping the injured Japanese at bay. Tarkington fired, his bullet slicing into a soldier who'd come seemingly out of nowhere. When he tried to work the bolt, it jammed and he dropped it. He felt for the .45 but he'd lost it somewhere along the way, so he drew the sword. The leather handle felt good and he leaped into the hole and finished off what Raker had started.

More Japanese came over the top, and he leveled the sword and cut through a man's arm at the bicep. The soldier stared in disbelief at the stump. Tarkington pushed forward, sinking the blade into his neck. The soldier's eyes rolled back in his head and Tarkington pulled the blade free, the metal snicking against bone.

Motion to his right caught his attention and he remembered the women. They were on the flank and all he could see were Japanese surrounding them. He watched in horror as a slumped soldier standing at the lip of their hole leveled a rifle and fired over and over. He briefly saw their faces in the muzzle flash but they quickly dropped out of sight under the onslaught.

Tarkington lost all reason. He screamed and ran headlong straight at the soldier, his sword raised in both hands ready to slice through the man stem to stern. At the last instant, the soldier saw him coming and brought his rifle up, blocking the blow. Sparks erupted at the juncture of metal, lighting up each of their faces. Through Tarkington's crazed mind, he saw the insignia of a captain.

The force of the blow sent the officer back and he fell down the hill, still clutching his rifle. Tarkington threw himself after him, but another soldier stepped in front lunging with a bayoneted rifle. Tarkington parried the thrust and tried to stop, but slipped on the muddy, blood-soaked ground. The soldier's blade sank into the mud and Tarkington slid past him, swiping with the blade and missing.

He stopped his slide as the soldier swept his bayonet toward his face, and Tarkington dodged and sliced his leg. The soldier buckled as the back of his knee was cut to the bone, his ligaments and tendons severed. He screamed in agony but Tarkington didn't finish him, instead he turned back to the officer who'd gunned the women down. He wasn't there, lost in the gloom. More Japanese were charging him and he looked frantically for a rifle. Shots from the ridge line sent the charging Japanese sprawling and Henry was sprinting down the hill, reloading his rifle. "Dammit, Tark. Get your ass up here."

29

Tarkington followed Henry back to the ridge but instead of stopping to fight, they continued running. The Japanese were among the holes and trenches slashing and firing point-blank into the defenders. The line was being abandoned and Tarkington realized they were falling back to the village, where they'd be slaughtered. "We have to stop and fight," he yelled.

Henry turned, continuing to run and gasped through heavy breathing, "We're overrun. We'll hold 'em at the village. The whole left side's been overrun."

Tarkington struggled to picture who was on the left flank. "Winkleman and Eduardo." he stated matter-of-factly.

"Wink's okay, haven't seen Eduardo. Come on, keep moving."

Tarkington stumbled on a boulder and felt pain lance up his leg. He cursed but kept running. He realized he could see the ground; the night was giving way to the day. Time seemed to have stopped, but it obviously hadn't.

He kept Henry's back in sight, focusing on keeping up despite bullets zinging past and smacking the muddy ground. Muzzle flashes continued but the further they ran, the less he saw. He wondered if it was because they were breaking away or that he simply didn't have many men left.

He noticed a crouched soldier up ahead and wondered who it was. He stood as they approached, keeping his rifle aimed beyond them. "Where we going, Tark?" asked Winkleman.

Tarkington felt his fatigue and foggy brain clear. "Wink. You made it." He shook his head, thinking about the question. The plan they'd come up with if things got this bad was to retreat to the outskirts of the village. They'd erected some rudimentary defenses, more foxholes, stacked logs and tipped carts. "We have to defend the village. Give them time to get out of there." He knew it wasn't true, the villagers were committed to staying, even if it meant their deaths, which it undoubtedly would.

Winkleman's eyes widened, he aimed his rifle and fired. The blast intensified Tarkington's already ringing ears and he cringed. Winkleman worked the bolt action and backed away. "They're coming."

Tarkington turned and saw fleeting shapes running headlong toward the village. In the growing light, he saw they were the surviving Filipinos, women and old men among them. Beyond them, he saw the uniforms of the enemy. Some were stopping to fire and they were deadly accurate. Tarkington stopped, aimed and fired at a darting shape wearing a green uniform. He missed. He worked the bolt and saw he was empty. He reached for his satchel of ammunition and realized he didn't have one.

Henry slapped a clip into his hand. He stuffed it into the breech and chambered a round. Before he could fire again, Henry grabbed his shoulder. "We'll have a better chance back at the village."

A bullet sliced past his head and for an instant, Tarkington wished it had killed him. He couldn't stomach the thought of watching his men die.

They ran. To either side the sparse jungle was filled with terrified running villagers. Tarkington thought he'd catch a bullet in the back at any moment. He heard someone calling his name. He kept running but looked to the side and saw Major Hanscom running. He had someone draped over his back and was struggling with the load. "Major," Tarkington yelled and veered his way. Henry and Winkleman followed and were soon beside him.

Sergeant Miller was unconscious, his back was shiny with blood. Henry handed his rifle to Winkleman and pulled Miller off the exhausted major and onto his own back. He hefted the weight and trotted forward, Winkleman right on his tail, holding both rifles.

Tarkington pushed Hanscom whose breath was coming in short gasps.

"Gotta keep moving." Hanscom nodded, not able to talk. He trotted, then ran, pumping his legs despite his fatigue. "Almost there," Tarkington urged.

Soon the firing behind them tapered off. They kept running, finally seeing the edge of the village emerge from the gloom. Forty feet from the first building, Tarkington saw the makeshift cover. He dropped into a hole and turned back the way they'd come. There was no sign of the Japanese. Henry kept going, taking Miller into the village. Winkleman was in the hole beside him, squinting over the rifle sights, ready to fire at the first hint of green.

It was early dawn and the mist was getting thicker, rising slowly from the sopping ground. Tarkington looked at the other defensive positions. Men, women and children were still filtering in, some dragging along wounded. He searched for Vindigo, but didn't see him. The line was thin. They wouldn't last long. Tarkington shook his head. "Wink, you got the energy to muster the guys? I mean our guys," he swallowed against a dry throat. "I gotta know how many of us are left."

Winkleman took his eyes off the sights and nodded. "I'll do it Tark." He slapped Tarkington's back and pulled himself out the back of the foxhole.

"Bring 'em back here," he said and Winkleman nodded. He knew it wasn't a sound tactical decision, having his veterans interspersed with the villagers, was better, but if this was their last stand, he wanted them to fall together.

Tarkington sighted down his rifle. The mist would allow the Japanese to sneak close. Before, he'd considered it an ally, allowing them to create separation, but now it was definitely no longer to their advantage. He figured he wouldn't see anyone until they were no more than thirty feet away. He had one clip and once it was gone, he'd be down to his sword. It had served him well so far, but it was inadequate against grenades, rifle and machine gun fire.

Soon he saw Winkleman returning with men on his tail, hunched over and looking dirty and battered. He saw Raker, Stollman, Vick and Skinner. Each man looked exhausted and most were bleeding, or covered in the blood of others.

He stood and faced them, happy to see each man. Hanscom trotted up behind them and Tarkington nodded at him. "Anyone seen Eduardo?" he asked hopefully.

Stollman answered, "Last I saw, he was with Vindigo at the machine gun." He looked around the group, "Where's Henry?"

"Here," Henry trotted up from the direction of the village, his off-white shirt was covered in dark blood. He saw the others staring in concern and he looked down at the mess and shook his head, "Not mine...Miller's."

Hanscom looked up, as though being woken from an all-nighter. "How — how's he doing?"

"Still unconscious. He's with the old women and babies. They'll do what they can," he drawled.

Tarkington nodded, "Split up the ammo and find some cover. They'll be coming soon." The men settled into fighting positions, some dropping into foxholes, others leaning against rocks and wood structures. Tarkington pocketed another clip and they waited.

The minutes crept by and the fog thickened. Tarkington could no longer see the whole defensive position. He figured a platoon could walk right through the middle of them and they wouldn't notice. Despite the imminent combat, he had to fight to stay awake. His body was slowly shutting down.

The brief respite came crashing to an end with the sound of sudden and intense fire. He couldn't see anything but he tensed, lowered himself and sighted over the rifle. He had to make every shot count.

When he still didn't see anything, he came off the sights, searching for targets he knew would be emerging from the fog any second. There were explosions. He looked at Winkleman, who he lifted his head and stared back. "What the hell's going on out there?"

Tarkington guessed, "Stragglers? Maybe a pocket of wounded or something."

Henry, on the other side of Winkleman added, "Awful lot of fire for a few stragglers."

All they could do was wait. The fire ebbed and flowed. A few bullets whizzed overhead but they weren't aimed at them, just stray bullets. They kept their heads down, a stray bullet would kill you just as dead.

Through the fog a figure emerged, running hard. It was a Japanese soldier, holding a bayoneted rifle. "Here they come," Tarkington said. Before he could fire, Henry did and the soldier seemed to trip and fall onto his face. "Make every shot count."

A few more soldiers appeared. They were running and looking back over their shoulders. Tarkington aimed and was about to pull the trigger, when his target turned away, dropped to a knee, and fired back the way he'd come. Tarkington and Winkleman fired simultaneously and the soldier pitched forward. "What the hell's going on?" asked Winkleman. The few other soldiers were cut down with rifle fire but no more emerged from the fog.

Another flurry of shots, followed by more explosions. Stollman yelled out, "Maybe MacArthur's returned."

The comment made Tarkington smile but he realized it wasn't such a half-baked comment. The Japanese soldiers were running from *something* and there was a lot of shooting going on. Tarkington yelled, "Hold fire unless you're sure it's a Jap." The order was repeated down the line.

The shooting tapered off and seemed to be getting further away, as though the battle was shifting back toward the creek. Winkleman looked at Tarkington. "What should we do? Move forward?"

He shook his head, "Stay put. Whatever's out there will come to us."

A tense hour later, the fog thinned. The morning turned overcast and the muggy stickiness enveloped them like a damp blanket. Tarkington welcomed it though. Every minute of life was a gift; he hadn't figured he'd still be alive by now.

Shapes emerged from the jungle. Henry was the first to notice. He tucked the rifle stock tight to his chin and centered the sights. "Someone's coming."

Tarkington and the others saw it at the same time. Tarkington heard rifles being put to shoulders and barked, "Hold fire! Don't shoot till we know what's going on." He left his rifle at his side and squinted as more shapes emerged. They weren't dressed like Japanese, but they held rifles and he quickly realized there were a lot of them.

He pulled himself out of the foxhole and he saw the approaching men stop and crouch. He thought he might be shot at any second, but he raised his arms over his head and yelled. "Don't shoot!"

An English voice called out and Tarkington saw the man speaking. He was indistinguishable from the others but he was stepping forward. He said something to the others and their muzzles dropped slightly. "Hello. Who am I speaking with?"

Major Hanscom, off to Tarkington's left, leaped out of his hole and exclaimed, "Gonzo, is that you?"

The man stopped, took his eyes off Tarkington and found the wildly gesturing officer. "Major Hanscom? Zeke?"

Hanscom ran forward dodging boulders, downed trees and bodies. They met and Gonzalez braced and snapped off a salute, but the major was having none of it, he embraced him and lifted him off his feet.

The rest of the defenders moved out of their holes, keeping their rifles ready and walking slowly forward, following Tarkington's lead. As they got closer to the joyous reunion, Tarkington could see the men were Filipinos, there were hundreds of them, spread throughout the jungle.

He walked to where Hanscom and Gonzalez were smiling and slapping each other on the back. He sized the man up. He was short and swarthy and looked Filipino, but there was something about him that screamed 'American'.

Hanscom noticed Tarkington and he introduced them, "Staff Sergeant Tarkington, meet Sergeant Gonzalez. He's the man we left behind in Manila to monitor the radio."

Gonzalez extended his hand and Tarkington took it and shook. He looked around at the Filipinos surrounding them. They didn't look as happy as Gonzalez, in fact, they looked downright dangerous. "You and your men took care of the rest of the Japs?" he asked.

A Filipino stepped forward. He had the air of a man in charge and spoke before Sgt. Gonzalez could answer. "*My* men, Sergeant Tarkington," he said with some bite in his tongue.

Gonzalez nodded and introduced him. "This is Major Nieto of the Filipino Communist Resistance."

Tarkington could tell the man required a salute, so he did so then quickly dropped it. "My men and the people of this village owe you and your men a debt of gratitude, Major. But if you'll excuse me, I need to find the rest of my people." He and the rest of Tark's Ticks moved through the Filipino fighters, back toward the creek. The Filipinos stepped aside, giving the mud and blood-covered GIs plenty of space.

They found Eduardo and Vindigo in the same hole. The machine gun was still smoldering upon its tripod, the barrel shredded by shrapnel. There was a line of Japanese bodies leading from the hole, some spilling in where Eduardo and Vindigo had made their last stand. The machine gun crew cadets, were also in the hole. Their bodies looked impossibly small in death.

The GIs stood around the hole, taking in the grisly scene. It was obvious they'd made the Japanese pay a heavy price. It was also clear, they'd decided to continue firing, giving the rest of the defenders the time they needed to separate themselves from their attackers.

Tarkington went to his haunches and pinched the bridge of his nose. He didn't think he had the capacity for tears anymore, but his vision blurred as he stared at Eduardo's body. Henry put his hand on his shoulder and held it there for a second before turning away, there was nothing he could say to ease the pain.

Minutes passed and Tarkington's body started to shut down. A feeling of overwhelming fatigue came over him, but he shook his head, stood and walked the ridge, making himself check each hole. Some were empty, most were not. When he got to the last foxhole, he looked at the two Filipino women curled at the bottom. He didn't know their names, although he remembered them from the village. They were certainly not the only women to have lost their lives that day, but they were the ones he'd tried to save. He'd failed them.

The Japanese captain's face flashed through his mind. He saw him firing into the women without remorse and he suddenly wanted to find him and throttle him. He looked down the hill, it was dotted with dead Japanese.

The warm muggy air was already making some of the bodies bloat and stink.

He walked down the hill, avoiding bodies but keeping his rifle ready in case a Japanese was playing possum. He'd seen it before. Where he thought the captain's body should be, there was nothing. He looked across the carnage. He could hear the creek through the trees. He was too tired to go any further, to see any more bodies. He fell to his knees and wretched, tasting the bile from his guts.

Major Hanscom and Sergeant Gonzalez watched Tarkington fall to his knees and empty his guts. Gonzalez asked, "So that's the leader of *Tark's Ticks.*" It was a statement more than a question.

Hanscom nodded. "Hell of a man. He's a warrior. A true leader."

"Guess that's why they want him back so bad."

Hanscom scowled. "Not sure how he's gonna take that news."

"He's got a ticket home," Gonzalez said incredulously. "They all do. We've got three days to get 'em to the coordinates before the sub leaves."

"They're asking him to leave these people. People who've put their trust in him. He'll feel like he's abandoning them to die."

Gonzalez shook his head, "They're not asking, sir." He looked him in the eye, "They're ordering."

Hanscom shook his head, watching the other GIs standing around the hole where Eduardo and Vindigo died. Their shoulders hung as though the rifles they held were suddenly too heavy. If he didn't know them, he'd never guess they were American soldiers.

He watched them gently pull the two fallen warriors from the hole and place them side-by-side. Eduardo was Filipino, but as far as the GIs were concerned, he was their brother, as were all men who fought beside them.

Gonzalez commented, "Don't look like much do they?"

Hanscom straightened his back and said, "They're the best we've got."

AFTERWORD

Unlike what I've portrayed here, the details of the Bataan Death March were not learned until much later in the war. The atrocity incensed the Allies and cemented the desire for Japan's complete and unconditional surrender.

GAUNTLET
Tark's Ticks #3

**After the hell of Bataan,
getting home was supposed to be the easy part.**

They battled the Japanese for months. Now Staff Sergeant Tarkington and his battered and bruised GIs are finally on their way out. Riding beneath the waves inside a Gato-Class submarine should be a relief from the constant strain of combat, but traversing hundreds of miles of enemy-infested waters turns out to be anything but.

Tark's Ticks find that the sea holds as many dangers as the jungles. With courage, unwavering commitment, and sheer tenacity, they meet the dangers head-on.

Can they fight through the ever-tightening noose of the Imperial Japanese Navy? Find out in the gritty third book of the Tark's Ticks Series.

ABOUT THE AUTHOR

Chris Glatte graduated from the University of Oregon with a BA in English Literature and worked as a river guide/kayak instructor for a decade before training as an Echocardiographer. He worked in the medical field for over 20 years, and now writes full time. Chris is the author of multiple historical fiction thriller series, including A Time to Serve and Tark's Ticks, a set of popular WWII novels. He lives in Southern Oregon with his wife, two boys, and ever-present Labrador, Hoover. When he's not writing or reading, Chris can be found playing in the outdoors—usually on a river or mountain.

From Chris:

I respond to all email correspondence.
Drop me a line, I'd love to hear from you!
chrisglatte@severnriverbooks.com

Sign up for Chris Glatte's reader list at
severnriverbooks.com/authors/chris-glatte

Printed in the United States
by Baker & Taylor Publisher Services